Killing November

ADRIANA MATHER

ALFRED A. KNOPF
NEW YORK

Text copyright © 2019 by Adriana Mather
Jacket art copyright © 2019 by Robin Macmillan/Trevillion

All rights reserved. Published in the United States by Alfred A. Knopf, an imprint of Random House Children's Books, a division of Penguin Random House LLC, New York.

Knopf, Borzoi Books, and the colophon are registered trademarks of Penguin Random House LLC.

Visit us on the Web! GetUnderlined.com

Educators and librarians, for a variety of teaching tools, visit us at RHTeachersLibrarians.com

Library of Congress Cataloging-in-Publication Data is available upon request.
ISBN 978-0-525-57908-3 (trade) — ISBN 978-0-525-57909-0 (lib. bdg.) —
ISBN 978-0-525-57910-6 (ebook)

Printed in the United States of America
March 2019
10 9 8 7 6 5 4 3 2 1

First Edition

Random House Children's Books supports the First Amendment and celebrates the right to read.

For my son, Haxtun Wolf Mather,

whom I call My Little,

but who lights up my entire world

One

MY NAME IS November Adley and I was born in August. The way my dad tells it, the Connecticut nights were unusually cool that summer, and the day I arrived our maple burst with color reminiscent of late fall—hence my name. He claims the leaves shone so brightly in the morning sun that it looked like our front lawn was on fire. Dad also says that's part of the reason I'm obsessed with the woods. I'm not sure there's any connection, but I enjoy the comfort of that story—a reminder of a time when the world was safe and so was my family.

The most disorienting thing about safety—my own in particular—is that it never crossed my mind before. My ex-CIA, now–financial manager dad often tells me I'm too trusting, all the while shaking his head like he's shocked that we're related. Which I, of course, remind him is one hundred percent his fault, since I've lived my entire life in the same small town with the same friendly people, who pose about as much threat as a basket of sleeping kittens. Dad argues that I *want* to believe people are good and that while that's admirable, it's also not realistic. To which I ask him how it helps anyone to believe that people are bad. He claims that having a healthy sense of suspicion prepares you for every possible danger. But until now, it was all just a theory. And if I'm being honest, even yesterday, with Dad insisting there was an imminent threat to our family, I still wasn't convinced. Nope, there was absolutely nothing indicative of danger in my life until a few minutes ago, when I woke up in this medieval-looking . . . parlor?

I frown. A man I'm assuming is a guard stands against the wall next to me. He's staring forward, blatantly ignoring me, as I consider the door. I push as hard as I can on the wrought-iron latch and even throw my shoulder into the dark wood, but it doesn't budge. I let out a huff from the effort and scan the room. There's a roaring fire in the fireplace and maroon velvet furniture that probably costs more than my entire house. But there are no windows and the door in front of me is the only exit.

"I know you hear me," I say to the guard, who so far hasn't answered a single one of my questions. He's dressed all in black, with a leather belt and leather armbands that put to shame the Roman gladiator costume I wore last year for Halloween. I toy with the idea of snapping my fingers in front of his face, but he's a good foot taller than me and his arms are more muscular than my legs.

He remains silent.

I try another angle. "You know I'm a minor, right? That you can't keep me locked up in this . . . Well, I'm assuming this is my new boarding school. But what kind of a school locks up their students?" Dad told me this place would be different, but I have a hard time believing he meant I'd be trapped in a windowless room.

Just then I hear a key slide into the door and it swings outward. My shoulders drop and my hands unclench. Another guard, dressed identically to the first, gestures for me to follow him. I don't waste a second. Unfortunately, the room guard comes, too, and walking between them, I feel almost as confined as I did in that room.

The guard in front pulls a lit torch off the gray stone wall and I take inventory of my surroundings—the lack of electricity, the arched ceilings, the heavy wooden doors that use latches instead of knobs. There's no way I'm still in the United States. This place looks like something out of a documentary I once streamed about medieval Irish castles. However, I find it nearly impossible to believe Dad would send me all the way to Europe, not to mention be able to pay for it. We almost never leave Pembrook, much less the state of Connecticut.

As we continue to walk, I notice impressive hanging tapestries depicting knights, royal courts, and bloody battles. It's also dead quiet, no sounds of people chatting or cars driving by.

The hall has a distinct chill, and I pull the sleeves of my sweater down over my fingers for warmth. I have no idea what happened to the coat, gloves, and scarf I wore onto the plane; they weren't in the room with me when I woke up. We pass under an archway and ascend a staircase with worn, uneven stone steps. I count two landings and three flights before we come to a stop in front of a door patterned with iron rivets. The lead guard unlatches it and warm air billows out.

The antiquated office reminds me of a somber scene in a movie about Mary, Queen of Scots. The only light in the room comes from an abundance of candles set in silver candelabras and in sconces on the stone walls. The windows are covered with heavy curtains and a fire blazes inside the fireplace, filling the air with the scent of woodsmoke.

A tall, thin woman stands behind a seemingly ancient desk. Her brown hair is pulled into a high bun so tight that it gives me a headache just looking at it. She's probably around Dad's age, but her severity makes her seem older.

She does a poor impression of a smile. "Welcome to Academy Absconditi. I'm Headmaster Blackwood. I trust your trip was agreeable?" Her voice and demeanor command obedience.

"I don't remember my trip," I say, feeling uneasy under her gaze as I pull a piece of fuzz off my jeans. The rant I was working up downstairs feels inappropriate in this formal setting. "I passed out on the plane and woke up on a couch in the . . . To be honest, I'm confused how—"

"Teachers' lounge," she says, and gestures for me to sit in an armchair in front of her desk. The frills of a white blouse spill out from the edges of her black blazer. The contradiction makes me wonder which one she is—uptight and trying to appear approachable, or soft and trying to look stern. "You were out for some time."

"I was locked up down there," I say, expecting shock, but it doesn't come. I turn and look behind me. Both guards are still with us, one on either side of the now-closed door. Whether they're protecting her or preventing me from leaving is unclear. Maybe both.

Blackwood nods as though she understands my unspoken question. "Guards aren't permitted to speak to students; they only speak to faculty and staff. Now, considering the lateness of the hour, I think we should dispense with the small talk, don't

4

you?" She glances at a dark metal clock on the wall that resembles a small Gothic tower with exposed gears.

It reads 1:30, and judging by her "lateness of the hour" comment and the empty hallways, I'm guessing it's a.m., not p.m. "Hang on . . . that can't be right." I look between her and the clock like someone is playing a joke on me. It was after midnight when Dad dropped me at the airport. And about two hours after that when I fell asleep. "Have I been out for a full day? How is that possible? And why didn't I wake up when I was being brought in here? Or when the plane landed?"

"I understand that you're disoriented, an unfortunate side effect of getting you here smoothly—"

"*Side effect?*" My stomach knots up as I narrow the possibilities as to why I was asleep for twenty-four hours. "Did . . . did someone drug me?" My voice has risen in pitch, and I fight off a sense of panic.

I file back through the sequence of events before I passed out. The last thing I clearly remember was having a lemonade on the plane. Dad must have told me a million times not to eat or drink anything that wasn't given to me by someone I trust, but refusing a drink from a flight attendant is like refusing something I ordered in a restaurant.

I look up at Blackwood for some indication of what's going on, but her expression is blank. She definitely isn't acting like the suggestion of a possible drugging is outrageous.

I stand up. My instinct is to run. Except I don't have a clue where I am, other than a vague sense that I'm in a rural area, judging by the lack of noise. "Ms. Blackwood, can I use the phone? I'm not sure this is . . . I just need it for a minute." I scan her desk, but there doesn't seem to be one.

"Unfortunately, no, you may not."

"I'm sure this is a great school, but—"

She puts up her hand to stop me, like she understands me perfectly but is unwilling to indulge my concerns at present. "Before you leave this office or communicate with anyone, you must understand and *agree* to the rules." She pauses. "Also, I'll ask that you call me Headmaster Blackwood. We pride ourselves on tradition here."

I stare at her, at a loss for words, something my best friend, Emily, will verify has only happened once before.

Blackwood gestures for me to sit down. "Now, I suggest you relax and pay close attention. Some of what you want to know, I'm about to explain to you."

I reluctantly sit. Dad told me this school would challenge me in strange ways, and even though I find it all wicked suspicious, I trust him. He wouldn't put me in danger. In fact, that's the whole reason I'm here—to keep me out of it. I lean back in the worn leather armchair, tucking one of my feet under me.

Blackwood raises an eyebrow as she takes note of my slouched posture. She stares down at me and lifts her chin almost like she would lift me up if she could will it through her thoughts. "Your sudden arrival was unforeseen. It's not our policy to admit new students midyear—midsemester, no less." She looks at me expectantly.

"Thanks for making an exception . . . ," I say, invoking my manners even though the words feel stiff in my mouth. I don't like the way she says *admit*, like this is a long-term thing. Dad told me it would only be for a few weeks, just until he could clear up the break-in at Aunt Jo's. Then I'd return to my house in sleepy Pembrook and everything would go back to the way it was.

Blackwood opens a black fabric journal marked with a satin ribbon and scans the page. "Before I tell you about Academy Absconditi and its student body, there are three rules that are absolutely nonnegotiable. They must be obeyed at all times and they apply not only to students, but to faculty as well." She folds her hands over her papers. "The first is that you do not speak, write, or in any other way communicate about your life outside these walls. Not what town you lived in, not who you're related to. Not your last name or the names of people you know. I understand that you're particularly gregarious, and I just want to make myself extra clear that if you break this rule, you not only put yourself in danger, but also put your *family* in danger."

I squint at her. "How would I put my family in danger here? This place is supposed to be the opposite of dange—"

"I also understand that you've been quite sheltered," Blackwood says, flat out ignoring my question and giving me a disapproving stare. "But time will correct that."

I don't respond because I'm not sure what she's referring to and I'm not sure I want to know. Maybe she's right about the disorientation, or maybe it's this conversation that makes me feel like I'm upside down.

"The second rule forbids you to leave the campus," Blackwood continues. "This institution is located deep in a forest that's rigged with traps. Going beyond the perimeter walls is not only unwise, but extremely perilous."

I sit up. Now, *this* is the kind of school perk Dad sold me on—tree obstacle courses, complex puzzles, knife-throwing tricks.

If this place turns out to be as Robin Hood adventurous as it is creepy, I guess I can forgive him for the long-distance travel, and her for the possible drugging. "What kind of traps? Has anyone ever made it through them?"

"No. Never," she says as though she's answered this question countless times and it never stops being exhausting. My eyes drift momentarily above her head to the maroon-and-silver crest on the wall, under which I read the Latin phrase *Historia Est Magistra Vitae*. Before I can work out the meaning, Blackwood starts talking again.

"The third rule is that if you harm another student, we adhere to an eye-for-an-eye punishment system. All sparring must be confined to the classroom under faculty supervision."

The momentary excitement I had over the booby-trapped forest disappears, and I feel my expression drop into a frown. Dad said that sending me here was only a precaution, that he needed to be with Aunt Jo for a few weeks, that he couldn't watch us both at the same time. He told me to trust him. I just assumed he was being overly protective like usual. But if there's danger *here,* then the whole thing reeks. A tiny knot forms in my stomach, not the type that overwhelms you in the moment, but the type that lurks and grows in the dark, quiet moments when you're by yourself.

I look again from the blotted-out windows to the guarded door. "Isn't that a given . . . the no-hurting-people bit?"

"There have been an unusual number of fatalities here in recent years. So no, it's not a given," she says like it's nothing more important than Taco Tuesday in the cafeteria.

My throat suddenly goes dry. "What do you mean, *fatalities*? How intense are the classes here? What exactly are people dying from?"

Blackwood looks at me like I'm a lost puppy that she has no intention of petting. "We do not offer basic studies like other preparatory schools; what we offer is a great deal more. The Academy builds on your skill sets and on your individual strengths. For instance, knife throwing is not simply about precision. It is a skill that is practiced while in motion and under duress. And deception is honed so that you may both read it in others and deploy it as second nature. Instead of languages, we offer an accents class and a cultural norms elective to allow you to better move between countries without your origins giving you away. It's a *privilege* to attend this school, not a right. Our professors are of the highest caliber and our students are hand-picked from all over the world. There are eighteen professors in residence, and you, November, make our one hundredth student. Every spot in this school is coveted and every student here knows that." Her tone sounds like a warning, like I will be out on my butt if I make a wrong move. "You'll need to undergo a psychological and physical examination before we decide which classes will best suit you." She leans back in her chair, the candles in the candelabra on her desk casting shadows across her face.

Academy Absconditi—definitely Latin. My brain whirls into motion. *Absconditi stems from* absconditum, *meaning "hidden" or "secret." So it's either Hidden Academy or Academy of the Hidden.* I can feel my eyebrows scrunching up as I try to take it all in. I'm not sure if I'm excited or terrified to be in a secret school with a bunch of knife-throwing deception experts with accent control.

The candles in the room flicker as though to emphasize Blackwood's long pause, and when she speaks I once again get the uncanny feeling that she's able to read my thoughts: "The Academy is true to its name. As far as the world's concerned, we don't exist. Not even your parents, who may or may not have been students here, know its location."

Well, at least Dad was telling the truth when he said he couldn't tell me exactly where I'd be going. Is it possible my mountain man of a father went to this school? It's suspicious that he didn't mention it, but he also never talks about his childhood, so it's not entirely impossible.

"As you may have noticed, there's no electricity here. There's also no Internet access and thus no communication with the outside world whatsoever," Blackwood continues. "Parental visits are organized through the school and approved at our discretion. Understood?"

I stare at her. That explains the lack of a phone and her refusal when I asked to make a call. But this extreme isolation makes me think one of two things is going on here. Either this is going to be the most intense survival training of my life or the threat to our family was significantly worse than the break-in Dad claimed it was and he wanted me far away while he dealt with whatever *really* happened. My heart beats a little faster at the thought; I don't want to believe he would keep something that important from me.

"Understood," I say cautiously.

"And you agree to the rules?"

"What choice do I—" I clear my throat. "I do."

"Very well," says Blackwood, and releases her breath like she's pleased to be moving on. "As I said, you've come to us late at seventeen. Most students start at fifteen, with the occasional admittance at sixteen. You'll have to make a concerted effort to acclimate quickly, although I've been assured you have the skills not only to keep up with the other students, but to excel here." Her look tells me she isn't sure she agrees. "Still, keep your head down. Watch and learn from the other students. Keep your socializing to a minimum. Be on time and be polite. And above all, do not disrupt."

I would laugh, except it's not funny. She just described the anti-me.

"You'll have meetings with our analyst, Dr. Conner," she continues, "who will help you assimilate. Now I think it best if you retire for the evening. Dr. Conner will begin your evaluation in the morning." She gestures toward the two guards. "These gentlemen will escort you to your room. Layla, your roommate, will act as your guide for your first week. She's been instructed to brief you on the basics, and I have full confidence that she will be thorough. She's one of our best students."

"How do you spell Layla?" I ask, my thoughts turning to one way I can get information without asking for it.

Blackwood hesitates and gives me an odd look. I would tell her that her own name in Old English means "black wood," but there's clearly no point.

"L-A-Y-L-A," Blackwood says, then closes the journal and stands up.

I stand up, too. I want to ask more questions, but it's obvious from her expression that she has no interest in continuing our conversation.

"Thanks, Headmaster Blackwood. Sleep well."

She gives a perfunctory nod and I head for the door. The guard with the torch lifts the latch and I follow him into the hallway. He towers over me, and I'm almost five foot nine. And once again, the guards orchestrate it so that I'm walking between them.

The only sound is my boots on the floor. Their footsteps are conspicuously quiet as we make our way down a flight of stairs and into a hallway lined with arched wooden doors marked by wrought-iron accents. There are no numbers or names to distinguish them. The guard in front of me stops and knocks on the third door on the left. Only a second passes before there's the muffled sound of a metal latch and the door swings open.

The girl behind it has long black hair to her waist, so straight and shiny that it reflects the torch flame. She has dark brown eyes and full red lips. She scans me head to toe and her eyebrows push together, reminiscent of Blackwood's sour pucker.

Even though she's in nothing more than a white nightgown, my boots, shabby and mud-stained from my usual outdoor antics, and my oversized cable-knit sweater suddenly make me feel underdressed.

"Layla, right?" I say, stepping in and breaking the silence with a smile. "I hear we're roommates. I'm November." I reach out my hand to shake hers, but she doesn't take it. Instead she does a quick curtsy. A surprised laugh escapes before I can consider it. Her gaze hardens and she latches the door behind me with a rough click.

"I'm sorry. I didn't mean to laugh. Really. Your curtsy just caught me off guard. Can we start over?" I can hear my best friend, Emily, scolding me for my poorly timed laughs.

"It's forgotten," she says like she's being forced to be polite to me.

The suite of rooms she shows me only reinforces my initial impression that we're in an old castle somewhere in Europe.

And now that I'm not locked in, I can better appreciate the medieval decor. The stone walls have candle sconces that look like they could be a thousand years old. There is a large fireplace, a light gray velvet couch and love seat, and a breakfast table in front of an arched window that's entirely covered by heavy maroon curtains. The gray and maroon remind me of the colors of the crest in Blackwood's office. "Daang," I whisper.

"Your bedroom's there," Layla says flatly, gesturing to my right. Her face shows no emotion whatsoever.

I follow her line of sight to a door that's a narrower version of the one I just came through.

Layla, I think. *It's a name that became popular in medieval times, and had something to do with a seventh-century poem. I'm pretty sure it's Arabic in origin, and if Blackwood's spelling was right, it's most likely Egyptian. The tricky part is that each spelling signals a slight variance in meaning. . . .* "So, um, did you know your name means 'born at night'?" I turn back to her, but she's gone. I stare at the closed door opposite mine. A lock slides into place on the other side of the wood. I didn't even hear her walk away. She's no Emily, that's certain. Who I'm sure by now is at my house, demanding to know where her best friend is and why I'm not returning her texts. I wish Dad had given me time to explain things to her.

I push open my bedroom door—*temporary* bedroom door. A candle's lit on my bedside table next to a carafe and drinking glass, and there's a basin of water on my dresser that I presume is for washing up. A white nightgown identical to Layla's lies across the end of my bed—which has a canopy made of wood and an intricately carved headboard. Unfortunately, though, my luggage is nowhere to be seen, and I'm too exhausted to try

13

to sort it out. I pull off my boots and my jeans, dropping them on the floor in a pile, and sit down on the bed. It's like sinking into a giant pillow.

I grab the bottom of my sweater to pull it over my head but change my mind and tuck my legs under the blankets. I blow out the bedside candle and fall backward into the mound of fluff. Only then does my chest tighten with homesickness.

I exhale and stare at the wooden canopy above me. *I can make it a couple of weeks anywhere,* I assure myself. *I made it through soccer camp last summer in a field that stank of rotten cabbage—I'll make it through this.*

Two

I TUCK A white linen shirt into a pair of black leggings that I found mysteriously laid out for me when I returned from my bath. I stare at myself in my vanity mirror. The only thing I recognize is my long braid. The rest of me looks like I've dressed up as a pirate for the Renaissance Faire. If Emily saw me, she would laugh for a year. I just wish I had my phone to take a picture.

There's a knock on my bedroom door.

"Come in!" I say, and the door swings open.

Layla's dressed in the same clothes as me, only the pirate gear doesn't diminish her grace. Her hair is in a high sleek ponytail that reaches most of the way down her back. If anything, she looks more regal than she did last night. "We'll be late if we don't go soon. And I'm never late."

"I'm usually late," I say in a friendly tone. "Maybe you'll be a good influence on me."

She frowns.

"Do you know where these clothes came from?" I gesture toward my black-laced boots. "When I got back from the bathroom, they were on the trunk at the foot of my bed."

Her frown deepens. "The maid."

"The maid?" I pause. "You're kidding." Dad never even hired a housekeeper and now I have a maid? This school must have cost him his savings. The knot that formed in my stomach last night tightens. Something about my dad's decision and this entire situation feels off.

She stands a little straighter, which I didn't imagine was possible with her already perfect posture. "Not in the least."

Sheesh. She's stiffer than my ninety-year-old physics teacher. "Well, any chance you know what happened to my clothes?" I ask. "Also, the things I brought with me from"—I remember rule number one—"home. I can't find my luggage anywhere."

"Personal items are forbidden on campus. Headmaster Blackwood keeps them locked up."

"Even my toiletries and my—"

"Everything."

I grumble. I already miss my pillowcase covered in pine trees that was part of a bed set I lusted after for months. And the scarf Emily knitted last winter that has become a staple of my wardrobe even though it's lopsided—all the familiar little bits and pieces from my life are locked up somewhere I can't get them.

"About that—the forbidden part. What's the deal with all the secrecy?" I ask.

Layla looks at me suspiciously. "Why would you ask me that?"

I definitely wasn't expecting her to dish on all the inner workings of this place, considering the severity of Blackwood's rules, but I also wasn't expecting such a defensive answer. Now she's piqued my interest. I smile the disarming smile that's always worked well for me. "I was just hoping you could explain it to me."

"Don't be absurd." She lifts her chin and turns around in one fluid motion. I wouldn't be surprised if she practiced that dramatic exit, waiting for someone to frustrate her so she could use it.

I follow her into the sitting room. She opens a tall armoire and pulls out two floor-length black coats with hoods and hands me one.

I examine the velvet-lined wool with interest. There are gloves in the pockets. "Is this a *cape*?"

"It's a *cloak*," she corrects me, "and the quality is impeccable."

At just about heart level on the left-hand side of the cloak is the crest I saw in Blackwood's office. It's embroidered with silver and maroon thread. "*'Historia Est Magistra Vitae,'*" I read out loud. I'm great with Latin root words—it's one of the things I picked up when I became fascinated with name origins—but I'm awful with the grammar. "History, Teacher, Life?"

"*History Is the Teacher of Life*—Academy Absconditi's motto," Layla says, and sighs like she's resigning herself to something tedious. "The maroon means patience in battle. The silver means peace. The oak tree signifies great age and strength. The torch represents truth and intelligence. And the sphinx symbolizes omniscience and secrecy." Layla opens our arched door before the last word leaves her mouth and walks out of the suite without pause.

I follow her and close the door behind us, thinking about

the crest as I put the cloak on. The stone hallway is brighter than last night, but the air is still cold, giving it an all-around gloomy feel.

That was a serious rundown of symbols Layla just gave me, not some generalized school motto. I chew on my lip. It's odd that someone chose colors that mean both "patience in battle" and "peace," which strike me as contradictory. Also, I don't know much about crests, but I do know that the sphinx is most commonly associated with Egyptian and Greek cultures. "So back to this secrecy thing—"

"No."

I take a better look at Layla. I wonder what would happen if she ever met my dad. I bet they would stare each other down, never saying more than two words to each other. I guarantee she's the type of girl who likes to pretend she never farts and if one did slip out she would pass out from overwhelm. I laugh.

Layla turns to me sharply. "What?"

For a brief second, I consider telling her. "Look, we're here together, right? In this, well, this castle, I guess, for at least the next few weeks until we go home for the holidays—" *And home forever.*

She huffs. "*I'm* not going home for any holidays."

I search her face for a hint of emotion but find none. I would be devastated if I wasn't with my family for the holidays. "Just the same, we might as well make the best of it. Don't you think?"

Layla turns away from me and down a stone corridor with a series of narrow arched windows cut into it. The stone is so thick that you could easily use the windowsills as seats. I can picture archers perching in them once upon a time, raining arrows down on enemy invaders.

"This building takes some time to learn," Layla says, completely ignoring my comment. "It zigzags, but the thing to remember is that the outside is a rectangle. So if you follow the outer wall, you can always find your way again."

It's like I'm having a conversation with the supermarket lady, Agnes, who hums incessantly and barely listens to anyone. Instead of answering whatever question you asked, she responds with whatever she's currently thinking about. Emily and I treat her like a fortune cookie. If she tells us the artichokes are running rampant or that potato sprouts look like zombie fingers, we figure trouble's afoot, but if she goes on about a new ice cream shipment, it's going to be an amazing day.

"And if you find yourself outside in a courtyard or garden, you're somewhere in the center of the rectangle," Layla continues in a monotone, like she's reading out of a brochure. "The entire structure is three stories tall, except for one tower that's four stories."

"Blackwood's office," I say, happy to recall a sliver of information about this place.

"Yes," she says, and takes a quick questioning look at me. "You can orient yourself by that tower. Think of it as north and the girls' dormitory as east. Directly across from us, on the west side of the building, is the boys' dormitory."

I count the doors and the turns as we go, a crack in a stone, a step that's steeper than the others, committing them to memory. I was the kid everyone followed around at carnivals because it only took me one go-around before I knew where everything was. Dad says it's from obsessively learning every inch of the woods near our home, which are a bazillion times harder to map than a building or a fair.

Layla reaches the end of the corridor, goes down three steps, and turns left. "I suspect the class schedule here is going to be different from what you're used to. While some classes are back to back, most are not because many of the courses involve physical exertion. Our heaviest days are Monday through Friday, with a lighter schedule on the weekend. But the professors have the right to call an impromptu challenge whenever they want." She pushes a flyaway hair back into place. "Now we're entering the north side of the building, which has classrooms and faculty offices." She points to the wall. "And the south side has common rooms—the dining hall, library, weapons rooms, and so on."

I stop abruptly. "Hang on. What kind of weapons rooms?"

She stops, too. "We have a fairly extensive sword collection. And the bows and knives are some of the best."

I can feel myself grinning. I've never used a real sword. Dad always made me practice with a wooden one, which I did so often that I broke my fair share of them. And a room full of knives? Sign me up.

"But the poisons aren't what they could be," Layla continues, almost to herself. "There's no point in talking about it now, though, because we won't get to that side of the building until lunchtime."

My smile disappears. "Poisons?"

"I hear they're expanding the curriculum next term, so it may improve." Her delivery is matter-of-fact.

As far as I can tell, the only reasons to teach poisons are because you plan to use them or because you think someone might use them on you—neither of which sits well with me. "Why exactly are we learning about poisons?"

She looks at me like I can't be serious. "You're excited by knives but wonder why there's a poisons class? If this is some kind of carefree, innocent act, you can do better than that."

I stare at her. "Using knives, arrows, and swords is a *skill*. Poisons are strictly about hurting people."

"Right. And knives are for cuddling," she says flatly, and starts walking again. "You have an appointment right now with the head of assessment. His office is just down this hall."

I grab her wrist, but she smoothly undoes my grip before I get a good hold. She glares at me, the first real sign of life I've seen in her. "Don't ever do that."

"Touch your arm? Sorry. But stop the tour for a sec. I'm serious. What's with the poisons and the archaic eye-for-an-eye rule?" My off feeling is escalating and I'm getting the distinct sense that there is something about this place I should know and don't. "And what about the student deaths Blackwood mentioned? I know I can't ask who the students are and all, but can you explain at least a little? Should I be nervous right now?"

For a second she looks confused. "I don't know what you want me to say."

"The truth. Why would our parents send us to an isolated school where all the rules have some imminent-danger theme?" I dislike the disorientation of not knowing where I am, but not as much as I can't stand the idea that my dad withheld information from me.

"There's less danger here than anywhere else," Layla says like I've offended her last sensibility.

"Not from where I'm standing."

She leans toward me and levels her voice. "I told you to stop playing this innocent game."

"It's no game." I hesitate. My instinct is to double down. "I'm sorry you're annoyed, but since my dad isn't here to grill—"

"Lower your voice." Her tone is commanding and fiery. She looks behind her down the empty hall and pushes me back with surprising force into the stairwell we just came out of. "Maybe this isn't an act. Maybe you really don't know. But stupidity isn't the answer." Her voice is barely above a whisper and is flat-out accusatory.

"Why would you think my questions are an act? What on earth would I gain from it?"

"My answer's still a resounding no," she hisses. "By referencing your father, and *only* your father, you just told me that it's likely your mother is dead. Now I know something about you, combined with the fact that you were clearly raised in America, based on your vernacular. The clothing you arrived in last night suggests you live in a northern climate, and based on the style of clothing, I'd say a rural area rather than an urban one. Your features suggest you're originally from western Europe; I would guess southern Italian because of your hair and eyes. That narrows you down to only a handful of Families you could be related to. Should I go on?"

I stare at her. Who, or what, is this girl? "Families? What *families?*"

Her eyes widen and her hands clench. "You're loud and you're reckless and there is absolutely no chance I'm giving you information. Good play, but you've lost." Her words are biting.

"Wait—"

"I'm done with this conversation," she says. "I can't *believe* Headmaster Blackwood matched us as roommates." She walks away from me at full speed.

Damn. I'm striking out here. Charm doesn't work; being pushy doesn't work. I raise my hands in surrender. "Look, I'm really not trying to piss you off. Honest. My best friend always says I push so hard that sometimes I push people right over a cliff. I get that you don't trust me. I'll do my best to chill out and stop attacking you with questions. But I'm not playing you and I don't know what I've 'lost.'"

Before she can respond, the doors around us creak open. Students pour into the hallway, all wearing the same clothes and cloaks we are. Did a class just end? I didn't even hear a bell. Where I'm used to shouts and laughter and pushing between classes, there are only hushed conversations and deliberate movements.

Layla weaves in and out of the creepily quiet students. The glances I get are so subtle that if I weren't looking for them I would assume the other students didn't even notice me. There's none of the openmouthed new-kid ogling that goes on at my school.

I shiver. There's something unsettling about this place, making me further question Dad's decision to send me here. It feels like a test, a way for him to prove the point he's always trying to make about me being too trusting. I can almost hear him saying: "Look, look at this place and tell me I'm not wrong—people *always* have something to hide." The strange part is, even though we had our disagreements when it came to trusting people, underneath it all I got the sense that he was secretly proud that I looked for the best in everyone. Maybe I was wrong.

"Layla," says a guy walking toward us, and I snap out of my thoughts. He looks remarkably like her, other than his height. Where she's three inches shorter than me, he's three inches taller. But they both have the same regal presence and the same pointed expression. "I'm surprised," he continues. "I would have thought you'd be at the assessment office by now." He winks at her.

Judging by his comment, it occurs to me she must have told him I was here early this morning. Either that, or they somehow knew I was coming, which worries me more. There's no phone or Internet here for communicating, so the only way they could have known was if this was arranged days ahead of time, days before I knew myself.

"Extenuating circumstances." Layla looks at me like I'm an unidentifiable cafeteria food. "Ash, this is November, my new roommate. November, Ash."

"Layla with a roommate. Who would have thought this day would ever come?" He looks directly at me and I involuntarily take a step backward. There's something about his gaze that makes me feel instantly exposed, as though he shined an unforgiving light on the pimple I was hoping no one would notice. Where Layla's cold, he appears warm, and yet there's nothing welcoming about his welcome.

"You didn't have a roommate before me?" I ask. Blackwood did say there were only a hundred students and this school is huge, so it's not surprising there might be singles. But it does seem like a lonely choice in this gray place.

"We're not all suited for it," Layla says, and it feels like a warning as much as an explanation.

"I imagine Layla's taking good care of you?" Ash says before I can respond. The more he speaks, the more I notice the similarities he shares with Layla—the way they move their eyebrows, their strong cheekbones, and even the curve of their hairline.

"She's an excellent tour guide," I say. "But so far I'm a terrible tour-ee. I'm mostly badgering her with questions." I pause, piecing together what little I know about him. "Is Ash short for . . . Ashai?"

His smile widens but looks forced. "Exactly. I'm surprised Layla was talking about me; it's unlike her."

You can say that again. "She wasn't. It's just that Ash by itself isn't an Egyptian name. And since Layla's name *is* Egyptian, I assumed that yours would be, too. I mean, you two are brother and sister, right?" I don't feel the same thrill I usually do when I do this. Instead, I get the sense that I've said something terribly wrong.

Ash looks at Layla and not at me. "You told her we're Egyptian?"

The *we're* tells me I'm also right about them being siblings. Layla lifts her chin. "Obviously not."

They look at each other for a few long seconds. They don't say a word, but even I can tell they're communicating in some way by the intensity of the looks they share.

Ash shifts his gaze back to me. "I have time this afternoon. Maybe I could join your tour or even take over for Layla if she needs a break?"

My instinct is to say no, apologize to Layla, and promise I'll stop talking if she just won't pass me off to him.

Thankfully, Layla shakes her head. "You know she's my responsibility," she says, and I'm grateful—not that being called someone's responsibility is a compliment.

"Well, then, I guess I'll just see you both at lunch. Oh, and Layla . . ." He holds up a small braid made of pine needles.

Layla checks the now-empty pocket of her cloak while Ash

25

grins victoriously. "Five, four," she says with a hint of annoyance. "You win."

Ash gives us both a small bow as he slips back into the river of students, who behave more like spies than high schoolers. Up close his intensity is almost overwhelming, but as he walks away I find that it's equally hard not to watch him. I'm not sure if I'm intrigued or intimidated.

Three

I TAKE A seat on one of the maroon couches in the assessment office, which is mostly lit by the glow of flames coming from a large fireplace. Portraits of sour-looking old men and women cover the walls, and the ceiling is crossed with wooden beams. I drag my boot along a faded rug and look out the tall, narrow window, which reveals nothing but thick tree branches.

Dr. Conner places a silver tray bearing steaming-hot bread, butter, and jam on the table in front of me. My stomach rumbles in response. There are few things in the world better than fresh bread. And because of the drugging, I'm not even sure how long it's been since I last ate.

"Now, November, I'm going to ask you a series of questions," Dr. Conner says as he lowers himself onto the couch across from me. His accent sounds British, and he wears a black blazer similar to Blackwood's, only his has a maroon pocket square. If I had to guess, he's about my dad's age or maybe even a few years younger.

"The most important thing is that you answer honestly," Dr. Conner says as he crosses his legs and opens a leather folder.

"It will greatly increase our chances of getting you into the appropriate classes. As it's unusual for us to accept a student midyear, especially one as old as you, we don't have the time to leisurely assess your strengths and weaknesses the way we normally would."

"Absolutely. Fire away," I say as my brain races through its own assessment. *Conner—deriving from* cunnere, *meaning "inspector," and* cun, *meaning "to examine."* "Did you get any transcripts from my school?"

He raises an eyebrow. "Certainly not. I can assure you that none of that information exists here. And everything said in this office is confidential and used only for teaching purposes. No one else has access to your files besides Headmaster Blackwood and myself."

Layla's and Blackwood's warnings ring in my head. Did he think I was testing him to see if any of my personal information was on record here?

"Oh, good. Then let's tackle your questions," I say with less pep.

He runs his hand over his short beard and frowns at me. "Are you an introvert or an extrovert?"

"Extrovert. Hundred percent," I reply.

"Do you have any injuries that currently limit your movements?"

"Nope. No injuries."

"Which level of balance most accurately describes you—the ability to walk a ledge, a tree branch, or a tightrope?"

I can feel my forehead scrunching as I consider my answer. *Where is he possibly going with this?* It feels more like an assessment for playing extreme sports than for a school. "Tree branch. Are there really people at this school who can walk a tightrope?"

"Climbing skills?" Conner asks, ignoring my question.

"Excellent."

He looks up for a brief moment. "How excellent?"

It's starting to seem like *none* of these questions are going to be about my academic strengths. "Trees are my best, but I can climb rocks, shinny up poles . . . basically, if there is a texture and a handhold, I can climb it. It's sort of a—" I stop myself before telling him that there's a running bet among my friends in Pembrook about what I can climb and how fast. *Rule number one,* I remind myself.

He lifts his eyebrows. "Nighttime or daytime?"

"Either."

"Nighttime or daytime?"

"Really, both are fine."

"I'm glad you think so," he says in a way that tells me he's not glad. "But when I give you a choice, I expect you to *choose*."

I shift my position on the couch even though I don't need to. "Nighttime."

"Why?" he says, and looks up at me.

"Well," I say, and pause. "Darkness doesn't bother me, and it can be really useful sometimes."

He nods and jots down a note, which by this point in this bizarre conversation I would really like to see.

"Which of your senses would you say is the strongest?"

"Huh, okay, let me think." When I was little, Dad and I started playing this game where one person was blindfolded and would follow the other through the woods and away from the house for five minutes. The leader would zigzag and go in circles, trying to confuse the blindfolded person as much as possible. But if the blindfolded one could find their way back to the house, they won. I always did it by listening and by touching the trees. Dad swore he did it mostly by scent, which I still think is unbelievable. He started designing outdoor strategy games like the blindfold game after my mom died when I was six. We'd go on camping trips for long weekends and he'd teach me all sorts of tricks—survival skills, I guess is what they really were, though they felt more like puzzles or games back then. He never admitted it, but I think he was trying to find ways to exhaust me physically and mentally and keep me from asking questions about my mom.

Conner clears his throat. "Next question."

"Wait, I have my answer."

He looks at me pointedly. "I said next question, November."

"Some combination of touch and hearing," I say quickly before he can start talking again, not because I couldn't pass on the question, but because I don't like to be silenced.

He doesn't react. "Would you rather climb a tree, go out to sea, or be pain-free?"

I hesitate. Dad used to give me these kinds of personality tests as a sort of riddle. I always teased him that it was a carry-over from his former life in the CIA. But what I want to know now is what going out to sea, my strongest sense, and whether I like day or night have to do with anything.

"It's not a difficult question," Conner says, and my brain snaps into motion.

Climb a tree probably means you just want to have fun or live in the moment. *Go out to sea?* Leave where you are, feeling unsatisfied with your current situation. *Be pain-free . . .*

other than the obvious meaning, I'm actually not sure about this one.

Conner pulls at his beard and looks between me and the folder as he jots down notes.

"Be pain-free," I say, even though *climb a tree* is definitely the most accurate for me. However, if there's one thing I get the sense this school doesn't value, it's having carefree fun.

He grunts. "And your capacity for spatial relations?"

"Solid."

"Athletic stamina?"

"I've always played a lot of sports . . . so I would say strong."

"Codes?"

"As in breaking them?" Boy, this guy doesn't spare a word he doesn't have to.

"As in breaking or creating."

I shrug. "No experience."

He looks up at me for a second and I get the sense that he doesn't believe me. "Okay, good. That will give us a starting point at least for class assignment."

Class assignment—I now take it that the classes Blackwood and Layla described aren't just electives, they *are* the curriculum. Not that I'm sad to give up math and English, but it's also shocking that a prep school wouldn't be more focused on academics.

Conner puts the leather folder on the table. He looks at the untouched tray of food. "Aren't you going to have some bread and jam?"

"Thanks, but I'm good. Feel free to eat without me," I say, trying not to make eye contact with the tempting bread.

"You must be hungry. You haven't had breakfast yet," he says, and smiles.

After they most likely drugged me on the plane, there is no way I'm eating this. I look at him squarely. "This is an assessment office and you're assessing me, right? The only thing I can think is that the food is part of my assessment, and I'm not sure I want to find out what's in it."

His expression shifts, like he's found something he was looking for. "You're suspicious. Or maybe it's just me that you don't trust."

For a second I'm taken aback. This is the first time anyone has ever called me suspicious. And somehow this comment feels different from the others, like he's probing my psyche as opposed to just collecting information. "I don't like to make the same mistake twice," I say carefully.

He waits a beat, and I can practically see the wheels in his head turning, making decisions about me. It's strangely uncomfortable to be assessed when you don't know what people are looking for or what types of conclusions they are coming to.

Conner leans back on the couch, and his casual posture almost appears welcoming, like I'm talking to one of my friends' dads, not an uptight assessment officer. *Dad.* A pang of homesickness grips my empty stomach.

"How much do you know about the Academy, November?" Conner asks.

"Very little," I say, and I can tell by his look that he takes it as the truth.

"Headmaster Blackwood asked that I speak to you a bit about our history and what is expected of you here," he says, and I lean forward.

"Yes, please." At this point I'll take all the info I can get.

He folds his hands in his lap. "But," he says with emphasis, "this brief introduction will not make up for the plethora of information that you have missed in your first two years."

I get the sense that he's warning me, which is baffling. Why would they let me in if they were so worried about everything I've missed?

"Before we get into all that, though—Headmaster Blackwood made rule number one clear to you, did she not?"

"Never reveal personal information about yourself or your family," I say.

Conner nods. "We also ask that you use precautions with any students you might recognize. We understand it's inevitable that some of you will know each other. But it's in those moments when you are most comfortable that you will be the most vulnerable," he says, and again I get the feeling that he's fishing for something.

"Not a problem," I say. "I don't know anyone."

He looks at me for a long moment and clears his throat. "Now, let's see here. . . . The Academy was designed and built by the original Council of Families as an elite institution for their best and brightest children. It was the first time that all of the Families worked together toward a common goal. It was agreed then, as it is still agreed today, that strategic excellence and safety among their children be prioritized above politics."

Now I'm officially lost. I want to ask him *What politics?* but he continues speaking before I can open my mouth.

"I cannot tell you the exact date this school was founded, as its secrecy has prevented some of that information from being recorded, although many estimate that it was approximately fifteen hundred years ago, roughly a thousand years after the first three original Families formed. What I can tell you is that

Academy Absconditi has been housed in this particular *building* since 1013." He lifts his chin a little higher, as though that's a mark of pride.

Families—there's that word again. When I questioned Layla about it, she acted like I was being intentionally annoying. Conner clearly assumes I know what it means, too, and I'm not sure I want him to know that I don't. I nod as if I'm following.

"All students have the same required core classes," Conner says. "And the choice of special electives like accents, martial arts, coding, boxing, archery, and horticulture. While levels of specific skills vary within each year of students, there is a strict divide between the elemental-level students in their first two years and the advanced-level students. If an elemental-level student cannot transition properly to advanced-level expectations, they are not permitted to stay." Conner pauses in a way that makes me think he wants me to understand the gravity of his words.

"And because I'm seventeen, I'm guessing I'm in my third year and therefore an advanced-level student?" I say.

"You are. Now, we've been assured that your physical skills are sufficient. But the core class that links everything we do here is history. Unfortunately, you have missed two and a half years of lessons that not only reveal the stories of the original Families but also analyze the major historical events they influenced. It's the strategy discussed in the context of these historical events that will shape your education here. Headmaster Blackwood only hopes that your tutors have been good enough that you do not slow down the other students. As I said, excellence is a must."

History Is the Teacher of Life now makes perfect sense as

the school motto. Also, I'm pretty sure my dad would kill me if he spent a ton of money to safeguard me in a remote private school only to have me sent home because I failed some cryptic history class. I rub my hands together. "And if I wanted to do some independent studying just in case? Is there a book I could read or something?"

Conner frowns for so long that I cough in the hope that the sound will make him stop staring. "I fear that if you don't realize there's no written record of that history, it may be altogether impossible for you to survive here with the other students."

The word *survive* sends a chill through me. So I laugh. I laugh because I'm good at it, because it's been my lifelong go-to in order to make people feel at ease, and because I get the distinct impression that I just revealed my hand and need to recover—fast. "I didn't mean a book about *Family* history. I meant a book that might help me with, you know, the subtleties."

He huffs like he's unsure, but the threat has disappeared from his eyes.

"Or anything else you can think of," I say. "I'm all ears."

He relaxes into the pillows behind him. "Well, now, that is something you will just have to figure out for yourself."

I open my mouth to respond but catch myself. What a jerk.

Dr. Conner stands. "Now if you'll follow me, I have one final thing for you to do this morning."

I get up off the plush couch and push my braid over my shoulder.

Conner pulls two chairs away from the wall and sets them up facing each other. I wait for him to sit down, but he doesn't. Instead, he straightens his vest and stands behind the chair on the right. "Sit, please, in whichever seat you like."

The chair he's not standing behind would put my back to the door. I don't know if it's a feng shui thing or not, but it's always bugged me to sit with my back to an exit. However, there's no way I'm going to sit in the seat he's standing two inches behind. I glance around, and instead of choosing, I sit on the floor with my back against the wall where the chairs originally stood.

I don't bother to explain my actions and he doesn't ask. No "I gave you a choice" speech this time, either. He just jots down more notes.

After a moment, Conner hands me a piece of paper with eight squares of color on it. "Please mark each color with a number, one being your favorite and eight being your least favorite. No need to overthink it. Just choose which colors you enjoy the most."

I stare at him. First all those odd questions, and now a color test?

Conner offers me a pen and a pencil.

I take the pencil and mark a *1* next to yellow and a *2* next to green. They remind me of the sun and the trees and are exactly the opposite of being in this gloomy gray building. I mark a *3* next to red and the pencil breaks in my hand; the entire point comes off. I look up at Conner, who is watching me carefully and without surprise. He makes no effort to offer me the pen or a different pencil.

Is he waiting to see if I'll ask for help? Screw that. I stick the pencil in my mouth and bite into the wood. Then I pull bits of it off with my fingernails until the exposed lead forms a crude tip and I continue marking the colors. Conner watches my every move.

I stand up when I'm finished and hand it back to him.

He nods at the paper, like it's telling him things he already knows. "You may go," he says over his shoulder as he walks back to his desk.

"Can I ask you something?" I say. "Was that food you offered me okay to eat?"

Conner turns around and pulls a small vial of something from his blazer. "The antidote," he says, and smiles.

I stare at him in horror. I figured the food might be part of the assessment, but I didn't actually predict that the guy who's been charged with making sure I acclimate here was going to poison me.

He takes a seat at his desk. "And now you must go," he says. "I have a schedule to keep."

I grab the door latch. I can't get out of his office fast enough.

Four

I RUN MY fingertips along the cold, uneven stone walls as I follow Layla down the stairs in silence. I asked her about the seat choice and the pencil thing, but she only asked me what actions I took. Which in turn had me wondering what information I would be giving away if I told her. So I shut up.

Layla leads me through the tapestry-lined foyer I walked through last night on my way to Blackwood's office. She stops in front of a broad wooden door and a young guard opens it. The guard is dressed in the same leather armbands and leather belt that the guys who escorted me to my room last night wore.

"Thanks," I say as I pass the guard, but she doesn't respond. I grumble under my breath.

My upset disappears, though, the moment my boot touches the soft grass in the rectangular courtyard. The temperature instantly drops, but not as harshly as I would expect for December. Of course the inside temperatures are lower than I'm used to, so I might not notice the difference the way I normally would. The humidity feels similar to home, which doesn't tell me much about where I am, considering that many parts of

Europe have winter climates comparable to what I have in Pembrook. And the air is thick with the earthy smell of damp soil and moss that's reminiscent of being deep in a forest.

The perimeter is lined by ancient oak trees with enormous trunks, which doesn't give me any clues, since oaks are also common throughout Europe and North America. But despite the lack of info I can glean from them, they are stunning. Their tops have been carefully groomed to create a dense arched canopy over the entire space, dappling the light on the ground. Thick vines hang from the branches at a variety of lengths, making the whole thing a Peter Pan–esque fantasy jungle gym.

I run my hand along one of the vines and give it a tug. "I guess this place isn't all bad," I say between dry lips, realizing my mouth has been hanging open as I've been taking it all in. Catching flies, as Emily would say.

"This courtyard is used as part of our athletics program, and it's strictly forbidden to climb the vines without an instructor present," Layla says, squarely putting the kibosh on my desire to shinny up them. But even she can't completely dampen this moment for me.

"When is that class?" I ask.

"Tomorrow," she says.

"For juniors and seniors, or for everyone?" I take a deep breath, enjoying the scent of freshly cut grass and bark.

"We don't use grade standings like that. Fifteen- and sixteen-year-olds are considered elemental. Seventeen- and eighteen-year-olds are advanced," she says. "And we don't share classes with the younger students. Generally, they have a lighter schedule than we do, giving them more time for practice."

I nod. That fits with everything Conner told me. "Question:

If everything here is so secret, how do people apply for college? I'm guessing there are no transcripts from this place."

Layla looks at me like my question is ridiculous. "*If* we go to college."

"Why go to a prep school described as only admitting the best if you don't plan on going to college?" I ask.

"And why waste four years studying inane subjects in college when you could just say you went and be done with it?" she counters.

My eyes widen. So then this isn't some bizarre supplementary prep school with a focus on survival skills, like I thought. It's the *only* education these kids seem to think they need. But what kind of a career can you possibly plan on having if your main skill sets are in weapons, history, and deception? Spies? Assassins? Secret service? I want to think I'm wrong and that Dad would never send me here if that were the case, but I honestly can't understand Layla's reply. "So what does everyone do if they don't go to college?" I ask carefully.

She looks at me sideways. "Whatever our Families need us to do," she says, and turns around. "Try to keep up. We still have a lot to cover."

I follow her to a gap in the wall of trees, trying to figure out if there is a better way for me to ask what I want to know without getting a cryptic answer or frustrating her. The part that's making me most uncomfortable is that from what I've heard and seen today, this doesn't seem like the type of place where you pop in for two weeks and leave. I'm now convinced that my dad omitted something important, and I really don't like the uneasy feeling I'm experiencing as a result.

We pass through an arched doorway formed from vines and into a garden bursting with color. It, too, has a thick tree canopy, well groomed like the last. Only, instead of vines for climbing, this courtyard is decorated with garlands of royal purple berries and white flowers. Purple profusion berries, if I remember correctly from the plant books I've always hoarded and refused to let Dad donate to the library. Giant, moss-covered rocks have been sculpted into benches, and blue, purple, and white flowers are arranged in intricate patterns.

"The garden lounge," Layla says with pride. "Students are allowed to spend free time here during daylight hours. The snow can't easily make its way through the thick tree canopy, and since there is a hot spring that runs under the school, we get to enjoy the flowers nearly all year round."

Off the top of my head I know that the UK, France, Iceland, Germany, and Italy all have hot springs, and I'm sure there are more that I don't even know about, so again the school gives nothing away about its location.

"This place is phenomenal," I say, breathing in the sweet flowery air. But I can't fully enjoy it because I'm still hung up on the spy/assassin worry and my dad.

"We have a resident horticulturist who teaches an elective in botany and also works with our poisons teacher," Layla says. "He never plants anything lethal in here, though," she adds, registering the look of concern that I'm sure flashed across my face. "*That* greenhouse is located in the outer perimeter."

"The outer perimeter?" I ask.

"Between the school and the outermost wall," Layla says. "Only select faculty members have access to it. It's also where the food is grown and the dairy cows and hens are kept." She points to another archway visible through the wall of trees. "Through that way is an open field. There's an archery class in there right now."

"By *open*, do you mean with no tree canopy?" I ask.

She shakes her head. "All outdoor space is camouflaged. There are even trees planted on the school's roofs, and vines on its walls."

I blink at her, and for the first time it really sinks in that I'm in an ancient building no one knows the location of, with no easy way for me to contact the outside world. "And that's to . . . keep the locals from spying on us, or to hide us from airplanes?"

"Actually," Layla says, looking skyward, "they say there's a kind of high-tech camouflage netting that encases the school and reflects radar, making the entire building nearly undetectable and appear like nothing more than a hill."

I'm now convinced that whatever Dad was trying to protect me from by sending me here must be really dangerous. Which only makes me worry about him and Aunt Jo. I'm seriously regretting not pushing harder to make him tell me the specifics.

Layla heads for the archway she just pointed at and waves her hand for me to follow.

And I do. "I thought you just said there was a class in there?"

"I did," she says, and enters the next courtyard with me right behind her.

I gasp.

To our left, five students in identical stances brandish bows and arrows. Behind them, another ten or so await their turn. And to our right is a wall affixed with wooden targets, not bull's-eyes but a series of Xs no bigger than a quarter.

"Release!" says a wiry woman with high cheekbones. She wears an all-black version of the outfit we're wearing.

Five arrows whiz past us so fast that I feel the wind on my face. They securely lodge in the top line of Xs. Not one is amiss.

"Easy enough," says the teacher.

I swallow. I can't believe how good they all are.

"Now try it with movement," the teacher says, and I detect a French accent.

One of the archers steps a few feet in front of the rest, and his gaze makes me just as uncomfortable as it did when I talked to him earlier—*Ash*. He gives Layla and me a knowing grin and spins a leg out to the side in a fast kick as he releases an arrow in midair. It not only lands in an X, it hits it so perfectly it splits the X in half.

My mouth opens. "That was incredible," I say to Layla.

The teacher turns and looks at me. "Since you're talking during my class, I assume you would like to try to top that."

And before I can get a word out, an arrow whizzes through the air and punctures the grass at my feet. I reflexively jump backward. A bow comes next.

"Um, I don't—" I start.

Layla snatches the bow and before I can finish my sentence she's loaded and shot the arrow. She not only hits the board, she splits the arrow her brother shot in two. "It won't happen again, Professor Fléchier," Layla says.

Fléchier—French for sure, but also related to Fulcher *in Old English, meaning "maker of arrows."* I'm starting to realize these professors' names must be pseudonyms, given their literal meanings.

There's the sound of metal hitting metal and I look back

at the target board. Another arrow is lodged in the same entry point as Ash's. The guy who shot it is tall, with hair that's bleached white and the type of confident posture that makes it hard not to notice him. He winks at me and I smile before I can consider it.

Layla practically pushes me back through the archway and into the flower garden. "How dare you embarrass me like that!"

I stare at her in awe. "I'm pretty sure I embarrassed myself. You, on the other hand, split an arrow *in half.* And after seeing that, I'm seriously regretting having pissed you off."

"There are rules, alliances, *manners,*" Layla says, clearly annoyed with me. "You *never* interrupt a teacher. And especially not . . . Professor Fléchier is . . . Do something like that again and I'm demanding a roommate change."

I press my lips together. I've never seen another student get this mad about talking in class. And I've also never seen a teacher react like that. I'm not only out of my element here, but my instincts are all wrong. "I'm sorry, Layla. I really am. I'm just not used to the rules here yet."

Her expression relaxes a little and she straightens out her already straight cloak. "That's the second time you've apologized to me today."

I half smile. "You'll know it's really bad when I start buying you presents," I say. "My best friend used to keep an ongoing request list."

Layla looks at me curiously. "Let's go," she says in a tone that tells me she's not *really* mad anymore.

She weaves through the flower beds toward the far wall, where gray stone peeks out between the tree trunks, and pushes through a wooden door. I reluctantly leave the cushioned grass, running my hand over a tree trunk as I go. A guard shuts the door behind us. He has an odd scar above his right eyebrow in the shape of an X. Even though he doesn't say a word, he doesn't try to hide the fact that he's scoping me out, either.

Layla gestures at the high-ceilinged foyer with shields mounted on the wall and a statue of an armored knight. "We're now in the south side of the building. These shields commemorate some of the most important achievements our Families have made—minus the past two hundred years, of course."

I take a good look at the shields. Conner's comments about history play in my mind. But the last time I asked Layla about Families head-on, she got annoyed. Plus, that guard hasn't taken his eyes off me and it's giving me the creeps.

"And you know who all these shields belong to?" I say as though I doubt her knowledge.

She scoffs and points to my left. "That one represents Aśoka's most trusted advisor, that one Alexander the Great's lover, Julius Caesar's aunt, Cleopatra's best friend, Akbar's cousin, Peter the Great's councilor, Genghis Khan's strategist, and Elizabeth the First's chambermaid. Need I go on?"

I shake my head, trying to convince her and that staring guard that I know what she's talking about. But the truth is, I'm more confused than I was before. What do chambermaids and best friends have to do with this school?

"Sit, Nova," Dad says, gesturing at the couch.

I plop down and pull my favorite red-and-cream-plaid blanket over my legs.

Dad sits next to me. He rubs the palm of his callused hand with his thumb and is silent for a few long seconds. "I don't have enough time to explain everything if you're going to get on that plane tonight. Besides, there's nothing you need to know right now. I'll take care of everything here. In the meantime, you go learn some new knife skills and survival tactics."

I frown at him. It's not unlike him to speak around things. But there's something in his voice that unsettles me, a crack in his confidence. "Did something happen to Aunt Jo that you're not telling me?"

He looks tired. "I don't know all the details. Which is part of the reason I need to go and help sort things out and make sure everything and everyone is safe."

"Okay," I say slowly. "But you told me she had a break-in. That's not the worst, is it? I mean, even if it has something to do with your old CIA life, do you really think it warrants sending me off to some—"

"Nova, I need you to trust me. Can you do that?" His expression doesn't give anything away, but there is a gravity to his tone.

"Of course," I say, and I want to push the issue, but every time he's ever told me to trust him, he's done it for a reason. And every time he's been right.

He nods and some of the tension seems to leave his eyes.

We're quiet for a few seconds, all the unanswered questions hanging between us like thick fog.

He watches me. "I understand that it must feel sudden, but I don't have a lot of good choices at present. I just know I can't take any chances where you're concerned. If your aunt is in any kind of danger, then we very well might be, too. I want to clear up whatever is going on and be certain it doesn't spill into our lives here."

I don't bother asking him what would happen if it did. Because I know. He would do whatever he needed to protect me, including move us. He told me that once when I was little and I've never forgotten it. There are few things I love more than living in Pembrook, and if I have to go to some remote school for a few weeks while he sorts things out to keep us from having to move away, I most certainly will.

He laughs suddenly and catches me off guard. "Do you remember the time that man kicked his dog and Aunt Jo kicked him? He threatened to call the police on her and she said, 'Do it. I hope they send me to jail. It'll give me lots of time to contemplate how I'm going to kill you when I get out.'"

I grin. "Tiny and vicious. Believe me, I know exactly why you want to go to Providence. Who knows what she'll do left to her own devices."

And just like that, we're back on the same page. No more fog. No more answers, either. But it's always kind of been that way with him. And it doesn't matter. Because even if I don't know exactly what's going on, I know him.

I exhale. "I guess a few weeks isn't the end of the world."

He nods like he knew I would come to this conclusion. "Good. We're agreed. And Nova, I know you've got a lot of questions. And I know how much self-restraint it's taking for you not to fight me tooth and nail on this. But I promise you that you know exactly as much as will keep you safe. And I will take care of whatever is going on."

I frown at the shields. No, I don't know what will keep me safe. And how did he hear about this school, anyway? I assumed it was some kind of wicked crazy program he knew about from his CIA days. But the students aren't American, as far as I can tell; they're from all over the world. And the figures on the shields that Layla named are from vastly different historical periods. I don't see how they could have any connection to American intelligence.

A girl and a guy enter the foyer, speaking in hushed voices. But instead of passing by, they stop.

"Aarya," the girl says, introducing herself, and does a curtsy. She's got a similar complexion to Layla's and loose wavy hair. *Aarya is . . . Sanskrit, I'm pretty sure. However, it's also a name that's used by a variety of cultures all over the world.*

"And this is Felix," Aarya continues, and I catch a British accent. The guy next to her bows. Where she's relaxed, he's stiff. And he has a scar across his cheekbone that reaches all the way to his ear.

"November," I say, placing my hand on my chest. "I'm not much of a curtsier."

Aarya laughs, even though what I said wasn't funny.

"If you don't already have plans for lunch, please feel free to join us," Felix says, also with a British accent. But his facial expression remains stiff, almost awkward. He and Aarya appear to have such different demeanors, it's hard to imagine them as friends.

"Oh, thanks," I say. Finally a normal welcome. "That'd be great."

And just like that Aarya and Felix give me a quick nod and move on without another word. Well, maybe it wasn't a *super*-normal welcome, but it's definitely among the friendliest interactions I've had so far.

I turn to Layla, but her expression has gone colder than before.

"Did I do something wrong?" I ask her, and the guard's head moves ever so slightly in our direction.

She speed-walks out of the high-ceilinged room and into the hallway. About halfway down, she stops and looks both ways to make sure we're alone. "Aarya's . . . She's a *Jackal,*" she says in a hushed voice.

I look at her like she's lost me. "But she's British, right?"

Layla shakes her head. "No one knows where she grew up. She's impeccable with accents. The best in the school."

I stare at Layla. "Did you just tell me something personal about someone?" I can't help but smile.

"What I told you is that Aarya's from the Jackal Family, and by your reaction to my analysis of you earlier, I can now say that you're Italian."

"I—" I catch myself before I tell her that she's only half correct—my mom was Italian and my dad's American. Jackal Family? Something about that feels oddly familiar. "What does that mean, that she's a Jackal?"

What looks like genuine shock appears on her face. "I told you to stop that."

I close my mouth, pretty sure that whatever response I give next will be wrong.

"You're not good enough to go up against Aarya," Layla says, "and you'll hurt all of us with your stupidity."

I exhale audibly. "I honestly don't know what to say to you right now. You won't let me ask questions. And you yell at me when I say I don't know what's going on. I get that maybe you

49

don't like Aarya, but if she wants me to have lunch with her, I don't see what's so bad about that. Unless you've changed your mind and suddenly want to explain it."

Layla looks at me long and hard. It almost seems like she wants to ask me a question. Then without a word she turns and starts walking faster than before.

"Layla?" I call after her.

"I need to *think*," she says, and I have to practically run to catch up with her.

For the next hour, Layla doesn't say one word to me that she doesn't have to.

Five

LAYLA WALKS ONE step ahead of me into the cafeteria, which looks like it was modeled after a royal banquet hall. There are three tables. The one at the front of the room seats about twenty and is arranged on a raised platform. And two long tables, seating at least fifty each, run perpendicular to it. All the tables have maroon velvet chairs in neat rows and crisp white tablecloths that are super impractical for a herd of teenagers. There are centerpieces made from sprigs of spruce and white flowers, and from the ceiling hang wrought-iron chandeliers with real candles.

Teachers take their seats at the elevated table and the students politely and quietly find theirs. There is a low buzz of conversation, but nothing like the chaos of my cafeteria.

I follow Layla down the middle of the tables. Each place is set with china plates and silverware that looks freshly polished, something I thought belonged exclusively to movies. As I'm gawking at the fancy place settings, I hear my name. I look up and find Aarya smiling at me from across the table.

"Sit, sit," Aarya says, and Felix pulls out a chair.

"Layla," I say. "Do you want to—"

"No," she says, and keeps walking.

I watch Layla's back as she gets farther away from me.

"Don't worry so much. Layla worries enough for all of us," Aarya says.

I accept the chair Felix pulled out for me. Although I can't help but feel weird that I didn't follow Layla, even though I'm pretty sure we could use a minute apart.

"Thanks," I say to Felix, who sits down next to me.

"You're quite the hot topic around here." Aarya pushes bowls of roasted cauliflower and carrots and a pan of lasagna in my direction, and I gladly accept them. "Not that anyone will tell you that."

A girl with long red dreads, braided down the center of her head like a Mohawk, turns and looks at Aarya.

"What?" Aarya says. "Problem?"

The girl shakes her head and returns her eyes to her meal, but she doesn't seem the least bit put off. In fact, if I had to guess, I would say she and Aarya are friends. Interesting that Aarya, who's obviously bold and fluid, would have one friend who's so reserved and another who's so stiff.

Felix pours me a glass of water, and now that I'm so close to him, I notice that the scar on his face is a clean line, like a cut from a knife or a sword, the type you would imagine belonged to a knight or a pirate in a children's book. And by the way it's faded, it looks like he's had it for a long time. Did someone really slice him in the face when he was a kid?

"It's funny," I say, "barely anyone here has even looked in my direction, much less spoken to me."

"We're not the most openly friendly bunch," Felix says, like he prefers it that way.

"Speak for yourself," Aarya says. "I'm a hoot."

He raises an eyebrow. "I bet most of this room would disagree."

"Says the gloomy Gus from the moors of gray and rainy," she says with her mouth full, which makes me think Felix's British accent is real even if Aarya's isn't.

He gives her a warning look.

"Okay, okay," she says in a dramatic surrendering voice. "You're *not* gloomy. Barrel of laughs, you are. No one can stop when they're around you. You must take after your—"

"Aarya," he says in a sharper tone, and his back straightens further.

She laughs. "You should really see your face, mate."

I look back and forth between them as I grab a piece of garlic bread. This school might be seriously questionable, but the food is outrageously good.

"Now, November," Aarya says. "Tell us all about you."

I smile. "I thought that was the first rule of this place, not to say."

"Did you really think for a second that we don't share personal things?" Aarya asks. "You know what else is a rule that no one follows? No dating."

I almost choke on my cider and Aarya laughs, a big relaxed laugh, which earns her looks from some of the nearby students. She glares at them until they look away.

"Well then, I'm glad I'm going home soon," I say.

"Home?" Felix asks.

"For the holidays," I say.

Aarya and Felix share a subtle look, and I get the feeling they've just made some sort of assessment. I glance down the long table at Layla and wonder if I should leave them and join her.

"It's hard when you first arrive here," Aarya says. "It was an adjustment for all of us. Granted, we've all been here awhile now. But you, you're what, seventeen?"

I brush off her question with a shrug. "Which for here seems to be wicked old."

Felix dips a piece of bread in tomato sauce and shakes his head. "It's not that, it's that you're the first student we've ever heard of who came in this late. How did you swing it? Must have been enormously expensive." His intonation and posture make me examine him more closely. I've never met anyone with all the awkwardness of a debate club nerd and yet the physical appearance of an attractive pirate.

Aarya nods.

"I . . ." If I tell them that we never had much money, I'll be telling them something about my family. And if I say I don't know, then I'm revealing how truly ignorant I am of my situation. Damn it. Conversation in this place is like navigating around land mines.

I laugh to distract them from my silence. "Secrets are secrets," I say. From the corner of my eye I catch an almost imperceptible smile from the girl with the dreads. "But enough about me. What about you, Felix? By the way you emphasize the *e* in your name, I'm guessing you're British?" I pause. "Did you know your name means 'lucky' or 'successful'? And Aarya, your name is actually Sanskrit for the goddess Durga, but it's a common name in lots of countries." I drum my fingers on the table as I dredge up what I recall about her name's etymology. "But Sanskrit is a dead language, not to mention that Aarya is a name given to both boys and girls. It's funny how your name is changeable, almost like your accent. Maybe it's even an alias?"

Aarya claps her hands together with exaggerated slowness and guffaws, earning her more hard looks from nearby students. "Game on! I like this girl."

I take a bite of lasagna.

"November," a male voice says behind me. I turn around to find Ash, whose posture is relaxed but whose eyes are focused. His black hair is neat and his eyelashes are longer than mine.

"Oh, go away, Ash," Aarya says. "We were just starting to have some fun." She smacks her hands on the tablecloth, rattling a few plates. The girl with the dreads looks up. "If you take November away, I'll be stuck with this church mouse"— she waves her hand at the girl—"and Eeyore," she adds, inclining her head toward Felix.

"As much as I regret spoiling your game—I mean *fun*," Ash says in a voice that would be charming if his demeanor weren't so piercing, "November has a lot to cover on her tour and it would be better to get a head start before lunch is over."

Aarya scoffs, but neither she nor Ash seems tense. Felix and I, on the other hand, radiate nervous energy.

"Why don't we ask November what she wants to do? Eh?" Aarya says, and looks at me. "Would you rather walk these isolated halls with this smooth-talking thief, who will be assessing your every move, or stay here and eat and laugh with us?"

"Oh, Aarya, you're not still sulking over losing your knife, are you?" Ash says, and a chill runs down my spine. The nicer his tone, the more intense he sounds.

Aarya stands up so fast that her chair screeches backward. "Oh, Ashai," she says slowly, "how is that studious twin of yours—so scheduled, so predictable? If there is one person I can always find, it's that darling Layla." She uses a perfect Egyptian accent, and I can see the threat in her eyes.

I put my white cloth napkin on the table. "And you know who's always with Layla? Me. Her roommate. The one who can get into this school after the cutoff age, midsemester. Wonder what else I can do that you all can't."

I move to push my chair away from the table, but Felix grabs it and pulls it out for me, jerking me backward. He whispers near my ear, "I *know*."

My heart pounds. "Excuse me?"

But Felix acts like he didn't say a word.

I start to walk away, but Ash stops me.

"Check your pockets, November," Ash says, and I do.

I pull a salad fork from my cloak pocket. I don't know what it means, but I get the feeling it's nothing good. Ash takes it from my hand and tosses it onto the table with a clang.

Aarya blows me a kiss.

I turn away from them and follow Ash out of the cafeteria, deeply regretting the fact that I didn't listen to Layla in the first place. The moment the door closes behind us, I start talking. "What the hell was that?"

"It's against the rules to take anything from the dining hall, especially silverware that could be used as a weapon," Ash says, and gives me a pointed look. "The kitchen staff counts it after every meal. A missing fork would trigger a search."

"But when—"

"When Felix pulled out your chair," Ash replies before I can finish the question.

"So they set me up?"

Ash watches me process the information, and it suddenly occurs to me that I'm alone with him.

I look both ways down the hall. "Isn't Layla coming?"

"No. She's finishing her meal."

"Shouldn't we . . . ," I start. "Didn't she want to be the one to show me around?"

Ash smiles and I reflexively take a step back toward the cafeteria. "You just chose to sit with Aarya when she told you not to."

"Maybe we . . ." I can't think of any reason not to go with him.

"Layla is a very capable girl," he says with an emphasis on *capable,* and I'm not sure if he's telling me not to worry about Aarya's threat or that it wasn't my place to stand up for Layla.

"I don't doubt it," I say.

Ash begins to make his way down the hall at a leisurely pace like he doesn't have a care in the world.

I watch him out of the corner of my eye as we walk. Even if he doesn't think I should have stood up for Layla, the fact that I did has to count for something, right?

"If you want to ask me something, just ask," he says with a voice like silk.

I frown. He's not even looking at me and still it feels like he's reading my every move. "Do I need to worry about Aarya now?"

"Yes," he says. "But not just because of that conversation. Attention from Aarya in general is a bad sign. What did she say to you? Maybe I can help you sort it out."

"Actually, right before we left, Felix whispered 'I *know.*'"

Ash nods. "Either he's telling you he knows who you are, that he knows something you don't want him to, or possibly he was just screwing with you in order to slip the fork into your pocket."

"Well, he can't know who I am because I've never met him before," I say.

Ash looks doubtful. "That's the most naïve logic I've heard in a long time. He could know who you are because he knows your family, or because he somehow knew you were coming to this school. There are lots of reasons people might deduce who you are here, and never having met you has nothing to do with it."

I stare at him for a second. I want to tell him that I'm nothing like the rest of these students and that he's dead wrong that people here could know me, but I'm sure I'd only be revealing information about myself if I did. "When did you know I was coming?"

The corners of his mouth turn up slightly. "Layla found out the night you arrived, just a few hours before you got here."

I stare down the hall, trying to make sense of his answer. The only thing it tells me is that the school knew I was coming, which of course they did. I find it hard to believe they would take me if I were dropped on their doorstep. But it doesn't tell me how long they knew and how much my dad didn't tell me.

"Did Aarya say anything else?" Ash asks, pulling me out of my thoughts.

"She wanted me to tell her how I got into this school so late."

He stops in front of a door, and for some reason, he looks amused. "Do you always tell the truth?"

Great, how do I answer that? "Do you always stare at people with those laser eyeballs?"

He laughs, but it doesn't lighten him.

We both stand there for a beat. I reach for the door latch, but he gets to it first.

He holds the door open for me. "The advanced students' parlor." He sweeps his hand in front of him.

My shoulders drop by an inch. It's the friendliest room I've been in so far, with its roaring fireplace, piano, and huge window streaming light. There are cozy couches around the fireplace and big armchairs with footstools next to reading tables. It's as lavish as the rest of this place, but it also feels lived in.

I walk right up to the picture window, which is larger than any I've seen in this castle, and place my hand on the cold glass. Below, a handful of cows graze or sleep lazily in dappled sunlight under the oak canopy. They remind me of the cows Emily's boyfriend, Ben, and his family kept.

Emily and I enter Pembrook's town square, which is pretty much the quintessential Connecticut postcard with its Victorian homes and brick storefronts with hand-painted signs. It's late Saturday morning and people are out walking their dogs, shopping at the farmers' market in the middle of the square, and sifting through treasures at the antiques store.

"What are you and Ben doing today that's so important you can't go to the movies?" I ask Emily.

She shrugs and doesn't look at me. "Not much. Hanging out at his house."

I stop in front of Lucille's—which boasts it's the best diner in Pembrook. It's also the only diner in Pembrook. "Not much? This coming from the girl who for the last two weeks has harassed me with details about every possible everything having to do with Ben?"

"I think he wants to show me something."

"What?"

Emily's cheeks turn pink. "It's nothing."

I smirk. "His ability to unhook your bra?"

Emily's cheeks go from pink to crimson and I can't help but grin. "No, idiot. You know he hasn't even kissed me yet."

I wag my eyebrows at her. "I can keep guessing."

She glances around at the other pedestrians, all of whom we know, and she gets hostile. "You better not."

I put on my thinking face. "Hmmm. Let's see here. Maybe Ben Edwards wants you to—"

"He wants me to milk cows with him, okay?" she yells at me.

I stare at her in shock. "Wait. Let me get this straight. Emily Banks, whose worst nightmare is getting dirty, and who wore high heels to last year's graduation bonfire in the middle of the woods, is going to do farm chores?"

"Shut up," she says. "It's not funny." But she's grinning.

"I beg to differ," I say, the beginning of a laugh shaking my words.

She attempts to keep her composure but cracks, and just like that we're both laughing loud and hard.

"Are you two going to keep acting like fools in front of my door, blocking my paying customers, or are you going to come inside and have some strawberry shortcake?" Lucille says, opening the diner door. Her silver hair hangs in a loose braid over her shoulder.

"Strawberry shortcake!" Emily says, and squeals.

Lucille hides her grin. She's Emily's godmother and she knows full well that strawberry shortcake is her favorite dessert. "Get *inside before you let out all my heat." She shoos us through the door.*

"Miss us?" I ask her, and kiss her on the cheek.

"About as much as I miss hemorrhoids," she says, leading us to our favorite table next to the window and plucking the RE-SERVED sign off it.

I feel Ash watching me as I stare at the cows. "Layla told me you weren't prepped for coming to this school."

My smile disappears and I immediately scan the room. The only door is the one we came through. "And Layla thought I was playing a game."

"Were you?" he asks, his invasive gaze intensifying.

I shrug and look back out the window, trying to appear casual, but my heart beats a mile a minute.

"Interesting," he says.

"Interesting, what?" I say with a little too much emphasis on *what*.

"You weren't prepped," he says.

I make eye contact with him. "I didn't say that."

"You did," he says. "If you were prepped and being strategic by pretending you weren't, you would never call my attention to that fact. You would keep up that game. Also, your pulse quickened when I questioned you, and you looked away from me."

My eyebrows push together. "How could you possibly know my pulse quickened?"

"The vein in your neck."

"You stay away from my neck," I say, channeling my inner Emily.

He smirks. "You also very subtly shook your head, telling

61

me your answer was no. And you took a fast breath through your mouth instead of your nose, indicating stress." He pauses, waiting for me to pick my chin up off the floor. "What you can do with names—piece them together and identify people with them? I can do that with body language."

"Okay?" I say, not really wanting to use any more words than that after his analysis.

"You're my sister's roommate," he says, his seemingly happy expression never wavering. "Don't lie to me, or I will know."

"Is that a threat?"

"Not unless it needs to be."

I rub my hands over my face. "You know what? I think I'm going back to the cafeteria."

"Dining hall," he corrects me.

My chest rises a little higher when I breathe, which I'm sure he notices. I turn away from the window.

"You don't like being here," he says, and I stop in my tracks. His ability to read me is annoying as shit. "If you weren't showing everyone your hand all the time, you'd probably like it more."

"I'd like it more if everyone in this school were less creepy," I say, frustrated, which only widens his grin. "And stop smiling like that. If anyone should make something less obvious, it should be you and your gloating."

He laughs, which seems to surprise him as much as it does me. He pauses. "It wasn't smart, what you did with Aarya."

I huff. "I was *defending* your sister."

"You think that's what you did?" He shakes his head and his expression turns serious. "You showed Aarya that you're loyal without being discerning. That you aligned yourself with your roommate after less than a day. That you're emotional, and that by threatening the people around you, she can get a reaction out of you. Maybe even hurt you. You didn't defend Layla, you made her a target."

My jaw tenses. "It's all head games with you guys. Deception. Why would anyone even *want* to hurt me? I've been here for one day. This school sucks. I can't wait until my two weeks are over."

His composure breaks ever so slightly, like I've startled him. "Two weeks?"

"Yeah, until the holidays."

"Holidays," he repeats with a look that again tells me I've said something revealing.

Do I even want to ask? "You know, Aarya looked at me the same way when I said that."

Ash lets out an "oh boy" whistle. "We don't go home for the holidays. Aarya now knows you don't have a clue how this school works or know anything about the culture here."

"Hang on. *We*, as in you and Layla, or *we* as in everyone?"

"Everyone," he says, and it's like someone stole all the air from the room. "Holidays—any of them, really, with the possible exception of New Year's—aren't celebrated. And New Year's falls on a variety of days for people at this school, so here we celebrate nothing."

This can't be right. My dad distinctly said *a few weeks*. I'll miss the lighting of the tree in the town square, the Pembrook carolers, the terrible play our local theater puts on every year, and Lucille's menorah lighting followed by her homemade spiced cider and fresh donuts. I rub my forehead and press my lips together. A lump forms in my throat. I got in when no one else could, so maybe I can get back out. Ash notices my upset, but for once, he doesn't rub it in my face.

He looks at me like I'm a Rubik's Cube. "I've never met anyone who didn't want to be here, who didn't consider it an honor."

I snort. "I find that really hard to believe. There's no laughter here. No easy attitudes. No *fun*."

"Oh, there's fun, all right. I'm just not sure you would think so. Or that you could keep up."

I study him for a second. "Try me."

He takes his time. "Let's see here. On Friday and Saturday nights curfew is extended to midnight. And from twelve to twelve-ten the guards change, reducing the active stations to about one-third. If you think you can handle it, meet me outside in the vines tomorrow night."

I study his face. Sneaking out to go climb some trees? He's got my number. Layla must have told him how I reacted to that courtyard.

"Or don't," he says with a smile.

I try to mask how much the idea appeals to me. "Why on earth should I trust you?"

"You shouldn't."

I grunt.

"But my guess is that if you weren't prepped to come here, then you have some questions."

I look at him sideways. Damn he's good. "Are you saying you'll answer those questions?"

The door creaks and Layla walks through, her graceful steps not making a sound.

I barely blink and Ash's demeanor has shifted. He's farther away from me and leaning lazily up against the window like we didn't just have that conversation.

"Hey, Ash," Layla says, holding up the braided pine needles. "One to zero."

Six

I LIE ON my bed and pick at the end of my braid. The candle on my bedside table flickers, causing the shadows on my ceiling to move around like cartoon ghosts.

"It just doesn't make sense," I say for the second time to no one.

Dad must have known about this school, because as far as I can tell you're either in the know or you're absolutely not. He got me in after the cutoff age. Plus, this is the place he chose above all others to send me to while helping Aunt Jo.

He said, *I promise you that you know exactly as much as will keep you safe.* Do I know something I don't think I know? It's possible this is a test, an extended version of one of our outdoor strategy games, but I can't shake the feeling that I should be worried—worried about Aunt Jo and my dad, and very possibly about being here in general.

I roll onto my side. When Blackwood suggested it in her office, I didn't think it was likely Dad went here, but I'm not so sure anymore. And *if* he went here, then does that mean all his stories about growing up in Maine and being your typical country boy were basically bunk? Has my dad been lying to me my entire life? The thought makes my stomach do a small flip. But I'll take the Maine lie any day as long as what he told me about fixing everything with Aunt Jo is true. There are a lot of things I can deal with, but my family being in serious danger when I have no way of getting to them quickly is not one of them.

I get out of bed and open my door. Layla's on the light gray velvet couch, reading a book with her legs tucked under her. I glance at the clock, which says 11:50 p.m., and head for the door. If I'm going to sneak out tomorrow night, I might as well get a sense of what kind of obstacles I'm in for.

My hand touches the iron latch.

Layla looks up from her book with its worn fabric cover and faded gold lettering. "It's past curfew."

"I'm just going to step into the hallway."

Layla shakes her head and her hair swishes like inky water. "Not unless you want a mark against you."

"A mark?"

"For being out after curfew, for trying to pick a lock to a restricted area, for opening a curtain at night and letting light out, et cetera. Get three and you get a punishment of their choosing."

"Like what?"

"Depends on the person. But they're always terrible."

I consider telling her that her brother suggested we meet in the vine courtyard *after* curfew, an offense probably worth twenty marks.

"Layla?"

She marks her page with her finger. "Yes?"

I choose my words carefully. "If I'm asking something I

shouldn't, don't tell me. You were right about Aarya. I made a mistake. And I don't want to misstep again."

Her expression loses a little of its ice.

I take a breath and pace myself. "I've never met anyone from a . . . Jackal Family before, and, well . . . I'm not sure how to say this . . . Is there anything you *can* tell me?"

She purses her lips and levels her gaze at me like she's trying to decide something. "Only that the stories are mostly true. We're ninety percent sure that the Jackal Family was responsible for Franz Ferdinand's driver taking a wrong turn in 1914, the turn that got him and his wife assassinated and instigated World War One. And we're certain they had a hand in 'accidentally' leaving the gate open at Constantinople in 1453, leading to the city's demise and the death of Emperor Constantine. Not to mention the 'accidental' bakery fire in London in 1666, which led to the destruction of more than thirteen thousand houses, and dozens of other incidents. I'm not saying Jackals only cause chaos, because as you know, none of our Families are perfect. We all have a long list of mistakes. But what I *am* saying is that Jackals are more likely to serve their own agenda than the Council of Families'. And because they are spread throughout numerous countries, it's much more difficult to identify them. They speak every language, and they blend in everywhere. They are more true to their characteristics than any other Family here. Deceptive. Innovative. Clever. They will cause you trouble if they can."

I freeze, and not because Layla just alleged that Aarya is likely related to people who helped start WWI, but because the description she just gave is ringing like a bell in my mind. *Deceptive.*

Innovative. Clever. And now I remember exactly where I heard about the Jackal Family. My mother.

The latch moves under my hand and I jump backward. The door swings open and on the other side is the guard with the X scar above his eyebrow. His eyes narrow ever so slightly when he sees me. For a second we stare at each other, and just as I'm about to open my mouth to ask him what his deal is, he walks away without a word.

I look at Layla questioningly, but she's already off the couch and moving. "Get dressed. Fast!"

I run into my room and grab my clothes off the floor. It takes me all of a minute to put them on, but even so Layla is standing by our open door when I finish like she's been lounging there for hours.

She tosses me my cloak and I follow her full-speed into the hallway, which is lit by the open doors that students are pouring out of. I want to ask Layla what's going on, but I don't need to advertise my ignorance in front of everyone.

We follow the other girls from our hall down three flights of stairs and to the foyer that leads to the vine courtyard. It's a mirror image of the one with the shields and the knight statue on the south side of the building, only it has nothing more than two torches and some faded tapestries hanging from its walls.

The girls are sitting cross-legged in a U shape and Layla and I are among the last to join them. I do a quick count and come up with twenty-five girls, including me. Maybe it's only the advanced students, then?

Aarya sits on the opposite side of the U, smirking at me while her quiet friend with the red dreads fidgets with the hem of her cloak. I stare back at Aarya, wondering what her Family has to do with a make-believe game I played with my mom when I was little. At least, I always thought it was make-believe.

"Welcome," Blackwood says, emerging from the staircase. She wears the same ruffled shirt with a blazer and black pants she did last night. It's eerie the way no one's clothes ever change in this place. Even her hair remains in the same forehead-abusing bun.

"I trust that when we search your rooms tonight, we'll find that everything is in order," Blackwood says, and scans the group of us. Everyone nods. I swallow, remembering the fork, and make a mental note to ask Layla if Felix could have somehow known they were doing a search tonight.

"As you all know, we have a new student," Blackwood says, and looks at me. "So I thought we would play a strategy game." She shifts her weight and smiles a strained smile. "We often talk about this school's best students, about their accomplishments and their awe-inspiring feats. But we seldom talk about their failures." She pauses. "Twenty-five years ago, there was a girl at this school who won every single midnight strategy challenge her fourth year. Every. Single. One. What's interesting, however, is that she lost so often in her first three years people would roll their eyes when they had to go up against her. How do you explain that?"

"She spent three years strategically identifying flaws in other people's strategies," Aarya says, now speaking with an Italian accent. "And when she accumulated enough information, it provided a map to people's strengths and weaknesses, allowing her to navigate them as she pleased. She also had the element of surprise after everyone assumed she would lose."

"Very true," Blackwood says. "There is untold advantage to true observation. Take Ines, for example—she catches details most of you miss." She looks at Aarya's quiet friend, who recoils ever so slightly from the compliment.

There's a petite girl on the other side of Aarya who shoots Ines a look that I can only guess is a sort of angry jealousy. Aarya looks at her and the girl turns away, but there is definitely something going on there.

"You all are trained in verbal and body language clues," Blackwood continues. "You analyze masterfully, but you also have egos. And if you allow your need to win to compromise your ability to truly observe, then you have missed a great deal. This girl did not make that mistake."

Blackwood braces her hands behind her back. "Consider this example, too: In the mid-eighteen hundreds, twelve-year-old Margaret Knight witnessed a machine malfunction at a cotton mill that resulted in the injury of a worker. As a result, she invented a protective cover for that same machine that wound up being immensely popular. Unfortunately, she never got credit because she was too young to apply for a patent. But the patent wasn't what concerned her in the moment of invention. It was the problem at hand. If you want to be truly great, you need to find solutions even when they don't directly serve you. What else can we surmise about our former student?"

Layla shifts subtly next to me. "To win every challenge for a year straight, she would have had to do more than accumulate information on the other students," she says. "She would have had to know the way each student thought, and then think differently. We always expect that people will react the way we do—that when we hit them they'll hit back, or that when we help them they'll be grateful—and when they don't behave the way we think they will, we're surprised."

Blackwood looks at Layla approvingly. "Leonardo da Vinci didn't limit his study to one thing. He was curious about art, anatomy, and engineering, to name just a few. He didn't see the world for what it was, but for what it could be. And he combined his interests to tackle ideas like human flight. He knew that there were *many* ways to solve the same problem if you were brave enough to dream them. So yes, Layla, this girl did just that. She did what no one expected over and over, and just when you thought you knew her next move, she changed again. She was the most breathtakingly brave strategist this school has ever seen."

Judging by their expressions, the other girls seem to take this lesson quite seriously. There is a mixture of what I think is admiration and an ambition to be better. I can't help but wonder if they know the identity of the girl Blackwood referred to.

"Now let's have a go at this challenge," Blackwood says, and her eyes land on me. "Stand up, November."

My heart starts beating so loudly, I'm positive the vein Ash saw in my neck is going wild.

Blackwood motions for me to approach her at the open part of the U. "Turn around."

I face the other girls, who all stare at me with blank expressions, except for Aarya, who looks amused. The girls appear to come from all over the world, yet I've only heard people speaking English. And I'm suddenly feeling grateful. The only thing that could make this place more baffling would be if I couldn't understand anyone.

"The rules will be as follows," Blackwood says, untying my

cloak. It swishes to the floor and the cold night air immediately seeps through my clothes. "No light, and no leaving this room."

I quickly glance around me. There is a guard by the courtyard door, one directly across from her by the bottom of the staircase, and one in each of the hallway exits. Behind the hallway guards, the torches have already been snuffed out.

"Each participating girl will get one of these cloths." Blackwood holds up two pieces of gray fabric. "They will be tucked into the back of your pants and will stay there. The idea is to steal the other girl's cloth. The first person to do that wins."

Oh man. I look around again, this time making a fast mental map of the room. The staircase is directly behind me. There's a tapestry to the right of it, and a hallway with a guard. Another tapestry, a chip in the wall a little lower than my waist, a torch holder above the chip, tapestry, door. And it repeats in a mirror fashion on the other side of the room, minus the chip.

"We'll need one more girl," Blackwood says, and Aarya's hand shoots up in the air. "Everyone else will stay seated exactly where they are. November, you'll be paired with"—her eyes scan the group and land on the petite girl next to Aarya who gave Ines the jealous look—"Nyx."

Nyx, my brain translates, *the Greek goddess of the night, mother of sleep and,* oh, right, *death.* And by the light gasps and someone's snicker, I guess her name is apt. She stands up without her cloak and joins me on my left. She takes one look at me and I can tell she's already decided that I'm not a challenge. Well, we'll just see about that.

Nyx is so short that she only reaches my shoulder, and now that I'm close to her, I notice a thin black line along the top edge of her lashes, winging out at the corners, giving her eyes a cat-like appearance. And since Blackwood doesn't let us keep anything personal here, I can only assume that Nyx either makes her own eye makeup, or had the line permanently tattooed on. Makeup isn't usually something I would look to in order to tell me who my opponent is, but in this particular instance it tells me she's resourceful and stubborn and does not bow to other people's will.

Blackwood tucks the cloths into the back of our leggings. I glance at the chip in the wall again. I'd guess it's just about as high as Nyx's gray cloth.

Blackwood takes our hands, pulling me to her right and Nyx to her left. She nods at the two guards behind us, and they move to the torches on either side of the foyer. The guard nearest me is the one with the X. Boy, that guy is everywhere I go.

Each guard lifts a metal-cone-topped pole above a torch and snuffs it out. The room goes dark—blindfold game dark. And I'm positive it's not going to get any lighter as my eyes adjust: there are no windows.

From the direction of the hallways come knocking sounds, which I can only assume mean that the guards have returned to their posts. The room is unsettlingly quiet. I can't even hear anyone breathe.

"Begin," Blackwood says, and lets go of my hand.

My heart jumps into my throat. There's nothing like the feeling of absolute darkness and being hunted by a probable Greek ninja to inspire nightmaresque fear. And if I don't prove myself in this exercise, the entire school will get the memo that I'm a fly in a sea of spiders.

I take a handful of careful steps until I'm just beyond the U.

I must pass awfully close to the end girl, because I can feel her body heat as I go. My boots don't make a sound on the stone. The problem is, Nyx's steps are silent, too. *If I can just make it to that torch holder* . . .

I loop around the U near the backs of the girls until I think I'm about lined up with where the torch should be. I carefully put my hands out in front of me, trying to detect body heat from Nyx, but all I get is chilled air. *Here goes nothing.* I take a step toward the wall and something hooks my ankle, sending me stumbling forward and making all kinds of noise. And there's a laugh, which I would bet money belongs to Aarya. That girl is seriously getting on my nerves.

"Way to cheat, Aarya," I say. Normally I would just continue without a blip, but I can't have Blackwood and these girls thinking I'm so bad at getting around in the dark that I tripped over my own feet.

"Who's cheating? It's not my fault you're wicked clumsy," Aarya replies with an American accent that's a perfect imitation of my own.

There is the sound of a match striking, and the room is illuminated.

Blackwood holds a candle in front of her face. "Enough. Aarya, you have no place in this challenge. I specifically said to stay where you were. And November, surprises happen. People don't follow the rules. Were you under the impression that this challenge was about being fair?"

We all look at her, including Nyx, who's standing next to me with my cloth in her hand and a grin that appears to say "I knew I would kick your butt"—not as a gloat, but as an obvious statement of fact.

Damn it all. I not only lost, I get the added benefit of looking foolish. "Let me try again," I say.

"You lost, November," Blackwood says.

"I know. But you just told us a story about a girl who lost in order to win," I say, and smile. "Let's see if Nyx can beat me when she doesn't have Aarya's help."

"No one needs Aarya's help to beat you," Nyx says, and I can tell that she's miffed I even suggested it. She's Greek, I'd bet, based on her accent.

The room is completely silent as everyone looks from me to Blackwood. Blackwood moves her mouth like she's rolling the idea around on her tongue, then gives a perfunctory nod. I immediately scoot back to my starting position before she can change her mind.

Blackwood resets our cloths and I glance at Nyx, who gives me a withering look that makes me wonder if I just made a very bad choice. After all, she came right for me; she didn't even try to go around the circle the other way.

Blackwood blows out the candle and throws the room back into blackness. My heart beats three times and she releases my hand.

I run for the wall, not even attempting to silence my footsteps. My hands slap against the stone and there are snickers from the girls. I pat the wall in fast circles, trying to find the chip. *Got ya.* I reach above me, yank the unlit torch out of the holder, and throw it with all my might across the room and away from the U of girls.

There are surprised gasps as it skids along the floor, and I yank at the edge of the heavy tapestry, pulling it toward me. Then I push it hard, sending it swishing in what I hope is the direction of the X guard in the hallway. There's the sound of squeaking leather that I believe is the guard attempting to re-adjust himself, and I'm grateful I hit my mark. In the midst of all the noise, I grab the now-empty torch holder above my head with both hands.

I can hear the girls whispering, and I pull my legs up to where my hands are on the torch holder. I get my boots firmly wedged between the wrought-iron rings for balance and to take some of the weight off my hands. The iron is surprisingly sturdy and easy to grip, but even so I won't be able to hold my-self in this inverted position for very long. Blackwood shushes the room and I have to smile: Dad always said that if you can't do something without being noticed, create confusion.

I carefully place my braid between my teeth and let my right arm hang down along the wall, finding the chip in the stone. And I wait.

It takes only two seconds before the air near my hand warms. I hold my breath. Nyx came directly after me *again*. Boy, this girl doesn't play games. If she's after you, she's after you, simple as that. Judging by the fact that I can't hear her breath and our heads should be fairly close together, I'm guessing her back is to me. I move my hand forward, miscalculating her height and grabbing her shirt just above the waist. Thankfully I catch the edge of the cloth, too, and secure it between my fingertips. I yank.

She lets out a surprised yelp.

Blackwood lights a candle and the entire room looks at us, blinking in the pale light. The shock on their faces is obvious. I unhook my feet from the torch holder and jump to the floor.

Nyx's eyes narrow. "Winning *second* is still losing," she says under her breath.

I grin at her. "But didn't we just learn that it's the most *recent* win that everyone remembers?"

"Nicely done." Blackwood nods at the cloth in my outstretched hand. From the tone of her voice I can tell that something in her has relaxed, like she's just decided not to throw me out.

"You can't win second if you're already dead," Nyx says so quietly that I almost miss it. I stop smiling. She's determined, focused, and straightforward and it's obvious she doesn't like me. I get the feeling that by winning tonight, I'm going to lose something in the near future.

Seven

I PULL OPEN my bedroom curtains and light dapples my room, giving it a soft warm glow. But the floor is like ice and the moment my bare feet hit it I jump, snatch up my discarded socks, and practically fall over trying to put them on.

The chill sobers me up and the events from the night before come rushing into my thoughts—the challenge, Nyx's threat, and the Jackal conversation I had with Layla. I don't see how it could be a coincidence that she used *deceptive, innovative,* and *clever* to describe Aarya—the same words my mom used to describe a family of stuffed animals in a game we played when I was small. It was a childish game—at least I thought it was. My mom said she used to play it with Aunt Jo and their mother back in Italy. Each animal family had three words to describe them, all of which are emblazoned in my memory like nursery rhymes.

I freeze and my stomach does a fast somersault. It didn't occur to me last night, but when Dad came to my room to break the news about going to this school, he picked up one of my old stuffed animals and said, "Do you remember that game you used to play with your mom? I could never get you two to take a break from it." Then he smiled at the memory, the way he often does when my mother comes up in conversations. I didn't think anything of it at the time, but now . . .

I open my bedroom door, caught up in my thoughts, and nearly jump out of the socks I just put on. On the other side, with a hand raised to knock, is a young woman who looks to be in her twenties, carrying freshly pressed clothes. She's wearing a maroon wool dress and a crisp white . . . I guess it's a bonnet? Her cheeks have a natural pink flush that reminds me of a rose.

"I didn't mean to startle you, Miss November," she says. "I was just coming to tell you that I've brought morning tea with bread and jam at Miss Layla's request." She takes a look at me like she's trying to log every detail, but not in the threatening way the kids and teachers in this school do. Her look is warm and curious.

I put my hand over my heart, like somehow this will slow down my pulse. "No, no. It's not you. Sorry. I just didn't expect anyone to be there when I opened the door."

She does a quick curtsy and gives me a huge smile. "I'm Pippa, your and Miss Layla's chambermaid. If you need any-thing, please let me know," she says, and I detect an Italian accent. She moves past me into my room and lays the clothes she's carrying over the trunk at the end of my bed.

Pippa, I think. *Could be a nickname for Filippa, the Italian feminine form of Philip, meaning . . . "friend of horses"?* Which I suppose suits her. Her upbeat demeanor reminds me of being outdoors in the sunshine.

"Thank you," I say as she begins to straighten my blankets. "But I mean you don't have to . . . I'd rather just . . . Thanks."

"Not a problem," she says, and makes her way back into the common room with me at her heels.

Layla is already sitting at the table near the arched window, and the sight of the freshly baked bread makes me want to hug everyone.

"Oh my god, Pippa, you just made my whole morning," I say with wide eyes.

I slide into my seat and put my napkin on my lap with enthusiasm.

"I got you the very freshest loaf," Pippa says with pride. "Grabbed it just as Cook was taking it out of the oven."

I break off a piece of the bread and steam escapes into the cool morning air. "You might be my new favorite person."

"Thank you," Layla says crisply before Pippa can respond and in a way that tells me it's an invitation for Pippa to leave.

"Yes, thank you!" I chime in as I scoop some golden butter onto my knife.

The door clicks closed and Layla's eyebrows push together.

"What?" I say as I chew.

Layla sips her tea. "Are you always that friendly with people you don't know?"

"Actually . . . yeah," I say. I would tell her that she sounds like my dad commenting on me being too trusting, but that would be violating rule number one.

"Well, don't be," she says.

I wipe my mouth with my napkin and take a good look at her. "Pippa seems sweet. And don't you think it has to suck to take care of a bunch of secretive people out in the middle of nowhere in some castle with no electricity? I'm sure she would appreciate a kind word or two."

Layla pauses like she's not sure what to make of me. "All Strategia serve their Families in one way or another, November. No one gets a pass. And besides, Pippa won't be here for more than a few years unless she chooses to be."

I pause, my bread halfway to my mouth, and my skin starts to prickle. I've definitely heard that word before. "So Pippa's Strategia?" I say, trying to make the word sound casual and natural.

"Yes. Everyone in the Academy is Strategia—the professors, kitchen staff, guards, the people who tend to the animals. You didn't think we would allow a non-Strategia to be *here,* of all places, did you?" She looks at me incredulously.

"No, I guess not," I say. Not only does she think I know what Strategia are, but if she's claiming *everyone* in this school is one, then where does that leave me? I pour myself some tea, trying to figure out how to ask her to define it without putting a spotlight on myself. "There's no technology taught in this school." *Assassins and spies need tech.* "Why is that?"

Layla shrugs. "Waste of time. We only get four years here. We can learn tech skills at home. And it's not really a priority when everyone has tech specialists in their Family."

Tech specialists, compulsory work for the Families, the Council of Families that Layla mentioned last night, and whatever the students are . . . It's sounding like these Families are self-governed, self-reliant, and *powerful.*

Layla gives me an odd look. "Now hurry up and drink your tea. We're still going to the dining hall to meet Ash."

"Do we need to bring textbooks or something for class?" I ask as we head down the stairs. Our entire day yesterday was eaten up with tours, assessment, and visiting various class options. But we never actually participated in one.

Layla shakes her head. "With the exception of poisons class, most of the advanced students don't use textbooks or take notes; we learn."

I follow her through the foyer and out into the vine courtyard. "What does that mean?"

"Why are you constantly asking me what things *mean*?" she says, still giving me the suspicious look she adopted over morning tea. "I wouldn't do that in front of other people if I were you."

I keep pace with Layla's fast steps. The coldness that crept into her demeanor yesterday after I sat with Aarya at lunch is still there.

I open my mouth to respond as we step into the garden lounge, and we almost smack into two guys having a quiet discussion. One is the confident archer with the platinum hair who winked at me yesterday. His friend is similarly tall and handsome and has a tattoo of ivy peeking out from the rolled cuff of his shirt. He doesn't have the same commanding presence his friend does, though. Just by seeing them talk together, you can tell there is an imbalance of power between them.

"So it's the new girl," the confident archer says, shifting his attention and flashing me a grin. His accent is British.

His tattooed friend crosses his arms. "You're not going to introduce us, Layla? Where are your manners?" He sounds French and has a lilting voice. I wouldn't be surprised if he was a singer in a band.

"Brendan"—Layla gestures toward the archer, and then toward the guy with the French accent—"and Charles. This is November." Layla's tone is flat, like she could be reading off a grocery list, just trying to accomplish the task at hand. Great. I'm a grocery list.

"A pleasure, I'm sure," Brendan says, and bows, but there's something duplicitous about his friendliness. He's nothing like Ash, who always seems to be assessing; Brendan's positive attitude feels like a lure. "Have you enjoyed your first two days at Phantom High?"

"Phantom High?" I say with a smirk. "Clever. Well, all I can say is the food's excellent . . . when it's not poisoned."

Charles laughs, but it's not an easy laugh and I can't help but feel like I'm participating in some elaborate dance I don't know the steps to. I look to Layla for clues as to who these guys are, but her expression remains neutral. I can tell by the tension in her stance, though, that she wants to get the hell away from them. And if she isn't doing it, I can only assume she doesn't feel comfortable dismissing them.

"Oh, great, the royals and the nerds talking to each other," Aarya says in an American accent, walking up with Ines. "What is the world coming to?"

"It's a world where you're irrelevant, Aarya," Brendan replies, and once again I sense something cruel behind his upbeat tone.

"Oh, boo-hoo," Aarya says as she walks away. Ines touches her arm, which seems to be a signal for Aarya to stop.

I take a better look at Brendan and Charles. There is clearly some dynamic here that I'm not understanding. Layla's tense around these guys and Ines doesn't seem to want Aarya to get into a conflict with them.

But of course Aarya turns back toward us just before they enter the building. "I don't matter to you, Brendan? However will I go on?"

"Maybe you won't," Charles answers, and unlike Brendan, the threat in his tone is direct.

Aarya rolls her eyes and goes inside like nothing happened, but Ines frowns.

Layla takes the distraction as an opportunity to walk away from them, and I follow.

"They're all running from us," Charles says, and they both laugh.

I look over my shoulder briefly before we enter the building on the far side of the courtyard, and the hair on my arms immediately stands up. Brendan and Charles are staring directly at me. If attention from Aarya is bad, my gut tells me that this is much worse.

I look at Layla with newfound appreciation. She might be uptight and closed off, but at least she lacks the menacing vibe these other students have.

"Layla, what I said last night . . . about you being right about Aarya," I say quietly.

Layla scans the foyer with the displayed shields, but no one is near us.

I keep my voice low. "I just wanted to say that I haven't learned my way around here yet. And yes, I definitely ask too many questions. But I'm going to do my best to keep up. I get why you think I was being reckless. And . . . my loyalty is to you.

One hundred percent." I mentally wince, remembering what Ash said about me being impulsively loyal. But this is who I am. I don't betray my friends, even the new ones.

Layla looks at me and I swear I catch a glimpse of vulnerability behind her stony expression.

"I just want you to know that I *am* listening to you," I say. "And I'm grateful you're taking all this time to explain everything in detail."

She gives me a quick nod, and I can already tell that some of the hardness has left her demeanor.

We walk toward the dining hall in silence. Then, casually, she says, "Ash told me what happened with Felix and the fork," and steals a glance at me.

I smile. I know an acceptance of an apology when I hear one. I walk a step closer to her, keeping my voice quiet. "What are the chances that Felix knew about the search last night?"

"I want to say he did," she answers. "Because the timing is suspicious, and if there's one thing we're *not*, it's random. But the only way he could know about a search is if a faculty member told him, which is forbidden. Unless he overheard something he wasn't supposed to. I just don't know."

I nod. "What about Ines? How does she fit in with Aarya and Felix?"

"Ines is Aarya's roommate," Layla says, and pauses in front of the dining hall door. "She's also one of the best tactical students at this school, but she doesn't talk to anyone except for Aarya and Felix, mostly Aarya. And she's probably right not to."

I want to ask her what she means by that, but she pushes open the door and I follow her inside. The dining hall at breakfast is nothing like at lunch or dinner. It's almost lively. Students congregate in groups, and there's even some light laughter—which I now attribute to the fact that the teachers' table is empty.

As we walk between the tables, I spot a broad-shouldered guy and a long-haired guy watching us approach. They exchange a few words, and it's obvious I'm the topic of conversation.

Just as we pass the broad-shouldered guy, his chair moves backward and smacks into my leg. Across the table, his long-haired friend smirks.

"Ow. Watch it," I say, rubbing my leg.

The broad-shouldered guy stands up, and he's a good six inches taller than me. "It's not my problem if your reflexes are bad," he says. He's got an Italian accent similar to my aunt Jo's, and his tone is just short of threatening.

Layla must hear it, too, because she looks from me to him like she's trying to sort something out. "And it's not *her* problem that you're too big for these chairs, Matteo," she says calmly.

My jaw drops. Layla didn't say boo to Aarya or Brendan and Charles, but she'll mouth off to this huge guy? *Matteo*, I think. *Italian for "gift from god" or, as it happens, "tax collector."*

He lifts a playful eyebrow at Layla, but when his gaze returns to me, it's not gentle. I get the sense he knows something I don't and he's not happy about it. Gift, shmift. This guy's a tax collector. "You're lucky you're with Layla."

"That I know," I say lightly, and I catch a glimpse of approval in Layla's expression.

He walks past me and his shoulder knocks into mine hard enough that I stumble backward.

"He's all bark," Layla says.

"Sure," I say, pretending it doesn't bother me as I watch Matteo walk away. "But what's all the hostility about?"

I turn back to Layla, but she's walking again and I need to pick up the pace to catch her.

"Everyone is testing you," Layla says. "Give it a couple of months."

She stops at a chair across from her brother, whose eyes are just as hard to meet as always. I audibly let my breath out. *Months? No chance.* My conversation with Ash about how no one leaves for the holidays replays in my mind, and my unsettled feeling cranks up a notch. I suddenly feel the need for some air and a place to quietly think.

"Is there a bathroom down here?" I ask Layla.

"Through the door to the right."

I walk back between the tables, careful not to make eye contact with anyone so I don't provoke any more aggression. I've never felt this way. My town is friendly. My school is friendly. There probably isn't a person in all of Pembrook I don't know by name, address, and pizza preference.

I open the door and slip into the quiet hallway, walking a little way down from the guard who stands outside the dining hall. I lean my back against the stone for a moment and close my eyes. This is the first time in my life that I haven't been excited about meeting people, when I've wanted to be *away* from the crowd instead of in the middle of it. I could go outside, maybe sit in that garden. I shake my head. That would take too long and I'd probably freak Layla out that I was messing up her schedule.

A door creaks and my eyes pop open at the sound.

"Shit," I breathe.

Matteo walks out of what I can only guess is the bathroom. His eyes narrow when he sees me. He probably thinks I followed him, but saying I didn't is only going to make it look like I did.

"You look like her," he says like he's disgusted, but keeps his voice low enough that the guard in front of the dining hall can't hear him.

My heart thuds. I can't imagine who from his life I might look like. The only person I've ever been compared to is my mom, who Dad claims I look exactly like. But how on earth would Matteo know that?

"I don't know what you want me to say." I keep my voice steady and neutral, imitating Layla, and I repeat her words in my thoughts: *He's just testing me.*

Matteo scans my face, searching for something. A denial, maybe? "You're an idiot for coming here," he says. "And even more of one for having followed me into this hallway."

My hands clench. "I didn't—"

But I don't get my rebuttal out, because a fist the size of a grapefruit is suddenly headed for my face. The impact with my cheekbone rattles my entire skull and I slam back into the wall, sliding to the floor.

My hands immediately fly to my face, the left side of which is already swelling. I can hear the guard's boots pound against the stone as he rushes over. My nose isn't bleeding yet, which at least makes me think it isn't broken, but the pain is unreal and tears involuntarily flow down my left cheek.

I peer up at Matteo with my unswollen eye. The guard is restraining him now, holding his arms behind his back, and a crowd is already forming in the hallway, spilling out from the dining hall. The guard pulls Matteo away from me and he doesn't resist.

Layla helps me up by my arm. I can see her questioning with her eyes if I'm okay, but she doesn't say a word. I grab at the wall behind me. My head pounds like someone's playing the drums on it. I want to scream at Matteo, but there's a lump in my throat and I'm afraid if I open my mouth I'll angry-cry.

The crowd parts to let Headmaster Blackwood through. She looks from me to Matteo, like she's trying to cherry-pick information from our body language.

"Down," Blackwood says, and the guard forces Matteo to his knees. She turns to me. "Well, go ahead."

No "Are you okay?" No "I can see that you've been knocked out by a guy twice your size—maybe we should get you to a doctor."

I stare at her in horror. "Go ahead?" I ask.

"An eye for an eye, just like I told you," Blackwood says, looking at me expectantly. "Only, I didn't expect it to be quite so literal or quite so soon."

This isn't just an odd school with creepy rules. The people here are actually vicious, even the ones who are supposed to be regulating law and order.

"You want me to hit him in the face?" My voice cracks in disbelief.

"Do it!" Aarya yells from somewhere in the crowd, and I catch a glimpse of Brendan's white shock of hair. He and Charles watch with interest.

My stomach flips. Blackwood raises her hand and Aarya shuts up. I look at Matteo. He seems calm, like he did exactly what he needed to.

"Uh, um," I stammer, still in shock.

"Well, get on with it," Blackwood says, and I can't believe how cavalier she's being about this.

"I . . . I'm not going to hit him," I say, and I can feel the surprise ripple through the onlookers. I've never hit anyone in the face in my life and I'm definitely *not* going to start with a guy whose face will probably do more damage to my hand than the other way around.

"Do you think the rules don't apply to you?" Blackwood asks.

"I didn't say that. I just . . . What will punching him prove?" And as I think about it, the answer occurs to me. "The real problem is that he hit me in the *first* place, not that I won't hit him back." I want to tell her exactly what I think of these students with their "tests," and her archaic punishment system, but my emotions are running too high and I can't get my thoughts clear enough to do it without sounding like I'm scared.

Blackwood lifts her chin and raises her voice. "Apparently November believes that retaliation is beneath her. So if any of you are looking to blow off some steam, she's an easy target. She won't hit back."

My mouth opens and for a moment I think I must be hearing things. Did she really just tell all the students that they could *hit* me? Frustration wells in my chest and a lump forms in my throat. Now I know exactly what Conner meant when he warned me that I might not survive here. I catch Layla's eye in the crowd and she frowns.

Matteo hasn't taken his eyes off me, and now he mutters, "Like I said, you're an idiot."

Anger begins to bubble inside my already clenched chest— anger that I was hit, that I haven't understood a single thing since I set foot on this campus, and that I'm even here at all. This is the most screwed-up school in the world.

"This is your only chance, November," Blackwood says, like maybe I don't get what she's offering me.

I step forward. I can't have people thinking that they can hit me whenever they want. I'm sure there are already about six onlookers who would jump at the chance. But I also can't believe I'm in a position where I'm being encouraged to hit another student in a school, and by the headmaster. All I want to do is walk away and fly straight back to Pembrook.

I pull back my arm and my fist shakes.

Matteo laughs, and the sound grates on my last nerve. The only thing worse than being punched for no reason is then being laughed at for it in front of everyone.

Screw this. I step forward with my left leg, pulling my right one back, and I kick him in the balls with all my might.

Matteo's eyes widen; he grunts and crumples to the floor. Blackwood raises an eyebrow.

"I slipped," I say with an edge in my voice.

"Well, now you're even," she says. "There will not, and I repeat, there will *not* be retaliation later. This is it. You walk away with an even score."

"Understood," I say, even though I really don't. And just like a switch has been flipped, everyone starts moving at once.

"That was your third mark, Matteo. Meet me in my office after class," Blackwood says. He stands up and I reflexively take a step back.

"Come on," Layla says. "Let's get you to the infirmary."

Matteo walks past me and Ash says something to him, only I can't hear what it is.

Eight

LATER THAT EVENING I sit in front of the fireplace in our room on an ancient-looking rug patterned with trees. I watch the fire pop and dance over the logs and lift my hand to lightly touch my bruised eye. The strong-smelling poultice the nurse left on my face all day brought down the swelling, but I'm positive I'm going to have a shiner for a good two weeks. If people weren't gossiping about me before, they will be.

I've decided to talk to Blackwood tomorrow. They might not have a phone here, but there has to be a way to get in touch with Dad. There's no chance he would want me staying at a school where students attack me in the middle of the hallway and teachers expect me to hit them in retaliation.

I look up at the dark wooden clock on the mantel, which looks like a cuckoo clock without the cuckoo: 11:54 p.m. I'm positive that sneaking out right now is a bad idea. But I'm also positive that I just got sucker-punched for some mysterious reason and if I don't go meet Ash I may never know the truth about this place.

Layla's bedroom door creaks open for the first time all night.

As far as I can tell, she's been avoiding me, and I just keep hoping she hasn't decided I'm too big a liability.

"I didn't know he would do that," she says quietly.

"What do you mean?" I say, turning toward her.

She holds her door open but doesn't actually come into the living room. "When I said Matteo was all bark, I just want you to know that I had no idea he would hit you."

My eyebrows scrunch together, pulling at my sore face in the process. "I didn't think you did."

"Well, I didn't," she says resolutely, and exhales.

"Do you know why he did it?" I ask carefully.

She shakes her head and her hair shimmers in the firelight. "Anyway . . . good night," she says, and disappears back into her room before I can get another word out.

I stare at her closed door for a few seconds after she shuts it. In the short time I've known Layla, I can tell that's all the information she's going to give me, maybe all the information she has.

It's 11:59 p.m. I drum my fingers on the rug, hesitate, and jump up off the floor. I'm not going to just sit around waiting for someone else to attack me. I'm going to get some answers.

I pull on my boots and tie my cloak around my shoulders. It's bulky, but it's also black and will help me blend into the low light. I lift the latch on the door as gently as possible and crack it open. The hallway's empty and everything's quiet. I slip out, closing the door gently behind me, and book it down the hall. I stop by the staircase and peer down it. It's mostly dark and there are no sounds of movement. Although I wish my heart would shut up so that I could hear better.

I take the steps quickly, pausing periodically to listen for the guards, and slink along the wall toward the first-floor entrance. I grip the cold stone and anxiously peek around the edge of the archway. There's a guard in front of the door that leads to the vine courtyard. Did they already change the post?

As I pull back from the archway, my shoulder collides with something. My mouth opens but a hand presses over it before I can make a sound, and someone turns me around. For a split second utter panic flashes through my body, until I make out Ash staring down at me in the near blackness. He's so close that I can smell the scent of fireplace on his cloak. He puts his finger to his lips and then points toward the entrance hall. We look again just as the guard is opening the door to go into the very courtyard we were supposed to meet in.

Ash holds up his hand, folding his fingers over one at a time. *Five, four, three, two, one.* He walks straight for the door, silently, at full speed. Oh, this is *such* a bad idea. I can't believe I'm doing this. Ash pauses midway through the room and gives me a demanding look. Someone clears their throat a flight or so above me.

Shit—another guard!

I'm out of that stairwell and headed for the door so fast you'd think I was on fire. Ash carefully lifts the latch and we slip through. The courtyard door closes just as the other guard walks out of the very stairwell we were just in.

Ash grabs my shoulders and pulls me to a halt before I can take another step. I can't see a thing, not one thing, and I don't dare move.

Ash takes my hand and lifts it. My fingers graze fabric that feels similar to the blackout curtains that hang on all the windows in this place. They must pull them across the doorways at night to prevent any light from showing when the guards go in and out.

We stand there for a few long seconds before Ash finally pushes aside the fabric. The soft glow of the moonlight shines through the tree branches and my tensed shoulders relax a bit. The air is cold, but the smell of trees is reassuringly familiar.

I have to run to keep up with Ash as he weaves around the low-hanging vines. He stops in front of an impressively large trunk on the opposite side of the courtyard and begins to climb one of the vines. I watch as he hoists himself onto a branch about twenty feet above me, and I can't help but be impressed. I follow him up and he offers me his hand, but I shake my head and pull myself onto the branch next to him. He takes a good look at the trees around us, then back at me, and we climb again, up and up.

Ash stops at two branches that have grown so close together they've melded into a kind of bench. The bottom branch is wide enough that I can sit cross-legged on it, leaning my back against the trunk. Ash lets his legs dangle over the side and swings them, like he's never been more comfortable. If I'd ever found a guy in Pembrook who could climb trees and shoot arrows the way he could, not to mention possessed the general elegant beautifulness he has going on, I would have proposed then and there. Why is it that all the good ones also have an Old-World-assassin-creepy-analysis thing about them? It's one of those mysteries the world may never solve.

He speaks then, keeping his voice quiet. "The acoustics are very good here. We're in the middle of the three courtyards, not near any rooms and far enough off the ground not to be heard as long as you don't raise your voice. I sometimes think it's the only truly private place on the entire campus."

I smile, my heart still racing happily from the climb. "You were right. This is fun." My breath billows out in a white cloud and I realize how much I needed this bit of adventure right now.

He watches me for a second. "You grew up near a forest?"

I hesitate. The moonlight reveals enough detail that he could probably see by my expression whether I was lying. And besides, telling him there was a forest near my home doesn't really give anything away. There are a bazillion forests all around the world. "I did. It was right at the edge of my backyard."

He nods. "Layla told me the only things on the tour you seemed to show an interest in were these courtyards."

I figured she told him as much. "Yeah, but even growing up near a forest doesn't mean I could make a climb like that. What made you think I could?"

He raises an eyebrow and tilts his head like the answer is obvious. "Because you're at this school, for one; athletic abilities are a given. And because I heard about the way you outsmarted Nyx."

Layla really does tell him everything. "All right," I say. "Since you already know so much about me, why don't you tell me a few things?"

He leans against the branch lazily and turns toward me. "What do you want to know?"

I catch myself smiling and consider how to approach all the questions I have without revealing how much I *don't* know. It doesn't take a genius to figure out that being clueless at the

Academy is the same as being vulnerable. "Tell me about the Families here."

He looks amused and I'm relieved that at least my question makes sense to him. "Now, that's a broad topic."

"Then tell me how the Families formed twenty-five hundred years ago," I say, recalling the bits of information I got from my interview with Conner.

He laughs. "You sneak all the way out here at night, risking marks, to ask me to tell you the origin story? Don't you think you should use your time more wisely?"

I shrug, like it's all no big deal. "Look, I know . . . I have lots of other questions. *Lots.* But when I was in Conner's office, he made me feel like I didn't know the history nearly as well as most of the kids here. And I want to be able to keep up in my classes. So just humor me," I say, putting on the persuasive voice I use to try to talk Emily into doing things she doesn't want to.

Ash looks at me for a second and his eyes seem to be asking a question. "I guess a deal's a deal," he says. Then he sighs and leans back, putting his hands behind his head. "The original three Families formed in an age where power and conquest were paramount. The Families started simply as key advisors and friends who had the ear of the Persian king"—he touches his own chest—"the Roman emperor"—he gestures at me—"or the Greek king. And these advisors influenced the rulers' decisions. But word of these invaluable advisors eventually spread, and the leaders of the other civilizations targeted them in attacks. What better way to weaken the emperor than to eliminate his wisest counsel?" Ash smiles to himself, as if ancient assassinations were a good thing. "And so the rulers in the

Greek, Roman, and Achaemenid Persian empires started hiding these men and women. And before long, the secrecy these advisors utilized became their greatest strength." Ash pauses and looks at me.

"Go on," I say, not sure what to make of the fact that if what Ash is saying is true, then the students here must be able to trace their lineages back to the time of ancient Greece.

"Over the next few hundred years, these secret advisors became more abundant and honed new skill sets. They not only counseled, but they also collected information, poisoned adversaries of the rulers, and helped to infiltrate other empires. As a show of gratitude, they were given properties, wealth, their own crests—with animals as the central figures, of course. The only things the advisors didn't possess were proper titles, but behind closed doors they were commonly referred to as the rulers' *Family*."

"Families" with animal crests. If I learn nothing else from this conversation, at least I have a starting point for understanding where Jackal came from.

"Over time the Families grew less dependent on the ancient rulers and began serving their own agendas," Ash continues. "They built their homes in secret locations, they elected their own governing councils, and they even worked with Families from other empires to bend and shift historical events to their will." As Ash talks, it's hard to ignore the enthusiasm in his voice, like he's been telling stories his whole life.

I catch myself leaning toward him and readjust. "Are you saying they were less dependent *on* the rulers or decided that they were strategically superior *to* them?" I ask.

Ash grins. "Well, perhaps a little of both. The rulers probably thought they were in charge at that point, but let's be realistic. *Vincit qui se vincit.*"

"*Beauty and the Beast,*" I say.

"Pardon?" Ash says, and takes his hands out from behind his head.

"*Vincit qui se vincit*—'he conquers who conquers himself.' It's etched on the stained-glass window in the Beast's castle," I say.

"Seriously?" he asks. "You're referencing a fairy tale?"

"An animated movie," I correct him, and he gives me a puzzled look, like I might be from another planet. "But I didn't mean to interrupt," I say in a rush. "Please finish your story."

Ash sits up a bit, and I can tell he's trying to sort something out about me. He's silent for a couple of seconds and then clears his throat. "So, as you know, the ancient civilizations eventually became too big and too politically complicated. They collapsed one by one. But by this time, Strategia had evolved, and as the great civilizations broke apart, Strategia saw the opportunity for true independence. Over time Europe divided itself into smaller kingdoms and the Greek, Persian, and Roman Strategia splintered off into further divisions—Britain became the Lions, making up the modern UK territory, the Franks became the Deer in France and Germany, and the Spanish became the Foxes in Spain and Portugal. Though, of course, these days you'll find Family members in all countries all over the world. We've gone global, as it were." He smiles.

I concentrate on what he's telling me so hard that I'm sure my face looks strained. So there are the three original Families and then the three newer ones, but nowhere in there did he mention Aarya's animal crest. "And the Jackals?" I interject.

He raises an eyebrow at me. "Thought I was going to miss a detail, did you?" His expression turns mischievous. "No one's sure exactly when or where the Jackals formed. They're the rebels of Strategia. They didn't originate in any one country but are thought to have come together from everywhere, and to have formed their own coalition independent of bloodlines. And like the animal they chose for their crest, they prefer to live in small groups. They proudly lack the organization the rest of the Families enjoy. Now, of course, it took centuries before Strategia formed their own UN, if you will, known as the Council of Families, to establish a central order. Around 500 CE was the very first time members of all the Families came together. It didn't take long before the Council agreed that passing down centuries of acquired knowledge could never occur in typical ways. And that brings us to the glorious Academy you have joined," he says, and spreads his arms out, gesturing at the courtyard.

I chew the inside of my cheek, fascinated. So *assassin* and *spy* weren't wrong, they just weren't right. Whatever these Families are is far more complex than that—they're nothing short of an ancient secret society that quietly pulls the strings behind the scenes all over the world. But the part that I can't get good with is why *my* family would put me here with all of these secret society kids. I'm from Pembrook, Connecticut. I drive an old truck with a worn bumper sticker that reads I'M ONLY SPEEDING 'CAUSE I REALLY HAVE TO POOP. And the most mysterious thing about me is whether I'm going to bring lunch to school or walk to the pizza place, for god's sake.

"Well?" Ash says, and I realize that I'm frowning into the dark branches.

"Right . . . thanks. That helps. I just . . . Stupid Conner, trying to make me doubt myself," I say, and force my face to relax. I press my thumb into my palm.

"Something else you want to ask?" Ash says, watching my hands.

I stop what I'm doing and casually rub my hands together instead. "Tell me whatever you think will keep me from getting punched again."

His expression turns serious and he nods, like I'm finally asking the right questions. "See, that's the thing. Layla and I aren't sure why that happened. You Italians have always bickered among yourselves. I'll admit that it's dramatic sometimes, but ultimately you all look out for each other. I tried to ask Matteo, but he wouldn't say a word. The only thing I can gather is that it was personal and important."

"But I've never even talked to him!" I say, frustrated. Again with the unspoken rules of this place. How could it have been personal when Matteo is a total stranger to me?

"Yeah, but that doesn't exactly matter. All the members of a Family are entwined whether they want to be or not," Ash says. "Bears especially."

The longer I look at him, the more serious I realize he is. I get that he's saying the Romans are Bears, but what I don't get is why he's implying I'm a part of that Family. I mean, the bears were my mom's favorite in the stuffed animal game we played, but that's not hard evidence that it has anything to do with me. Is it? My heart starts to race.

When I don't respond, Ash starts talking again. "All I know is that Matteo radiated frustration. His fists were clenched the entire time Blackwood was talking to him." Ash pauses and looks off into the trees for a moment. "The interesting thing was, though, I think he respected you."

I take a breath and attempt to calm myself down. "Why would you think that?"

"Because he lifted his chin," Ash replies. "Classic sign of deference to an opponent in battle."

I choose my next words carefully. If Ash thinks I'm flustered, he may start questioning me instead of the other way around. "So besides Matteo, are there any other Families I need to avoid?"

Ash raises an eyebrow, like something I said was off. "You need to pick your allies for yourself. But as Layla has already told you, it's generally not smart to trust a Jackal, especially coming from an influential Family like the Bears. There aren't many Jackals here, but they always seem to make their presence known. And their alliances are unpredictable."

I measure my voice to hide my flurry of concerns. The only thing worse than the upside-down feeling of potentially being a member of a deadly secret society I know nothing about is these assassin-trained kids finding out how ignorant I actually am. "What about Felix?"

"Ah, Lion. His immediate family used to be quite powerful, from what I hear, but lost standing some years back—hence his alliance with Aarya and that Fox."

"Ines?"

Ash reaches up and rests his arm above his head. "Right. Those three aren't the norm. No one is quite sure what the long-term goal of their alliance is. But if you ask me, Felix has been in love with Aarya for years, even though *that's* never going to happen. And Ines uses Aarya as a mouthpiece so she doesn't have to deal with the rest of us."

"Makes sense," I say, even though *sense* is the last thing any of this makes. I need time to think over that game I played with my mom, figure out what else I know that I didn't realize I did. I remember the Family descriptions perfectly, but not all of the complexities of their relationships.

"And your Family?" I ask.

He gives me a quick look, like I'm asking an obvious question. "You know I'm a Wolf. But look, I think I can simplify this. Instead of going through all hundred students one by one, why don't you just tell me where you stand?" He says this last bit casually, but I have a gut feeling that it's significant.

"Stand?"

"For, against, or neutral?" he says, emphasizing each word in such a way that I'm sure he's asking me something important, something I should know.

"You're going to have to spell it out," I say carefully, aware that he's watching my every move. Although I don't know why I'm surprised that Ash had an ulterior motive for inviting me up here. Everything about him screams strategy, and the worst thing is, I knew that the minute I laid eyes on him. I could kick myself for thinking otherwise.

"Are you trying to make me think you're not involved in Family politics?" He's still lounging, but his eyes are focused.

"I'm not. I mean, not that I know of," I say as neutrally as possible, wondering if I'll regret my answer but not seeing a safer alternative.

His voice is smooth and steady. "That makes no sense. You

came in late, midsemester. Aarya sought you out. Brendan challenged you. Matteo punched you."

"See? Your guess is as good as mine," I say.

He's silent for a second, studying me. "Either you've suddenly become a good liar or you're telling the truth. I don't know which is more unbelievable."

It has to be better for him to think I don't know about Family politics than for him to catch me lying about what side I'm on, despite the fact that I don't know what the sides are. I lighten my voice. "Believe what you want."

He shakes his head. "There's something more going on here. Something you don't want me to know . . . And don't think I missed that there was also something about that origin story that bothered you." He scans my every feature, taking his time reading me, and making me wish I had somewhere to hide. "What are the Bear Family attributes?" he asks suddenly.

I attempt to unclench my shoulders. "What are the Wolf Family's?" I shoot back.

"Intuitive. Loyal. Diligent," he says without pause, an answer that—I remember with a jolt of recognition—is exactly what we used to say in the game I played with my mom.

I smirk to keep the mood from becoming too serious. "Loyal to who?"

"Ah, isn't that always the question?" His eyes look mischievous, like I just became his new favorite game. "Now . . . what are the attributes of the Bear Family?"

I maintain eye contact with him though my heart is pounding. "Inventive. Protective. Courageous."

"Hmmm," he says. By the look he's giving me, it seems he finds something about me suspicious, but from the way this

105

conversation has unfolded, he also assumes I know way more than I do, making him less likely to guess the truth.

"Here's the thing," I say as nonchalantly as I can. "The origin story was really just a test to see how you were with history. The reality is, I came in late and missed two and a half years of history class. I just want to make sure I'm keeping up." Less is more here.

Ash shifts his position on the branch. "Well, now, things just got interesting. Are you asking me to tutor you in Family history?"

"You're a strong analyst and a good storyteller," I say truthfully.

He smiles. "Flattery will get you everywhere. But what do you have to trade?" Something in his expression relaxes and a bit of warmth leaks through his usual focused intensity.

I hesitate, not only because I'm not sure how to answer, but because I find it hard not to smile back at him. "What do you want?"

"Information," he says. "What else is there?"

Crap. I don't know what I could possibly tell him that would be valuable. And if I do know something worth telling, would it even be safe to tell?

"Like for starters, how you got into this school so late," Ash says, and tilts his head expectantly.

I stay still, hopeful that he'll read my expression as indecision instead of ignorance.

He smiles. "Look, you were paired as my sister's roommate. That's not an accident, because *nothing* at this school is random. It's likely that we're more alike than not."

No wonder everyone advised me to just stay quiet. I suddenly think Ines might be the smartest person in this whole school.

After a couple of seconds of silence, he starts talking again in an upbeat way. "You're probably wondering where the Academy is located, right?" He adjusts his position again so that he's looking directly at me. "Everyone who comes here wonders that. It doesn't matter how much we were trained to never mention this place. Curiosity is human instinct, *especially* for Strategia. The Council of Families knew this, and after a few failed attempts in other buildings where the school's secrecy was breached, they settled on this location. Additionally, they came up with an elaborate camouflage system that has kept the Academy hidden for more than a thousand years. Can you even imagine?" Ash shakes his head. "Now, the most common guess is England, based on the seasons and the foliage alone. But if you start paying closer attention, the seasons and the foliage match so many places it's not funny. There is every likelihood that the school was built to look like it's in England because that is exactly where it *isn't*. Everyone here speaks English now, but that wasn't always the case. You'll find that students here stop asking these questions after their first year because it's a futile pursuit. If some of the greatest minds over the past thousand years haven't figured out our location, you won't, either. And besides, there is nothing to gain by knowing where we are. You only put yourself and all of us in danger."

He pauses to make sure he has my attention, which he most certainly does.

"The analytical minds and ambition that drive us to figure

out the school location also make us look at history *differently*. In history class we're not just learning dates and events. We're taught about our Families' greatest victories and most catastrophic failures. And not the way we learn about Family origins as children. The lessons are broken down to illustrate specific strategy and maneuvering details, and the deeper you look, the more you see patterns. At first you don't think much of it, but then, all of a sudden"—Ash snaps his fingers—"it clicks. You start seeing the cyclical nature of historical events— the cause and effect—in a way you've never analyzed it before because you never stopped to consider that a member of your own Family was not only responsible for those events, but was strategically maneuvering them."

Ash gestures with his hands, and his expression is more animated than I've ever seen it. "Take Pope Gregory the Ninth, for instance. After he decided that cats were associated with devil worship, he had them killed in droves throughout Europe, right?"

I nod, vaguely recalling this from world history class.

"But because he took away the rat's natural predator, medieval Europe found itself with an overpopulation of rats, resulting in nothing less than the bubonic plague, which killed *twenty million people*." Ash shakes his head, as if in disbelief. "We see that misstep as obvious *now*, looking back. But what is unique about studying history here is that you realize our Families saw it as obvious back *then* and tried to stop it. When you're paying attention, history isn't linear; it's a web of interrelated events, each domino toppling the next. You learn to predict instead of react. It's the backbone of everything we do at this school. If you can figure out *what* someone is going to do, not just in a single moment, but five steps down the line, you can be effective."

His enthusiasm is infectious and I find myself nodding. How could twins be so entirely different? He's talkative. Layla's not. She follows the rules to the letter. Ash seemingly breaks them every chance he gets.

"For my part of the deal, I'll give you the highlights, make it easier for you to stop embarrassing yourself," he says with a smirk.

"I'll think about it," I say, even though I know I probably won't get a better offer. I just have no idea what I'll trade with him or how everything I've heard tonight makes sense with what I know about my own family—who are clearly not who I thought they were.

"Hey, look, it could be worse. You might have been paired with a different roommate and not had the good fortune to talk to me," he says with a grin.

Again, it's pretty much impossible not to smile back at him. "Is that so?"

He leans toward me. "Who else in this school would tell you secrets?"

"And who else would encourage me to break all the rules?" I say, matching his playful tone.

"Speaking of which, it's time to go," Ash says, sliding off the branch and onto a smaller one below.

"You're kinda good at that," I say, climbing down to meet him. "I'm *better*, but you're still good."

Ash nods approvingly. "Do that. Exactly that and you'll survive here." Then he grabs the branch in front of him and swings down to a lower one.

I mimic his move, but using only one hand instead of two.

He laughs and so do I.

"Race you down?" he says, and before he gets to the end of his sentence, I'm already moving.

In no time we're at the vines, me arriving a split second before he does. I give him a gloating look, since talking this close to the ground is out of the question.

He grabs the vine I'm hanging on and yanks it toward him. I put out my hand to stop us from colliding and wind up with my palm on his chest, which I can't help but notice is muscular. I can feel his heart racing under his linen shirt.

He whispers in my ear, his breath warm on my cold skin, sending goose bumps down my neck. "The guards are about to make their rounds again. And just before they do, we'll stand on either side of the doorway and tuck ourselves behind the curtain. Then as the guard parts the curtain to exit, we'll slip behind him along the wall into the recessed doorway. As long as you don't make any noise or pull the fabric, we'll go undetected."

All my thoughts of our nearness, his breath, and his chest under my fingertips disappear and I drop my hand. "That's a terrible plan," I whisper back. "Why can't we just wait for the guard to clear the courtyard and *then* sneak behind the curtain?"

"If we do that, we won't have enough time before the next guard takes up the post at the door."

"I thought you said they cut the number of guards at midnight?"

"They never cut the number of guards," he whispers. "That's just when they rotate. Their stations are reduced because they're in motion, not because they're off duty."

I pull back and look at him so that he can see that I think he's an ass for misleading me. He winks and lowers himself silently, hand over hand, down the vine before dropping the last few feet onto the lawn. I do the same and reluctantly follow him to the heavy fabric shrouding the courtyard door.

He stands on one side and I on the other. I imitate his movements and tuck myself behind the curtain, pressing my back flat against the uneven stone wall, trying to stay as far away from the arched doorway as possible.

A minute ticks by and my breath slows, but my stomach does constant somersaults. Then comes the sound of a latch lifting, and instantly every hair on my body stands at attention. The door clicks shut and the fabric moves. I slide into the archway and hold my breath in the darkness, afraid that if I even blink, the guard will hear me and skewer me with a sword. Not that I've ever seen them with swords, but still.

Five horrible seconds pass before Ash opens the door. I practically trip over myself to get inside. The moment the door closes, I start to run for the stairs, but Ash pulls me to a halt. He pushes my hair back and cups his hand over his mouth and my ear.

"You'll get caught that way. Take the far right hallway all the way to the end, and then take that staircase up. Stay against the left wall." He pulls my hood up over my head and releases me.

I take off without pause, my boots making a muffled patting sound against the stone. The hallway Ash told me to take is almost entirely shadowed, making it hard to see. As much as I'd like to maintain my sprint, I slow to a jog to silence my steps. Dad always said that if you're rushing and making noise you'll completely miss what's going on around you. I hug the left wall just like Ash said. And even though it's cold, my hands are sweating from the spike of adrenaline.

Halfway down the long hallway, the shadows ahead of me appear darker, different. I pause and steal a glance over my shoulder. No one is there and everything is still. I squint at the shadows ahead, trying to make sense of the dark shape. It doesn't appear to be moving or giving any indication that it's animate, but there also shouldn't be anything on the floor of this hallway. Layla took me through it earlier and it was completely empty—no furniture, no rugs, no tapestries. I inch forward, keeping my steps perfectly silent.

For the last couple of feet, I hold my breath. I tentatively nudge the long shape with my boot, and it gives slightly but there isn't a sound. I bend down and squint in the dark and that's when I realize what I'm looking at. *Feet.* My boot touched someone's foot. *Oh no. No.* I rub my eyes. *This can't be right.*

I inch along the body, my pulse drumming furiously in my temples. From what I can tell from the clothes, it looks like a guy, lying on his back. And there's something . . . *Oh god,* I think. *It's a* knife. *A knife is sticking out of his chest.* As I continue to stare, I notice that the entire front of him is dark, but the student uniform shirts are white. . . . "Blood," I breathe almost inaudibly. My throat is bone-dry.

I kneel down next to him, my knees nearly giving out, and I force myself to stretch a hand toward his neck. My fingers are shaking when they find it—cold skin, no pulse. His long hair sticks to his cheeks. *Long hair . . . Oh god, it's Matteo's friend from the dining hall.* I look around me for an answer, for help. There's nothing and no one. Dead. He's *dead.* My mind loops the realization and my vision blurs. For a moment I think I'm going to pass out.

I open my mouth to call for help but freeze before a sound escapes my lips. There is no one to call. If I run to get a guard there's every possibility they'll think I did it. Not to mention the eye-for-an-eye punishment system here. I take one more desperate look around, like an answer might somehow pop out of the shadows.

I shake my head, trying to get my bearings. I can't stay here. Being caught with the body would be a thousand times worse than calling a guard. Not to mention being caught by the killer. There's no guarantee that whoever did this isn't lurking nearby.

Instantly, I have that unnerving sensation of something dangerous looming behind me, the kind that used to send me running out of our basement when I was a little kid. I stand up, feeling sick at the thought of leaving him in the dark, drenched in his own blood, but equally terrified to stay. *Who can I—*

Layla. Layla will know what to do.

I run along the wall, fear pushing me forward faster than is cautious, and I duck into the stairwell. Every detail of my surroundings comes sharply into focus, the worn third step, the oddly shaped stone by the ceiling, the silence. I methodically make my way up the stairs, listening for all I'm worth and examining every shadow.

I peek around the corner at the entrance to the third floor and find the hallway empty. Unfortunately, I'm also about as far from my room as I can be. And now that I'm this close, I just have to go. Run. I have to *run*. I close my eyes for a second, take a breath, and bolt out of the stairwell. I slide in front of my door and fumble it open. I duck inside, my heart raging in my chest, and just as I'm closing the door, I spot the guard with the X coming up the other staircase. He makes eye contact with me as I click the door shut. *Shit!!!*

I lean my back against the wall, my breath fast and heavy, and stare at Layla's door. I open my mouth to call out for her, but I can't even think of the words to describe what just happened. I want to scream at myself for not telling her I was meeting Ash in the first place. And now that there's a dead body, what if Ash denies meeting me at all? She'll definitely believe him over me. Hang on. It was Ash who told me to take that hallway. He was the one who said to keep to the left.

Could Ash have set me up to take the fall by intentionally sending me the long way around? That guard would have caught me outright if I hadn't decided to run the last few feet. Ash knows their schedules to the second.

I sink to the floor and put my head in my hands. I'm so screwed.

Nine

WOOD CREAKS AND my head shoots up off my knees. Layla steps out of her room, not blinking and groggy like I would expect, but clear and focused.

She takes note of my crouched position and my strained expression. "You went out." Her tone is accusatory.

"I did," I say, my voice unsure and too fast.

Layla watches me, and I swear I can almost hear her thinking: *You went out when I warned you not to.*

"I met Ash in the vine courtyard."

Her eyes widen and her lips momentarily press together before she says, "You got caught."

I rub my hands over my face and press them into my temples. "No. Well, kind of. Not with Ash." I stand up so fast that I see spots. I look at Layla for a long second and will myself to focus. "We went to those branches, the ones that make a bench in the sky, and we talked about the school, about nothing really. Then on the way back to the room, he told me to take the long way around to avoid the guards. And I . . ." My voice catches.

Layla glances at the door and back at me. "November." There is an anxious edge in her tone now.

"My foot hit something in the shadows. A body. My foot hit a *body*." I cover my mouth with my hand. "I think it was Matteo's friend, the one with the long hair." My words gargle and twist.

For just a second, Layla's completely still.

I move toward her, my words tumbling out. "He was dead, Layla. *Cold*. I didn't know what to do. I didn't want to leave him there. But I panicked and ran back to our room. I think one of the guards spotted me as I was shutting the door."

"How did he die?" Her voice is small and quiet.

"A knife in his chest. And blood. There was so much—"

"Stop." She closes her eyes and takes a breath.

And I do.

"You know our rules," she says with a steady voice.

I nod, squeezing my hands together until they hurt.

"If a guard saw you, they're going to question you. And then they're going to question me. We need to go to our bedrooms. *Now*."

"Oh god, I just left him there on the floor, Layla." I look at the door to the hallway.

"Go to sleep, November," she says in a harsh tone. "If they find us here talking about a dead body, you can bet anything they will throw us in the dungeon."

"*Dungeon?*" My voice rises sharply and I immediately pull it back down. "Shouldn't we at least—"

"There is absolutely *nothing* we can do about it right now that won't further complicate the situation," she practically spits at me. Her eyes turn fiery and her graceful fingers clench

116

into fists. "*You* left the room, *you* took the risk, and now you've pulled me into this mess with you."

I take a step backward, her burst of emotion sobering me up. "Ash—"

"Ash nothing. I don't want to hear that name right now. And I don't need all your teary words, either. You didn't even know Stefano!" She turns on her heel and disappears inside her bedroom before I can react.

I stare after her, my heart beating steady, heavy thumps, my palms slick. Stefano's bloody chest flashes in my mind, his hair sticking to his face, his lifeless skin. My stomach wrenches and I run for the bathroom.

Ten

MY EYES SNAP open at the sound of my bedroom door creaking. I sit up so fast that Pippa looks startled as she enters my room. Her hair is tucked under her bonnet and she carries pressed clothes on hangers.

"Good morning," she says cheerfully.

"Hi," I say with a voice so rough from crying that it makes that simple word feel wrong and foreign. I'm sweating even though it's chilly and I'm not sure that I slept for more than a few disturbed minutes at a time.

Layla bustles into my room and when she sees me she laughs. "Trouble sleeping again? You look terrible. Don't worry; you'll adjust to the bed soon enough."

I blink at her. Who is this friendly creature who took over Layla's body?

"You can put the clothes anywhere you like, Pippa," Layla says with an implied "and then you can leave" after it.

Pippa lays the fresh outfit over the trunk and looks at me like I'm a puzzle that needs solving. She barely takes notice of

Layla. "Breakfast is laid out in your sitting room. The word is that they're cleaning the dining hall. But if you ask me—"

"Lovely. Thank you," Layla says before she can continue.

Disappointment shows on Pippa's face when Layla doesn't ask any follow-up questions. Normally I would give her a big "Thank you" and tell her how much I appreciate everything, but I have no enthusiasm to offer this morning. All I can think about is Stefano's cold neck below my fingers and his blood-covered chest. Pippa does a quick curtsy and leaves.

The moment our suite door closes, the friendly expression drops from Layla's face. "You might as well walk around with a guilty sign on your back if you're going to act this emotional. Did you imagine that they weren't going to question our maids about our behavior?" Disgust flashes in her eyes and she walks out of my bedroom.

I throw back my covers and follow her to the table near the window in the common room, which is laid out with cloth napkins and fragile-looking china. "I wasn't expecting—"

"I don't care what you were expecting," she says, and sits down, placing a napkin on her lap. "There is already a bull's-eye on both our backs."

I sit down, too, trying to reconcile the horrifying reality that I found a dead body last night with Layla's expectation that I act like nothing happened. "If we're supposed to be acting normal, then why did you say I look terrible in front of Pippa?"

Layla looks up from her cheesy eggs and frowns. "Because by calling it out, I instantly normalized it. I made her read your demeanor as nothing more than a bad night's sleep on a lumpy mattress. And by smiling, I sent the impression that I approve of you. Pippa knows that I'm discerning, that I wouldn't accept you if you weren't trustworthy." She pauses and levels a look at me. "Seriously, what's wrong with you? This is first-year deception." Her upset and anger from last night have been replaced with her usual cool demeanor.

I poke at the potatoes on my plate, trying to muster an appetite. I have no idea how to process the events of the past few days. Saying I'm freaked out doesn't even begin to cover it.

All night long I've been replaying the moment when Ash told me to take that hallway. And I can't ignore the fact that Stefano had a knife sticking out of his chest when Aarya and Ash had just talked about a missing knife at lunch. She even accused *him* of stealing it. Not that I would put it past Aarya to lie about the knife for exactly this reason.

"The dining room is being cleaned—" I say.

"They don't want to give us an opportunity to talk in a group. They're probably trying to see who searches out who," Layla says, and spears a roasted potato wedge.

My stomach twists. "Is that why they didn't question us last night after that guard saw me?"

"I don't know," she says, and I can see stress in her expression. "There is a tactic here, I'm just not sure what it is yet."

I put down my fork. I wish I could erase this whole event from my memory. "Okay, tell me. What do I do if they question me? I haven't taken deception classes for years like you have. I don't know what you know."

Layla makes eye contact with me and pauses. "Exactly."

"What?"

"Play the 'I don't know what's going on here' approach.

You've been using it well so far. At least it will be consistent." She doesn't offer any more information.

If I can't manage to lie to Layla and Ash, then I can't lie to Blackwood, or whoever is doing the interrogation. They'll know immediately. But I can't exactly tell them I found a dead body, either. "Do I say anything about what I saw?"

"If that's a joke, it's not funny," she says, and a bit of anger creeps back into her tone.

I have no idea how I'm going to get through this day or the possible questioning without making myself look guilty. I want to cry every time I think about Stefano lying there in the dark. I push my plate away.

Layla watches me. "I suggest eating. You'll need energy for whatever is coming next."

I walk behind Layla as two lines of silent students in black cloaks file through the vine doorway and into the courtyard where the archery class was held. I can't help but think that it looks like we're going to a funeral.

"Professor Messer," Layla whispers to me like a warning.

I immediately translate Messer as German for "knife," triggering the image of Stefano's bloody chest to flash through my mind. I squeeze my eyes shut for a second and when I open them again the teacher is looking straight at me.

Professor Messer is a short muscular woman with lots of small scars on her hands.

"I've been told you're skilled with knives and will be able to keep up," Messer says, and takes a good look at me. She speaks with a German accent. "I have no intention of spending part of my class reviewing things already learned by the elemental students."

Everyone looks at me and it's obvious from the disdain on their faces that not being able to keep up here is humiliating.

"I'll keep up," I say, and my voice sounds weak. Layla shoots me a disapproving look.

I drop a small knife toward my foot and try to kick it back up in the air with my toe, but it arcs out and away from me before I can grab it.

Dad watches me from the porch and laughs. "What in the world are you doing?"

I hold the knife in the air above my foot. "I learned this thing in soccer today and I thought maybe I could do it with my knife."

He shakes his head and smiles. "Well, no one can accuse you of not having an imagination."

I manage to kick the knife up, but it's a little too far away for me to catch it. "Imagination, shmagination," I say. "This is going to be so cool."

I hang my cloak next to Layla's on the vine-covered wall. She leans in. "Unless you want to explain why you didn't report a dead body last night and go to the dungeon, you need to stop wearing your emotions all over your face." Her voice is fierce even in a whisper.

I take a deep breath and we join the nine other students. Of course the first day I'm expected to perform in class would be the morning after I stumbled upon a dead body. And to make things more interesting, Nyx, Brendan, and Charles are here, and so are Aarya and Ines. I find it strange that none of them have made a snide remark or thrown me any pointed looks, which they all have made a habit of these past few days. The change in behavior makes me wonder if they already know about Stefano. I glance at the arched doorway; I keep expecting one of the guards to come pluck me from class and shackle me.

Messer holds a rolled-up piece of leather and taps it against her other hand. "In Persia in 522 BCE, a pretender stole the throne. The rightful ruler, King Cambyses the Second, gathered an army to march against him. But he never succeeded. And why was that?" She pauses. "Because he accidentally stabbed himself with his own knife and died from the wound."

There are a couple of amused scoffs.

Messer smiles. "While this story may sound absurd, it elegantly illustrates the diabolical nature of knives. They can be your best friend—they're easy to conceal and easy to maneuver. But with one tiny mistake they can be your death. They are a weapon that requires complete confidence and perfect timing. There's no room for error. What do I mean by that?"

Brendan cracks his knuckles and takes a step forward even though it's not necessary. I've seen him only a handful of times, and already it's obvious that he likes to take up space. "If you throw a knife at the proper time, you can deliver a death blow or incapacitate your opponent without having to engage in a fight. But if your timing or aim is off by even a fraction, you'll wind up giving your weapon away," he says.

"Very true," Messer says. "And while learning precision in a relaxed environment is cozy, it won't prepare you for a stressful one. You have to learn to be so focused that the walls could be crumbling down around you and you'd still hit your mark."

Messer inclines her head toward Brendan. "Step forward and take the first shot."

Brendan approaches Messer and rolls back his toned shoulders. Out in the field I spy three staggered targets similar to the archery targets, with a series of tiny Xs on them instead of the usual bull's-eye. The first target is an easy distance, but the last is a serious challenge at what looks like more than thirty-five feet.

"Charles, you too," Messer says, and it's clear the two of them are her go-tos when she's making a point. Charles smirks; I can tell he likes being lumped in with Brendan. He even takes a quick look back at the class to make sure we all notice. Charles rolls his sleeves up, exposing his ivy tattoo, which appears to move as his muscles flex.

Messer hands them each three knives.

Brendan immediately pulls back with no hesitation and throws his first knife, wedging it perfectly in an X on the closest target. He smiles and stretches his arms over his head. As they come down, he pulls back and throws again, so fast that I can hear the knife slicing through the air. He hits an X on the second target as neatly as the first.

Making a show of it, he licks his finger and tests the wind. He throws at the farthest target, but his knife strikes a couple of inches off. He's skilled, but given Messer's favoritism, I expected more.

Charles steps up next and hits the first two targets as cleanly as Brendan. His form is good, but almost too good—like he needs it to be perfect. I wonder if he could do as well if he were hanging upside down from a tree branch.

Charles looks over and smiles at Nyx before he readjusts to throw his third knife, and her eyes smile back so subtly that if I weren't watching her closely, I would have missed it. Emily gives Ben that look all the time when she's trying to keep a smile off her face in front of a teacher. Which makes me wonder if Charles and Nyx are a couple. Then Charles releases his knife and it zips through the air with a crisp buzzing sound, like a loud fly. It lands in the farthest target an inch away from the X.

When my gaze returns to Messer, I'm startled to find her watching me.

"By the look on your face, you think you can do better," she says like it's a statement of fact and not a question.

My eyes momentarily widen. I can practically feel Layla radiating tension next to me about my inability to act normal.

"Well?" Messer says.

I clear my throat. "Better than their third shots? Yeah, definitely," I say, and the whole class turns to look at me.

Aarya smirks. "I would *love* to see this," she says, then covers her comment with a cough as Messer gives her a stern look.

Charles locks me in his gaze. "We welcome the challenge," he says. He reminds me of this hipster I dated for a split second last year before I realized he was never going to like me more than he liked his hair.

By the way Charles and Brendan look at me, I can tell they don't welcome the challenge one bit.

Messer is holding out three knives, but Brendan doesn't move and I have to step awkwardly around him to take them. Maybe there's a fine line between sadness and anger, or maybe I just don't like bullies, but suddenly all my emotions from the past twenty-four hours are directed at beating these two.

I make eye contact with Brendan. "Well, I was going to go easy on you to make you feel better. But now I think I won't," I say.

I glance at Layla, who looks like she can't decide if she's horrified by my comment or relieved that I'm not weepy.

Charles scoffs and I turn toward the target. I hold my first knife up, pull back, and let it soar. It knocks Brendan's knife right off the target.

"Oops," I say. "Let's try that again. Maybe I'm just stiff."

I bounce on my toes and shake out my body. I pull back my arm and send the next knife flying. This one knocks Charles's knife clean off the second target. There are a few whispered comments behind me, but they're too quiet to make out the words.

"I don't know why I'm missing so much today. I must be—" I stop, like I've just realized something. "I know what it is." I shake my head and flash Brendan and Charles a rueful smile. "I'm not left-handed."

There are a couple of uncomfortable-sounding snickers from the students that stop the moment Messer looks at them.

I take the last knife in my right hand and throw it in one fast and fluid motion at the farthest target. My knife not only splits an X directly down the middle, but it splits the same X that they both missed.

Brendan's fist clenches near his side and Charles's jaw is tight; they both look decidedly put out. Aarya, on the other hand, laughs, and when I look over, there's even a hint of amusement on Layla's face.

Messer's expression remains stony and unimpressed. "Well, well. Let's see how you do when the stakes are real." She scans the students. "Ines, go stand in front of the farthest target."

I swallow and Aarya abruptly stops laughing. Charles and Brendan now seem to be the ones who are amused.

Messer waits while Ines walks across the field. "Hit the X

an inch above Ines's head," she says. "With the way you've been showing off, that should be no problem for you."

All the bravado I had fifteen seconds ago disappears and is replaced with a stomach-twisting panic. I glance at Ines, who stands calmly in front of the target, and I can't meet her eyes. This is crappy on so many levels. God forbid I miss. On top of the horror I would feel, I'm pretty sure Aarya would skin me alive here and now.

"You look like you're about to faint," Charles says, and makes an exaggerated frown.

Brendan chuckles. "Maybe she's only comfortable fighting inanimate objects."

I look at them. "You think this is funny? If my shot is one inch off the way both of yours were, I could kill her."

"Yet they're right," Messer says, and holds out a knife. "Under pressure, you can't perform. Are you refusing to take the shot?"

Shit. I've backed myself into a corner here. "I'm not taking the shot," I say.

"Very well, then. Brendan?" Messer says, and my eyes widen. She's asking *Brendan* to throw? He's even worse than Charles.

"Obviously," he says, and flashes me his confident smile.

I snatch the knife from Messer's hand, and there are a couple of surprised gasps behind me. I throw quickly, before Messer can object, and the knife lodges a good six inches above Ines's head. She never even flinches.

"You missed," Messer says, and by the tone of her voice I can tell that the class I was really looking forward to has just become a nightmare.

Eleven

AFTER A LONG morning of dreading I might be escorted out of each of my classes by guards, I take a seat next to Layla in the dining hall. The tables have been removed except for the one on the raised platform where the teachers eat, and the high-backed wooden chairs have been arranged in rows. With the large chandeliers fully lit above our heads, the ornate arched ceilings, and the decorative stonework on the walls, it looks like we're about to meet some sort of dignitary. But from what I can tell, the entire school has been assembled, and I would bet anything we're not here for entertainment.

Three rows ahead of us, Brendan looks at me like he knows something I don't and takes a seat next to Nyx and Charles.

"About what I did in knife throwing—" I whisper to Layla.

"Not now, November," she says, and her tone is harsh. She doesn't look in my direction.

Headmaster Blackwood stands on the platform in front of the teachers' dining table, watching us all like a bird of prey. She clears her throat even though the room is already silent and doesn't remotely resemble the mob scene that ensues every time we get called to the auditorium in my school at home. My stomach does a quick flip.

"Some of you are wondering why you've been called from your classes this morning. Some of you are not," Blackwood says, scanning the room. A handful of teachers stand against the stone walls between the somber portraits and arched windows—they stare at us and not at Blackwood. Conner is one of them, and he has the same probing look he wore when he was assessing me. I want to sink down in my chair, but I'm sure one of the teachers would notice and interpret it as an admission of guilt.

"A student was murdered last night," Blackwood says without any fanfare, and surprise ripples through the crowd. "Stefano," she continues. The students throw questioning glances at one another, shifting in their seats, and it seems like everyone starts whispering at once.

Layla looks at me in shock and I do my best to mimic her. Damn she's good.

Blackwood clears her throat once more and the room instantly falls back into uncomfortable silence. "I am severely disappointed that we find ourselves in this position yet again." She sounds more annoyed than upset. "You all have become too comfortable here, too sure that you are untouchable. I assure you that you're not. Our tactics during the course of this investigation will not be typical, so do not presume. The guilty party or parties may think they've evaded discovery. But in the end, we will find you out and you will be made an example of." For a split second, her eyes settle on me, and I can feel the blood drain from my cheeks.

When Blackwood mentioned student deaths to me in her

office the day I arrived, I didn't for one minute imagine she meant *murder*. My stomach churns uncomfortably, and I fight the urge to shift around, rub my hands over my face, do anything that might show how sick I feel about this whole situation.

"Your privacy is revoked, and you'll be subject to tests and observation whenever and wherever Dr. Conner and I choose. And just because you can't see guards, that doesn't mean they're not following you." Blackwood smooths a wrinkle in her blazer. "For the time being, all meals will be served in your respective suites rather than the dining hall. That is all you need to know; you may go."

I look at Layla, hoping she'll explain the brevity of that speech and the cold cruelty of Blackwood's demeanor. There was no sensitivity to the fact that students have just lost their classmate, no reassurance that we'll be safe; in fact, it felt like the opposite—we've been assured that we're not only in danger, but also potential suspects. However, Layla just stands and heads for the door like all the other students. No one says a word. No one looks at anyone else.

Someone taps my shoulder and I nearly jump out of my skin. My heart sinks when I whip around to find Conner right behind me.

"Follow me, November," he says, and I catch Ash watching me from across the room.

Conner leads me back to Blackwood's office. I take a seat in the armchair in front of Blackwood's desk while Conner settles into a chair near the wall, his folder and pen at the ready. The fireplace is ablaze with crackling and snapping wood—a familiarity that I would usually find comforting. But the coldness in Blackwood's and Conner's expressions and the heavy stillness suck any sense of comfort out of the room.

We all sit there silently for so long that I wonder if this horrible moment somehow got frozen in time.

"So . . . ," Blackwood finally says. "You left your room last night after curfew, November."

My pulse throbs in my temples and my stomach twists uncomfortably. I've always been good in conversations with principals and deans. And I've definitely been in trouble enough to know my way around them. But that was back when the worst thing that could happen to me was suspension, not an eye-for-an-eye punishment system. "Yes, I did."

Blackwood folds her hands on her desk. "And a student is dead."

"I know."

"How do you know?"

I hesitate. "You just told us in the assembly."

"Hmmm," she says, and Conner takes notes.

I immediately regret my answer. I feel like I'm not only sweating all over her office, but that every single thought I'm having is knowable by her. The only tactic I really have is to take Layla's advice. "Hang on. You don't think I had anything to do with what happened, do you?"

"Oh, don't I?" Blackwood says, and gives me a warning look.

"You read people or analyze them—you both do." I wave my hand to include Conner. "And I know I'm new. But if you're any reader of character, you know without a shadow of a doubt that I didn't do it."

"Don't you dare suppose what I know or what I don't," Blackwood says.

"Don't you remember what happened with Matteo? I didn't even want to hit him in the face. You practically had to threaten me to get me to retaliate. If I'm uncomfortable *punching* someone, killing a person is an impossibility."

Blackwood purses her lips and sits back in her chair. "Actually, if you planned to attack Stefano, the very first thing you might do is create a situation meant to illustrate how non-aggressive you are."

I try to adjust my position, but there's no place to shift to and I just wind up looking more agitated than I did a few seconds before. "I wouldn't even be able to think of that, much less—"

"Enough," Blackwood says, and her word is like a slap, which at least tells me that my naïveté must be convincing enough to frustrate her. "What were you doing out of your room last night?"

My heart races. There's no way around it. "I was meeting Ash," I answer.

"Where?"

"In the vine courtyard."

She pauses a moment. "Why?"

I cringe reflexively. I'm in murky freaking waters right here. "To find out more about the school."

"You were told that anything you need to know about the school, you could ask Layla."

"I . . . well . . ."

"Unless you mean to learn more about the students, which I have already told you is strictly forbidden." Her tone harshens and she leans forward.

"I just . . . I wanted to learn more about what the school is *really* like." Here we go.

"By breaking the rules."

"No," I say carefully. "I'm not saying that it's good to break the rules. But if I'm going to live here with these people who've known each other for years and understand the way this place works, I have a ton of catching up to do. And I'm the only new advanced student. Fifty percent of me was just curious."

"And the other fifty percent?"

"I didn't mean that literally."

"But you did mean there was another reason."

Great. I'm stepping in one sinkhole after another. "Ash is interesting . . . I, well . . . He's cute." True, but totally meaningless. And it places me well within the clueless range.

Blackwood leans back in her chair like she's wondering how deep I'm going to dig myself in—I'm wondering the same thing. "Dating is not allowed," she says flatly.

"But looking is, right?" I know I'm pushing it here, but if I don't sell this reason, she's going to go digging for another.

For a second, she doesn't move. Then she says, "I'm going to lay this out for you as plainly as I can, November, because otherwise I fear you will yammer on about every kind of nonsense, and I don't have time for nonsense. Last night you were out of your room. Last night one of our students was murdered. If there is some evidence or reason that I should not suspect you, you should state it now."

"I . . ." I'm completely at a loss. "I'm sorry I left my room and broke the rules. I shouldn't have. But I absolutely did not kill anyone. I wouldn't do that. I just wouldn't."

"Did Layla know you were gone?"

I resist the urge to rub my forehead, because I can't show them how rattled I am. This is bad. Real bad. "No. But she heard me when I came back."

"Did you speak?" Blackwood asks.

I nod. "I told her I was out with Ash and she got angry."

"Did she report you?"

"I told her she didn't have to because a guard had already seen me."

"Which hallways did you take that night?"

It takes all my willpower to stay still. "I took the staircase closest to my room." *Does she know I'm lying? Can she see it?*

"And Ashai?"

I pause. "I don't know."

"But you were with him."

"I was paying too much attention to not getting caught myself that I honestly couldn't say which way he went."

"But he came and left when you did?"

"I assume so."

"But you don't know."

I want to say something that prevents Ash from looking suspect. The last thing I need in this dangerous situation is to make an enemy out of him. But for the life of me, I can't think of anything. "No, I don't."

"Whose idea was it to go to the vine courtyard?"

I tense. "Ash's. Well, both of ours, really. It's my favorite place on campus."

"And Ash was generous enough to break the rules to show it to you?" There is an insistence in her tone, and I know that I've somehow made this worse, not better.

"We just thought it would be fun."

"And how was Ash benefiting from this arrangement?"

She clearly knows him. I shrug as casually as I can in this tension-filled room. "I can't be sure, but my guess is that he wanted to be the first person to figure out the new girl."

Blackwood glances at Conner, but her expression reveals nothing of what she might be thinking.

Conner levels his gaze at me. "Did Ashai tell you which way to go?"

The image of Stefano's body lying on the cold hallway floor flashes through my thoughts. *What's Conner fishing for with a question like that?* "Like I said, we were both in a rush to get to our rooms when we got inside. We didn't really talk."

By the way Conner looks at me, it's clear he knows I've evaded the question. I also know that he's not going to let it go unless I turn the tables on them.

I shift the conversation back to Blackwood. "The bigger question no one seems to be asking is why a student died here at all. Because based on what you told me the day I arrived, this isn't the first death. I know you'll find me innocent. I have no doubt about that. And whenever you clear my name, I want you to get in touch with my dad. I'm not staying in some remote castle where people attack and kill each other." I hadn't realized how badly I'd wanted to say that until it just came tumbling out.

Conner looks at Blackwood. Her hard gaze doesn't waver. "That's not for you to decide," she says.

My voice rises. "Like hell it's not—"

"No." Her tone is commanding. "Your family, just like every other, signed a waiver when you were admitted giving the

Academy final say in what happens to you while you're here. I will decide who is guilty. Just as I will decide how much freedom you will have during this investigation. And I most certainly will decide when you can leave. So if I were you, I would stop before I also decide you're being disrespectful and give you a night in the dungeon to sober up."

I swallow. The reality that I'm trapped here at Blackwood's discretion with deadly secret society kids and no way out makes it hard to breathe.

Blackwood holds me in her stern glare. "You may return to your schedule, November. But this conversation is far from over. Also, you'll have to get by without Layla taking you to your classes for the time being."

I freeze, instantly worried about Layla and whatever Blackwood is planning. I want to ask, but I'm positive I won't get an answer.

"And congratulations," Blackwood continues. "You're the first student in modern history to accumulate three marks in their first week. Stay tuned for your punishment."

My stomach drops and I stand up quickly. I can't get out of this room fast enough.

She pauses. "Unless you're guilty of Stefano's murder, in which case your punishment is already decided."

Twelve

LAYLA IS STILL nowhere to be seen and it's well into evening. And with each hour that she's gone, my anxiety gets incrementally worse. I push the last of my dinner around on my plate as I fidget in my chair at the round table in our common room. Everywhere I went this afternoon the guards were watching me like hawks. To top it off, I've been so tense I haven't had an inch of space to process what I saw and what's happening.

The door to the suite swings open and my head snaps up from my plate. Only it's not Layla, it's Ash. I stand up so fast I almost knock my chair over.

"Are you *insane*?" I hiss at him. "Don't you think it's basically the worst idea in the world for you to be here right now—especially alone, without Layla, on the day that they're questioning everyone?" The shock is obvious in my voice.

"It would be, if I were the type to get caught. But fortunately, I'm not that type," Ash says, sounding as calm as I am nervous. "Or at least I wasn't until someone talked to the headmaster and I received three marks." He walks past the couch and fireplace, stopping a few feet away from me.

I rub my forehead. For a second I wonder about Conner asking me if Ash told me which way to go and if Ash did have something to do with the murder. Could Ash have set me up? "You know I can't lie without it showing on my face."

"So you didn't lie during your interview?"

"Well . . ."

He looks at me like I'm an open book. "You lied for you, just not for me?"

I fidget. "That's not exactly how it went, either."

Ash takes a step closer and I'm suddenly aware that there are a table and a window behind me and nowhere for me to go if I need to. "As far as I understand it, you didn't do me the courtesy of telling Blackwood that I was headed to the boys' dormitory. And not in any way headed in the direction of the hallway where you found Stefano's dead body."

I can feel the color drain from my face. "Oh god, you didn't tell her that—"

There's a light knock on my door, and we both turn. "May I come in, miss?" Pippa's voice calls, and as the latch starts to lift all I can think is *Please don't let her have just heard Ash say that I saw the dead body.*

Ash ducks into my room and I sit back down at the table, trying as naturally as I can to push my food around on my plate the way I was doing before he showed up.

"Oh, you're not finished," Pippa says. "I'll just turn down your bed and refresh your water—"

"No, I'm done," I say quickly, and stand up. I smile to ease the nervousness in my rushed response. "Please feel free to take the plates. And there's no need to turn down my bed. I've got it."

She looks doubtful as she collects the rest of my dinner onto a silver tray. "It won't take more than a minute."

"Really, truly," I say, and keep up my smile until she pulls the door closed behind her.

I run into my room, my heart pounding a mile a minute, only to find Ash lounging on my bed with his arm tucked behind his head.

He reaches out and touches my water glass on my bedside table. "You should have let her give you more water. You're actually running low."

My mouth opens. "What is your . . . What are you doing?"

He looks amused. "Talking to you."

"How can you be so damn nonchalant about this? Do you know how serious this all is?" The words coming out of my mouth take me by surprise. Usually it's Emily saying some version of this to me.

Ash props himself up on his elbow—the picture of leisure. "I understand better than you do. But flailing about like a ball of nervous energy isn't going to make any of it better."

"Oh, and letting Pippa come in here while you're lounging on my bed would have been a fantastic idea. You could have gotten us both in trouble *again*," I say in frustration.

He stands up. "It's funny, I didn't take you as the risk-averse type."

I run my teeth over my bottom lip. "Normal risk? I'm all in. Death risk? Not a chance."

Ash steps past me and locks my bedroom door, and I immediately realize my mistake. I willingly sent Pippa away, which means I'm now alone with him when I have every reason to be suspicious of him.

He raises an eyebrow, and I'm guessing that my nervousness at being locked in this room must show on my face. "Then what are you doing at this school? Our entire lives are a death risk."

Ash is standing so close I could count every one of his long eyelashes if I wanted to. And when I hold my breath for a second too long, I'm positive he notices.

"You know what I mean," I say in the steadiest voice I can summon.

"No, I really don't."

I look from him to the locked door and back again. "Why are you even here, Ash?"

"Layla made it clear to me that I had to take responsibility for asking you to meet me last night." His expression actually looks sincere for a moment, not like he's trying to charm me or analyze me.

I feel an immature twinge of relief that Layla's also mad at him and not just at me.

We stare at each other for a few seconds.

"Did she tell you that I found Stefano?" I ask, even though I already know the answer.

"She did."

"Please tell me you didn't repeat that to Blackwood." I can hear the fear in my voice and I'm sure he can, too.

He hesitates for a second before answering. "The only thing I told Blackwood was that we were both in such a rush I didn't see which way you went."

I exhale. "I said essentially the same thing."

"I know you did. I could tell by her expression," he says.

I shake my head. "I'm a little jealous of you right now. You know these people. You know how to be strategic in a situation like this. And here I am left spewing half-truths and blabbering confusion to get through it." I rub my forehead near my eyebrow.

He considers my words. "I'm pretty sure I know most of what you said, and you didn't do as badly as you think you did."

"How do you know I think I did badly?"

"Are you saying I'm wrong?"

"No, I'm saying you're annoyingly right."

"The way you just touched your forehead."

I stop fidgeting. "What?"

He imitates my gesture. "This. You did it with your fingers out, shielding your eyes. It's often linked with the shame of lying—metaphorically trying to hide yourself from being looked at."

My eyes widen. "Doesn't it get old always knowing what people are thinking? Don't you want to be surprised sometimes?"

He scans my face. "The third mark I got was for conspiring to date another student. Now *that* was a surprise."

"Oh man," I say, and laugh, even though there is nothing funny about this situation. "Yeah, well, telling them I was breaking the rules because you are attractive seemed less likely to cause a tizzy than telling them I wanted to learn as much as I could about the other students."

Ash looks far too pleased. "So you told Blackwood you're attracted to me? I have to say that's not a usual tactic. I'm fairly impressed."

I put up my hands. "I totally see what you're doing, changing my words and then watching my response. I said you're attractive, *not* that I'm attracted to you. There's a big difference."

By the look on his face I can tell that he's used to girls admiring him and that this whole situation just became more interesting. And I know this, because I would do the exact same thing. In some ways Ash is more similar to me than I would like to admit, and I want to tell him to step off my personality. I'm supposed to be a snowflake.

"I want to propose something to you," he says, turning serious as he sits down on my bed.

I give him a wary look. "The last time you proposed something we wound up sneaking outside on the same night someone got murdered."

"That's exactly my point," he says. "As of right now, I don't know who killed Stefano or why." I can feel him reading me. "But I do wonder about the timing. Strategia are never random, and I would bet anything that *you* were meant to find Stefano."

My stomach drops like I'm on a bad carnival ride. "You think someone is setting me up?"

"Or me. I don't know. I'm just saying that we can't ignore that possibility." He looks way less put out about the whole thing than I am feeling.

I brush some flyaway hairs back from my forehead. It's suddenly hard to breathe. "I'm stuck here," I barely whisper, thinking back on Blackwood's refusal to contact my dad.

"Pardon?"

I rub my hands over my face. "Nothing. What are you proposing?"

"That we find Stefano's murderer," he says.

142

My heart thuds. I've always thought of myself as a thrill-seeker, but in less than one week here that's been proven wrong in every conceivable way. "You want to actively seek out the person who stabbed another person with a knife and possibly has reason to set *me* up for it?" I pace back and forth. "Can't we just, I don't know, let Blackwood do her investigation? If she's half as good as you are at reading people, don't you think she'll be able to sort it out? If we just keep our heads down and don't break any more rules, as difficult as that might be for you, don't you think it will get resolved?"

Ash's expression turns hard. "I know you use your open and seemingly trusting demeanor to disarm people, but if you actually believe half of what you just said, you'll without a doubt take the fall for this."

I don't need Ash's people-reading skills to know that this time he means exactly what he says. The room spins and I sit down next to him on the bed. Under normal conditions, if I were sitting on my bed with a boy who looked like Ash, all I'd be able to think about would be flirting. But right now all I'm thinking about is whether I could be executed for a murder I didn't commit.

"We're going up against the best-trained deception and tactical experts in the world. So I suggest you get in the game immediately. Everyone else is on the playing field and you're sitting in the stands eating popcorn. Don't think for a minute that your interview today with Blackwood was the end of it. The worst is coming." Ash's usual smooth-talking charm is absent.

I nod, because as much as I'd like to hide under my bed until this all goes away, his point is fair. "Okay. I'm obviously going to do what I have to in order to avoid taking the fall for murder. But I'm not going to do this dance with you, where you try to pull information out of me in ten kinds of sneaky ways. First nice, then serious, then pushy." I pause. "If you're right that someone wanted to implicate me, then someone knows or thinks they know something about me personally. And yes, gathering that same information is probably ninety percent of the reason you're here right now, offering to work with me on this."

Ash opens his mouth, but I raise my hand before he can say anything.

"No, let me finish. You know this school and these people better than I ever will. You've also had the training to give you tools to deal with this. You don't need my detective skills; you need information on me. But I need information, too. You said you would tutor me in history if I told you personal things. Well, I'm not going to make it that easy. If I agree to do this with you, *you've* got to give something up, too. And you need to stop manipulating me."

He watches me closely with his "I see your inner soul" expression that drives me nuts. "Perhaps."

"I'm serious. No more toying with me. The first day we met you told me that I shouldn't trust you, but here you are asking me to work with you to find a murderer." I point at him. "And I don't like that you look at me like you're reading my mind. I feel like I'm always on the edge of a cliff when I talk to you."

For a split second there's something akin to shock in his expression. "You really enjoy bringing things out into the open, don't you?"

"As much as you enjoy hiding them."

He spreads his hands and holds them out like he has nothing to hide. "What do you want to know?"

I look at him pointedly. "Something of equal value to whatever I tell you."

"As long as I get to be the one who decides what is equal," he says.

"You are a piece of work," I say.

He smirks. "At least I'm not predictable."

"You can say that again." I chew on the inside of my cheek and shift my focus to the flickering candle on my bedside table, watching it cast shadows on the maroon blackout curtain behind it. Part of me fears I'm making a huge mistake. But if I'm stuck here with no way to talk to Dad and the administration suspects I was involved in a murder, I can't just sit around and wait for the chips to fall. Especially after what I learned from Ash last night: Strategia have managed to shape world events for the past two thousand years. Compared to manipulating world leaders, I must seem like easy pickings. I sigh and look back at Ash. "So, who was his roommate?"

"I beg your pardon?"

"Stefano's roommate. If we're going to figure this thing out, wouldn't that be a logical place to start?"

Ash looks at me sideways, like he's surprised I had to ask. "Matteo," he says, and the moment his name comes out of Ash's mouth I'm positive this is the worst deal I've ever made.

Thirteen

LAYLA AND I walk toward class, and even though I've been up for some hours now, I still feel groggy from lack of sleep. Also, I've been getting more looks than usual all day, making me wonder if my conflict with Brendan and Charles is now public knowledge. And as though they knew I was thinking about them, I hear Brendan's and Charles's voices behind us.

Layla pushes through a classroom door and I exhale in relief. But it's short-lived, because not five seconds later Brendan and Charles enter, too. And to make matters worse, Nyx is with them.

The five of us are the first ones in the classroom, where the desks, if you can call the large wooden tables that, have all been pushed to the edges of the room. There are two ropes tied securely around a thick dark wood ceiling beam, and hanging between them is a flag bearing the school crest.

"I can't say I'm not disappointed, Layla," Nyx says, and her gaze is direct and probing. "I thought you were the smart twin. But every time I turn around I think you're less neutral than the day before." There is no showmanship in Nyx's approach the way there is when Brendan is toying with someone. And she doesn't look back at her friends for approval and solidarity the way Charles usually does. She's direct. You can tell she says what she means and a threat is a threat.

I look from Nyx to Layla, and it's obvious by Layla's expression and rigid posture that whatever Nyx is talking about is important. Then it clicks. *Neutral.* Ash used that word when he asked me about my Strategia Family politics—he said "for, against, or neutral."

Charles is standing next to Nyx, and he's a good foot and a half taller than she is. He's also right between us and the door. "I think maybe Layla always fell on the wrong side of politics, and that it just took her sloppy friend here to shine a light on it." The contradiction between his silky voice and the words he chose makes me do a double take. He's like a toddler, cursing with a smile.

One look at Layla and it's clear she wishes she could disappear.

"Sloppy?" I say, boisterously enough that the whole ominous mood breaks. "Pshhht. If you're trying to insult me, you're going to have to be more creative than that." They all look at me with dagger eyes, but I don't care. I'm just happy to take the heat off Layla for a second. I owe her that much at least. "I met an eight-year-old a couple of weeks ago who called me a Skittle fart. Now *that's* creativity."

"Every time you open your mouth," Brendan says, spreading his hands out like he has an audience of four hundred instead of four, "it only confirms the fact that you don't belong here."

"Just because you—" I start, but the door opens and a middle-aged woman I'm assuming is the professor walks in with three more students behind her. I shut my mouth and the five of us break apart, like we were never talking in the first place.

I knew these three would be a problem for me, but I never thought they'd target Layla *because* of me. I watch Layla, who seems to be just as uncomfortable as I am, and wish I could apologize. But I know that at this point the situation has escalated beyond what an "I'm sorry" can fix.

"So you're all here but you're still wearing your cloaks," the professor says. "I shouldn't have to remind you to always be prepared."

The room goes silent and we move quickly to hang our cloaks on the far wall. Everyone returns to form a line in front of the professor, who looks directly at me. "I'm Professor Liu, November. Welcome to your first day of psychological warfare—or, as we affectionately call it, mind games."

I nod my consent, careful not to speak out of turn like I did in Fléchier's class. *Liu—the name of the Chinese emperors of the Han dynasty . . . it means "destroy."*

Professor Liu begins to roll up the sleeves of her black linen blouse in nice, even folds. "Last class we were speaking about perception—how reality can be immaterial because what matters is what your opponent *thinks* is real. For instance, if you can convince someone that you are more powerful than you really are, you can potentially scare them out of battle. Anyone?"

Brendan answers before the others, which seems to be a pattern of his. "At night, Genghis Khan would order his soldiers to light three torches each to give the illusion of an enormous army and intimidate his enemies. He also tied objects to horses' tails so that when they rode through dry fields they'd kick up clouds of dust and further enhance the impression of their numbers." He delivers his answer with a clear voice and a smile. Upon first encounter, I thought Brendan, Charles, and Nyx were the equivalents of the popular crowd at Pembrook, but I'm now thinking Brendan's confidence comes from being well trained and prepared.

"Right," Lui says. "Influence perception and you have the ability to change an outcome without fighting." She clasps her hands behind her back and looks up at the ceiling. "Today, we're going to do something unusual and start class with a physical challenge. As you can see, I've hung a flag from the ceiling beam. There are two ropes and eight of you." She opens a container of what looks like hand chalk for climbing and walks down the line of us; I watch as the students dip their hands in and pat them together. "You'll have to be fast and you'll have to be smart. There are no rules about the types of tactics you might use against one another. The only rule is that the first person to reach the desk directly behind you is the winner."

I want to think I misheard her, but I didn't. What I can't wrap my mind around is the fact that Liu is encouraging us to fight our way up two ropes to a beam that's at least fourteen feet off the ground. There's no safety net, no rules. In fact, she gave us permission to fight it out any way we need to, which, knowing this bunch, probably means a lot of martial arts moves I'm not prepared for. Stealing a cloth in the dark was one thing, but this is something else entirely. And after last night and the conversation we just had with Brendan, Charles, and Nyx, this is basically worst-case scenario.

"Boxing," I say, and take a jab into the air on our front porch. "Or wushu." I throw a kick.

Aunt Jo sips her lemonade with her feet up on the porch railing.

"You know defensive moves, Nova," Dad says as he whittles away at a walking stick with his favorite knife. It's got a silver

149

handle in the shape of a wolf's head. "And you know how to get out of someone's grip if they grab you."

I groan. "Are you kidding? Those aren't remotely the same as what I'm talking about. You've taught me about knives, swords, booby traps, and survival skills"—I count the items off on my fingers as I go—"but you won't teach me boxing? Do you hear yourself?"

"Christopher is probably scared you'll kick his butt all over town," Aunt Jo says, and I giggle. "Embarrass him in front of all his buddies."

Dad tries to contain his smile, but it sneaks into the corners of his eyes. "I'll teach you when you're older."

"How old?" I say.

"Eighteen," he says, and I nearly fall off the step I'm balancing on.

"Seven years? Seven?" I look pleadingly at my aunt. "Aunt Jo?"

"Don't use that cute face on me," she says. "I see what you're doing."

"Nova," Dad says. "I'm intentionally not teaching you how to fight."

"Because you think I'm going to get hurt?" I say.

He pauses his whittling. "Because you already have the skills to be an excellent fighter. You're fast and strong. You have good reflexes. You'll pick up boxing easily. But I don't want you to think like a fighter. I want you to think differently."

"Differently how?" I ask.

"I want you to think of unusual and creative solutions. And I want you to see the world in your own unique way. If you learn to hit a certain way in boxing or to jump a certain way in wushu, your brain will immediately default to them as an answer. I don't want you to rely on the same answers every other person does. I *want you to make up your own. If you learn how to approach a fight from an unexpected angle, you will become the weapon your opponent can't predict."*

Liu has stopped in front of me and offers me the hand chalk.

"I . . . ," I start, but I have no idea how to tell her that I don't know how to fight properly.

"Afraid to join in?" she says, and everyone looks at me.

"No, I just . . ." I look at Layla for help, but her expression is unreadable. Reluctantly, I dip my hands in the chalk.

"Everyone stay where you are," Liu says. "November, take three steps toward the ropes."

Nyx shoots me a disgusted look.

Oh, this is just getting worse by the second. "I really don't need an advantage," I say.

"Take three steps forward, like I said." The professor's voice has a commanding edge and I scoot forward.

If I lose now, it's going to be ten times more embarrassing. My whole body tenses as Liu drags out the next couple of seconds in silence.

"And go!" she says loudly, and everyone makes a dash for the ropes.

I don't get two strides in when a boot strikes the back of my knee, sending me flailing onto the floor. Nyx snickers and all seven students pass me full-speed.

Near the ropes, Charles takes a fast swing at Layla. She dodges gracefully, though I'm not sure how she could have anticipated his punch. But just as Layla eludes Charles, Brendan lands a kick to her stomach. She doubles over, and from the way she's gasping, I know he knocked the wind out of her.

I jump up from the floor and start to move toward her, but

as I do Brendan turns to face me. I somehow see everything at once: Charles has reached the rope, and when he grabs for the guy who's clinging to it, he gets a swift kick in the face. Layla is upright and her breathing seems easier, but then my view of her is temporarily blocked by Brendan, who is now running toward me. From the little I've witnessed of his fighting skills, there is every likelihood I'll end up with broken bones if he attacks me. His eyes narrow as he closes in, and I don't think anymore, I run, too—all the way back to the tables near the wall. I arrive a split second before he does.

"Halt!" Liu says, and Brendan stops just before he collides with me. As the sparring at the ropes subsides, a few frustrated groans escape the fighters' lips. Did Liu stop the challenge because I ran? I look from Brendan to the professor. I doubt Liu is going to let it pass without broadcasting my fear in detail to the whole class. And after the confrontations I've already had with Brendan, this might be one of the most embarrassing moments of my life. I can almost feel myself shrinking.

"November is the winner."

Hold on, what? My head whips toward Professor Liu so fast, I'm lucky I don't wrench my neck. I open my mouth but quickly shut it again before an admission of complete confusion comes tumbling out.

Brendan looks at me like I just solidified my role as competition, and I get the sense that the last place I ever want to be is between Brendan and his glory. I would back up another step, but the table and the wall make that impossible.

"Make a sound in the east, then strike in the west—from the Thirty-Six Stratagems," Liu says. "We will be studying them closely over the next few months. These psychological tactics aren't new. In fact, they were compiled somewhere around 500 BCE. What is interesting here is that you all are still falling for the same tricks people used twenty-five hundred years ago. People don't change, the props around them do." She smiles an amused smile. "I spoke so much about the flag that the only thing you focused on was how to beat each other, *not* on what I was actually saying. Think about it: I never said you needed to capture the flag to win. I said you needed to touch the table. However, I must admit that I'm shocked that only two of you were truly listening."

I want to laugh at my pure dumb luck, except it's not funny. Had I actually participated the way I intended to, and the way most of the students had, I would be knocked unconscious right now.

"And I'll hand it to you, November," continues the professor. "You acted naïve, and the way you protested about getting an advantage was brilliant. You demonstrated tactics in keeping with this class's lessons. I look forward to seeing what else you'll contribute."

The other students' frustrated expressions intensify, and I'm now getting openly nasty looks. I wish I could crawl under the table and pretend this never happened.

I try to catch Layla's eye to see if she's okay. But she won't look in my direction. Brendan does, though, and he winks at me. But it's not a friendly, flirty wink. He's throwing down a gauntlet—he's powerful, he's smart, and he's after me.

Fourteen

I DIDN'T IMAGINE anything could be worse than stumbling upon a dead body in the middle of the night, but as I stare at the fireplace from my sprawled-out position on the couch, my conversations with Blackwood and Ash have started to cast the situation in an ominous new light. The only thing is, I can't think of a single substantial reason someone would want to frame me for the murder of another student. Unless *maybe* someone had wanted to kill Stefano for a long time and I just happened to come along and get into a fight with Matteo, making me an easy target. *Matteo*. I reflexively touch my bruised eye.

Of course, there's always the possibility that Ash's in on whatever happened. He did tell me to take that hallway. And if he is, and I give him the personal information he wants, I'll be making it so much worse. This is an absolute nightmare situation.

The door slams and I roll off the couch and into a standing position to find a fuming Layla marching into the room.

"Get ready," she demands. "We're apparently going to the

parlor." There is so much frustration in her voice that I know it's the last thing she wants to do.

"I'm ready," I say, watching her with caution. I'm well aware of the signs indicating someone is about to erupt. I've learned that lesson with Emily a few too many times.

"Well then, get your damn cloak if you want it," she snarls.

"If you don't want to go to the parlor, we don't have to go. Though I'm guessing Ash suggested it," I say in my most mellow voice.

Her eyes spark at his name. "Not want to go?" She laughs and it sounds sinister. "I *hate* that place. You know what else I hate right now?"

She points her delicate finger at me. "You, and my stupid brother. How dare you two drag me into this catastrophe! You know you could die, right? Or he could die? Maybe I'll murder you both myself and save everyone the trouble of a trial!"

I stay perfectly silent and as still as possible.

"It's bad enough I have a twin who begs and borrows trouble every time I turn around. But then I get saddled with a roommate who encourages him! I'm only one person; I can't watch you both at once. And I don't want to. Do you hear me?"

I nod with purpose.

"You both have some nerve." She huffs. "You do realize they held me all afternoon, don't you? Endless hours in a room without windows, only to be assaulted with five thousand questions about the two of you. And to be told like a child that if I cover for either of you there will be serious consequences. I had half a mind not to, and to let you both stew in this absolutely abominable disaster you've gotten us all into. But I *know* Ash didn't kill him, and as much as I wish I could say otherwise, I know you didn't, either. So there you have it, screwed by my own conscience. And you know what really gets me?"

I shake my head.

"Stefano was my friend." Her voice softens, and I can tell that she has nearly worn herself out. "And instead of being able to mourn him and process how I feel about all of this, I have to worry about you two idiots." She plops down on the couch.

I carefully sit next to her. Who knew this fiery girl was under all that studious perfectionism? For once she doesn't seem a million miles away behind a wall of ice, but vulnerable. I reach out and touch her hand and am pleasantly surprised when she doesn't pull it away.

Layla shakes her head and her eyes glisten slightly. "We better get to the parlor. Keep your eyes and ears open and don't walk off with anyone for any reason." She removes her hand from mine, but even tolerating five seconds of a friendly gesture is enormous progress in my book.

"I have some questions—"

"Of that I have no doubt," she says, and stands. "But there is no time for them."

✴ ✴ ✴

A guard opens the door for us and Layla and I make our way into the parlor. Even though I've decided the kids in this place are seriously questionable and the present circumstances are as bad as they can be, I'd still rather be with people than be alone in my room stressing.

The parlor is full, with more than thirty advanced students

sprawled out on a rug in front of the fireplace or draped over velvet couches quietly talking. It reminds me of those cocktail parties you see in movies about old European families. One person who is noticeably absent is Matteo. I exhale in relief. Layla, however, is stiffer than usual.

Charles, Brendan, and Nyx are playing cards at a round table and take immediate notice of us.

"Well, this night just got better," Brendan says, leaning back in his chair and pushing his platinum hair out of his face.

Nyx lowers her cards. "Not so much better as car-crash fascinating," she says. Even though she uses the word *fascinating*, her tone suggests that she couldn't be less interested in us. Like she wishes we would just disappear.

"What's the occasion?" Charles smirks at Layla. "Did you ladies miss me?"

Nyx frowns at Charles.

Layla doesn't spare them a glance. I open my mouth to respond, but she gives me a sharp look and I close it again. I hate that she lets them get away with that BS. Not that we don't have bigger problems right now.

The three of them watch us as we pass their table. Out of the corner of my eye I see Charles and Brendan exchange a few remarks that I can't hear, and they laugh. No wonder Layla didn't want to come here.

Layla takes a seat at an empty table near a big window that is now completely covered with a curtain.

"Are you sure you don't want me to say something to them?" I ask, keeping my voice quiet and light. I know she doesn't want to be in this parlor or in this situation, and I also know that it's partially my fault that she is. "Because I will. They act just like dumb jocks in a locker room—only not dumb at all and with terrifying skills. But they don't frighten me one bit."

There is a hint of a smile on her face. "More like arrogant royals, and they *should* frighten you."

I pull back to get a better look at her. "Aarya called them royals, too. How literal are you being when you say that?"

She sighs, then says in a hushed voice, "Brendan, Charles, and Nyx are all legacies—they're the firstborn children of the leaders in their Families and will eventually take over leadership when they get old enough. And Brendan's British. Hailing from the most powerful Family in all of Strategia makes him act like a prince who can do no wrong."

I remember Ash told me that the UK-based Strategia were Lions. And their being the most powerful Family explains some of Brendan's confidence and the way he always seems to be taking up more space than necessary.

"Yeah, but this is a *school*. How powerful your Family is shouldn't matter, your skill level should."

Layla looks at me directly, like I just said something important. "No. It shouldn't matter. And it didn't used to." She hesitates and I can tell that she has more to say. I hold my breath, hoping she won't decide to shut down.

"Nyx and Brendan have been allied for as long as we've been here," she continues. "Charles, however, only started hanging around the two of them this year. It happened a few months after he got close to Nyx."

"Are Nyx and Charles dating?" I ask.

She gives me a curious look. "A lot of people think so. Why do you ask?"

"Just the way she watches him," I say. "And the way Charles

always seems like he's trying to win favor with Brendan, almost like someone would try to impress their girlfriend's popular older brother."

"Nyx and Brendan are as close as any two allies can be. So you're not that far off. And Charles is always trying to ingratiate himself, but more importantly, he wants to ingratiate his Family. He tries too hard, if you ask me."

I can hear in Layla's voice that there is something she's not saying about the whole situation with Charles, but I'm not sure I should push her, since this is the most open she's been with me yet. She's not gushing or anything; she's mainly telling me things about people she doesn't like, but it's a good start.

I lean back in my chair and attempt to casually take in the room. Only in doing so, I accidentally make eye contact with Aarya. She's near us on a couch, sitting with Felix and Ines. Aarya is looking far too pleased with herself, Felix is doing his best to appear annoyed even though it's obvious he thinks she's amusing, and Ines is drawing on a sketchpad.

"So . . . November," Aarya says, and elongates the words for dramatic effect. "I heard something *very* interesting." She's using her American accent tonight, and her eyes sparkle with mischief. She projects her voice so that the people around us can't help but listen. "Can you guess what it is?"

Layla tenses next to me.

"No, but I have a feeling there's no way to avoid having you tell me," I say.

She laughs and leans back into the couch, like she feels certain she has everyone's attention and wouldn't want it any other way. "You're fun. I'll give you that. Way better than most of these pompous know-it-alls," she says, and looks at a table of four girls, who avoid eye contact with her. "Now where was I? Oh yes"—she slaps her knee—"what I heard about you." She pauses to draw out the reveal. "You, Miss November, were out last night after curfew. Very naughty, if you ask me."

The entire parlor turns to me as if on cue. *Shiiiiit.*

To my utter shock, Layla scoffs. "Good one, Aarya. Nice presentation. You must be really bored these days."

"Well, now, you're *covering* for her, Layla? How did you ever manage to let someone get on your good side that quickly? You must be slipping."

"Or just desperate to have a friend, since she can't seem to make any that matter," Brendan chimes in, and I see a flash of anger in Layla's eyes. Aarya's eyes, however, are brightened by this whole exchange. And I have to wonder what he means by *matter.* All I can think is that it has something to do with the Family alliances Ash was talking about, but I'm not sure.

"Layla's laughing because you're ridiculous, Aarya," I say to her, and then turn to Brendan. "And whoa there, Brendan. Let's not talk about *desperate* unless we also talk about your embarrassing knife skills. Or did you just get into this school because you're the firstborn of a leading family?" I'm taking a shot in the dark here, but how dare he come at Layla like that?

By the way his eyes narrow, I know I've struck a nerve. But the surprised and tense glances from some of the other Strategia make me think I may have gone too far.

Aarya claps and hoots. "This is the best time I've had in months. Look at Brendan's face." She laughs. "Look at *Layla's.*"

Layla stands up like she's had enough of this whole night, and I get up with her. Whispers vibrate through the room like a swarm of locusts, though I notice Ines drawing uninterrupted in her sketchpad, like nothing at all is happening.

"But my real question is"—Aarya pauses to bite her lip and raise her eyebrows—"who were you meeting? You must have been meeting someone, right? You just got here and haven't had time to learn the guards' schedules."

"Ah, that's a good point, Aarya," Charles says, and he puts his cards down, eager to jump in. "Why don't you enlighten us, November?" He steals a glance at Brendan.

I shake my head and smile, like their assumption couldn't be more absurd. I only hope a roomful of deception experts can't tell that my actual thoughts are anxiously racing. Even I know that denying something outright makes you look guilty.

"It just strikes me as odd that on the same night Stefano was killed you were out of your room. Details. Details," Aarya says, and sighs.

The room gets noticeably quiet at the mention of Stefano's name, and even Ines looks up from her sketchpad.

"So many details," I say. "Why, just a few days ago at lunch someone mentioned that you had lost your knife. Do we know yet how Stefano died?" I keep my tone casual.

Layla shoots me a look that is somewhere between admiration and horror.

"*Touchée, mon amie.* Now you're in the arena," Aarya says, switching to a perfect French accent. Then she growls and slashes her fingers at me like she's a big cat.

Brendan hasn't taken his eyes off me, and now I stare right back at him. I can feel the danger there, only it's not the vicious playfulness I get from Aarya, but a cold power that is prepared to crush me. I refuse to bend, though. There is nothing I hate more than an idolized bully.

Just then the door to the parlor opens and Ash walks in with a girl and a big grin.

"Come on," Layla mumbles, and I don't miss a beat. I can feel everyone's eyes on us as we walk toward the door.

Ash opens his mouth to say something, but Layla cuts him off. "I don't want to hear it."

Layla and I walk right past Ash, who makes no attempt to follow us. We pass the guard and are most of the way down the hall before Layla speaks again.

"He did that on purpose," she says with an edge to her voice.

"Who, Ash? Do you mean showing up late?"

"The whole thing. Sending us there to see what kind of trouble it would cause, probably knowing that Aarya was going to call you out, showing up late with that stupid innocent look on his face. Ugh," she says as we make our way up the stairs.

"So he set us up?" My mind reels at how Ash could have orchestrated a fight when he wasn't even there. I'm not sure if I'm impressed or disturbed.

"Yes, of course. He put *us* in the hot seat to see what kind of information he could pick up in the aftermath." By her tone, I can tell Ash is going to get an earful from his twin tomorrow. She stops in front of our door. "November?"

"Yeah?" I say.

"You did well in there. You held your own and you didn't let them force you into guilt." She opens the door and walks in.

I smile. "Thanks, Layla. That means a lot."

"But they also pried information out of you and out of me. And everyone is now wondering if you did kill Stefano. That wasn't a win by a long shot," she says, and pauses. "Also, if you ever again publicly spout a piece of personal information I give you, we're going to have a serious problem."

I lock the door behind me. "What personal information? The firstborn thing? Isn't that something everyone knows?"

She frowns. "Everyone *but* you, which means the only way you could have found out is if I told you. In their eyes, it means we now have some sort of alliance. You also took a shot at Brendan's ego. There's no way he's not going to retaliate."

Fifteen

LAYLA AND I walk through heavy wooden double doors into an ancient-looking library. Rolling ladders are perched against walls of bookshelves, balconies that zigzag along the second floor contain small seating areas, and the ceilings arch high above, plastered in intricate patterns. The filtered light coming from the enormous stained-glass windows highlights the dust from the worn fabric and leather books and makes the air sparkle, giving the whole room a magical feel.

I've been trying to talk to Layla about what happened in mind games yesterday, but every time I attempt to bring it up, she just tells me to wait.

We walk past a row of tall bookshelves and climb a spiral staircase to the second floor. The library is virtually empty, not that I think everyone would be racing to get here on a Sunday, but then again, who can really tell with a school like this? We make our way to the rounded back left corner of the second floor and Layla stops.

"Pay attention," she says as she checks the surroundings to make sure no one is looking, even though we are entirely shielded by a bookcase. She pulls two bluish books from the third shelf, a thick torn brown one from the fourth shelf, and a faded red one from the fifth. Then she pushes the center of a carved leaf on the dark wood molding and the bookcase pops open to form a door.

My eyes widen. "That was so freaking cool," I whisper.

I make a mental note of the books she used and which leaf she pressed. Layla holds the bookcase door open for me, and I enter to discover a cozy little room with a rug and two armchairs around a table stacked with books.

"What is this place?" I ask in awe. A secret room behind a bookcase? Emily would die of excitement over this. She's not only a book lover, but was also the type of kid who would talk to an odd-shaped hole in a tree, convinced that fairies were hiding in it.

"Our private study," Layla says. "Each dorm room is assigned one." She grabs a box of matches off the table. "They're scattered all over the library. Of course, you would never leave anything secret here. They're clearly not impossible to break into. But we mostly leave each other's spaces alone to avoid retaliation." Layla lights the candles in the wall sconce, brightening the little study. "Besides, they give you a place to think without someone reading your facial expressions every two seconds."

"Not to mention the stone walls make them virtually soundproof," Ash says, sliding through the door right before Layla closes it. He must have been following us, and the fact that I didn't notice worries me; I wonder what else I'm not noticing.

Layla scowls at him, which only makes him put on his most innocent expression.

"Aw, don't be mad, Lay," he coos.

"I most certainly will be mad." Her look is icy. "That was a sneaky, horrible trick, sending us to the parlor. You could have come up with another way to get the information you were after."

Ash slides up to her. "You would never have agreed. And you have to admit that if I had been there, the interactions wouldn't have been as revealing."

She pushes his hand off her elbow. "I really don't care, Ashai."

"You do care. You also know that sending November by herself wouldn't have had the same effect," he says.

"But if it did, you'd have been happy to let me take the heat? Gee, thanks," I say.

"Apparently he'll do anything that benefits his strategy," Layla says. "He's practically Machiavellian these days."

"Don't be cruel, Layla. I said I was sorry. Look, I'll make it up to you. I promise."

"And how do you plan to make up for the fact that Nyx said I seem less neutral every day?" Layla asks, and Ash's face falls.

All of his earlier playfulness disappears. "Hang on. Back up."

"You heard me," Layla says, and I desperately want to ask about these political divisions, but I know this isn't the time.

"Luckily, November shifted the conversation and it ended," Layla says, and Ash looks at me, not like he's grateful but like I'm the root of the problem.

"Okay, Layla. We'll fix this," he says in a reassuring voice. "But in the meantime, let me try to make it up to you. Anything you want."

Her stubborn expression wavers slightly. *"Anything?"*

"Yes," he says, and with some dramatic resignation, he adds, "Even my sword trick."

Some of the tension in her face disappears. There is a long moment where they just look at each other, at the end of which he grins.

"Oh, shut up," Layla says. "The least you can do is not gloat about it." And I realize they just had an entire exchange using nothing but facial expressions, which I only caught a sliver of.

Ash grabs two pillows from the armchairs and hands them to us. Layla sits down on the rug near the wall and places her pillow behind her back. I do the same thing opposite her, and Ash plops down lazily in the middle of the floor, leaning against one of the cushy chairs.

Layla levels her gaze at me. "We need to discuss what happened last night, but first we need to set some ground rules. I know all about that agreement you both made without me, and I have to say that you're not only reckless, but I honestly don't know which one of you gets carried away with ridiculous notions faster. Just the same, it's done. And whether I like it or not, we've each covered for one another somehow, so we're in this situation together. November, you were right to ask that we tell you things in return for your personal information. Secrets should always be traded at equal value. Fair is fair. But don't think for a second that the trust we're establishing is unbreakable. If you betray us in any way, you will regret it way more than we will."

I glance at Ash and back to Layla. I don't doubt that for a second. "I understand."

"And the tutoring you asked for," she continues. "I'll help. Ash and I have different strengths in analysis and you would benefit from learning from both of us. Besides, asking for tutoring when you need it isn't shameful; it's smart."

I breathe deeply. "Please. I'll take all the help I can get. The last thing I need is to pick a fight and then embarrass myself in class."

"You embarrassing yourself might be unavoidable," Layla says, and Ash chuckles. She gives him a warning look. "Your training in a few areas clearly needs work. But we can't afford for people to think you have weaknesses, either. They will attack them. Or exploit them like *some* people."

Ash makes a face like "Who? Me?" which Layla pays no attention to.

"So then where should we start? You guys know better than me who might have motives," I say.

"Yes," Layla agrees. "We'll tell you what we know. But we also need to talk through the sequence of events surrounding the murder. Lots of people could potentially have motives, but only some will make sense in context."

"Stefano's murder happened right after you got in that fight with Matteo," Ash says.

I nod. "Right. I was thinking about that, too. Do you think the murder is somehow connected to Matteo?"

"Yes, in a way," Layla says. "Matteo and Stefano are from the same Family, they were roommates, and they spent most of their time together. Whatever punishment Blackwood gave Matteo because of your fight has kept him out of classes. So it's possible that someone knew Matteo would be occupied and saw it as a good time to strike."

"I see," I say. "If they were always together, getting Stefano alone was an unusual opportunity?"

"Exactly," Layla says.

"It's interesting that someone would try to frame you for killing another Bear, though," Ash says. "Your Family tends to stick together—through love, hate, infighting. They don't usually kill one of their own unless it was ordered and agreed upon." He looks at me in a strange way and it dawns on me what he's asking.

"Oh god, no. Definitely no. I was *not* sent to kill Stefano." Asking someone to assassinate someone else in your Family is a *thing*? I want to laugh, it's so ridiculous, except that apparently, I'm part of a Family that has been known to commit contract killings and I feel sickened by it.

"We know you weren't," Layla says, and rolls her eyes at Ash, "otherwise we wouldn't be helping you."

"My point is," Ash says, "that whoever did this might have reason to think they could make *Matteo* believe that you would kill Stefano."

I push my hair back from my forehead, not because I need to, but just to clear my thoughts. I went from living in a town where I know way too much about everyone to being in a castle where I don't even know who I am. It's like trying to figure out the rules of football when you're already on the field with the ball in your hand and have twenty players running at you. "Okay, I see what you're saying. Someone thinks my family and Matteo's have some kind of long-standing grudge or grievance—potentially explaining why he punched me, and also making it believable that I might retaliate by killing his friend. Except, if there's a problem between our immediate families, I don't know anything about it."

Layla looks at me oddly, like she's not sure what to think.

"Well, it's likely that whoever set you up is aware of some sort of issue. It's just hard to believe something so serious would have been kept from you."

I'm starting to think that *everything* serious has been kept from me my entire life. "So then we start by looking at people who might know something about me? Honestly, I'm not sure who that would be besides . . ."

"Matteo?" Ash says, finishing my thought.

I hesitate. If I tell them Matteo thinks I look like someone, and that the only person I've ever looked like is my mother, I'll be revealing practically *all* I know. On the other hand, keeping his observation to myself probably isn't going to help me survive this. "He said I look like one of my family members, a dead one."

"Huh," Layla says.

"What?" I say, watching her reason through something.

"Matteo is the firstborn in the Bear Family and is in line to lead it one day," she says slowly, like she's still putting the pieces together. "But you, you don't recognize any of the other students, which, combined with your American accent, means you probably grew up largely outside of Strategia society. It's just odd that the future leader of the Bear Family would feel he knows you well enough to come after you, while you're totally unaware of who he is."

"However," Ash continues, "if Matteo recognized the resemblance to your relative, then other students and teachers might, too. More people here might know you than you realize."

I know Ash said that I'm part of the Bear Family, and as difficult as that is to believe, I can only assume there must be some truth to it, given that I was admitted to this school. But until this moment, the possibility of being one of them—a *Strategia*—always felt like some far-removed idea that didn't really have anything to do with me. "Okay, well, if you're right, and someone other than Matteo recognizes me, who would benefit from pitting me against him?"

"The Lions," Ash says like it's the most obvious thing in the world. "Even living in America, you must know how much your Families hate each other."

"Yeah, of course," I say, even though I have no clue what he's talking about. But if the Lions and the Bears are known enemies, then my interactions with Brendan are starting to make a lot more sense. "I was asking who *specifically* from the Lions. Do you think Brendan killed Stefano and set me up?"

"Brendan could have a motive," Layla says. "*But,* with so many other Families falling over themselves to please the Lions, it's hard to tell what Brendan does himself and what he manages to get others to do for him—Charles, Nyx, and a whole list of students could owe the Lions favors or be in debt to them in some way that allows Brendan to manipulate them."

"What is the deal with Charles and Nyx?" I say, purposefully leaving the question open-ended.

"As I told you," Layla says, running her fingertips over the edge of the rug, "they're both in line to lead their Families one day, and therefore pretty secure in their own right. Still, both of their Families depend heavily on alliances with the Lions. Especially Charles's. His Family's ties to the Lions don't go back as far as Nyx's do, so taking down key members in the Bear Family would definitely serve him."

Ash looks from me to his sister, and there is something in his expression that makes me think he's not totally comfortable with Layla giving me all this information.

"When I first met Blackwood," I say, "she told me that there had been a few deaths here recently."

Layla sighs. "It's no secret that the Lions have been killing off the very best and most skilled members of Families who won't bow to them."

I immediately think of Ines and how everyone says she's one of the most skilled in our class. Maybe she has more reason to be standoffish than I originally thought. Layla, too.

"In recent years it's spilled into this school—some students have been killed off before they even graduate," Layla continues. "This place was always respected by all the Families as a safe space. Sure, there were deaths now and again, but nothing like this."

"So if everyone suspects the Lions are behind the student deaths, why isn't anyone doing anything about it?" I ask, which wins me another smile from Layla.

"Who's going to stop them?" Ash says.

"Well, I . . . I don't know," I say.

"Exactly," he says, and we're all silent for a second.

"What about Aarya?" I say. "How's she involved? I mean besides that stunt in the parlor last night, she also announced to everyone in the caf—dining hall that Ash stole her knife last week."

Layla turns to her brother in horror. "Tell me you didn't."

"I didn't," he says, and they stare at each other until she's convinced he's telling the truth. Strange that he didn't tell her that. I thought they told each other everything.

"But from what I hear, November flipped it on her by announcing the knife to everyone last night in the parlor," Ash says. "Brilliant, by the way."

"Thanks," I say, and smile. "So then you think Aarya could be part of it or have a motive?"

"I'm not sure," Ash says. "But she's at least partially in the know, which makes her suspicious."

"What about Felix?" I ask. "He's a Lion, right?"

Layla nods. "If Aarya's involved, then Felix is," she says. "For now, I think we should pull on that thread and see where it leads, since getting near Aarya and Felix is exponentially easier than getting near Brendan, Charles, and Nyx."

"By *pull on that thread,* what do you mean exactly?" I ask.

"That we follow her," Ash says. "Try to find out what she knows."

My pulse quickens. "We?"

Ash smirks. "You and I."

"What about Layla?" I say, and I can hear the nervousness in my voice. Following Aarya does not sound easier than following Brendan.

"Afraid you can't handle all that time with me?" Ash says, clearly finding the whole thing way too amusing.

I scoff. "More like I can't handle your ego."

He smirks. "Humility isn't a virtue."

"Neither is self-adoration," I say.

"It must be an odd feeling for you, Ash," Layla interrupts, "not having a girl fall all over you in two seconds. I think I'm going to enjoy this. And to answer your question, November, I'll be working another angle. I'm much better at research than Ash is."

"By *better*, she means more patient," Ash says.

"By *better*, I mean better," Layla says, and Ash grins at her. If they were typical siblings, I could see him bribing her to help him with his homework and her asking him to teach her how to flirt. But there is nothing typical about them.

Sixteen

I GLANCE FROM Brendan, Charles, and Nyx on my left to Aarya, Felix, and Ines on my right, wondering if one of them murdered Stefano and figured they could blame it on me. Layla gives me a look that tells me I need to stop staring, and I lean back in my chair.

Professor Kartal spins an ancient-looking globe in a wooden stand. Her shoulders are pulled back and her chin is held high, giving her a commanding presence. She watches the globe and not us. *Kartal . . . her name means "eagle" in Turkish.*

"Strange things happen by accident every day . . . every single day," Kartal says, and sighs. "King Umberto the First of Italy once ate in a restaurant where he discovered that the owner was born the same day he was and in the very same town. What is further puzzling is that they both married women named Margherita. Then in July of 1900, King Umberto learned that the restaurant owner had been shot and killed in the street. Later that same day, the king was assassinated."

I'm not sure where she's going with this, but so far, this isn't like any history class I've ever had.

Kartal looks up at us, still spinning the globe under her finger-tips. "And during World War One, the British army turned the passenger ship RMS *Carmania* into a battleship. They then disguised the *Carmania* as the German passenger ship SMS *Cap Trafalgar*. Are you following? This is all about to come back around. In 1914, this disguised British ship sank a German ship. That ship was in fact the real *Cap Trafalgar*"—she laughs—"which the Germans had disguised to look like the British *Carmania*."

A laugh bubbles out of me and a couple of people look my way. Apparently I'm the only one other than Kartal who enjoyed the story.

Kartal takes her fingers off the globe and tucks a stray piece of her black hair into the braid that wraps around her head. "And have you read Edgar Allan Poe's only novel? *The Narrative of Arthur Gordon Pym of Nantucket,* it's called. It tells of an ill-fated Antarctic voyage where four shipwrecked survivors wind up adrift on a raft and, of all things, decide to eat the cabin boy, named Richard Parker. Well, in 1884, the ship *Mignonette* sank, leaving four survivors. They, too, decided to eat the cabin boy to survive. And what do you suppose his name was? Richard Parker. I can't help but wonder if they were Poe fans."

I've never really been one for history, and I was kind of dreading this class because of my meeting with Conner, but I think I've just changed my mind. Maybe that tutoring from Ash and Layla won't be so bad.

Kartal looks directly at me. "Strange things also happen on purpose," she says before breaking eye contact. "During the Middle Ages, King John of England wanted to build a highway right through Gotham. And the residents were required to pay for this highway themselves. At the time, madness was considered contagious. So the good people of Gotham decided to fake insanity to discourage people from wanting to pass through, trying to eliminate the need for the highway they didn't want. A whole town gone mad." She smiles. "Would anyone like to tell me where I'm going with this?"

"There's something about coincidences that people are attracted to," Nyx says, and she sounds annoyed by it. "The stranger the coincidences are, the more people want to believe them. An entire town gone mad is a good story; people will actually go out of their way to verify it rather than examine the motives."

I take a better look at Nyx. I can't help but feel like this particular conversation is somehow related to the murder.

"Absolutely true," Kartal says. "Anyone else?"

"It's easy to talk people into believing coincidences and into not believing them," Aarya says.

"Explain," Kartal says.

Aarya leans back in her chair. "If the coincidence gets reinforced, people will attach to it and expand upon it. They'll try to understand every last detail about what makes it so strange and believe it even beyond reason. However, if the coincidence is argued against, it will forever be clouded with doubt, whether it's real or not."

"I quite agree," Kartal says. "Which makes orchestrating one of these events extremely risky, but glorious if you can pull it off. Now tell me: Which story isn't like the others?"

"The first," Layla says. "Someone who knew about King Umberto's meeting with the restaurant owner might also encourage the telling of that story at dinner parties or social gatherings.

Once the story became commonly known, it would be fairly easy to shoot the restaurant owner, tell the king, and then orchestrate an assassination. It builds on the oddity and lends credence to the coincidences, suggesting fate as a possible reason for the king's death."

I look at Layla and I'm a little in awe. Ash was right when he said they analyze history, understand how one domino topples another, and use that information to predict future events. It's not unlike the way he reads my mannerisms.

"And furthermore," Felix says, "Layla's analysis has created the very doubt that Aarya was talking about. So even if the restaurant owner's and king's deaths were pure coincidence, we've just been introduced to new variables that mean we can't deny the possible intentionality of the events."

"Quite so," Kartal says. "The framing of history impacts its credibility as much as the facts. Just like a portrait painter who hides his subjects' flaws changes our impression of them. Peeling away those layers to find the truth is often difficult. And if the person who framed the story is skilled enough, there may always be doubt, so much so that the truth is lost forever." She says this last part slowly.

I swallow. A week ago I would have thought this conversation was a coincidence, but as I just learned, coincidences can be carefully orchestrated events.

"Let's talk about a specific plot that centered around the discovery of a body rather than the body itself," Kartal says.

I fight the urge to scan the room, to see if anyone is reacting to Kartal's doublespeak. Layla stays unnaturally still, with a blank expression, and I immediately realize that they all hear it. I'm just the idiot who is about to be obvious about it. Damn it. Every time I think I'm catching on, I discover I'm a step behind. Ash was right when he said I was in the bleachers eating popcorn while everyone else was on the playing field.

"During World War Two, British intelligence dropped a body dressed as a British officer into the Mediterranean Sea," Kartal says. "On this body, they placed the plans for an invasion of Greece. The thing was, Greece was a decoy; they were actually planning to invade Sicily. The Spanish found the body and bought the ruse, believing that the invasion would occur in Greece. What made the entire thing work, though, is that while the Spanish gave the documents to the Germans, they never handed over the body. Spain was chosen as the target of this plot because of their particular aversion to autopsies. Had the Germans discovered the body, they would have conducted an autopsy and would have potentially figured out that the person hadn't died from drowning and that it was all a fake." She looks around the room. "The entire plan relied on the fact that the people finding the body wouldn't do the inspection they needed to."

The questions Kartal is raising make my head spin, especially if there's a chance that she's referring to the way in which Stefano was found and by whom. Blackwood did say that her investigative methods would be unusual and unpredictable. So part of me can't help but wonder if some of the staff are simply trying to stir the pot and get us to question what we think we know—exactly like I'm doing right now.

Seventeen

"WHY DID WE leave the parlor? Aarya's still in there," I whisper to Ash in the middle of an empty hallway lit by a single torch.

Ash pulls me into the shadows and talks so quietly that I can barely hear him, and I'm right next to him. "Because I saw Felix tell her in sign language that he would meet her."

"Meet her where?" I ask, a pit forming in my stomach. Ash's nearness isn't helping with my nerves. I'm sure if anyone came through the hallway they would think we were having a romantic moment. But the last thing I need is more marks. I'm probably going to be scrubbing toilets with a toothbrush as it is.

"I'm assuming her room," he says.

I pull back slightly to get a look at him. "What are you saying right now?"

"I'm saying I want to hear that conversation," he whispers, and I can tell by his tone that he's serious.

My eyes widen as I realize what he's implying. "No. Forget it. That is so not what I signed up for, Ash. I'm not breaking into . . . I'm not doing that."

"Then stay here and be scared," he says. "Any minute now they could come out of that parlor and we'll lose our window of opportunity. But that's okay; you go to bed. I'm sure you'll sleep well knowing that you will likely be blamed for a murder you didn't commit." And he walks away.

For a second I just watch him with my mouth open. I've clearly met my match in Ash when it comes to being creatively pushy.

"Damn it," I say under my breath, and walk quickly down the hall to catch up with him.

When I reach him, he's wearing a small smile, like he knew exactly what the result of that conversation would be. I scowl and consider saying something biting, but as we pass into the stairwell, my annoyance with Ash is eclipsed by my fear of what we're about to do.

Ash stops in front of the second-floor entrance to the girls' dormitory, checking for guards, and I immediately get a feeling of déjà vu from the other night. Only then it was all still a game.

Ash motions for me to follow him and we dart into the hallway, keeping our steps silent. He stops at the fourth door on the right and silently lifts the latch of Aarya and Ines's door. We slide inside, my heart beating a bazillion miles an hour.

I've never considered how easy it is to get into someone else's space at the Academy. The doors can only be locked from the inside. But then again, I'm not sure what use locks would be with this group. Instead of making it harder to break in, I suspect locks would incentivize this group to try.

"What now?" I whisper, scanning the common room, which is a replica of Layla's and mine. Between the stone floors and antique furniture, the only good space to hide is under the beds, and there is absolutely no way I'm risking getting trapped in one of their bedrooms.

"What's now is that you pick up that piece of grass you tracked in," Ash says, looking at the floor like he can't believe I'm so careless. "Unless you want to immediately alert Aarya that we're here, and if that's the case, I hope your fighting skills are good enough to handle a three-on-two fight."

I look down at the floor, and sure enough there is a single blade of grass that must have been stuck to the bottom of my boot. I pick it up and shove it in my pocket.

Ash makes his way across the room to the window blotted out with a heavy curtain. "The sill is big enough. Go from below and try not to pull the curtain out too far. If light gets through, the guards outside might see it and come up here. Don't sit down on the sill—stand and press your back against the side of the window arch. And get yourself into a position that you can stay in for a few hours and where you have flexibility of movement without making any noise. If someone pats the curtain, you have to be ready to move so that the fabric doesn't touch your body and give us away."

For a moment I just stare at him, thinking he can't possibly mean what he's saying. But he gives no indication that he is anything but serious.

I gulp. "So I'm going to be hiding for *hours* against a second-story window in a room with someone who probably wouldn't think twice about pushing me out of it? And there is a real possibility that someone is going to check the curtain, and I'll have to avoid their hand?"

"Yes," Ash says, as if it's the most normal thing in the world.

Then he pulls out the curtain just enough for me to shinny under it. "You first."

"How are we going to get back out?" I ask, and realize I've taken a step away from the curtain, not toward it.

"We wait until they go to sleep and we're quiet about it," he says.

"And if someone sleeps on the couch?"

"Then we're stuck here for the night, or we have to take our chances with sneaking past them," he says, and pauses. "You need to get under this curtain now, unless you want them to walk in and catch us outright."

I walk toward him, dreading the moment when Aarya returns.

Ash watches me carefully. I bend down, hesitantly touching the curtain.

Ash sighs. "Go back to your room, November," he says, and I stop what I'm doing.

"Excuse me?"

"Seriously, go back. You can't do this if you're not confident. You'll give us away in a minute. Go. Quickly, before this is all a waste."

I stand, pushing my hair back from my face, and he gives me a hard look. I want to say something, to protest, but he's right. There's no time. And the only thing that would make this whole thing worse would be getting caught because I'm lingering stupidly.

I peek into the hallway and, luckily, it's empty. I slip out of the room, closing the door behind me. It's not the silent exit Ash would have made, and that only makes me feel crappier about the whole thing as I dart into the stairwell toward my room. This is the first time anyone has ever suggested that I'm not confident enough to do something, and it's screwing with my head. He didn't say I wasn't good enough. He wouldn't have brought me if he didn't think I was capable. But that piece of grass was a huge oversight.

I tiptoe down my bedroom hallway, careful to avoid all the creaky boards. I drop to my hands and knees and crawl across the living room floor until I get to the back of the couch.

"I can hear your breathing, my onesie-wearing spy," Aunt Jo calls from the couch, where she's playing cards with Dad.

I stand up. "Dang it."

"And I saw you slinking around on the floor, Nova," Dad says. "What have I told you about that?"

I put my hand on my hip, annoyed that I have to repeat things back to him like a little kid when I'm almost eight. "That my small size is an advantage, but not if I can't stay completely hidden."

"And how would you have stayed hidden?" he asks.

I huff. "By staying in the hallway and not coming all the way to the couch."

He nods.

"But I couldn't hear you as well from there," I protest. "And the floor in the hallway is cold."

"But you could hear us," he says. "And yet by coming all the way into the room, you've been caught, letting Aunt Jo and me know that we're being spied on. So what good did it do you?"

"None," I say, annoyed.

"It wasn't a bad effort, though, little one," Aunt Jo says, and puts her elbow over the back of the couch to get a better look at me. "And I'm entirely flattered that you would go through all *that trouble to get out here just to overhear our conversation. I won't leave you empty-handed. For your efforts, I'll reward you by letting you know that I'm beating the pants off your father in rummy."*

Dad shakes his head. "The imagination is an amazing thing, Jo." He looks at me. "Now, back to bed, Nova."

"Fine," I grumble, and Aunt Jo gives me a kiss on my forehead. She looks down at my ankles and laughs because I've unevenly cut the noisy skidproof plastic feet off my onesie.

At seven years old I was more confident, more willing to take risks, than I just was in Aarya's room. And I know better than to track things in and linger indecisively like that. Dad told me a million times that you either do something or you don't, but hesitating is never an option.

When I get to my room, I immediately check behind the curtains and under the beds. Emily always thought it was weird the way my family encouraged me to be better at sneaking around, instead of scolding me. I used to tell her it was because Dad believed that survival skills were just that—for survival. But until I came here, I didn't actually realize how right he was.

Eighteen

LAYLA HANDS ME my cloak as she recaps what Ash over-heard last night. "Apparently, Matteo only just returned from the outer perimeter, so Felix was telling Aarya he's not sure Matteo even knows about Stefano yet," Layla says. "Although I'm certain he figured something was wrong when he returned to his room and Stefano was missing."

"Outer perimeter?" I ask. "What are you talking about?"

"Blackwood has been known to send students to the outer perimeter as part of their punishment," Layla says. "The tasks vary, but it's frustrating because you miss all your lessons."

I try to keep the fear off my face that Matteo is back. He already punched me for no reason that I can tell; I really don't want to find out what he will do if he actually believes I killed his friend. "How did Felix know Matteo was in the outer pe-rimeter?" Only in a school as competitive as this would people be upset they missed their classes.

Layla shrugs. "Ash didn't say. Maybe Felix spotted him com-ing back in and assumed, or maybe he overheard Matteo telling someone that was where he'd been. Felix also told Aarya that

Charles spotted Ash out on the night of the murder. And if Aarya knows that, you can pretty much assume the entire school will know by lunchtime, leaving us vulnerable to possible sabotage by the other students who might have reason to further the idea that you or Ash was responsible."

"Great," I say with no enthusiasm as I slip my arms through my cloak. "Is it weird that Charles would tell Felix about seeing Ash? I didn't get the sense they were friends."

"They're not. But the passing of information is about strategy, not friendships." Layla opens the door and we make our way into the hall, cutting off our conversation.

As I walk alongside Layla, I instinctively look over my shoulder for Matteo, even though it's unlikely he'd be in the girls' dorm. I can't help but be a little bothered that Ash didn't tell me what he heard last night; he must have come to our room this morning to tell Layla and not included me. I know his sister is the obvious go-to, but I wonder if he's lost a little faith in me for being so hesitant about hiding in Aarya's room. And I can't really blame him. In a situation where so much is at stake, I dropped the ball.

"If you keep looking over your shoulder, the entire school is going to know you're afraid of Matteo, which only makes you look guilty," Layla says under her breath as we walk through the downstairs foyer.

"If I don't look over my shoulder and Matteo jumps on my head, I'll be squished," I mumble, trying to make light of my raging nerves.

We walk into the courtyard with the vines and stop. About seven students are already there.

"I'll come get you before poisons class," Layla says, and I

can tell by the way her eyes dart to the side that even she is concerned about what Matteo's return will mean.

I feel like I've been flipped into an alternate universe. Just a week ago I had nothing more on my mind than how to talk my way out of detention and the dress shopping Emily wanted to do for the winter formal. Now my thoughts are full of murder, deception, and classes that teach me how to poison people. I've never been so homesick.

"So are you going to the dance with Jack or what?" Emily asks as she turns her marshmallow over the fire pit on my back deck.

"Not sure," I say, tucking in the blanket around my legs. I bite into my s'more.

"Not sure, nothing. I have no intention of babysitting you all night," Emily says.

"Me? I'm the most social person you know," I say, and push her hand a little closer to the flame so her marshmallow browns faster.

She gives me a look. "Oh, I'm not worried you're going to get stuck against the wall all night. I'm worried that you'll have too much time on your hands and decide to scale the building and parachute through the skylight with your dress over your head."

I laugh. "And you think Jack is somehow going to dazzle me so hard that I won't want to misbehave? The bigger problem is that if I do go with him, I'll probably end up having to babysit him all night."

She shakes her head. "I don't get you. You think he's cute."

"He is cute. But he's boring, you know?" I pause. "I'd way rather make out with him at parties and just call it a day."

She laughs. "You're the worst."

"The worst, but not boring," I say with a grin, and wipe chocolate off my lip.

The back door opens and we both look up.

"You know, you girls can roast marshmallows just as easily inside by the fireplace without freezing your butts off," my dad says.

"That's what I keep telling her," Emily replies. "But you know what she's like."

"We have like ten blankets and it's a balmy forty-eight," I argue.

"Practically tropical," Emily groans.

"Well, I'll put the kettle on if you want some tea to warm up with," he says.

"Thanks, Dad. We'll be in soon."

He starts to pull the door shut, then pauses. "I forgot to tell you. I'm headed over to Aunt Jo's after work tomorrow. So I won't be home for dinner."

"She can eat at my place," Emily volunteers. "No problem."

"Glad to hear it," he says, and closes the door.

"Your dad's been going to Providence a lot. That's the second time in two weeks, right?"

"Third," I say. "He's been helping her with some home repairs. I keep telling him he should go on a weekend so I can go with him."

Dad went to see Aunt Jo three times in two weeks, which was unusual enough, but on top of that he always went on days I couldn't go. And then right after all these unusual visits, her house got broken into. Which raises the question: Did Dad know something was going on even before the supposed break-in? I can't believe I never picked up on this. And now that I'm painfully aware that I don't know squat about my family, I *am* worried—worried about what's really going on with them and that I have absolutely no way to get in touch and find out if everything's okay. Damn this school's archaic isolation.

Just then Matteo enters the courtyard and snaps me out of my thoughts. He doesn't look puffy and red-eyed from crying the way I would be if I'd just lost my close friend. Instead he looks focused and . . . furious. Ines and Felix enter the courtyard right behind him.

On instinct, I check my distance from the two exits just in case I need to make a run for it. But Matteo has yet to look in my direction. Charles and Brendan, however, are staring right at me.

The professor smiles at me and places her hand on her chest. "Professor Basurto," she says, and just like that the silent standoff among the six of us is broken. "You must be . . ."

"November," I say.

"November. Right, of course. All you need to know is that I move quickly, I expect the best, and I encourage you to be creative."

Basurto—a Spanish name, and one I've always loved because it means "the middle of the forest."

"Sure. I love to climb," I say, but it sounds less peppy than it normally would.

"Then we'll get along just fine. Why be on the ground when you can be in a tree, no?" She winks and claps her hands together.

Matteo still hasn't looked at me. I'm not sure if that's a good or a bad thing.

"Throughout the ages, trees have played an integral role in plotting and trickery," Basurto says. "There is the Major Oak in Sherwood Forest, whose hollowed-out trunk supposedly served as the hideout for Robin Hood and his Merry Men. There's the arrow that killed Ponce de León because it was tipped with poison from the sap of the manchineel tree. There are the weapons made from wood and the deadly codes written on paper, and then there's my favorite use of trees—evasion. They are the perfect escape route because they offer unpredictable terrain, they provide coverage, and only the very skilled can move through them swiftly without falling to their death or suffering grave injury."

I steal a glance at Matteo again, but it seems like his thoughts are a million miles away.

Basurto smiles and there's a spring to her step as she paces through the grass. Her shirtsleeves are rolled up, revealing well-toned arms that she no doubt acquired from years of climbing. "So today we're going to start off with a chase exercise. You must show me how uncatchable you are—or the opposite, as the case may be. For my first group I'll take Charles, Matteo, Nyx, November, and Kiku." Basurto points to each of us, ending on the girl Ash was with when he came into the parlor the other night. "Go ahead and form a line. The front person should start one vine ahead of the next person, and so on."

I try to maneuver my way to the back of our group without making it obvious, but Matteo cuts me off and steps behind me, taking the last spot. My stomach drops so fast that I gulp. Charles looks back at me and smirks.

"When I say so, you'll climb three-quarters of the way up your vines," Basurto says. "And when I say go, you'll move as fast as you can to the far end of the courtyard. The first person in each group to reach the other side wins. Those of you at the back of your lines can only advance if you catch the person in front of you. Being the first has its advantages but also means everyone is after you. Hence the chase. If you get tagged, you're out. Likewise, if you fall to the ground, you're out. We will do this more than once, changing the order each time we go."

Kiku is in front of me, then Charles; Nyx is in the first position. Behind me, I hear Matteo crack his knuckles. I wipe my hands on my pants to make sure they're dry and grab hold of the knobby vine. I can feel my pulse through my fingertips.

"You may start climbing," Basurto says.

The second my feet lift off the ground I feel the familiar rush of excitement. Unfortunately, it's coupled with my dread of having Matteo directly behind me. All I want to do is look over at him, but Layla's warning about showing fear rings in my head.

"Go!" Basurto yells unexpectedly before we're even halfway to the trees.

I book it up my vine to the first available branch and swing my legs up. Two branches away from me, Kiku is just getting a grip. I stabilize myself and jump to the next branch, but Kiku's branch is too far to reach. I spot a vine and quickly sidestep to my left to grab it. Kiku has gotten her balance, but she's still gauging her next move, and while she does, I swing over to her branch, keeping the vine in my hand for safety. She jumps as my feet make contact, but not before I graze her elbow with my fingertips. *Gotcha.*

She gives me a death stare.

I glance back to find that Matteo is only one branch away and my heart starts pounding. If I hesitate, he'll catch me for sure.

Still holding the vine, I yank it more firmly toward me and hook it securely around a nub on the trunk, effectively pulling it out of Matteo's reach. That should buy me some time. Then

I start to climb, looking for Charles as I maneuver through the branches. When I spy him, he and Nyx are about six feet above me in the trees and heading for the middle of the courtyard, where the branches are thinner. I watch as Nyx makes a daring leap, just managing to stabilize herself as she lands. Charles isn't far behind.

All the time they've spent chasing each other up into the canopy has slowed their progress, which means I have a shot at catching up. I balance myself on a big solid branch and snag a new vine, holding it as I race along, only stopping when I'm under them.

I hear boots on bark and the sound is too close for comfort. I look left, discovering that Matteo has just stepped onto my branch and there's only about twenty feet between us. I whip my vine at him, hoping it will slow him down, but he leans out of the way and it goes sailing past him. Knowing Matteo is mere seconds behind me, I scramble onto a higher branch so fast that I give myself bark burn. Just as I get my balance, Nyx jumps from a branch above my head and I instinctively duck. But Charles is only a beat behind her, and as he lands I reach up and tap his ankle. The look of horror on his face is rather satisfying.

He snaps a twig above my head, sending down wood and leaves into my face.

I sidestep and grab a higher branch. Only, before I can get a good hold, a big hand wraps around my calf. I look down, and as we make eye contact, instead of letting go of me, Matteo yanks on my leg. My hands scrape against the bark and my stomach slams onto the branch I was standing on just moments ago. My legs flail and I desperately try to steady myself, but my momentum is too great and I tumble past Matteo, frantically grabbing on to his ankle to keep from dropping.

For a split second we stay frozen like that—me dangling from his boot and him looking down at me—before I manage to hook my legs around a vine and let go of him.

I'm so mad I want to scream, but Matteo's already moved on, chasing after Nyx.

I steady myself with the vine, shaking from anger and exertion, and climb my way back down to the ground. If I weren't so used to falling in trees, Matteo could have killed me back there. He probably meant to.

"Beautiful first go," Basurto says as I land in the soft grass— only, I barely hear her compliment because I'm moving toward the end of the courtyard where Matteo will land any minute now.

I pace back and forth in the grass.

"Why is it that so many people seem to want to hurt you?" Brendan says, his voice like silk. "It must be your shining personality."

Charles joins us and smirks.

"Whatever," I say. I don't get mad often, but when I do, I want to tear the world apart at the seams. I look at the burning scrapes all over my arms. Spots of blood stain my white shirt.

As I examine my cuts, Matteo drops down from a vine, and the moment he lands I shove him with both hands, sending him back a step.

"You could have killed me," I growl. "Basurto said *tag*, not yank the person you catch down to their death. What the hell is your problem? And don't try to tell me it's because of Stefano, because you know I wouldn't kill someone in my own Family to get back at you for a punch!" I'm taking a chance, but I hope my indignation over Family rings true to him. I need to undermine whoever is trying to pit us against each other.

"Hey, now!" Basurto yells from the middle of the courtyard as she starts to march toward us. "This is not how we use our energy in my class."

Matteo stares me down, breathing hard from the climb, daring me to hit him. "Save it for someone who cares. Your words don't mean anything to me." His voice is calm but his eyes are anything but.

Basurto steps between us. "I see you two have a flair for the dramatic today. I saw your little maneuver up in the trees, Matteo. It was bad form, I'll grant you that. But if he really wanted to kill you, November, he could have shaken you off his boot before you could reach for a vine. But go ahead and continue. Fight it out. Throw yourselves on the ground like children if you need to."

Matteo and I stare at each other for a long moment before I eventually look away. He did have the opportunity to kill me, I realize, and he chose to let me get my grip. But that doesn't prove that he doesn't want me dead—only that he wasn't willing to kill me in front of everyone.

"No takers? Well, I'm going to get back to this beautiful day, then," Basurto says.

The entire class watches us, with Brendan and Charles looking particularly interested in the exchange. I'm left feeling oddly exposed.

Nineteen

STILL WORKED UP over my exchange with Matteo and my worry about my family, I take a seat in Conner's office. I focus on the flames crackling in the fireplace, the only thing in the whole room that has movement and doesn't feel stale.

"Is there anything you would like to tell me, November?" Conner asks from the couch across from mine. Ten things that I don't want him to know flash through my thoughts.

"Not particularly," I say.

His eyes focus on me in a way that tells me he doesn't accept my answer. "Why don't we talk about your friendship with Ashai?" he says slowly.

I hate these vague leading questions. I much prefer Blackwood's direct ones. "Where's Headmaster Blackwood?"

"Not here," Conner says, and offers no clarification.

I lean back into the couch, trying to give him the impression that I'm comfortable and have nothing to hide. "What do you want to know?"

"You and Ashai have been spending a lot of time together," he says like he's daring me to disagree.

"He's my roommate's brother. It would be hard to avoid him if I wanted to," I say.

"*Do* you want to?" he asks.

These mind games are the worst. "Not particularly."

"Because you find him attractive?" he says.

"You already heard me say that to Headmaster Blackwood," I reply casually, as though there's nothing more to the story.

"But I didn't believe you when you said it," Conner says, and I hold my breath for a brief second.

"Are you kidding?" I say in a slightly brighter tone. "Even someone with terrible vision could see that Ash is attractive."

"I'm not debating his looks. I'm simply saying that I don't believe they're a contributing factor to your leaving your room after curfew."

I instinctively glance toward the door, which I'm sure he notices and interprets as me wanting to avoid his question.

He waits.

I sigh, trying to show him that I'm going to tell him what he wants to know. "You told me you were worried I might not be able to keep up in history. Well, I'm competitive, like everyone else here, and I didn't want to be behind. I noticed that Ash is a strong analyst and I wanted to convince him to tutor me."

Conner considers my words. "Hmmm. I see. And that night, after you met with him, which route did you take back to your room again?"

Oh, shit. Ash was wrong—I did not do well in my first interview. "When I spoke with you and Headmaster Blackwood, we covered—"

"Take me through it step by step," Conner says, and puts his pen down to watch me more closely.

I take a deep breath, trying to slow my heart, but it doesn't work. "The moment I came back in the building, I was moving fast. I—"

"Which door did you come through?"

"The one at the east end of the vine courtyard."

"Uh-huh, go on," he says. "Details, please."

"As I said, I was moving fast because I knew it was late, and there's really nothing to tell. I went up the stairs and down the hallway. And when I got back to my room, that guard spotted me," I say, attempting to keep my voice light and my hands from fidgeting.

"When I said *details*, I meant details, November." Conner's tone is sharp. "Which staircase? Which hallway?"

It feels like the temperature suddenly went up ten degrees. I roll up my sleeves. "The hallway that my dorm room is in and the staircase by way of the courtyard." I only hope that my leading with the thing that's true means he won't get a clear read that I'm lying.

"Blackwood and I questioned the guard who saw you," he says, and my palms start to sweat. "And unfortunately for you, *that night*, the guard patrolled the girls' dormitory from a different direction than he usually does." He adds this in a way that makes me think he's closing in on his one-two punch.

I make a conscious effort to stay still and not let him see me squirm.

Conner is silent, drawing out the time, knowing that I'm hanging on his every word. "The guard usually enters the dormitory area from the west end of the hallway. But that night he used the staircase and hallway at the east end." Conner smiles.

"The same staircase that you supposedly took to return to your room. If you did in fact take that staircase and hallway, you would have been right in front of him. Unless you expect me to believe that you were in that staircase with him, yet so quiet and so invisible that he didn't hear or see you?"

My pulse races, but I stay silent. I know by now that not talking when you get caught is way better than covering a lie with another lie.

"Well?" he says.

"I don't know," I say, and I feel a bead of sweat form above my upper lip.

"You don't know or you're lying?" he says with a smugness that's infuriating.

My mind is racing. "It seems strange that a guard who takes the same route every single night suddenly decides to change his routine," I say to throw the focus off me. But now that I've said it, it does seem odd.

With that, the smugness in Conner's expression disappears, like I just disrupted his favorite game. His eyes narrow slightly. "That doesn't change the fact that he was in that staircase and you could not have been."

"I'm sorry, but I don't know how to explain it to you. I'm just as confused as you are. Maybe you should question the guard further. Perhaps he's not telling you something."

We stare at each other for a few more seconds, and I know in my gut that while I may have won this round, the fight is only beginning. Conner is out for blood, and right now he thinks I'm guilty. Not that I entirely blame him, with all the lies I've told.

He puts his folder down on the maroon cushion and

readjusts his blazer, picking a piece of lint off his shoulder. When he speaks next, his voice is smooth and calm. "Tell me about your conflict with Matteo."

"It's simple. He hates me and I don't understand why," I say, relieved to have something completely true to say.

"I'm surprised you don't understand, considering who you are to each other."

My heart skips a beat. "What did you just say?" Ash and Layla were right. Even though I don't know who people are here, that doesn't mean they don't know who I am.

Conner gives me a look. "Pay attention, November. I said, I'm surprised you don't understand, considering how you are with each other. I heard about your little altercation in the courtyard earlier."

I give Conner a sideways look. That is *not* what he said. It's also entirely possible he knows and is messing with me, trying to see how I'll react. "He nearly pulled me out of the tree."

"So you tried to start a fight with him?" Conner says.

"No," I say, scratching my arm even though it's not itchy. "I just wanted to get him to stop attacking me."

"By attacking him?"

"By *confronting* him," I say with sincerity.

"Well, I would stay away from him if I were you," says Conner. "I don't think causing more conflict is wise at this juncture. Do you?"

I just look at him, knowing that anything I say right now will only make it worse for me.

Conner crosses his legs and leans back. "You also told Headmaster Blackwood that you wanted to go home."

My heart thuds.

He takes his time. "It's odd that you would ask to go home after everything your family did to get you into this school so late. Unless . . . possibly you're running away from something?"

"I'm . . ." I desperately want to ask him what my dad did to get me in here, but something tells me that letting Conner know I'm ignorant of that would be a very bad idea. I rub the back of my neck. "I don't know."

"You don't know?" he repeats, leaning into the words.

"I'm actually not sure why I said I wanted to go home. I think I was just frustrated at being questioned so intensely about a murder I didn't commit."

"If you didn't commit the murder, the questioning shouldn't frustrate you," he says.

"Well, I'm not perfect," I say.

Conner seems like he doesn't buy it. "I look forward to our next talk, November. I believe you have a lot to think about. Although I don't suggest lying to Headmaster Blackwood again. It will end badly for you if you do."

I'm not sure which lie he's alluding to, and I get the sense that might be the point—to make me nervous about all of them. I get up. "Can I go?"

He nods and I don't hesitate. The moment his door closes behind me, I shudder. They actually think I did it. And the truth is, even *I* think I look like a suspect. I had a reason to get back at Matteo, I was out that night, and a guard saw me coming from the hallway where Stefano's body was discovered. Ash warned me I might take the fall. But somehow I never expected that I would get punished for something I didn't do.

I head full-speed away from Conner's office, and almost walk smack into Aarya.

"November!" she says in a bright tone. "Just the girl I wanted to see. I hear you're missing something."

I take a good look at her. If she's in a happy mood, it can't mean anything good. "Besides losing my patience if you don't move, I'm not missing a thing," I say, stepping to the side to go around her. But she steps with me, blocking my path.

"Oh, I think you might be. It's a little something, but it says a lot." She's using her American accent again.

"Either spit it out, Aarya, or get out of my way," I say, not in the mood for her games.

"*Mrrrow.*" She curls her fingers at me like a cat. "Someone's testy today. I take it your meeting with Dr. Conner didn't go well? Tough luck. I bet mine will, though. I think he'll be very interested to know I found one of your hairs in my room this morning."

I laugh to cover the stomach-sinking horror I'm feeling. "You're really obsessed with me, aren't you, Aarya? Don't get me wrong, I'm flattered. But analyzing some hair you found is going a little too far, don't you think?" I scan my memory of the moments I was in her room. Did I touch my hair? I guess I could have knocked one loose. Or maybe it was on my cloak and dropped off.

"There's good news and bad news, Ember. Can I call you that?"

"No."

"The good news is that I wasn't actually sure the hair was yours. The bad news is that you just convinced me that it is. I'm *shocked*"—she makes a dramatic display of widening her eyes and touching her heart—"that Ash and Layla didn't teach you how to sneak around properly. I was sure we had higher standards at this school. But I guess we're slipping, letting any old body in this place." She sighs.

I step around her, and this time she lets me pass.

She laughs. "You really shouldn't break into other people's rooms, Ember, unless you're prepared for the consequences." There's something joyfully threatening about her tone, like a psychotic clown in a horror movie.

I keep walking.

"Kiss kiss!" she yells after me.

Twenty

I WALK DOWN the hall to my room, my brisk pace fueled by my uneasiness. "Layla?" I say as I unlatch the door and walk in, but there's no response.

I close the door and head for my bedroom.

"She's in the library," says a voice, and Ash steps out from behind my door, sending me flying two fast steps backward.

"Geez, Ash. You almost gave me a heart attack!" I say.

"Then stop being so easily surprised," he says, and I cringe inwardly. An image of him telling me to leave Aarya's room last night flashes in my thoughts.

"You're right. You're totally right. I need to stop being so jumpy. I need to stop being a lot of things," I say, and head for the window, patting the curtain with my hand.

"I already checked there," Ash says, and I walk toward Layla's room. "And I checked your bedrooms."

"Oh," I say, and stop.

He takes a good look at me. "You're practically shaking. This isn't just about finding me here. Something happened."

"Aarya knows I was in her room," I say. "She claims she

found a piece of my hair." I look at him for some sign as to whether Aarya might be bluffing, but he gives nothing away.

"I warned you about covering your tracks," he says.

"Believe me, I definitely learned that lesson. Not that I think I can stop hairs from ever falling from my head. But I agree on the grass. I won't be making that mistake again. Or hesitating the way I did, either," I add, frowning. "I could have gotten us caught by Aarya. I *did* get myself caught."

"Mmmm. I see. And you're scared of her?"

"She's completely unpredictable."

Ash shrugs. "True. But Ines is a better fighter. If I were you, I'd be more worried about Ines."

"This really isn't a joke."

He plops on the couch. "Welcome to Academy Absconditi, November, where the scheming never stops, and where someone is always trying to push you off a ledge. You're in a dangerous situation. You're taking calculated risks to get out of it. But risks are still risks."

I rub my hands over my face.

"You need to get yourself together," he says, his voice serious once more. "I'd like to think that this is just you getting out your emotions in private. But I'm here, so clearly it's not. Unless this display means you've decided to start trusting me, which as of yesterday I would say wasn't the case."

I study his face for a few seconds, but his expression is as calm and hard to read as usual. "Can I?"

"*Trust* me?" He laughs. "You're actually asking me if you can trust me. You're a fascinating girl, I'll give you that."

I sit down next to him on the couch. "I'm serious. Layla's a good person. You, on the other hand, are less of a good person.

Everything is a game to you," I say, and Ash starts to respond, but I stop him. "The other night in the trees, up on that sky bench, you told me that you're a Wolf and that Wolves are loyal. And I asked you who you're loyal to, remember? I know that at the very least you're loyal to your twin. Two minutes with you guys and that's obvious. Now, Layla has decided to help me. Who knows why, as I've proven to be troublesome ever since I got here. But she has anyway. And I don't know if you're on board just because Layla is making you, or if it's because you were out past curfew and helping me helps you, or if maybe you do hope that I'll get blamed and get the hell away from your sister."

Ash watches me curiously.

"But what I do know is that every single thing I tell Layla, she tells you. Even if I wanted to filter information to you, I can't without filtering it to Layla first. I won't make it on my own without her. As much as I hate to admit it, I'm too vulnerable. So yes, I'm asking you if I can trust you."

For the first time since I met Ash, he actually looks unsure. "That depends."

"Okay, I can work with that," I say quickly, relieved that he's at least taking my question seriously now. "What does it depend on?"

He looks at me for a long moment, searching for something. "Well . . . you're the one student at this school I know nothing about. I don't know where you stand on important issues or where your immediate family stands or even what kind of people you're aligned with. Rule number one isn't a joke. Handing out information about yourself and your family at this school is dangerous. But that doesn't stop us from trying to learn the basics about one another. Not knowing anything about you makes you more interesting for sure, but it also poses a potential problem."

I'm reminded of the way Ash looked at me after Layla repeated Nyx's accusation about Layla being less neutral. "Then why was Layla so adamant about me not talking about myself?" I ask. "If you guys don't know who I am, wouldn't Layla be trying to figure it out?"

"Layla cares too much and is far too moral, if you ask me. Plus, she already told you. She thinks you're reckless," Ash says, and smiles. "Not that that's always a bad quality. And even though she doesn't know why, Layla knows you were paired with her for a reason. Nothing at the Academy is random, especially not roommate assignments. It's likely that our immediate families are aligned in some manner, so by revealing unknown information about yourself in the middle of a hallway you could be compromising not just yourself but her, too."

I nod. "I actually really appreciate her shutting me up. I'm not sure what would have happened if she hadn't."

He leans back but doesn't take his eyes off me. "See, that kind of naïveté is exactly what confuses me about you. I find it nearly impossible to believe you really didn't know what would happen to you. Strategia are never clueless. Yet the entire time you've been here, you've been asking questions everyone else knows the answers to, performing brilliantly in some classes and blundering your way through others. Layla told me what you did in mind games and that you fretted about it for an hour afterward. She said she couldn't tell if you'd actually planned to win the challenge or won by default because you were simply running away from Brendan. Sometimes I think you're the worst liar I've ever met and other times I think you might be a genius."

I exhale. I got lucky when Layla and Ash thought my naïveté was intentional.

"I'm going to need you to tell me the truth," Ash says. "Not the abridged version, or there can't be any trust between us. Why don't things add up about you?"

I steel myself and I look him squarely in the eyes, so that he can read me, so that he knows I'm not lying. "I am really good at some things," I start, "and completely untrained in others. Layla guessed correctly. I did run from Brendan because I don't know hand-to-hand fighting the way you guys do. All those questions I asked you, I asked for real. My cluelessness isn't an act."

He listens intently, frowning. "That's exactly the problem. How could you not know how to fight or not know the answers to basic questions every Strategia learns as a child?"

"Because I wasn't raised the way you were raised," I say carefully.

"And how were you raised?" he asks.

I take a deep breath. *Time for the truth.* "I had no idea I was a Strategia before I came here. I still don't really believe it."

He stares at me for a long time, his invasive look on hyper-drive. He opens his mouth to say something but closes it again and frowns more deeply.

I tuck one of my legs under me on the couch. "I only ever heard the word *Strategia* once before, as a kid, and even then I was eavesdropping. I swear I didn't know what it meant, or who they were, until you told me. And I still have absolutely no idea why I'm here."

His frown is practically a scowl. "But you recited the Bear Family attributes the night we snuck out."

"Because of a game I played with my mother when I was little. I had all these stuffed animals, and we used to group them into families. The three words that described each family were something I thought my mom just made up. No one was more shocked than me to discover that those words actually mean something in real life." I level my gaze at him. "Admit it: you must have suspected something was off with me then or you wouldn't have had me recite them."

This time Ash's eyebrows go up. "No. Asking a Strategia to recite their Family attributes would typically have resulted in a snarky response. I was just feeling you out. I suspected something was off when you actually took me seriously."

"Yeah, well, see what I mean?"

He stands up and walks around the rug in front of the fireplace. I can almost hear him replaying our conversations in his thoughts, looking for discrepancies. After a good minute, he turns to me with a serious expression. "Your behavior matches what you're saying, but how in the hell did you get in here? We're prepped from before we can speak, and lots of kids don't make the cut. Only the very best get in, with some exceptions made for ruling families and their firstborn children. And if you belonged to one of those, even if you were a distant cousin, everyone would know who you are."

"Well, that's not me," I say.

"I know."

"And there are things I'm not trained in."

"Yes. Obviously. It's just so strange." His seriousness doesn't disappear, and his intense look returns.

"Knock it off with that look, Ash. At this point I'll tell you anything you want to know, just ask me," I say.

He doesn't respond with a sarcastic remark or a laugh like I was expecting. "You're certain you're part of the Bear Family?"

"Well, my mother was Italian and, yes, I'd say she was definitely a Bear. At least based on the games we used to play. But my dad is American," I say.

"American?" Ash says like he has a bad taste in his mouth. "But still Strategia?"

"Honestly, I didn't think so when I first came here," I say. "He's just a regular guy. But he used to be part of an intelligence agency, so—"

Ash groans and shakes his head.

"What?"

"Intelligence agency? November, your dad's Strategia. Please tell me that you can see that." He gives me a concerned look. "Being an intelligence officer is one of the most basic covers for our particular . . . skill sets if we're ever caught doing something."

I frown. When he says it like that, it all makes sense. In fact, it all seems terribly obvious. But the idea that Dad lied to me all these years isn't funny in the least.

Ash sits back down next to me. "There are some Strategia in America, but we don't tend to settle there. As I told you, most Families originated in what's now Europe, the Mediterranean, and the Middle East. It's not that it's never happened; it's just rare. We do our job, whatever it is, and then we go back to our Families. I would have heard if there was a highborn girl from the Bear Family who ran off to America. It would have been a huge scandal." He pauses. "It was your mother who Matteo recognized, right?"

I nod. I've thoroughly broken Blackwood's sacred rule number one, and I still don't know any more about my family, except that apparently I don't know them at all. "Okay, wait, back up. Start from the beginning."

"The beginning?"

"Am I right that you're a secret society?"

"*We*, November," Ash says gently. "You're part of this, too." There is amazement in his look. "And yes, I suppose that's what most people would think about us."

"And . . . are we assassins?" I say, and almost choke on the word.

"When we need to be, but we're also so much more than that. We can be selfish and competitive in advancing our own agendas, for sure. But we also help the world avoid catastrophe. Most people look forward, without ever bothering to consider the cyclical nature of history, and inevitably re-create the same disasters over and over again. Strategia stop the mechanisms that create those disasters."

I nod and jump into my next question before he decides to stop answering them, because for the first time since I got here, some of what I've observed at this school is starting to make sense. "So there's a system in each Family, right? Different jobs within Strategia—governing, leadership, servants, guards?"

"Yes," he says slowly, and he sounds different, like for once he's present and not five steps ahead. "Strategia Families grew in numbers after they stopped working for the rulers of their given empires and became independent. Everyone needed to pitch in to keep the Families functional and hidden."

"And what about us specifically, what about people who go to this school?" I ask.

"I can't believe we're having this conversation," he says, more to himself than to me. "We're the heartbeat of Strategia—the best strategists in our Families."

I hear him, but it still feels like he's talking about other people, not my family, not me. "Layla was saying something about the firstborn kids of the leaders of each Family taking over for their parents. So that means you have to be born into Strategia, right?"

"Well, most of us are born in, yes. But outsiders can be approved by the leaders of any given Family," Ash says.

I think about that. "And you said that Layla and I were likely paired as roommates for a reason?"

"Well," he says, and pauses. "When I said that, I meant that generally the Bears and Wolves don't have any animosity between them, and there's every likelihood that our immediate relatives have some kind of an agreement. But I'm not so sure anymore."

An image of my dad's favorite whittling knife flashes through my thoughts; the hilt looks like a silver wolf. He said his childhood best friend gave it to him when he was growing up in Maine. But now I'm pretty sure the Maine part was total bunk.

"And when you asked me if I was 'for, against, or neutral'?" I say without fully explaining what I want to know.

Ash exhales audibly. "It's complicated."

"But it's also important and something I need to know," I say.

He's quiet for a second. "I won't tell you the nuances of Family politics because we would be here all night if I did. But I can tell you that there are Families and individuals who support curbing the Lions' activities, which essentially means curbing their power, through force if necessary. And you can probably guess what *neutral* and *against* are. Strategia Families don't regulate one another—it's just not who we are. But historically we've also never experienced this type of power imbalance."

I open my mouth to ask another question, but Ash starts speaking again.

"The fact that you were admitted is shocking," he says. "How did someone who doesn't know anything about Strategia pull that off?"

I shake my head. "I honestly don't know. I've been trying to figure that out since I got here." I pause, feeling exposed, but also closer to him somehow. "So now that you know the whole truth, can I trust you?"

Ash looks at me, and he's more relaxed than he was before, but he's also still hesitant. "I don't think you have a choice at this point except to assume that you can."

"Really? That's all I get after telling you my secrets?" I shake my head. "You're such an ass."

"I'm such an ass because you don't like the truth?" He grins, and his eyes twinkle with mischief.

"No, because you *are*, like, at your core," I say.

He clutches his heart like I wounded him. "I almost thought you meant that. But then I didn't, because I can read you and it's obvious that you secretly love me."

I laugh and realize it's the first time I've laughed in days; the weight of Stefano's murder and the fear of being a suspect have darkened everything. "Well, you're not boring, I'll give you that."

He leans slightly toward me. "Never boring."

For a moment we are both quiet.

Ash sighs, and his look is gentler. There's none of his usual analysis or distance. It almost seems like he's seeing me for the first time, and for just a moment, I get lost in his gaze. My stomach flips in a good way, and for once he's the one to break eye contact.

I clear my throat. "I asked you in the vine courtyard what I needed to know to survive here," I say, and readjust my position on the couch. "Well, now you know what I meant. So I'm asking you again."

He pauses. "If I agree to tell you what you want to know, I need you to also do something for me."

"It's always a trade with you."

"I'm completely serious about this."

"Okay, fine. What do you need me to do?"

His eyes get intense again. "Not tell my sister what you just told me."

"What?" I lean back slightly. "Why wouldn't I?"

He presses his lips together for a brief second. "Because it's dangerous."

"For me, sure," I say. "But how would it be dangerous for Layla?"

"The fact that you don't know who you are tells me that there's something to hide, something important. And once that gets uncovered, I don't want Layla to be at the center of it."

I look at the fireplace for answers. It feels wrong not telling Layla. And it puts me in a place where I have to potentially lie to her. Plus, I trust her way more than I trust him—don't I? If she had been here instead of Ash tonight, I'd probably be having this conversation with her.

"The choice is yours, November. If I help you figure out who you are, Layla can't know the truth. Or tell her, and I promise you neither of us will help you. You need us way more than we need you, and you know that, otherwise you wouldn't have told me any of this."

"Don't bother saying the choice is mine, if there isn't a choice," I say.

I can't help but think about the talk Layla gave me in the library, when she said our new trust arrangement was completely breakable. I feel like I'm already destroying it.

Just then the door latch struggles against the lock. "November?" Layla says, her voice muffled by the thick door.

"I still need an answer," Ash says.

I huff. "Yes. Okay? Yes."

"Then we have a deal," he says, and there's nothing playful in his tone.

I get up and open the door.

Layla comes in carrying a huge stack of books. "Oh, good. You're both here."

Ash takes them from her and puts them down as Layla removes her cloak and hangs it in the armoire. "I got a book on knives for you to go through, November, to see if you can recognize the one that Stefano . . . well, the one used in the murder. And a medical book that should help us pinpoint how long he'd been dead by the time you found him. And some just for you on deception and body language. No offense, but I think you could use a refresher."

"Great," I say. "Sounds like a plan."

She looks between me and Ash. "Did something happen? You both look uncomfortable."

Ash looks at me, daring me to break our agreement.

"Well, Aarya knows I was in her room—at least she thinks she does. She found a piece of my hair," I tell her.

Layla frowns. "That's not good news. We'll need to be on guard. Aarya's the kind who believes in retaliation for fun as much as anything else."

"And I met with Conner again," I say.

"Dr. Conner?" Layla repeats, and her tone is more worried.

"He claims that the guard who saw me used the same staircase I did, so it was impossible for us to both be in it at the same time. That I must have gone a different way," I say.

"What did you tell him?" Layla asks.

"Nothing. I said I didn't know."

"Good," Layla says. "That was the right response."

"He also said that the guard used a different route than normal. I thought that was weird, considering how precise everyone is around here," I say, and Ash and Layla look at each other.

Layla's eyebrows draw together. "It's not entirely impossible, but it's not typical, either. Although I'm not sure you could prove that the guard did or didn't do anything unusual that night, especially since they don't talk to students."

I exhale. "That's what I figured." I hesitate. "Tell me honestly, how bad a spot do you think I'm in right now?"

Even before I hear her answer, I can see the worry on her face. "Bad," she says quietly.

Twenty-One

LAYLA AND I sit at the breakfast table in our room, which is covered with open books and food. I'm looking through pictures of knives and she's reading about rigor mortis. It's like a twisted version of the old couple you see in movies flipping through the newspaper and drinking coffee.

"So far, the closest thing to what I remember seeing is this," I say, pointing at a picture of a plain metal-handled knife in my book.

"A common kitchen knife?" Layla says, and frowns.

"Well, I can't say positively. It was dark. But I do remember it being silver," I say.

Layla's frown lingers.

"What?"

She swallows a bite of her toast. "It's just . . . I don't know how someone could have gotten hold of a kitchen knife. Those are locked up and guarded at all times, and not even in the kitchen, in a different room altogether."

I smear butter and jam on my bread. "The night I went up

against Nyx in that challenge, Blackwood said they were doing a search. Could that be what they were looking for?"

"That's what I was just wondering," she says, and we fall silent again, reading and eating.

Layla runs her finger under a few lines in her book. "You said his body was cold."

I nod. "Not icy cold, but like when you touch someone's cold hand. *Lukewarm* might be more accurate. All I know is that it was noticeable."

"You had just been outside," Layla says, half to me and half to her book. "You were wearing your cloak—it gets pretty cold here at night, even with a cloak and even with the activity of climbing trees. . . ." She looks up at me. "Can you remember if you were feeling hot or cold when you found his body?"

It's amazing to watch her consider all the factors. She'd make an excellent detective. "I tend to run warm," I say. "And by the time I had gotten to him, I was running and my adrenaline was pumping. I was definitely sweating."

"So he was cold compared to you, but would you say he was warmer than the air temperature?" she asks.

I nod.

"And you touched his neck, right? Did he feel stiff at all?"

"Well . . . ," I say, trying my best to recall that terrible moment and not get queasy. "I knew right away that he had no pulse, but he wasn't rock hard. Maybe a little stiff."

"What about the blood? Where was it?" Layla asks, and as relaxed as her expression is, I can see in her eyes that she doesn't like picturing Stefano dead any more than I do.

"He was in the shadows, so it was really just varying degrees of darkness, but I remember clearly that his chest was

covered in blood, or rather his white shirt was. He was wearing his cloak, too. But I didn't see any blood on the floor. If there had been, I would have gotten it on myself when I knelt down."

She stares out the window.

"What are you thinking?" I ask.

"A dead body loses heat at about zero point eighty-three degrees Celsius an hour—that's one point five degrees Fahrenheit, if it's easier for you. That's not quickly at all. Although if a body is kept in a cold place, it will lose heat faster. But regardless, he couldn't have been newly killed when you found him or you wouldn't have noticed a temperature difference. Also, for you to feel signs of rigor mortis, even just a little, he would likely have been dead for three to eight hours," she says, and my mind spins at the implications.

"But obviously he wasn't in that hallway for hours or someone would have found him before I did," I say, following her train of thought. "Are you saying you think he was *moved* there sometime after he'd been killed?"

Her forehead tenses with concentration. "That's the thing, you said you didn't see blood on the floor, but there *was* blood on his shirt. Even if your temperature readings were off because of adrenaline and exercise, and even if you aren't a good judge of stiffness, it's strange that there wasn't any blood on the floor. So yes, I think we can assume that he was placed there."

"You mean he was killed somewhere else and then put in that hallway specifically for me to find?" I'm trying to wrap my mind around the lengths someone went to in order to set me up.

"That's what it looks like from where I'm sitting."

"Ash knows the guards' schedules to the second, right?" I say, considering her words. "So are there specific windows of

time where we would be more likely to go to the vine courtyard and then to leave it? I guess what I'm asking is, would someone be able to make an educated guess about the time we would be coming back from those trees?"

Layla nods. "Definitely. The easiest time to go anywhere is right after curfew, because the guards always make rounds then. And then again about forty-five minutes later—which would be your most likely time to return. If you miss that window, you have to wait for another hour and fifteen minutes, when the guards go again."

No wonder Ash was insistent that someone set me up. "We need to find out who saw Stefano after his classes. It will give us a timeline to work with."

"Ash is already working on that," Layla says. "We also need to think about where Stefano was killed and where his body was kept before it was placed in that hallway."

There's a brief knock and the latch lifts on our door. Pippa comes in, looking at us in an almost sad way that sets me on edge.

"Your presence has been requested in the dining hall," Pippa says. "Immediately."

"Thank you," Layla says, and Pippa, who is usually chatty, leaves without another word.

I look at Layla for answers.

"I don't know," she says, "but we don't have enough information yet to prove it wasn't you."

✳ ✳ ✳

The dining hall has once again been transformed into an auditorium and is nearly full by the time Layla and I take our seats.

The teachers stand against the walls as before, watching us, and Blackwood is sitting behind the teachers' table. However, there is one noticeable difference—two guards stand next to her holding crossbows. And there are two more guards by the exit.

My stomach twists so violently that I have to stop myself from running to the bathroom.

"Stop fidgeting," Ash says under his breath as he takes the seat next to me.

I drop my hands into my lap. I look from Ash to Layla. They both stare forward with matching blank expressions, but the tension between us is so thick that it's hard not to panic. The two armed guards next to Blackwood loom over us all like angels of death.

Blackwood stands up and does a slow sweep of the room with her eyes. "Good morning," she says, and the room echoes a "Good morning" in response.

"It is a good morning indeed," she says with a small smile, so contrary to the general feeling of the room that my shoulders tighten. "We have concluded the investigation into Stefano's death, and the guilty party is now known. There will not be a trial. There will be no fanfare."

I look immediately to the exit. *An eye for an eye. There's no mercy here, no negotiating.*

When I shift my gaze back to the front of the room, Blackwood is staring directly at me. Every muscle in my body tenses, and out of the corner of my eye I notice a few of the students turning to look at me. Aarya smiles like she's about to see a magic show, but Matteo seems strangely uncomfortable. Dread inches up my body, making it hard to breathe. I want to scream that I didn't do it, that she has to know I didn't, but I can't seem to move a muscle. Instead the words lodge in my throat, unsaid, tightening my chest. Even Conner looks at me like this was all disappointingly inevitable.

Blackwood holds my gaze for so long that my eyes start to water from not blinking. Then suddenly she shifts her line of sight away from me. "Charles, you are hereby charged with Stefano's murder."

Gasps roll through the rows of students. I look at Charles and he looks right back at me, like he would kill me this instant if he could.

Nyx abruptly stands, and everyone turns to her. Charles, on the other hand, continues to watch me like he's trying to solve a math problem.

"Stefano and Charles attended this school for two and a half years without a single fight between them," Nyx says, her chin held high. "He's exactly the same as he's always been. And Stefano hasn't changed, either. What is not the same in this school, the *only* thing that is different, is November."

The students look from Nyx to me. I've never wanted to disappear so badly in my life. Ash leans slightly forward.

Blackwood sighs, like this is tedious for her.

"We all know there's something wrong with her!" Nyx exclaims, thrusting a finger in my direction. Her voice has taken on a wild tone.

Charles stands now, too, and touches her arm, but Nyx doesn't calm.

"Even her own Family members attack her," Nyx says, and I can hear the ragged emotion in her voice. "Mark my words, if

Charles is taking the fall for her this time, any of you could be next."

"Guards," Blackwood says, seemingly unbothered by the scene that's erupting. She gestures for them to take Charles.

The two guards by the door step forward. Charles looks across the room at them and takes a step in the opposite direction. He glances at Blackwood and then at Conner, his body tensed, like a caged animal. I wonder if he's contemplating running, and my heart beats wildly—only seconds ago I was thinking the same thing.

Suddenly Charles stops moving and looks over at me. The moment our eyes meet I can feel all his fear and anger. His chin juts out and his jaw is set in a hard line. He reaches under his cloak to his back and yanks out a knife. The steel blade shimmers in the candlelight. Gasps ripple through the room, and the students nearest him pull back. Behind him, Aarya's eyes widen, and it occurs to me that perhaps this is the knife she lost.

The next seconds blur as Charles pulls back his arm and Blackwood yells "Stop!" But her command has no effect because the knife is already whizzing through the air, and I find myself frozen in the moment, waiting for it to strike. My heart gives one deafening thud and I close my eyes as the blade slices through skin with a tearing sound. Only it's not *my* skin. My eyes fly open to find that Ash's arm is in front of me, the knife protruding through his forearm, sticking an inch out the back.

I look down at the blood that drips into my lap—Ash's blood—and when I look back up, Charles's face has twisted into something primal, something filled with hatred. For a second, I can't make sense of any of it—the chaos among the other students. Ash's arm with the knife in it. Charles. I touch my leg and my fingers come up bright red. Then all at once it seems like everyone is moving again. The guards run for Charles, Brendan blocks their path, and Nyx topples chairs into the aisle.

Ash stands and pulls the knife out of his arm, spraying the ground in front of us with droplets of red. Charles's glare is still fixed on me and I can feel his determination in my bones. *He wants to kill me.* Ash holds the knife in front of him, but Charles doesn't slow. Just when he's about to collide with us both, I hear a low whistle and a thud. Charles's chest arches forward unnaturally and his eyes widen before he slumps to the floor.

The guards have already brought Brendan and Nyx to their knees. Blood begins to pool under Charles. His mouth opens, but he doesn't manage to form any words. He takes one final strangled breath, his eyelids closing and his chest deflating. My own chest heaves, like it's trying to breathe for him, and my eyes fill.

"No," I say barely above a whisper. "No. No. No." Because now I understand. That whistle . . . that *thud*? It was an arrow, and it must have hit an artery, and now he's . . .

I look up at the platform, where Blackwood lowers her bow, giving it back to the guard on her right. "As I said, there will be no trial."

Nyx wails helplessly and struggles against the guard, who drags her out of the room. Brendan follows, also restrained. The metallic smell of blood fills the air, and I can't seem to get my bearings.

"With the guilty party dealt with, your schedules will resume as per usual," Blackwood says. "Go to your classes, everyone."

Still in a daze, I turn toward Ash, who is holding his injured arm up, blood dripping down his elbow. Conner and the armed guards are next to us in a flash, retrieving the knife.

"Let's get you to the infirmary," Conner says to Ash without sparing me a glance.

I want to thank Ash for saving my life. I want to sob and scream and throw up. But I just stand there frozen, unable to utter a word.

Twenty-Two

I SIT ON my bed, where I've been ever since dinner, trying to read by candlelight, except the words swim in front of my eyes and I can't make sense of them. But sleeping is out of the question. Every time I close my eyes, I see Ash's blood dripping on my lap and Charles taking his last breath.

"So Layla's got you studying deception and sparring, huh?" Ash asks, and I jump.

He comes into my room and closes the door behind him. I quickly put the book down on my nightstand and move my legs so that he has room to sit. His arm is all bandaged up, but he seems in good spirits.

Ash lowers himself onto my bed and grins. "Your mouth is hanging open."

I can't help it, I lean forward and throw my arms around his neck in a hug. For just a second, he tenses. Then he relaxes and puts his arms around my back. He holds me carefully, like this is the first time in years that someone's hugged him. Maybe it is.

"Thank you," I say into his neck. "Thank you so much. I

should have said something right away. I just didn't know how to process what you did." I give him a squeeze and let go. "All day I've been thinking about how to repay you."

"It was no problem," he says quickly, formally, like he's not sure what to do with my outpouring of emotion.

"Ash, you took a *knife* through the arm for me," I say. "It's a big deal. I can't even tell you how . . . I would be *dead* if you hadn't been there."

He looks more uncomfortable. "Need help?" He nods at my book, changing the subject. "Eighty percent of fighting is being able to predict which way and when someone will move or attack. Twenty percent is knowing how to combat that move effectively."

"Wait, hold on," I say. "I mean, yes, I do want your help. But what the heck was that chaos today? Layla's barely talked to me since."

"Well, Layla goes quiet when she's thinking," he says, and I can't help but wonder if she's reconsidering her friendship with me after what happened in the dining hall.

"Blackwood didn't even explain how she knew Charles was guilty," I say, and the image of the arrow hitting him replays in my thoughts, making me shudder.

"Technically, she doesn't have to explain," Ash says. "His reaction made it clear he was the guilty one, not you. But also, she may have *chosen* not to explain his motives in detail because she doesn't want to emphasize the divide between the Bears and the Lions. Everyone assumes that Charles killed Stefano because of politics—that's the obvious reason. As you may have noticed, everything comes down to politics and alliances when you're Strategia. And I'm sure a handful of people figured out that he tried to pin the murder on you, with the intention of taking out two Bears at once. It could have been three if Matteo had reacted to you differently and dropped you out of that tree. The bottom line is, Charles was trying to weaken your Family, which is nothing new."

"But Blackwood"—I can barely get the words out—"executed him in front of the whole school."

Ash nods slowly and gives me a thoughtful look. "Yes. But it was a fast death, and she could have lost another of her students if she hadn't reacted quickly. Almost did." He watches me. "That really shook you, didn't it?"

"I . . . Yes," I say, but I don't explain further. What's there to add when you've just seen someone killed in cold blood?

We're both silent for an awkward beat.

"So then is it over?" I ask. "Now that Charles is . . . now that Blackwood caught the murderer."

"Weeell," Ash says. "Layla's worried that we haven't been given our punishments for those marks."

"Wait, we? Meaning me and you? For being out past *curfew*?" It seems like such a small worry in comparison to what I witnessed today.

"Me and you," he repeats, and I can tell by his voice that something's wrong. "We should have been assigned a punishment by now. Charles was accused and proven guilty; everything's supposed to go back to normal. Except it hasn't."

I readjust the pillow behind my back. "Okay. What does that mean?"

"I don't know yet," he says, although I get the sense that there's something he's not telling me. He takes his cloak off. "I need you to tell me more about your father."

My uneasiness increases. "What do you want to know?"

"Did he grow up in a major city? Do you remember which countries he traveled to?"

I clamp my lips together and start to fidget. "Look—"

"I know," he says, and I stop.

"You know what?"

"You're rubbing your hands together in a self-soothing motion, which tells me that my questions made you nervous. And your lips are pressed together, indicating you're physically trying to resist giving me any information. I know you can't tell me details. Keep it as vague as you need to, but find a way to answer, and think about your body language," he says. "It says more than you realize and to more people than just me."

"Hmmm." I shift my position, trying hard to just act normal. "I know he lived in New York very briefly, but he always said he preferred a quiet life," I say slowly, thinking through my answer so that I don't give away anything traceable. "And he never travels or even talks about other countries or having distant relatives." I would say that he has an American accent, but having met a language virtuoso like Aarya, I now know a person's accent doesn't necessarily mean anything.

"What about his immediate family?" Ash asks.

"Well, his parents are dead and he's an only child. He claims to have some second cousins or something, but I've never met them." I frown, despite myself. How did I not find *any* of this suspicious before?

Ash nods. "If we figure out who his Family is, we might be able to figure out who has a vendetta against you and why they set you up. Right now, the only person who seems to know about you is Matteo. And I've already tried that. It's a dead end."

I blink at him for a second. "You spoke to Matteo?"

He looks at me curiously. "That upsets you?"

I know it shouldn't, but it kind of does. "Well, I'm obviously not his biggest fan after he punched me in the face for no reason. I'm half his size!"

"There are many, *many* reasons one of us might take a swing at someone here," Ash counters. "And your size doesn't mean a thing. If you think it does, then you're a fool. Nyx and all of her five feet can take down ninety percent of the biggest guys in this school, and she frequently does."

I open my mouth to argue, but he's right. This system is completely different from what I'm used to. People act differently, retaliate differently.

"As of this moment, Matteo seems to be the only person who knows who you are. Don't you want to figure this out?"

"I do. I do want to figure this out," I say, and tuck a loose piece of hair behind my ear.

Ash grins.

"What?"

"Oh, nothing," he says, but he doesn't mean it.

"Spit it out, Ash. Why are you grinning at me like that?"

"I just find it curious that you got all bent out of shape that I talked to Matteo. If it wasn't for a logical reason, then it had to be an emotional one," he says, and scans my face. "You feel some ownership over me."

My eyes widen. "Wrong. I do not want to own you. You're more trouble than you're worth."

"Uh-huh," he says. "I buy that. That's why you said 'do not want to own' when I merely said 'feel some ownership.' Sounds like a classic Freudian slip, if you ask me." He's enjoying this way too much, and if I thought I could push him off my bed without hurting his arm, I would.

Instead I settle for giving him a withering look.

He laughs. "It's been a crazy day, and we could all stand to get out of our heads for a minute. How about I show you some moves before I have to go back to my room? We really don't need a repeat of this morning."

"I really am sorry about that knife," I say, looking at the bandage on his arm.

"The knife is only part of a bigger problem—the message. This isn't ending with Charles. Nyx named you as an enemy. And if you're Nyx's enemy, you're also Brendan's, and thus the Lions in general, plus everyone who has an alliance with them. You need to prove that you have a place here and establish yourself or they'll crush you. Like Layla said, you can't let them think you have weaknesses."

"I'll work for it," I say, and I mean it. If things get any worse, I worry he and Layla will abandon me. "I've got a lot of energy. I'll read about history and deception in my downtime and do tutoring with Layla, if you can teach me sparring, poisons, mind games, and anything else you think I'm missing. I can practice as much as you're willing to teach me. I'm great with knives, trees, and fencing . . . although I've only ever used a wooden sword."

He looks at me in a way that tells me I said something odd again.

"What?"

"You're just so . . . trusting, I guess would be the word. So open," he says, and he almost looks sad about it.

I shrug. "But you're you. You're my friend. How are you

supposed to help me if I don't tell you what I need help with? I'm not going to advertise my weaknesses to the rest of the school . . . just to you."

He smiles a small smile. "It's not that. It's just . . ." He shakes his head. "Never mind."

He almost looks emotional. "Tell me," I say, and put my hand on his and squeeze it. The moment I do, I'm aware that it's not a normal gesture. But before I can pull my hand away, he takes it in his. He holds it carefully, looking at it like it matters, and rubs his thumb over my fingers. Goose bumps run up my arm.

"I just wish we weren't all in this mess," he says, and looks up at me. "That you could have come here and we could have met . . . I don't know what I wish. I'm just sorry, I guess, that all this is happening to you. You're probably the happiest person in this place, and even though every time you turn around someone is attacking you, you still trust people. I'm not sure I'll ever understand. But there is something beautiful about it."

I smile at him. Did Ash just let his guard down with me? His eyes are as intense as ever, but in a very different way. My stomach flutters, and despite myself, I feel my cheeks get hot.

"My best friend always says that even when I'm down, I'm happy," I tell him, and smile. "You never know how much time you have, so screw it—I'm going to live in every way I can. And the one thing I'll never agree with is how you guys seem to push each other away. I don't know what my life would be like without my best friend or my friends in general. I hope I have a thousand over my lifetime."

"Best friend," he repeats quietly to himself like I've just named some mythical creature. And I can't help but wonder if he's lonely under all his jokes and confidence. I want to pull him close and wrap my arms around him. But he gently lets go of my hand.

As he smiles at me, I can tell that something between us has changed, like he just made a decision to let me in a little. "Stand up," he says, and I do.

"Now, get in the position you would use if you wanted to hit me."

I smile. From heartfelt conversation to sparring in one beat. I step back with my right leg, put up my fists, and tuck my chin.

He nods at me, assessing my form. "You'll notice that most people step back with their dominant leg and lead with their dominant arm when they hit you. Your stance isn't bad. You're protecting your organs by positioning yourself sideways, and your neck by keeping your chin tucked. But you're too tense. And when you're too tense, you can't move fast enough. You need to be alert, but not so stiff that you can't maneuver."

"Makes sense," I say, and loosen my shoulders and knees a bit. "It's the same for fencing."

"Exactly," he says. "Now go ahead and take a swing."

I lead with my left and he blocks me before my arm even gets halfway to him.

"Blocking is going to be your friend in the beginning. Even if you can't win a fight, you can keep yourself from getting seriously hurt if you pay attention to people's eyes and movements," he says. "Go ahead and think about where you want to punch me next."

I picture hitting him in the stomach with my right hand, and for a split second my gaze shifts to his stomach. "Ahhh!" I laugh. "You're right. Eyes give you away. That's so helpful."

"Do it once more, only pay attention to the arm you plan to hit me with."

He's correct again—my left arm pulls slightly backward as I'm thinking about a jab. It's an involuntary tell.

I look up at him, happy to be learning something useful. "You do it. Think about hitting me and let me see if I can pick it out."

He glances at my face, and his left shoulder twitches ever so slightly.

"Face shot with your left arm," I say, and he nods.

"Charles looked at your chest before he threw the knife. People with weapons will always look exactly where they're aiming," he says. "But every once in a while . . ."

He looks at my face and his right arm twitches.

"Face shot, right—"

"This happens." He sends his left fist toward my gut instead, barely touching it. He doesn't take his hand back right away, and I can feel my blood pulsing under his touch.

"Every once in a while you'll run into someone who'll intentionally mislead you by looking somewhere they're not going to hit," he says. "But that only really happens in a relaxed environment. If someone's moving quickly and is in the moment, they will almost always give themselves away. Of course, if they're moving fast enough, the tells are also much harder to pick out. But the whole idea is similar to the way people look at your lips when they want to kiss you."

I raise an eyebrow. "Or want to punch you in the mouth."

"Or that," he says, and smirks. "I'm going to walk you through blocking in slow motion and then we'll do it at proper speed." He throws a punch at my face and I put up my left arm.

"Not bad, but you're still too stiff," he says. "A punch or a chop or anything directed at your face is going to come with force. But that doesn't mean you need to use a great deal of force to repel it. Use their momentum against them by redirecting it."

He takes my arm in his hands and bends it. "When I take a swing, you move my arm away from you. Like this. Tensing will never help you when you're fighting. But that said, feel free to flex your muscles if you take a hit to the abdomen. It can shield you from injury."

We're standing so close that my heart speeds up and I actually do look at his lips.

"I saw that, you know," he says.

I smile. "I have no idea what you're talking about."

"Uh-huh. Well, let's try this again. And be ready for the second punch, which you can also block, but it would be easier to lean out of the way." He throws a right at me and I block. He throws a left and I lean, his fist soaring past my cheek.

He nods approvingly. "Now, be careful to keep your distance. If you get trapped in close-range fighting, you'll be overpowered quickly. I'm showing you basic boxing, but a lot of us are skilled in multiple forms of martial arts, and can cause a great deal of pain with very little—"

I glance at his stomach but then lightly smack him on the cheek. He looks so shocked that I start laughing. "Gotcha."

He looks at my lips.

"I saw that, you know," I say.

"I know exactly what you're talking about," he says with a grin, and my stomach drops in a good way. For a second, I think he's going to lean forward, but then he steps away.

I return to my fighting stance. "What's with this no-dating

rule, anyway?" I say, aiming for nonchalance. "Is it a boarding school thing? 'Cause they obviously can't keep you guys from sneaking out of your rooms even with all these guards."

He shakes his head. "Our Families have approval over marriages. Especially those of us whose immediate families are in higher positions of power. A marriage can signify a major alliance, so they're arranged with care."

I look at him sideways. "Hold on. You all have *arranged* marriages based on political alliances? What is this, the fifteen hundreds?" Although I don't know why I bothered saying that, considering everything at this school is like the 1500s. "And marriage is one thing, dating is another."

"Not really. Not when you consider the number of secrets we keep and the things we can glean from one another through nonverbal communication. Getting close to someone emotionally and having it end badly could mean a breach of all kinds of information."

"You mean like all the information I'm leaking to you right now," I say.

"Not exactly," Ash replies. "You don't know Bear secrets. You can't even be sure who you are."

"Fair point. So you guys don't date until you're ready to get married?" I'm having trouble swallowing this one.

He smirks. "I didn't say that. I just said we don't get attached to each other. Nothing serious."

I want to tell him that's crazy, but given my own dating history, I don't have a leg to stand on. "So then has your Family already picked someone out for you?" I say jokingly, but he doesn't smile in return.

"Layla and I are also the firstborn of the leaders in our Family." From the expression on his face, it's obvious he has mixed feelings about that. "The alliances Lay and I make here will definitely influence my Family's decision. But yes, they have been narrowing down the possibilities ever since we were kids. Being the firstborn has its benefits, but also its obligations."

No wonder Brendan and the other guys give Layla such a hard time. If she's also in line to lead her Family, it's less that she's an outcast and more that she's a rival. "Are they trying to match you with another firstborn?" I ask.

"No. Never. Firstborns are required to stay with their Families. We tend to marry someone with good skills and a lesser station in another Family who is willing to join ours and relinquish theirs. Both Families benefit from the improved relationship."

My eyebrows push together. "Give up your Family? Why would anyone ever do that? And how could giving up your Family even be enforced?"

"With penalty of death," he says, and I lean back.

"You kill people for not having perfect loyalty to their new Family?" The astonishment in my voice is obvious. "What if you wanted to marry someone who isn't Strategia?"

"Unless that person is previously approved by your Family, it's forbidden. And if you go ahead and do it anyway, then . . . the penalty is death."

Did I just find out that the only people I can marry are either in this school or need to be approved by some Strategia in Europe I don't even know? This isn't happening. "What if someone wants to stop being a Strategia?"

He looks at me in almost a compassionate way. "Also forbidden."

I can't think of a single thing to say that doesn't involve panic. All this time I've been thinking that this was something I could walk away from, that I would have a choice. After I dodged a bullet this morning, I thought that if I just learned enough to blend in and stayed quiet, I would make it out of this school and never come back.

"Here, let me show you some kicks before I have to leave," Ash says, and by the look on his face I can tell that I'm not hiding my emotions at all.

Twenty-Three

THERE'S A FAINT clicking noise. I pull the blankets up over my shoulder and bury my head in the pillow. *Drip. Drip. Drip.* It's as if someone forgot to turn off a faucet somewhere in the distance.

I yawn under my thick comforter and rub at my eyes. I couldn't fall asleep for a long time last night, and all I want to do is roll over and burrow farther under my comforter. But the light is already peeking through the edges of the heavy curtain and I want to talk to Layla about that horrible assembly before we have to go to class.

The books Layla gave me are with me in the bed, where I passed out reading them. I stretch and wince. My muscles are sore from all the sparring exercises Ash and I did.

I toss off the covers and swing my legs out. When my feet hit the cold stone, there's something gritty under my toes, and I yank them back up. Something's wrong. There's never dirt on the floor; they keep this place spotless. I kneel on my bed, my mind racing through every terrible thing that could possibly be on that stone, and I pull back the curtains, letting the morning light spill in.

When I look back at the floor, I start to scream but stop myself so fast it sounds like a strangled yelp. Next to my bed, written in dark brown smears, are two words: *Sarete ridotti.*

Italian. My mom and Aunt Jo spoke in Italian when I was little. Aunt Jo still does sometimes. I'm not amazing with it, but I can translate this: "You will be reduced" or possibly "You will be eliminated"?

I immediately look at my bedroom door. The lock's no longer in place. My adrenaline spikes and I run to get Layla. I knock on her door and vigorously brush off the bottom of my feet.

Within two seconds she unlatches her door. She takes note of my spooked expression. "What happened?"

"I don't . . . Come here," I say, leading her back to my room.

She walks in, freezes as though someone pressed a pause button, and then resumes her fast pace. She kneels down on my floor and sniffs at the brown smears and scattered droplets. "That's . . . blood," she says, confirming what I already suspected.

I immediately think of Charles and Ash and the whole traumatic bloody scene in the dining hall yesterday. I swallow. "I can't imagine that anyone is walking around carrying blood to write a message in," I say mostly to myself.

"No," Layla confirms. "It's highly unlikely."

"Which means someone must have cut themselves in my room?" I shudder, immediately pulling up a mental image. "So creepy. Who would do that?"

Layla shakes her head. "Someone who was going out of their

way to scare you, that's who. And someone cocky. It took time to write this while you slept, as opposed to slipping in with a message that had already been written out and just placing it on the floor."

The thought that someone was in my bedroom, bleeding a warning onto my floor while I slept through the whole thing, makes me want to march right back to Blackwood's office and demand to leave again. If she hadn't threatened me with that dungeon, I would head there in my nightgown, etiquette be damned.

"The worst part is, I vaguely remember hearing something," I admit to Layla. "Although what would I have done if I had woken up and found someone here? Fought them?"

She looks up at me. "I can't imagine that would have gone well for you. And whoever it was probably had something sharp with them."

"Brendan or Nyx?" I ask.

"It's possible," she says. "They have every reason to be angry with you after the way things ended with Charles yesterday. Even though he was a newish addition to their group, Nyx was dating him and Brendan fully accepted him as part of their unit. That alliance was a bond. They would do almost anything to protect and defend each other."

I nod and find myself wondering if Layla and Ash might ever feel that way about me. "What about Aarya? Given the unpredictable factor?" I ask.

Layla exhales audibly. "This *is* her kind of game, but it's clear that the letters were formed by someone who is right-handed, and Aarya's left-handed. Granted, she could have written them with her right hand to confuse things, but she, unlike most people, typically likes to take credit for her threats. And the width of the stroke is bigger than her pointer finger. It's either someone with larger hands than hers, or she used her thumb. Or there was more than one person—Felix, for instance. But all things considered, I would say that Brendan is more likely."

I blink at her. Her brain is amazing.

"We need to clean this up," she says. "Pippa is going to be here any minute."

My eyes widen. "Clean it up? Don't we need to tell—"

"No," Layla says forcefully, and takes the washcloth off my dresser. She dips it in the basin and starts scrubbing up the blood. "If we bring Blackwood into this, we will get hit with retaliation twice as hard. It's just not how we do things here."

"But how do we explain that much blood on the—" I whisper, and Layla hushes me. The latch on the main door rattles.

With lightning speed, Layla grabs my empty water glass, wraps the cloth around it, and uses a book from my bedside table to crush it.

In the next second she somehow scatters the glass without making a sound, motioning for me to join her on the floor. Then she picks up a shard and grabs my hand. My eyes widen. She nicks me on the palm and I wince but refrain from yelping.

Pippa knocks lightly and comes into my room. Her eyes widen at the sight of the blood dripping down my palm onto the floor. But I have to hand it to Layla: there is nothing all that out of the ordinary about a sleepy girl who knocked over her water glass and then cut herself trying to clean it up.

Twenty-Four

"THE MORE YOU learn in deception class, the less you will have to learn in others," Professor Gupta says from the end of the antique conference table. He's a short elderly man I might take as unassuming if it weren't for the fact that he's teaching deception and could come off that way intentionally.

Gupta, I think. *Sanskrit originally. And a common name in India meaning "protected."*

The two torches on the walls make the small room dance with shadows. It looks more like an office where medieval war strategists would plot an invasion than like any classroom I've ever been in. The walls are covered in dark wood paneling, and ornate wooden arches bracket the ceiling.

I sneak a glance at Brendan, wondering if he was responsible for the blood in my room this morning, and check his hands for any stray cuts. But I can't see anything from here. And of course there's always Matteo. The message was written in Italian. Only he's not in this class for me to scrutinize.

I catch Ash looking at me from across the table and remember everything he read in my body language yesterday. I immediately relax my face and shift my gaze.

"Some of you will mistakenly believe that your fighting skills are what will help you most when you're out in the world." Gupta looks around the table. "But I assure you that your fighting skills will only get you one one-hundredth of the information that a mastery of deception will. Also, the more effort you put into concealing your intentions and reading others, the better prepared you'll be when you actually get to the fight. Now, the opposite is also true: deception can get you into situations that you can't back out of."

I swear the teachers, Conner, and Blackwood have figured out a way to subtly weave manipulative strategies throughout all the classes. And what's more, I feel like they're secretly directed at me and my shortcomings. But maybe everyone feels that way.

"In 415 BCE, the Athenian statesman Alcibiades was convinced that conquering Sicily would win the Peloponnesian War. The prudent general Nicias considered the idea rash and chose to deal with it by telling him a lie. He greatly overestimated how many men would be required, thinking it would dissuade Alcibiades. But the lie backfired. The Athenians took Nicias's word and sent nearly the entire army to Sicily, when a guerrilla tactic would probably have been far more effective. Nearly everybody died. The only survivors were the deserters, and not surprisingly Alcibiades was among them. Many blame Alcibiades for his arrogance, but Nicias was just as much at fault. He didn't take into account the personality of the man he was lying to, nor did he predict how his lie would be received, both of which were more important factors than the lie itself. Had Nicias conquered Sicily, his bluff would likely have been forgotten or gone undetected, but his lie was sloppy, and despite his good intentions it makes him responsible for thousands of needless deaths." Gupta pauses to look at all of our faces before his eyes fall on someone. "Felix, come up to the front, please."

Felix stands and makes his way to the end of the table.

"I would like you to tell the class two truths and a lie. Keep them short. I don't want you making it easy on them by giving too many details. And try your best to conceal your lie."

Felix takes a deep breath. "I've broken seven bones, eight if I count my nose twice. I would prefer to be hot rather than to be cold. And I can hold my breath underwater for nine minutes and thirteen seconds." I study him for any of the lying tells I've been reading about. But he doesn't make any hand movements or weird facial expressions that I can detect, and his voice sounds steady and normal to me.

"Now, which was the lie?" Gupta asks. "Jaya?"

Jaya's eyes are narrowed, like she's concentrating too hard. "The first one?"

"I know you're not confident in your answer by the way your pitch raised at the end of your sentence. You sounded like you were asking a question instead of giving an answer," Gupta says, and I feel some relief that Felix's lie wasn't so easy to detect that everyone but me spotted it.

"Does anyone disagree with Jaya's assessment?" Gupta continues.

The room falls silent for a beat.

Just when I think no one is going to answer, Ash says, "The lie was his second statement."

Gupta smiles. "Explain, please, Ashai."

"His nose had a tiny twitch, as though it were itchy. And

when you lie, blood flows toward your nose, away from your cheeks. People touch their noses more often when they're lying than when they're not," Ash says. "And his right shoulder ever so slightly lifted. One-sided shrugs are common nervous tells."

It's clear that Ash is in his element here.

"Correct," Gupta says. "And additionally, there was a linguistic cue, which we'll be studying more closely over the next couple of months. He said 'I would prefer' as opposed to 'I prefer.' The use of *would* is considered hypothetical, as opposed to a statement of truth. You may sit down, Felix. Jaya, you're on deck."

She stands and makes her way to the front of the room. "I accidentally burned my finger on a candle two weeks ago and the burn resembled a star. I can't stand the smell of blood. I did not finish my breakfast this morning."

"Which was the lie, Brendan?" Gupta asks.

"The third one," he says, and Gupta nods for him to go on. "She overemphasized her last statement, making it louder than the other two, pushing us to believe it."

I actually did notice that. This class is kinda fun.

"Good. Anyone see anything else?" Gupta asks.

"She also briefly rubbed her fingers together when she finished," Ash says, "a soothing motion to make herself feel better about the lie. And she spoke faster during her last statement than the others, like she was trying to rush through it."

Holy crap, Ash is good at this. An image of him flirting with me last night flashes into my thoughts and I groan in my head. This is so like me, to be attracted to the most complicated person in the room—the one I promised myself I wouldn't like and who I'm positive will only make my life more problematic. If

Emily were here, she'd be rolling her eyes hard right now, telling me to stop being such a wimp and just go for it. And I would probably tell her that everything was fine and that I didn't care that much, but we would both know I didn't mean it.

Gupta gives Ash a look of confirmation. "There was also a linguistic cue in Jaya's lie. Did anyone detect it? In her second, truthful statement, she used a contraction, the way most of us do in casual speech. But in her third, untruthful statement, she said 'did not' when she might have said 'didn't,' reinforcing the overemphasized nature of her lie, which Brendan spotted. Okay, Brendan, you're up."

Brendan stands. He doesn't wait for Gupta to say go, which isn't surprising.

He rolls his shoulders back and takes a breath. "I like November. But since I was a child, October's been my favorite month. And I find the long nights in December peaceful."

Oh, come on. And he doesn't even glance at me. So sneaky.

"Anyone?" Gupta asks.

"The first one," Felix says without missing a beat. "He said he 'likes' November but revealed a microexpression of disgust, pulling just one corner of his mouth back, making his words and his emotion incongruent."

Disgust, huh? Brendan shoots me a smile that makes the hair on the back of my neck stand up.

"I'm disappointed in you, Brendan. You're usually better than letting a microexpression trip you up," Gupta says. "This pitiful display makes me nostalgic for the students of twenty-five years ago. Do you know that one girl went an entire year without anyone being able to detect her lies?"

Brendan rolls his eyes, like "Here we go again with the bragging about past students" thing.

However, it's interesting to me that this is the second time someone's specifically pointed out a record set twenty-five years ago. I can't help but wonder if this was the same girl Blackwood claimed won all those midnight challenges.

"If confronted with the average person, you all will dance circles around them. But what about when you're in a situation with another Strategia? At the rate you're going, you might as well just tell one another the truth and save yourselves the hassle." Gupta sighs. "Ashai, please come up here and make me feel better about my purpose as a teacher."

Ash makes his way to the front of the class, appearing perfectly confident. His eyes sweep across the room and he smiles. "I like being surprised, even when the consequence is me being outmaneuvered."

Hmmm. I would guess that he does like surprises, but nothing about Ash makes me think he likes to be outmaneuvered.

"I'm better at cards than Layla is."

Something about his voice reminds me of when he's trying to charm me. But I can't imagine that Layla would be better at cards, considering his ability to read tells. Although I wouldn't put it past Ash to lie about the one thing we're all sure is true.

"And I'm not easily *eliminated* from a fight."

I cough from surprise at hearing the word that was written in blood on my floor this morning. *What are you doing, Ash?* He scans the room again, and I can't tell if he's trying to read people or if he's sending a message to whoever did it. Probably both.

Gupta smiles and his eyes crinkle. "Finally. Now, there is

248

a well-delivered lie. Did anyone see or hear anything in there that would indicate which of Ashai's statements was the deceit?"

The room is silent.

"Anyone?" Gupta says, and looks around the table of students. I look at them, too, trying to pick out a sign that might indicate the culprit. But I see only relaxed expressions and neutral postures.

No one answers Gupta. They must hate to be wrong so much that they won't even guess. "Well, then you stumped them, Ash. Nicely done. Moving—"

"It was the second one," I say, and everyone turns toward me.

Ash gives me a curious look.

Screw it. Better to jump in when there are no clear indications of a lie than when there are and I can't see them. Plus, I have a fifty percent shot, since Ash would never have made the last statement or overemphasized the word *eliminated* if it weren't true.

Gupta looks at me with newfound interest. "Go on."

"Ash uses charm as a tool. And although he was smiling through all of the statements, the second one felt more like he was luring us in, telling us something so obvious that it had to be true."

The look Gupta's giving me tells me he knows something I don't. "Well, now, feeling is more of an emotional instinct than identifying a tell," Gupta says, and turns to Ash. "But let's just see here. Is she correct, Ashai?"

Ash nods, and he looks at me with respect. I guess he really does like surprises.

Gupta claps his hands together. "Deception is about

practice, about making it part of your nature. If you have to use all your energy to focus on it, you'll miss everything else. And as we've just seen, being able to identify deception goes beyond being able to read signs; it goes to an analysis of the person. A good deceiver will make you see a lie where there isn't one and truth when it doesn't exist, which is what we saw displayed here. November used an analysis of Ash's personality to determine that the most truthful-sounding statement *was* the lie." Gupta nods to himself like he's remembering something. "That is all for today."

Everyone pushes their chairs back, but they don't scrape them against the floor. They calmly put on their cloaks and exit quietly, with no commotion. I'm not sure I'll ever get used to a pack of teens being so graceful.

I fall into step with Ash and we head down the stairs to the main foyer. "Want to take a walk through the garden on our way to lunch?" I ask. "I've been inside all morning and I'm starting to feel claustrophobic."

"Sure, November, I'd be happy to go on a date with you."

I laugh. I don't know how Layla puts up with a brother like him. Although I've often wondered how Emily deals with a friend like me. "You think you're so clever," I say playfully, "but as it turns out, I don't like you at all, not even a little bit."

He holds the door open for me and we step out onto the grass. "Apparently I'm not clever. The girl with the least deception training is the first one to spot my lie."

I smile. "Is that your way of telling me that you find me impressive?"

"You could say that," he says as we walk through the vine courtyard. "It's just a shame that you don't like me at all. I guess that's something I'll have to deal with." His amusement is infectious, and the way he glances at me makes my heart pound a little harder.

I clear my throat. "Does Gupta usually reminisce about old students that way?"

"You caught that, huh? Yes. He does it all the time. And he's not the only one. About twenty-five years ago there was a group of students who were considered particularly gifted. You'll sometimes hear teachers refer to them as the best this school ever had. There's a rumor that Blackwood was part of that group." Ash takes quick inventory of the space as we enter the garden lounge.

The afternoon light dapples the grass, and the bright purple berries pop against the canopy of green. The only other people here are two girls, chatting in one of the far corners.

"Blackwood? I'm not sure if that's good news or bad news," I say.

"She's apparently the youngest headmaster this school has ever had. Some say she took the position because of the escalating tensions between the Bears and the Lions, preferring a life of solitude." He keeps his voice low as we walk around the flower beds filled with blue, white, and purple blossoms. "You do know she's a Bear, right?"

My eyes widen. "But I thought Bears were mostly Italian? She speaks with a perfect British accent and her last name is British—I just never . . . Although now that I've said that out loud, I realize how ridiculous an assumption that is."

Ash smirks. "The Bear Family originated among the ancient Romans. But you know, throw in a few land campaigns, some exploration, and several hundred years, and you'll find that the

Bear Family has far greater reach than just Italy. And besides, every headmaster here for the past thousand years has been called Blackwood. It's just a title."

I let this sink in for a minute. "Why exactly do the Bears and the Lions hate each other?" I ask.

Ash starts walking toward the door at the other side of the building. "Come with me. I'll show you something."

I pick up my pace.

As we move through the arched doorway into the foyer with the knight statue and all the shields, my step falters. The guard with the X-shaped scar is on duty. He looks right at me, and I'm reminded of the first day Layla brought me through here, when I kept getting the feeling that he was assessing me. I haven't seen him since he caught me out of my room on the night Stefano was murdered, and his gaze has changed. He seems to be watching me more directly, and it makes me want to run.

I break eye contact with the guard and follow Ash down the hall and into the library.

The stained-glass windows are mostly covered with heavy curtains, and in the absence of natural light there are torches and large candelabras that illuminate the high-ceilinged room.

Ash leads me to the far right, to a wall of mounted scrolls, one of which is pinned open. As I study the scroll, I realize that it lists most of our classes and has a Family name next to each one. The first column reads:

Deception	Bear
Historical Analysis	Bear
Knives	Lion
Poisons	Bear

Strategic Sparring	Bear
Tree Climbing	Lion
Fencing	Lion
Psychological Warfare	Lion
Languages & Accents	Jackal

"What is this? Some kind of class ranking?" I ask in a whisper, even though I don't see a single other person in the library.

"You could say that," he says. "Since Academy Absconditi was started, they've kept track of the best students in each discipline. It's an enormous victory when one Family bests a record that's been held by another Family for years. Sometimes generations."

"How can the school possibly keep track of students from the past thousand years and actually rank them?" I ask.

"The core challenges haven't changed. We do things exactly the way our Families have always done them," he says. "And there are records set within each class. The one Professor Gupta mentioned today about someone eluding lie detection for an entire year was established by a Bear."

I look back to the wall. "It looks like a lot of titles were won by Bears."

Ash, too, is studying the scroll, but shifts his gaze to me. "For thousands of years there was a balance of power among the Families—each had its own specialties, skills, and styles. There were alliances and rivalries, but there was also a general respect for Strategia order and the Council of Families. However, in the last couple of hundred years, one Family has gradually risen above the rest—the Lions."

That makes sense with what Layla said about everyone

catering to Brendan and the Lions. "Has that power shift changed things within Strategia?"

Ash nods like he's often considered this same question. "In the beginning it simply meant that the Lions had deep pockets, vast numbers, and large resources. But they often sought the advice of the Council of Families in using those tools. Other Families would call on them for assistance, and there were a great deal of mutually beneficial alliances. So the power imbalance was present, but the abuse of that power was not."

"And that's changed?" I say, and for some reason, even though Ash hasn't mentioned anything bad yet, this story makes me nervous, like watching someone slowly lose their grip while hanging from the side of a cliff.

"Jag," Ash says flatly, and I give him a questioning look. "He's the current leader of the Lions." He smiles and shakes his head. "I know you told me you weren't raised the way I was, but I still find it incredible that you don't know certain things. Certain people."

"How do you think I feel?" I say, and he looks at me like I make a fair point. "So Jag . . . what was different about him?"

"Weeell," Ash says, dragging the word out. "Forty years ago he lost both his parents unexpectedly. He was only nineteen when he ascended to a leadership role, which is unusual in the Strategia world. Typically, a new leader would have been chosen by the Family and ratified by the Council of Families. But Jag's direct line had been ruling for more than a century, and for reasons that are still debated today, and probably partially due to the existing power imbalance, the Council of Families voted to let him take the seat, with the understanding that he would be aided by seasoned advisors."

"Like old European courts," I say, having very little reference for these things beyond what I've seen in the movies.

"Much like that," Ash says. "For some time it was assumed that Jag would honor the guidance from the Council, that Family dynamics might shift back to their previous amiable state. But the opposite happened. Jag rejected the Council, and he and his immediate family changed the Lions' culture even more dramatically. With each passing decade, the Lions infringed more aggressively on other Families' territories until the abuse of power was so great that many Families started aligning themselves *with* the Lions for protection. The Bears were among the few that refused. They resisted the Lions every step of the way, and the two Families became the worst of enemies."

"Wait, so why didn't the Council of Families or whoever replace Jag once they realized things had taken a turn?" I ask.

"This is where it gets complicated," Ash says, and I can almost hear the years of debate he's witnessed over this exact question. "As you pointed out, Strategia rule is similar to that of old European royal courts—a given lineage stays in power until they can no longer sustain their rule. Sometimes it's because they had no offspring and the line died out, or because they were killed at a young age, or simply because they weren't trained here and failed to fulfill the duties required."

I pull back and study him. "Are you telling me that attending school here is *required* for leading your Family?"

Ash looks thoughtful. "If you can't excel at the Academy, you're seen as unfit. Even after you're admitted here, you're not done proving yourself. It's just the opposite. If your younger sister bests you in everything while here, the rule will likely go to her. We may have our differences, but the one thing all future leaders understand is the pressure of responsibility."

"That puts Brendan, Charles, and Nyx in a new light," I say, half to him and half to myself. "But sorry I interrupted. You were saying . . ."

"Even though Family leaders can be replaced, that *does not* happen in the middle of someone's rule unless the current leader agrees to step down, which, as you can imagine, Jag did not," Ash says.

"Okay, but if things are as bad as you say, how come no one has taken the rule away from him by force?" I ask.

Ash shakes his head. "Under no circumstances do Strategia assassinate the leaders of other Families. With our given skill sets, can you imagine the chaos that would ensue if an all-out war happened between Families?" There is so much weight in Ash's voice that I can almost feel how personal this all is to him.

Currently, all I know are these young Academy Strategia. I can't even imagine what it might be like with entire Families of well-trained strategists and assassins trying to kill one another.

I exhale. "So what about now? What's being done about the Lions?"

His expression almost looks sad. "There's little we can do. Over the years, Jag has manipulated his advisors, his children, and his grandchildren, so this isn't just about deposing him; it's about figuring out how to break his hold over an entire Family. And the Lions are vicious; they rule with terror, killing off members of other Families that move against them. Those who are willing to stand up to them are dwindling."

"Is that why there have been so many deaths at this school?" I pause, trying to take it all in. "Are the Bears still fighting them?"

He nods, and I feel a strange surge of pride. If I'm going to be a Strategia, at least let me be from a Family that stands for something good.

Ash looks up at the scroll. "Even with the power imbalance, this list has always been populated by names from all the Families . . . except for when that gifted group I told you about swept nearly all the titles twenty-five years ago."

"Let me guess, they were all Lions?"

He shakes his head. "It was *one* Lion and *one* Bear that bested the whole class. They were both the firstborn of the leaders of their Families, and against all odds, they had formed an alliance. At the time, it was thought they might actually change things between the two warring Families and for Strategia as a whole. But a year after they left the school, they were both found dead."

"Found dead or murdered?"

"Same thing," he says.

"Um, not really." I pause. "But if there was one Lion open to changing things, there have to be others. Right?"

Ash lightly laughs. "Do you ever stop being so positive?"

"You know, I've never understood why people accuse me of being too positive. I think they're just missing possibilities," I say.

Ash's eyes smile. "We should be heading to the dining hall." He turns.

"Ash?" I say, and he stops. "Thanks for explaining."

"Don't thank me yet," he says. "If we figure out your Family secrets, dodge the attacks that will definitely be coming, *and* manage to stay alive . . . then you can thank me."

Twenty-Five

AS I WAIT for the fencing teacher to start our lesson, I roll up my sleeves and look around the open courtyard nervously. The last time I had a class without Layla or Ash, Matteo almost dropped me out of a tree. I can't help but wonder what's in store for me next.

Nyx is here and her eyes are puffy, like she cried all night. She hasn't looked in my direction yet, but I can tell she's tracking my movements—which I think is worse. In my short time here, I've noticed that when people won't look at you directly, they are paying even more attention. Felix and Ines are also subtly watching me.

"Today, we will have the honor of welcoming Dr. Conner as our guest," Professor Odd says, taking his place in front of the class. I would think it was a funny name except I happened to recall that *odd* is also Norwegian for "the point of a sword." True to his name, Odd is a tall, thin man with a long face who overenunciates everything he says in a theatrical way. "So let's be *quick* about getting our fencing gear. I would like you all to give Dr. Conner your *very best* performances."

Professor Odd claps his hands together and we form two lines behind him. This time, I make sure to take one of the last spots and not let anyone be where I can't see them. Unfortunately, Nyx is in the line next to me. She practically radiates anger, and I force myself not to look at her. Judging by how she reacted yesterday to Charles's death, if I even step wrong she might break my nose.

We follow Professor Odd through the garden courtyard and into the foyer with the shields, where we find Dr. Conner. Every minute standing next to Nyx makes me more tense.

"Ah, Dr. Conner. We'll just be a moment getting our gear," Odd says, and makes a small bow.

Conner smiles. "No rush, Professor Odd. In fact, I'll join you. It's been a long time since I've been in the weapons room."

"As you like," Odd says, and we make our way down the hall. A guard unlocks a door and we file into a high-ceilinged, windowless room chock-full of armor, swords, and shields. Locked glass cases display every type of knife imaginable, plus arrows and an assortment of compound and recurve bows. It feels like I stepped back in time to a medieval battle room. What is noticeably missing, however, are those weird Kevlar protective fencing uniforms you always see people with on TV—not that I really expected any safety gear.

Mounted on the wall are dozens of swords, and I watch as each person in line approaches the wall and selects one, which they then present to either Odd or Conner for inspection. My unease takes the joy out of choosing a sword, and I wind up just grabbing the one nearest me and following suit. I breathe a little easier when I notice that the double-edged blades appear dulled for practice. I wait behind Felix for Conner to inspect mine.

I run my finger down the blade as I walk out of the room. I would have died for a sword this nice in Pembrook, but Dad wouldn't let me have anything but those wooden practice ones. Emily used to joke that I saw *The Princess Bride* and decided to make it a lifestyle choice by learning all bladed weapons and constantly trying to re-create some dramatic adventure.

We all walk silently back to the courtyard. I notice that Nyx's hand periodically clenches around her sword, and Felix and Ines seem on edge. Between the dark cloud of general anxiety created by Charles's death yesterday and Conner looming over us, it's not really a surprise, though. I'm just grateful Brendan isn't here. My money is still on him for the "You will be eliminated" message.

"We'll start today with some freestyle sparring to get your blood moving, and then we'll begin our lesson," Professor Odd says, and clasps his hands together. "Dr. Conner, would you like to choose the pairings? And remember, everyone, no boxing or martial arts, *just* swords."

"How thoughtful, Professor Odd," Conner says, and looks us over with a smile. "How about . . . Felix with Kiku. Ines with . . . Jaya. November with"—he scans the group—"Nyx."

My stomach drops. He goes on pairing students, but I don't listen.

Professor Odd tells us to spread out and then promptly turns to Conner. The two men start chatting, and I reluctantly follow Nyx to the far end of the open courtyard.

She stops close to the dense wall of trees that separates us from the vine courtyard and turns to face me. Her curly hair is pulled back in a messy ponytail and her eyes are just as wild as mine would be if I had lost someone I cared about. As much as I don't like her, I also can't imagine how awful it must have been for her to see Charles die like that. I could barely handle it, and he was trying to kill me.

"Look, I know you must—" I begin, but she swings at my left side with her sword. I parry and our blades ring. "Whoa, I wasn't even in position yet."

She immediately goes for my right side. I deflect again. She's hitting me with surprising force, and I remember what Ash said about her taking down people much bigger than her.

She makes eye contact with me, and the hair on my arms stands up.

Nyx swings at my knees. I jump over her blade and give her a good whack on the shoulder.

Her eyes practically smoke with fury. "This is your fault," she spits at me. "All of this is because of you."

"Are you kidding? Charles tried to kill *me,* not the other way around," I say in a low voice, but it only seems to make her angrier.

She lunges forward, slicing her sword in one direction and then the next. I parry, our swords hitting each other in a constant stream of clangs.

"This is supposed to be—" I start.

Nyx fakes right and swings left. Again I deflect her, but I'm nervous. She's really good and she's coming at me like we're dueling to the death, not warming up. With the force she's using, if she does land a hit, I'll be lucky if she doesn't break one of my bones or give me a concussion.

"—*practice,* Nyx. You're gonna wear us both out before we

ever get to our lesson." I glance momentarily at Professor Odd and Conner, but they're laughing together and not paying any attention to how aggressive she's being.

Looking away was a mistake, because Nyx sidesteps and slices at my head. I just manage to block and step, but now my back is to the tree wall.

"Wear us out?" She laughs, but the sound is anything but happy. It almost verges on a sob. "Screw you, November. You and your family should have died a long time ago. Now we're all suffering for that mistake."

For a second I think I misheard her. Is she talking about my Bear Family or my immediate family?

She runs at me and angles her sword at my ribs. I block, but her momentum forces me to backstep again. Nyx slashes high at my head and I duck. Her sword hits the tree trunk behind me and I ready myself for another blow, but her blade is lodged in the trunk. She screams in frustration, and Professor Odd and Conner turn in our direction.

My heart starts to pound so hard that it blots out all the noise in the courtyard. *A dull blade wouldn't do that.*

Panic shoots through me and I move quickly away from the trees as she yanks her blade out of the wood. Sure enough, her sword is razor-sharp. I've been so busy dodging her blows that I didn't notice.

"Nyx!" Odd yells from across the courtyard, and her name is suddenly like a bell in my mind. *Sarete ridotti* could also mean "You will be nixed." My Italian is rusty or I would have considered it earlier—a clever play on words.

Nyx rushes at me, slashing her blade three times, fast and

hard. I block, but only barely. She grunts in frustration and aims at my face. I move to deflect, but she doesn't follow through. Instead, she throws a kick at my legs and I land hard on my back. In an instant she's standing over me.

She lifts her sword over her head and jabs it at my heart with both of her hands. I roll, but not fast enough, and the blade catches the edge of my upper arm. I swing my sword at her, forcing her back so I can scramble to my feet.

I can hear Odd and Conner screaming at her, but she doesn't pause.

Nyx slashes at me before I regain my balance. I get my sword up, but at an awkward angle, and she hits it so hard that it flies right out of my grip. For a split second we make eye contact and the corner of her mouth twitches upward. One swing and I'm dead.

I turn and run for the trees. The trunks are mostly smooth bark and the branches don't begin until a good twenty feet up. But there are some nubs where the lower branches have been cut off.

Nyx's boots pound the grass behind me and I jump for one of the sawn-off branches, only just pulling up my legs as her blade hits the wood. I manage to climb a few more feet and she screams, pacing at the bottom of the tree. But I can't go any higher. The next handhold is too far to reach, and my arm and leg muscles are already straining from the awkward position I'm in. My cut upper arm throbs and I know I only have about a minute before I lose my grip.

Nyx wraps her fist around her sword hilt, and I can see she's switched tactics. She's going to throw it like a spear. *Shit*. She narrows her eyes as she calculates. But just as she pulls back her arm, Professor Odd grabs her wrist. She turns around, swinging.

Conner pulls a needle out of his blazer pocket and jabs her in the arm. She stumbles two steps, drops her sword, and falls into the grass.

"Get two guards and tell them they're to take her to the dungeon," Conner says, and Odd takes off at a jog.

I let go of the tree and drop into the grass. For a couple of horrible seconds everyone is completely still. And it occurs to me—none of the other students tried to help me.

Conner dabs his forehead with a handkerchief and frowns. "Go to the infirmary, November."

I look down at my arm. Blood is dripping off my knuckles and into the grass.

Twenty-Six

LAYLA AND I walk down our empty dorm hallway, carrying books. There's only a single wall torch to light our way and it's burning low, casting long sections of the hall into dark shadow. My arm throbs from the stitches the nurse gave me, and I've learned that this place doesn't believe in painkillers. I glance over my shoulder, but everything is silent and still.

I unlatch our door and Layla and I put our books down—some on European history for me, which Layla said would give me the basis of understanding for what she needs to teach me, and more on criminology for her. She also threw in some regular books about poisons and swords just in case Pippa is taking note of our reading.

I'm not sure why Layla's still obsessively researching Stefano's murder after we found out Charles was the culprit and Ash and I were cleared, but she seems to be fixated on the details. Maybe she just wants to understand what happened to her friend? I would ask Ash if this is normal behavior for her, but I haven't seen him all evening.

We check the room to make sure no one is hiding anywhere, and Layla sits on the couch in front of the fireplace.

"If Brendan took the time to break in and write that message on your floor, why didn't he just kill you when he had the chance?" she asks.

I sit down next to her. "I don't know." I reflexively touch the bandage on my arm. "Maybe Nyx wanted to be the one to do it, to cut me down publicly?"

Layla chews on her lip. "Yeah, but she didn't succeed. And from what I heard, you held your own, which, against Nyx, is saying a lot. I think she saw an opportunity and took it, simple as that. Because why would she chance fighting you in the open if she could just sneak in and slit your throat?"

I shudder. "No knife?"

"That's possible," she says. "But how did she manage to come by a sharpened sword? The sparring blades are kept dull for a reason. Something here doesn't add up." She stares at the crackling fire.

"Conner said they were taking her to the dungeon," I say. "Are they going to enforce the eye-for-an-eye rule? And how would that even work? Because technically she cut my arm, but obviously she was trying to kill me."

Layla turns toward me. "I'm not exactly sure. I've never seen a situation play out this way before. They'll do something. The dungeon is miserable, from what I've heard, but I'm sure you'll get a chance to retaliate as well."

I frown, wishing all this retaliation business would just stop. "What about Brendan? Whether he was the one who broke in or not, I'm assuming he's got to be pissed now that one of his friends is dead and the other is in the dungeon."

Layla's fist clenches for just a moment. "Oh, this definitely isn't over. I'm not trying to scare you, but if the Lions want you dead, they're not going to stop until you are."

Knock. Knock. Knock.

Before I even turn around, Layla is off the couch.

"We're coming," she says as she lifts the latch.

The guard on the other side of the door looks around, and once she sees me, she turns and goes to the next room to knock.

Layla hands me my cloak and I slip it on.

We follow the other girls down the hallway and into the foyer where Nyx and I competed in the dark. It's hard to believe that was only a week ago; I feel like a year's worth of chaos has ensued since then. Blackwood stands by the wall, and the twenty-four of us girls assemble on the ground in front of her and form a U.

"We have some new challenges for you tonight," Blackwood says, and her tone makes it sound like a carefully concealed warning. "You will find these challenges different from any you have been presented with thus far. And there will be serious consequences for not completing them properly."

She looks behind her at the guards, who step aside to let six faculty members pass, including Liu, Gupta, and Conner. Blackwood nods at them and they begin to move around the U like we're playing a creepy game of Duck Duck Goose, each one selecting a handful of students.

Conner taps the girl on my left and Gupta taps the girl next to Layla. The girls get up and walk off in small clusters, following the faculty members who selected them, until only Layla, Aarya, Ines, and I are left.

"Follow me," Blackwood says with no warmth. I want to

protest, but I don't dare show Aarya that I'm nervous about whatever is about to happen.

Blackwood leads us two doorways down to the teachers' lounge I was kept in when I first arrived. The fireplace isn't lit like it was then, and the only source of light is a single torch by the arched doorway.

Four large guards follow our group into the room, and the X guard is one of them, which only escalates my unease. Layla and I glance at each other, and I can tell by the look in her eyes that she's worried, too. I want to ask her how extreme these challenges get, but no one is talking right now—not even Aarya.

I immediately take in the details of the room. There are two big couches near the fireplace, with a wide, sturdy coffee table between them. Two sets of armchairs with footstools separated by small end tables. A sideboard with a pitcher of water, clean glasses, and a bowl of apples. A round table with four chairs. Tapestries on the walls, and a couple of empty torch holders. A large fireplace with decorative stone trimming. A shelf full of books. A wrought-iron candelabra hanging from the ceiling. And no windows.

"Your first challenge is simple," Blackwood says, standing directly in front of the door with two guards on either side of her. "There are six objects hidden in this room. Find them and it will make completing the second challenge easier. Don't find them and you will wish you had—some of you more than others. I will be the one to decide when your time is up."

That doesn't sound remotely comforting and pretty much tells us nothing except that Blackwood makes the rules and unless we move quickly we'll regret it.

"Begin," Blackwood says, and everyone springs into action.

Ines goes to the bookshelf and methodically starts taking down every book. Aarya moves to the sideboard to inspect the apples. Layla drags the coffee table to the center of the room. She grabs a chair from the round table and places it on top, climbing up to the candelabra.

I turn in a circle. The furniture is the obvious go-to and most likely contains more than half of the objects. And I have no doubt those three will find whatever is there. But there has to be at least one object that isn't hidden in the furniture. I run my eyes over the walls, looking for anything that could be shifted or manipulated. I yank on the empty wrought-iron torch holders, but they are firmly attached. I lift the tapestry, but there's nothing behind it.

I stop at the fireplace. The stones are large and seemingly mortared in place. There are no logs in the fireplace, but there is some leftover ash. I sift through it with my fingers.

"Found one," Aarya says with a gloating tone. She pulls a hairpin out of the end of an apple and places it on the marble top of the sideboard.

A hairpin? They hid things that small? I smack my hands together and a cloud of soot billows out. I run my fingers along the brick-sized decorative stones that make up the mantel, looking for any crack or groove that shouldn't be there. My sooty fingers leave a trail, particularly in the tiny imperfections. Well, now, there's an idea. I scoop up the ash and smear it on all of the small stones by the fistful, painting the whole mantel with dark gray.

"Metal nail file," Layla says, and we all briefly turn to see her pulling it from the end of an unlit candle in the candelabra.

Aarya is removing the drawers from the sideboard and inspecting them for false backs and bottoms.

I look around me for a piece of spare fabric, but there's nothing but the heavy tapestry. Screw it. I grab the end of my cloak and start wiping the excess soot off the stones in a circular motion.

"Two paper clips," Ines says, pulling them from the loose spine of an old book.

Paper clips, a metal nail file, and a hairpin—there's definitely a theme here and I'm pretty sure it has something to do with locks. Except that the door in this room, like all the doors I've seen, closes with a latch.

I rub at the stones faster, and a soot line forms around a fist-sized stone in the upper left corner of the mantel. I drop my cloak and grip the rock with my fingertips, wiggling it back and forth. Slowly it comes out in my hand, and I catch Ines watching me from where she's checking the seams of a couch.

I peer into the small stone cubby and glimpse a dark metal object pushed all the way to the back. "Got one," I say, and pull medieval-looking pliers from the hole, placing them on the mantel.

Layla slides out an inch from under the coffee table, where she's inspecting the wood.

"Time's up," Blackwood says.

And just like that, the torch goes out, smothering the room in complete blackness.

"Layla?" I say.

"I'm—" she starts, but gets cut off by what sounds like a blow to the stomach. Wood scrapes against wood, and there is a squeak I can only guess belongs to moving metal.

I take a fast couple of steps toward Layla's voice, my arms out in front of me, and smack into the coffee table with my shins, pitching forward.

"Get the hell—" Aarya starts, and her voice is muffled.

Layla coughs and wheezes, only instead of coming from the floor, the sound seems to be coming from above my head.

There are a few rough thuds of what I can only imagine are people hitting each other, and I cringe, wondering if I'll be next. Something crashes to my right, and books topple to the floor from one of the bookshelves.

I recover my balance and climb onto the coffee table, moving toward the sound of Layla's labored breathing. My heart beats a mile a minute.

There is the whine of an old hinge as the door briefly opens and slams shut. A latch slides into place from the outside, and then the room falls into complete silence besides Layla's wheezing.

"Layla, where are you?" I say, waving my hands in front of me.

"Light. We need light, November," Layla manages between breaths.

I hear a couple more books fall. *"Mierda,"* Ines breathes, and I'm pretty sure it's the first word I've ever heard her say.

For a split second I stand there with my heart racing, lost in the darkness. There are no matches. There aren't even coals to work with. And I'm pretty sure whoever left the room took the torch with them, because I can't see any embers glowing from where the torch holder should be.

Ines gasps. "Aarya?"

I can hear the fear in her voice, and it brings my awareness into sharp focus. "Paper," I say with urgency, "the older and drier the better. Bring it over to the fireplace, Ines."

If I'm not wrong, some of the stones making up the mantel are actually flint, including the one that was loose. And there's a chance those old pliers are made of steel. I step down from the table and run back to the fireplace faster than is cautious, my hands in front of me.

I collide with the stone and quickly feel around the mantel. "Got you."

The sound of paper crumpling next to me makes my heart skip a beat.

"Here, find my hand," I say, reaching out, and Ines does.

I take the crumpled paper, secure it on top of the stone with my thumb, and hit the edge of the stone hard with the old pliers. A few sparks fly. *Yes!*

"If you could—" I start, but Ines is already blowing on the paper.

I hit the stone a few more times, and by my fourth go one of the sparks catches, creating a tiny burning hole in the paper.

"C'mon, c'mon," I coax it impatiently while Ines continues to blow gently on the flame. Little by little the burning circle widens until at last we're rewarded by an actual flame. Ines has rolled up another paper and tips it against the flame, giving us a small but definite torch, and my heart soars. It's not much light, no brighter than a birthday candle, but hopefully enough to get the general outline of things. As I squint through the gloom, Ines puts the knocked-over chair back on the table and climbs onto it.

"What in the . . . ," I say in horror. Layla's legs are wrapped around the candelabra branches in an awkward position and there's something tied around her wrists, preventing her from using her hands to hold on to anything.

Ines doesn't say a word to Layla, and to my shock she doesn't try to help her. Instead, she just grabs two candles and jumps down to the floor, returning to me and lighting the candles with the paper. She gives me one and the room gets instantly brighter. Blackwood and the guards are definitely gone, not that I thought any differently.

I quickly drip some wax onto the mantel and stick the bottom of the candle in it to free up my hands. "Hang on, I'm gonna get you down," I say to Layla.

"It's a zip tie," Layla says, having regained most of her breath. But I can tell she's struggling. "It's wrapped around the iron. If I take any weight off my legs, it's going to cut into my skin more than it already has. And it's so tight that if we use fire to try to melt it, I'm going to get seriously burned."

"Layla, the file. Where did you put it?" I say. But before I finish my sentence, I spot the piece of metal on the floor next to the table. I reach for it, but Ines is quicker. Only instead of handing it to me, she walks away.

"Hey, where the hell are you go—" I snap, but abruptly stop.

I follow her line of sight to Aarya, who's lying on the ground. There's a metal and leather contraption covering her mouth and nose that's secured by five metal chains reaching behind her head.

"Holy shit. Can she breathe?" I ask.

Aarya's eyes are closed.

Ines places a hand on Aarya's chest and shakes her head in a way that lets me know that whatever she's observing isn't good.

Blackwood said there'd be serious consequences, but this is extreme. Life-and-death extreme.

I look between Aarya and Layla. If Aarya can't breathe and I don't help Ines, I could be partially responsible for suffocating her. But I have no love for Aarya, and if I let Layla get sliced up because of her, I won't forgive myself. However, fighting Ines for the file will only ensure that everyone loses.

"Layla, how long can you hold on in that position?" I ask.

"Maybe two minutes?" she says, and I can hear the strain in her voice.

"Yell out when you're reaching your limit," I say, and crouch down next to Ines and Aarya.

For a split second, Ines looks up at me, surprised.

"Tell me what to do," I say as she files the last inch of a partially straightened paper clip.

"Unravel the second paper clip and fold it exactly in half," she says, and I find myself marveling at the sound of her voice, which is surprisingly soothing and self-assured for someone who so rarely uses it. "Bend the last half inch in a ninety-degree angle to form an L shape."

I start working while she explains.

She holds up her own paper clip. "See how I filed this to be flat instead of round? Do the same with the bent part of yours."

Ines hands me the file and uses the pliers to bend the flattened end of hers first one way, then the other, creating three little waves in the straight line.

I file away at my paper-clip L for all I'm worth, my fingers clumsy and trembling with nerves. "You okay, Layla?" I call.

"Yeah," she says, but the strain in her voice has deepened.

Ines turns Aarya over. There's a padlock on the back of

her head, holding the chains together like a medieval torture device.

Ines grabs the lock. I give her the L paper clip I filed and she shoves it into the bottom of the keyhole, sliding the wavy end of hers in on top of it. I take the file and run for Layla, climbing the chair so fast that it wobbles.

Whoever put her up here was taller than me, and I can barely reach her wrists. I squeeze the file between her skin and the plastic and saw at it as fast as I can. The plastic is thick and resistant and I can see the desperation on Layla's face.

"November?" Layla says. "I can't—"

A chair hits the table, and within a second, Ines is on it. She positions her shoulder under Layla's butt and supports her.

Three more seconds of filing and the plastic snaps. Layla grabs the candelabra, and Ines and I move out of the way so she can jump down onto the table.

Layla rubs her wrists, which have cuts on them, but nothing like what she would have had if she'd fallen. "I have no idea how they got me up there so fast. I've never fought a guard before. They're—"

"As agile as giant ballerinas," Aarya says. She's sitting up and rubbing her head. "I feel like I got clobbered by an ogre."

I grab the candle off the mantel and climb back up to the candelabra to light the others.

"You're pretty banged up, too, Ines," Aarya says, and in the brighter light I can see that Ines has two bruises forming, one on her hand where she potentially landed a punch and one on her cheek surrounding a scrape that I can only guess is from colliding with the bookshelf in the dark. "In fact, the only person here who doesn't look like they fought is November. How is it you were magically spared in this challenge? And wasn't Dr. Conner also there to save you right before Nyx tried to skewer you? Sounds like a big fat conspiracy to me. Maybe you're not a Bear at all, but a Lion sent to screw with everyone."

I open my mouth to respond, but the door creaks and we all turn toward it.

Blackwood stands in the doorway. "I see you girls managed to get yourselves in order," she says flatly, like she left us drinking tea and eating cookies. "You may all return to your rooms now. These gentlemen will escort you back." She gestures to two of the four guards who attacked us, one of whom is the X guard.

"*Gentle*men, that's one way to describe them," Aarya says in an Italian accent that drips sarcasm.

Blackwood gives her a hard look. "Perhaps you would prefer to continue with the challenges?"

Aarya doesn't flinch. In fact, she looks like she's about to accept Blackwood's offer.

"Say the word and you and Ines will get your wish," Blackwood says.

Anger flashes in Aarya's eyes. She almost imperceptibly glances at Ines and then reluctantly shakes her head. So Aarya does have a weakness. And it's another person. I have to admit that I'm surprised. I always got the sense she would throw her own mother off a building if the thought occurred to her, so this hint of loyalty is something unexpected.

Layla and I file through the door before Blackwood can change her mind.

The X guard takes up his position behind us, and I can't get up the stairs fast enough. Layla opens our door, and just as I'm about to follow her through it, I feel warm air graze the back of my neck.

"You're next," the X guard whispers, and I whip around, but he's already walking away down the hall.

I close the door behind me, my hand shaking.

"Did you hear that?" I ask Layla.

She looks at me expectantly.

"That guard just whispered 'You're next.'"

For a second she just stares at me. Then her mouth drops into a frown. "You're absolutely positive he spoke to you?" There's worry in her voice.

"Positive." I search Layla for answers. "Was that a threat? Did he just threaten me?"

Layla chews on her lip. "He's the same one who caught you the other night?"

I nod.

"Guards don't talk to students. Yes, we break lots of rules here, but that's not one of them. I told you I thought there was something off. Now I'm sure of it," she says.

"And that exercise Blackwood just had us do, is that a normal—" I start.

"No," Layla says, shaking her head vigorously. "It was typical as far as the psychology of those challenges goes, but not in its execution. Students have died in the occasional accident or . . . homicide, but never from being suffocated by the *headmaster*." By the way Layla's looking at me, I can tell she's as scared as I am. "Having a challenge like this on the heels of two students dying is . . . well, I don't know what it is, and that's what worries me."

I take my cloak off, but she doesn't. "Are you going some-where?"

"Ash's room," she says. "He needs to know."

"You're going to Ash's right after the guard said someone's coming for me? Can I go with you?" I ask.

"No, but I'll be back soon," she says, and slips out the door, leaving me all alone.

Twenty-Seven

THE MORNING LIGHT creeps through the edge of my curtains. I toss and turn under my comforter. I've been in and out of sleep all night, afraid that if I actually passed out, someone would come in and attack me. I'm fairly certain that this past week is going to make me the lightest sleeper in the world.

Between the guard's bizarre comment and the terror of Blackwood's challenge, the events of last night have only compounded my list of fears. Plus, I still can't get the sight of Stefano's body, the gasping sound Charles made when the arrow pierced his chest, or the hate in Nyx's eyes when she attacked me out of my thoughts. If Layla and Ash are right that the Lions want me dead, there has to be a bigger reason than me failing to take the fall for Stefano. Matteo is clearly a more important Bear than I am, and they're not going after him like this. Ash said that people in this school might recognize me, and all I can assume is that Brendan and his crew must think they know something about me, and that something could be the difference between my life and death. And on top of everything, I'm getting more stressed by the day about my dad and Aunt Jo.

Suddenly, there's a muffled scream and I launch out of bed so fast that my legs nearly get tangled in my blankets. I shove aside the trunk that I placed in front of my door and bolt into the common room.

Layla already has our main door open, and Pippa's on the other side in the hallway with a horror-stricken expression on her face and her hand pressed to her heart. I follow her eyes down to the body of the X guard by her feet. His throat is slit and blood is pooled on the floor below him.

"Oh no . . . no," I breathe, grabbing my stomach.

I look from the body to Layla, who's staring at the guard and is so still that I can't tell if she's in shock or logging every single detail. She went to Ash's room last night and told him the guard had threatened me—and possibly her. Now that same guard is dead and laid out in front of our door. I know Ash is fiercely protective of his sister, but even he wouldn't have done this . . . would he?

Up and down the hall, doors open and girls peer out to see what the commotion is all about.

I can tell by the way Layla's leaning that she wants to bend down, probably to touch him and figure out how long he's been dead. But she doesn't dare with this many onlookers. I try to focus on anything else, but my eyes keep involuntarily returning to the guard.

"Everyone back in your rooms! Immediately!" Blackwood has appeared, and the girls and their maids quickly shuffle into their rooms.

Layla closes our door, and I'm grateful to shut out the bloody image. I open my mouth to say something, but she shakes her head.

"Not now, November," she says, heading for her bedroom.

"We need to talk about this," I say in a demanding whisper. "We need to—"

"What I need to do is *think*," she says, and closes her door. Is she, too, wondering if Ash did it?

I hover in the common room for a while, but I can't make out any talking coming from the hallway. Eventually I hear some rustling and what I assume is water sloshing on the floor, then silence again. I spend the next hour pacing, biting my nails off, and watching the day brighten outside the window. Just when I'm certain I can't stand another minute of silence, Pippa opens our door.

Her face is red and blotchy and she can barely make eye contact with me.

"Pippa," I say, wanting to offer her some comfort but unsure how to go about it.

She wipes her nose. "He was a nice man. A good guard."

"You were close?"

She nods. "He was planning on leaving here in a year and—" She stops herself and takes a breath, like it's all too much.

She places a tray of breakfast food on our table.

"I'm really sorry," I say, but she looks at the table and not at me.

"After you eat, you're to go straight to class," she says, and, having delivered her message, promptly turns around and leaves.

Layla's door remains closed. I frown. Class instead of a summons to Blackwood's office? Not even an assembly to announce what happened? And poor Pippa. Layla was right—something is very, very off.

Twenty-Eight

AS LAYLA AND I exit strategic sparring, I rub my ribs, certain I have a serious bruise forming. I spent the entire class holding my breath and sweating over the possibility of getting paired with Brendan, but it never happened. He shot me taunting looks whenever he could, though. The moves Ash has been showing me definitely helped, but I still have a lot to learn. And to top off this horrible morning, Layla still isn't talking.

Everything feels on edge and upside down, like we're all collectively waiting for the next unexplainable horror. And now I have another dead body seared into my memory, another image I won't be able to erase from my mind. It's obvious everyone knows what's happened. People keep stealing glances at me and Layla when they think we're not looking.

I turn toward Layla, who is walking so slowly in the direction of the library that I wonder if she's having some sort of meltdown. But she doesn't look at me, and she also doesn't push through the library door. She just walks right past it at a snail's pace.

"Layla?" I say, walking slowly next to her, and she shushes me.

Her eyes are alert, and she's silenced her footsteps.

We make a turn and I realize where we are—the first floor of the boys' dorm. I turn to her in shock. I want to say something to dissuade her, yell at her that this is a bad idea, but I don't dare draw attention to us.

Three doors down she lifts a handle and slips inside a room. I hesitate for a split second and she grabs my arm and pulls me inside, closing the door silently behind us.

"Damn it, Layla, you should have warned me," I whisper at her. "And tell me we're not where I think we are right now."

"We only have forty-five minutes before these hallways will be populated again and before Matteo will be headed back," she says. "We'll start in Stefano's bedroom."

Everything inside me sinks. "You don't say anything all morning and now you sneak us into *Matteo's* room?" I say with frustration. "Don't you think that's a supremely bad idea when another murder victim just appeared in front of our door? You're supposed to be the sensible twin."

Her dark eyes flash the same fire they did that night she was angry about the parlor. "I didn't *warn* you because you wear your thoughts on your face like a child—something we *really* don't need right now. And I haven't spoken all morning because I was thinking, watching, observing—maybe if you and my brother did more of these silent activities we wouldn't be in danger every other damn day!"

I swallow.

She narrows her eyes. "And I am well aware that there was a body in front of our door this morning. Did you see a murder weapon with that body? No, you didn't. So where is it?"

"I—"

"Exactly!" she says. "It's still out there. And as far as I can tell, none of this makes any damn sense. Not Stefano's murder, not the blood on your floor, not the guard. Yes, there have been deaths in this school before, but nothing like this. *Nothing* on this scale has ever happened here. So I'm going back to square one. We are very obviously missing something and I want to know what it is before one of these people succeeds in killing you."

"Layla—"

"I don't want to hear it. Either help me or don't. But I need to get to work." She turns around and walks away from me.

I stand in Matteo's common room for a couple of seconds. As much as I don't want to admit it, she's right. And as much as I hate this, I can't leave her here while she's trying to help me. I huff once and follow her, noting exactly what position the door was in so that I can put it back before we leave.

At the sight of Stefano's room my stomach clenches and my heartbeat pounds in my temples. It's set up exactly like mine, except the air feels stale, like there hasn't been anyone in here in days.

Layla lifts her head from the storage trunk she's been examining. "Look for any trace of blood," she says, still with an edge to her voice. "If Stefano *was* killed here, then the killer would likely have had to keep his body here before planting it in the hallway. There are only a handful of places he would fit." She looks up for a second. "The way you used the soot from the fireplace last night made me think of it. Even if someone cleaned and covered their tracks, there's every likelihood the blood would get caught in the imperfections of the stone or wood."

I nod and dedicate myself to examining the base of his nightstand and the feet of his bed, but there doesn't seem to be any discoloration.

Layla moves on from the trunk to inspecting the perimeter of the room itself. She takes a small piece of white paper out of her cloak and runs it along a couple of cracks in the stone.

I stick my head under the bed, but with the dim lighting in this place, it's hard to see. "How risky is it if I light the candle? Will someone notice?"

She purses her lips for a second. "Someone may notice a match is missing, but it would be unlikely for Matteo to think it wasn't his butler or for his butler to think it wasn't Matteo."

"Then come hold the candle for me? The last thing we need is for me to burn something," I say.

Layla puts the paper back in her cloak and I slide under the bed. The mattress is resting on a frame of crisscrossing rope. Layla lights the candle and angles it just under the edge of the bed, with her other hand held below it to catch any dripping wax. The problem is that I can only see one section well at a time.

I slide my fingers along the wooden frame. "Move the candle closer to my head," I say as I scan the rope and the underside of the mattress. "Okay, now move it slowly toward my feet." I shift with her as the light moves. "Wait, hold on, go back."

On the rope, about an inch long and half a millimeter wide, is a brown mark. I grab the rope and separate the fibers between my fingers as best I can. Brown flakes fall onto my shirt. "Oh god."

"Slide out slowly," she says in a commanding voice, and I listen, even though all I want to do is wiggle and run away like

Scooby-Doo. Layla blows out the candle and puts it back where it was as I shimmy out from under the bed.

She kneels down next to me and licks her finger.

"Tell me you're not going to—" But she's already picked up a couple of the flakes on her fingertip and stuck them in her mouth. "Ohhh . . . that is so . . . You're nuts."

"Blood," she says. "Someone definitely hid Stefano under this bed. Which means he *was* killed here and put in that hallway hours later for you to find." She frowns in concentration.

I sit up and smack at my shirt, trying not to think about the fact that a dead guy's blood was just on it. "Layla, how is figuring out the details of Stefano's death going to help us sort out the bigger picture here? Isn't the important part that we know who committed the murder? And why is knowing where his body was kept so urgent that we would sneak into this room today of all days?"

She looks at me for a long second. "From what you described, Stefano was stabbed in the heart. And in order for Charles to avoid making a huge bloody mess all over the furniture and the rug, there couldn't have been much of a struggle. And for there not to be a struggle, Charles would have had to stab him in an instant kill zone, like the aorta. But it's extremely difficult to get a clean shot like that. And Stefano was a good fighter. So the only thing that makes sense is that Stefano was taken by surprise."

"Okay . . . so then Charles killed him right when he walked through his door, or something like that, before Stefano even realized there was a threat?" I say, trying to follow her train of thought.

"Something *exactly* like that," she says. "Remember how we were talking about figuring out a timeline for who had seen Stefano last? Then there was that assembly and Charles was accused and it became a moot point. Well, last night I asked Ash to check anyway. He told me that no one saw Stefano after his last class, not at all."

"So Stefano was killed right when he got back from class that day?" I say. "Actually, that does fit your timeline for how long he was dead, considering he was only a little stiff. But I still don't understand."

"Hear me out," Layla says. "Matteo's last class ended at six-thirty that day. But no one saw him after that, so the only thing we can conclude is that he went straight to Blackwood's office and was sent to his punishment without being allowed to return to his room. Now, Stefano's class wasn't supposed to end until six-forty-five—he was in boxing with Ash, and Ash said that the teacher let them out twenty-five minutes early." She looks at me expectantly.

"Hang on," I say, and hold up my hands, my mind spinning. "You're saying that whoever was here was actually trying to kill *Matteo*, not Stefano?"

"That's exactly what I'm saying," she says. "I think Charles was trying to take advantage of the fight you got in with Matteo by murdering him and making it look like you did it in retaliation. Which makes far more sense if you think about it. However, Charles wasn't aware that Matteo had been sent to the outer perimeter, rather than being allowed back to his room. And Stefano's class got out early, putting Stefano in the wrong place at the wrong time."

I brush my hair back from my forehead. "So Charles wanted to take out the firstborn of the Bear Family? I guess that does make more sense. A neat crime that he could pin on someone else. But why me? Because I got into that fight with Matteo and it was a good opportunity?"

"It was a good opportunity for sure, but my guess is that there's more to it than that. Otherwise why put that blood in your room? Why send Nyx after you publicly? And why was that guard killed?" she says, and for the first time I fully understand why she's been so insistent that things don't add up.

"You were right, Layla. We did need to come here. I'm sorry I fought you on it," I say.

She smiles a little. "But now we need to go," she says, and I don't hesitate.

I jump up and straighten out the comforter. Layla wipes fingerprints off the trunk with her sleeve.

She checks the floor for stray hair or anything we might have tracked in, and we make our way to the door. Layla cracks it open, peering out. She nods and we slip back into the hallway, closing the door quietly behind us.

Class must have just let out. I can hear doors opening and hushed conversation. We round the corner and come face to face with Dr. Conner.

He eyes us both. "The boys' dorm?"

"Yes," Layla says with a neutral expression. "Just passing through on our way from the library."

"I see," he says, but I can tell he's reading more into it.

At which point Felix and Aarya pass and give us a look, also assessing which direction we came from.

Layla makes a small curtsy to Conner and we continue walking.

"Conner knows something, doesn't he?" I whisper to her as soon as we're out of hearing range.

"Unfortunately, yes. He's the head of assessment. He misses nothing. And Aarya seeing us doesn't help. I would bet money she tells Matteo just to stir up trouble. That missing match could become a problem. We didn't burn the candle itself long enough for there to be a noticeable difference in height, but if someone checks it soon they will discover the hot wax."

My stomach does a quick flip. "Can we at least replace the match?"

Layla shakes her head. "No. If a match is missing and then shows back up, it will look a hundred times worse. We're stuck."

Twenty-Nine

LAYLA AND I walk into poisons class and take a seat at our table. It feels like a medieval version of the chemistry lab back at Pembrook. There are two students to a table with various metal instruments and glass jars. Only, instead of individual Bunsen burners, there is a fireplace used to heat things, and there are no safety glasses or plastic gloves to protect us. Layla says everyone learns the hard way what not to touch, which means I'm not touching anything I don't absolutely have to.

We're now in our second class of the day and there hasn't been a word about the guard's murder. No one's questioned us or announced that there will be an investigation. It's obvious the other students are on edge, too. Except for Aarya, who, as far as I can tell, seems to find everyone else's discomfort amusing.

Brendan stops in front of our table and picks up a glass vial of god knows what. He twirls it and studies the liquid inside like it's captured his complete interest. "Two murders since you've arrived, November—and I hear one was right outside your dorm room. Yet you're sitting here, while Nyx is in the dungeon." He looks over at me and I can see the threat in his eyes. He was close with Charles, but it's clear that what happened with Nyx is a much bigger deal to him and he'll make me suffer for it if he can. "But I'm sure that will be corrected soon enough." He drops the vial carelessly on the table, sending it rolling along the wood, and goes to take his seat.

Layla grabs the vial before it crashes to the floor, and by the look on her face, I know whatever is in it is definitely something toxic.

"Sit, my beauties," says Professor Hisakawa.

Hisakawa . . . Japanese in origin and can be broken down into two parts, hisa, *meaning "a long time ago," and* kawa, *meaning "river" or "stream."* I was fascinated by the name as a kid because of one translation I found that listed the meaning as "river of forever."

Hisakawa stands in front of the fireplace humming while everyone settles. She's a tall thin woman with blunt-cut bangs and hair that reaches all the way to her waist. "We often talk about poisons in terms of their specific formulas and intentional implementation, but today I would like to discuss poisons a little differently. You all know King George the Third, who was born in 1738 and held the British throne through the American Revolution? Well, it's been proposed that he had a genetic condition that caused him to suffer periodic attacks that the royal physicians at the time were treating with tartar emetic—an antimony-based medicine used to induce vomiting. Antimony is frequently found in nature with arsenic . . . and often contaminated with it." She pauses. "Ahh, I can see the lights turning on in those brains of yours. In the 1960s there was an analysis of King George's hair and it was found that the arsenic concentration was seventeen times the lethal limit.

"The physicians' notes described both forcing the king and deceiving the king to take this poisonous medication. Wickedly fascinating, isn't it? Now, his medical condition at the time disrupted heme synthesis. And what does arsenic do?" She rolls up on her toes and back down again. "It also disrupts heme synthesis, making his condition worse and ultimately making the king more dependent on the royal physicians who were poisoning him." She looks at all of us to make sure she has our attention. "Now, this is a curious situation because what outwardly appeared to be a caregiving tactic was slowly killing the king. And with the effects of the poison mimicking his preexisting condition, some might say it was a perfect crime."

Hisakawa smiles. "This is an example of a larger idea I want you all to mull over. But let's talk about arsenic for a moment. It was wildly popular in the Middle Ages; everyone fell in love with the agony and romance of it all. Who knows why?"

I've never seen anyone so delighted by poison before and I really don't know what to make of it. She's like a Tim Burton version of my kindergarten teacher.

"The Borgias were the stars of arsenic poisoning," Aarya says from her seat next to Felix. "It's said that arsenic improves the taste of wine, and the Borgias hosted a great number of dinner parties. Lucrezia Borgia carried the poison around in a secret compartment in her ring."

"Oh yes, the wine bit is one of my favorites," says Hisakawa. "And I've always liked that Lucrezia. What a name. Anyone else?"

"Arsenic was widely available in the Victorian era and was even sold in grocery stores. Women used to eat it or mix it with vinegar or chalk and rub it on their faces because they thought it would improve their complexions and reduce wrinkles," Felix says, and I notice he has a cut on his hand that wasn't there yesterday in fencing when Nyx attacked me.

"Absolutely. Arsenic has been used for any number of things—in cosmetics, to preserve food, as a pesticide, to dye fabrics. Still, there's something specific I'm thinking of," Hisakawa says.

"Arsenic poisoning resembles cholera," Layla says. "Often-times people would be pronounced dead of natural causes."

"Ding ding ding!" Hisakawa says, and Aarya rolls her eyes, clearly annoyed that Layla got the right answer. "A poison is truly great when it leaves no evidence behind, when its effects pass for an illness or when it's already present in someone's life and you only need encourage the interaction with it." She looks around the room. "The sixteenth-century philosopher and toxicologist Paracelsus famously said: 'All things are poison, and nothing is without poison. Only the dose permits something not to be poisonous.' What we learn from that profound statement is that there's poison in every environment. While something can be helpful in a small dose, it can be lethal in a large one. I'm not only talking about substances here—medications someone might be taking or cleaning products they use. I'm asking you to look beyond what is obvious to the more subtle and, if you can master them, the best of the poisons: emotional and psychological. If you can dose someone strongly enough with either one, death is likely to follow with no physical evidence left behind. The tactics with these are hard to detect, and it's only in the subtle changes that any real pattern can be discerned."

I'm not sure if that's the most disturbing thing I've ever

heard or if she's merely shining a light on something important. People can drown in sorrow, kill a friend in mistaken rage, and isolate themselves out of paranoia. But if someone is purposefully pulling those strings, would you detect it if you were on the receiving end? Again I have this nagging feeling that I'm hearing more than just lessons. Not to mention that my dad used to say something similar about detecting patterns. It feels like every time I turn around I'm realizing how little I understood about my life in Pembrook.

The smell of French toast and warm blueberries wafts into my room and I practically fall out of bed as I run for the kitchen. I wrap my arms around Dad's back as he mans the frying pan.

"Happy seventeenth, Nova," he says, and turns around to give me a big hug and a kiss on the forehead. "Aunt Jo's already called . . . twice. Even though I told her you were sleeping." He smiles and shakes his head. "She'll be here by the time you get home from school—with some ridiculous present, no doubt."

"Speaking of ridiculous presents," I say, and swipe my finger through the freshly whipped cream on the counter. "Where is it?"

"Where is what?" he says, but by his tone I can tell he knows exactly what I'm talking about.

"The surprise you've been promising!"

"Oh, right," he says. "I decided against it. I thought maybe you've gotten too old for presents."

I give him a hard look and he laughs. "No dad jokes right now. This is my birthday we're talking about."

"Well, I'm sure it's around here somewhere," he says with a mischievous grin.

I groan. "You hid it, didn't you?"

He shrugs.

"Okay, give me a hint," I say.

"Look for the subtle things that are different, a pattern. They'll point you in the right direction."

"Oh man. What if I don't find it before I have to go to school? This is child abuse, you know," I say.

He grins and flips the French toast. "Well, I suggest you do find it, otherwise you won't have the keys to drive your new truck to school," he says, and my mouth drops open.

"My new what? My . . . No! Seriously? No!" I scream and jump up and down. "I have a truck? Is it green? Tell me it's green." I run to the window, and sure enough there's an old green Bronco in the driveway with a cage in the back that tells me it probably belonged to a forest ranger. "I will love you forever for this!"

How many of these moments were there, where Dad was teaching me something Strategia-esque and I thought nothing of it? What I really can't understand, though, is why he didn't tell me who I was all these years. And what the hell is going on with him and Aunt Jo right now that would have him suddenly catapult me into this school?

He was right when he said I know things that will keep me safe, but if I can't identify them, they don't do me any good. *If only I could talk to him,* I think, and the thought makes my heart ache. I've never missed him and Pembrook so much in my life.

Thirty

THE DINING HALL is buzzing with conversation by the time Layla and I arrive, and even though the other students' body language is subtle, it's obvious they keep looking in our direction.

The teachers are paying more attention to us than they normally do, and Blackwood and Conner are sitting with them, which is unusual. The air feels electrically charged, like one misstep and the whole place could spontaneously combust.

Ash sits down across from us and immediately starts piling fettuccini Alfredo onto his plate, like everything is perfectly normal and he's starving.

"Any word on the guard?" I ask, keeping my voice low.

He shakes his head. "From what I've heard, no one has even been questioned yet. It's not like Blackwood. She usually goes right at an issue without hesitation."

"Like I keep saying," Layla adds, "something is off with this whole situation."

A girl and a guy sit down next to us and we all fall silent. Layla scans the room in a way that tells me she's lost in thought, and Ash looks up periodically to where Brendan and the other Lions sit.

I dip some crusty bread in the cream sauce on my plate, flipping through my memories to find anything that might explain who I am and help me understand the missing pieces. I actually felt safer when I thought I might be accused of Stefano's murder than I do now. At least then I didn't think people were actively trying to kill me.

I keep replaying my conversation with Ash about how Strategia don't get to decide to be anything else. Part of me refuses to believe it, but I know that part of me is wrong. If I manage to avoid my own death until I get home to Dad, I'm still trapped. I could try my best to fly under the radar, be so unimportant that no one would be interested in what I do for the rest of my life. But if I stay in Pembrook, I'll need to follow the rules or I'll put myself and the people I care about at risk. And even if I spend my life following the rules, that doesn't mean I'll be out of danger.

I have to believe that Dad had no choice but to send me here or I don't think I can forgive him. He said I had to go to this school for my safety—now there's a laugh. I no longer know what I can trust or which of the things he said were actually true. Although by the time I get through the intense study regimen Layla has me on, I'm sure that will change.

I hold my hands out toward the campfire, warming them. The air is crisp with the scent of cold weather and leaves, even though they have only just started to change color.

"Why haven't I ever seen you dating anyone, Aunt Jo?" I ask, looking up at her. "You're hilarious and tough and I can't imagine that people don't fall all over themselves to ask you out."

Aunt Jo sips her cider and rum, which I suspect is mostly rum, and leans back in her folding chair. "Not all fabulous people have long-term relationships, Nova. Some of us are just too bright to be tied down," she says. "Besides, can you imagine me tolerating something like that for the rest of my life?" She nods her head in the direction of my dad's tent, from which comes a loud snore. "I have half a mind to go throw a rock at him as it is."

I laugh. "But you always said that when you were a girl you thought you'd have five children."

"Ah, but then Matilde had you, and you were perfect with those pink cheeks and that laugh. That laugh . . . ," she says, and shakes her head. "It used to make me cry, you know. I see you looking at me like I'm a sentimental fool, which I very well might be, but it did. Your father would come into a room and find the three of us in hysterics. You laughing and us crying because we could not stand how adorable it all was. And since you were such a perfect baby, I figured that unless I had one exactly like you I would be forced to call it Secondo and dress it up in your old clothes."

"Stop, you would not," I say, grinning.

"You doubt this face?" she says, and wags her eyebrows at me.

"Never," I say, stirring my hot cider with a cinnamon stick.

"Why the sudden interest in my love life, eh? Have you got some passionately romantic story to tell me?" she asks mischievously.

"What? No. I wish. I just . . . You know my best friend, Emily? She has a huge family and they have these big festive holiday parties. Sometimes I get jealous. I kind of wish there were more of us, you know?"

She snorts and takes a sip of her drink.

"What, you don't?" I say.

"No," she says, spilling more rum into her cup. "I have relatives in Italy I would rather forget. First there's that self-serving father of mine, and then all the family members who won't admit that he's self-serving, which in my opinion makes them even worse." She raises her cup. "To hell with the whole lot of them."

I want to tell her that I meant I wish we had more family members like us, but I know better than to do that while she's ranting and damning people. She blames her dad for my mom's death, even though everyone—and the autopsy report—said her death was an accident.

"And don't get me started on Christopher's family," she says, pointing again in the direction of the snoring. "Putting my family and his family in a room together for a holiday party sounds about as much fun as shoving a Christmas tree up my backside. It would be nothing but fighting."

"Did they ever get along? Or did your family always disapprove of Dad?"

"From the moment your parents got together, it went downhill. Nonstop feuding before you were born."

"But not any more since Dad's parents died, right?"

"Good riddance."

I choke on my hot cider. Sometimes I wonder if there is any line Aunt Jo won't cross. "What made you choose Providence, of all places, when you left Italy?"

She smirks. "Please tell me you're joking, Nova. How you break my heart. The statue of the Independent Man? The fact that Providence was founded by rebels and rabble-rousers? And, well, the Italian food is good."

I open my mouth in fake shock.

"What? I said I didn't like my family. But our food is perfection."

I push my pasta around on my plate. I wish I could ask Aunt Jo about what's going on here and about my parents in general, such as why they chose to live in the middle of small-town nowhere. From everything Ash and Layla have told me, that couldn't have been accidental. And it makes me wonder what they were trying to get away from—their deadly Families in general, or was it more specific than that? I used to think Aunt Jo's hatred for her relatives was mostly theatrics, but considering what I've seen here so far, blaming them for Mom's death doesn't seem entirely off the wall anymore. A Strategia Family could definitely make a death look like an accident.

Without meaning to, I look around for Matteo. If the Bears did have something to do with my mom's death, if she broke some Strategia rule or something, it's entirely possible that his relatives were involved in making that decision. Is that why he knew what my mom looked like? I drop my fork with a loud clang and Layla and Ash both look at me.

Matteo meets my gaze, and something in me just snaps. The injustice of everything that's happened since I arrived here, the overwhelming horror of what I've seen, and the constant uncertainty and fear have finally caught up with me. All I want to do is scream at the top of my lungs.

I push back my chair, furious not only with Matteo but with the whole school. I bet my mom wanted out, too, wanted to get away from all of these Strategia and their deadly games. The question is whether or not they killed her for it.

"November?" Layla says.

"I just need some air," I say, and walk away before either of them can ask me any questions. I'm sure Ash will figure out that I've remembered something, and the last thing I want to hear from him is a detailed analysis of my parents' Families and my mother's probable murder. No wonder Aunt Jo was always so angry when the topic of family came up.

I head between the two long dining tables, my eyes trained on the door, anything to avoid looking at Matteo again or I'm positive I'm going to do something I regret.

I'm almost to the door when Conner cuts me off. I didn't even see him get up from the teachers' table. "November, I need to speak with you," he says, and touches his beard.

"Right now?" I say, not even trying to hide the annoyance in my voice.

"Yes, I have some . . . news," he says, and I stop dead in my tracks.

"What news?" I say quickly. I can't help but wonder if he saw me looking upset and decided it was the right time to shit on me further.

"If you'll follow me to my—" he starts.

"No, just tell me," I say, already running through a list of terrible possibilities in my head and agitating myself even more.

"I must insist that we at least step out of the dining hall." He pushes through the door before I can reply. I follow, but he doesn't stop until he's halfway down the empty hallway. "Do not ask me questions about what I'm about to tell you, because I do not know the answers. It's customary that this type of news is delivered by family members, but considering the recent circumstances, you are not permitted a visit."

My entire body tenses. I want to yell at him to just say it already.

He evaluates the hallway to make sure it's empty and levels his gaze at me. "Jo is dead."

For a second, I'm completely still, trying to make sense of his words. Jo? *My* aunt Jo? "No," I say, and shake my head. "No. That can't be true."

"As I said, I cannot tell you any more. That is all I know. Jo is dead," he repeats as though he can see that I'm resisting accepting it.

Someone killed my aunt? My aunt is dead. *She's dead.* The hallway spins. My chest feels like it's constricting and soon there will be no air left. My vision blurs with tears, and with each excruciating heartbeat I back away from him. I see his lips moving, but I can't hear a word he's saying.

If the Bears were responsible for my mom's death, who's to say they aren't responsible for Aunt Jo's? She wasn't just living in America, she *hated* them all. Ash said it was forbidden to leave your Family. Was this what my dad was trying to stop when he shipped me off here? My fists clench, my grief mixing with my anger explosively.

All of a sudden, I'm running, tears spilling down my cheeks. I slam through the door into the dining hall, and as if on cue, the whole room turns to look at me. But I'm not watching them; I'm looking straight at Matteo. I run full-speed toward him, jump onto a chair, and dive over the table. His eyes widen as I collide with him, slamming us both onto the floor. He grunts and tries to fling me off him, but I'm screaming and clinging to him for all I'm worth. For a brief moment, I see Conner towering above us. Then there is a sharp pain in my head and the world goes black.

Thirty-One

THE ROOM COMES into focus little by little, the flickering candle, the wooden canopy, a face. And I remember what happened.

"November?" Layla says with concern in her voice.

I turn away from her and shut my eyes. "Go away."

Someone shakes me. "Get up," a voice says.

I open my swollen eyes. "Stop."

"I'll stop when you get up," Ash says.

"I'm not getting up. Just leave me alone." I put a pillow over my face, but he yanks it away from me.

"It's been a day. Everyone gets a day to feel sorry for themselves. But no one gets two. You need to get up and eat something and drink some water."

"Feel sorry for myself? Feel *sorry* for myself? Screw you, Ash," I say, and my voice wavers. "I don't care about this damn school or being a Strategia. I just don't care."

He sighs. "Well, whether you care or not, your stunt in the dining hall yesterday made you even more of a target than before. So you don't really have a choice."

All I want is for this heart-crushing feeling to stop, for my life to go back to the way it was before this school, when my aunt was alive and my dad and I had a quiet life in Pembrook. I put the blankets over my head. "People are already trying to kill me—how much worse can it get?"

"They will succeed," he says, and pulls the blankets off me. I swipe at him, but he catches my wrist. I try to pry his fingers loose but he grabs my other hand.

"Let go of me, Ashai," I say.

"No. I will not let you do this to yourself."

"Well, you don't get to make that choice."

His intensity increases. "And what choice are you making? To stay in bed until someone comes and slits your throat? Believe me, you're not far off from that. Or maybe you want to stay here until Blackwood hauls you off to the dungeon, too?"

I yank at my wrists, trying to pull them out of his grasp.

His jaw is set. "You're sad and angry and you can't think past your emotions. But at some point those emotions will fade and you'll realize you've made the biggest mistake of your life. Only by then it'll be too late."

I'm getting so mad I want to scream or cry or both. "Why do you even care? It shouldn't matter to you."

"It does matter."

I scoff and try to get my feet free from the blankets.

But he doesn't let go—in fact, he hoists me out of the bed. I kick at him, but he blocks and turns us around so that he's standing between me and the bed. He lets go of my wrists.

"Really? You're going to prevent me from getting into my own bed?" I say, and I'm furious, all that anger I felt toward Matteo and this awful school rushing back.

I try to step past him, but he steps with me. I push, but he pushes back. My heart is racing and I can feel tears returning to my eyes. I want to tear him apart, and this room, and this school.

"You want to hit me, don't you?" he says. "Go for it."

He pushes my shoulders.

"Stop."

"Defend yourself," he says, and pushes me again.

"Knock it the hell off, Ash."

"If you're not going to hit me, I'm going to hit you," he says. "I suggest you block or do something other than stand there."

And before I can really think it through, I pull back my arm and punch him *hard* right in the jaw. And he doesn't stop me.

My hands fly to my mouth and I take a step backward. I shake out my hand, which now hurts like hell. I focus all my attention on it, trying to keep my lip from quivering. Punching Ash zapped my anger, and now that it's gone, all that's left is this bottomless sadness.

Ash rubs his face. "Not bad. I think there's a chance I'm actually going to have a bruise."

Tears roll down my cheeks. "I'm sorry. I shouldn't have done that."

He takes a step toward me and I start to cry harder, all my grief pouring out of me. His arms wrap around my body and he pulls me into a hug. I push back, but when he doesn't let go, I bury my head in his shoulder. Feeling the warmth of his arms around me and his hand rubbing my back makes me realize how much my life here has lacked in basic human comfort. No one touches anyone in this school unless it's to hurt them.

"Actually, I'm not sorry. You deserved it," I say.

He laughs into my hair. And when his laugh stops, we're both silent.

"It was someone really close to you," he says after a few seconds, but it's not a question.

I nod against his chest.

"I'm so sorry," he says, and squeezes me a little tighter.

I take a deep breath. "So am I."

We're like that for a long minute until my tears stop and my sniffles become less frequent. When he finally lets go, some of the edge is gone. The loss hasn't diminished, but the pain and the helplessness feel lighter.

I wipe my eyes with the heels of my hands. "Do you let everyone in this school who's sad punch you?" I ask, because I'm not sure what else to say to him right now and verbally sparring with him feels more normal than talking about my emotions.

He points to the wet spot on his shirt where my face was. "Only if they agree to snot on me afterward," he says with a sly grin.

"Are you making fun of me while I'm grieving? Do you have any shame at all?" I say, but there isn't any frustration in my voice.

"Shame is for other people," he says. "You know, I've never seen anyone fling herself over a table in a crowded dining hall quite like that before. It was fairly epic. I think you startled the hell out of Matteo. You should have seen his face. Even after you were carried out, he couldn't quite get over the whole thing. Wouldn't talk to anyone."

"He'll have his chance to get even, I'm sure."

Ash shakes his head. "He knocked you out cold. Blackwood called it even."

I touch the side of my head where I felt the sharp pain yesterday, and sure enough, there's a bump. "Oh."

I sit down on my bed.

"Don't you dare think about lying back down," he says.

I take a swig of the water on my bedside table. "If I do, are you going to let me punch you again?"

He sits next to me and smirks.

I look at him squarely. "Why did you do it?"

"Get you out of bed? Who would pine after me if you weren't around? It would get depressing."

I shake my head. "Did I really make things worse for myself?"

His smile fades. "Yes. With Blackwood and in general. Between Charles's death and Nyx being in the dungeon, the school is turning on you."

"And again, why are you here, dragging me out of bed . . . caring about any of this? Is it just because I live with your sister? Are you trying to make sure this doesn't spill onto her?"

"Well, that's certainly the reason I slept here last night," he says.

You slept *here?* is what I'm thinking, but what I say is: "So if I'm such a liability, why don't you just get me assigned to a different room?" I instantly regret my words. I don't want to leave Layla or stop spending time with Ash. But I also don't want to live with the constant fear that they might walk away from me at my weakest moment. I've always been sure where I stood with people and who I could count on, but at this school I have no idea.

"Why are you so impossible?" he says.

"You should ask my best friend. She'll give you a long list of reasons," I say.

He smiles, but there is sadness in his expression.

"Look, I'm not saying I'm not grateful. I'm so grateful. You and Layla . . . well, I don't know what I would do without you. And when you and I were caught after curfew together, it made sense that you guys stood by me. But at this point I don't understand why you're helping me, especially if the Lions are as powerful as you say they are."

"As I told you, Layla's more moral than I consider healthy. She's also unshakably curious. Once this situation became a puzzle, she was going to solve it whether you were here or not. And, well, she finds you infuriating, which, as you can tell"—he spreads his arms to indicate himself—"is a quality she greatly admires." He laughs. "She's come to think of you as a friend."

I sigh, and I can feel tears returning to my eyes. It seems like there has been nothing but hostility and death since I came here, so a few kind words go a long way. Not long ago my life was full of love and laughter. "And you?"

He doesn't answer right away and looks down at his hands. "You remind me of someone."

"Oh."

"Someone I grew up with." He looks over at me. "She was fast and strong and funny as all hell. And there was something so free about her, like the whole world was hers if she wanted it. I used to be envious of her, how she always saw the best in everyone, even when they disappointed her."

"You guys aren't friends anymore?"

"She wasn't Strategia," he says, and his voice tightens.

"What does that mean? You stopped being friends with her for that?"

"I was told to, warned," he says, and pauses. "But I was just a kid. I was stubborn, and I thought if I could just keep her away from my Family until I was supposed to go away to school, it wouldn't matter." He sighs. "And then one day she snuck into my house while there was a Family meeting going on, and my father caught her. He was furious. I swore to him that she didn't hear anything. I promised I would talk to her, end our friendship. . . ."

I have a sinking feeling in my gut. "Oh no."

He doesn't meet my eyes. "There was a fire in her house the next day." He rubs his forehead—the kind of tell he never shows. "And a month later Layla and I came here."

I don't need to ask if she died, because I can see the guilt written all over him. I'm fairly certain he was in love with her.

I smile.

He frowns. "Don't you think smiling at a story like that is bad form?"

"I'm smiling because it proves that under all those carefully controlled looks and that distracting flirting you're capable of real emotion."

"Wait just a minute, my flirting is not distracting. My flirting is captivating, weak-knees quality."

"And I'm smiling because that story shows you also think of me as a friend," I say.

"I do think about you," he says, even though that's not what I said, and for a second we just stare at each other. Then all of a sudden he looks away.

I clear my throat. "Where's Layla?"

"Library," he says.

I suddenly feel guilty. I'm sure she's doing research, trying to figure out how to get me out of this mess, and I'm hiding in my bed.

"In the dining hall earlier—" he says, as if reading my mind.

"Yes. I remembered something. A conversation with"—my voice catches—"my aunt. My mom's sister."

He nods and it's clear that he understands she was the one who died.

"She said that my parents' Families were fighting before I was ever born. And after what you told me about the Lions and the Bears—"

"Your father could definitely be a Lion. That would certainly have complicated their entire relationship and would explain why your parents chose to raise you off the grid. In fact . . . your mother may have been a Bear with decent status, and your father may have agreed to join *her* Family when they married, which in turn gives us a better idea of why you were able to get into the Academy so late." He's speaking fast and his eyes are bright.

"Maybe my mom's status got me considered for admission here, but why would they make an exception for me when I lack all the training everyone else has been getting since birth?"

He looks at me like he's considering the question. "Maybe you weren't brought up steeped in Strategia culture, but you've clearly had training. You bested Nyx in the dark, you're a phenomenal climber, you picked out my lie on instinct, and you managed to save both Aarya and my sister in your last challenge. Not to mention your skills with knives and swords. You're a perfect candidate to come here, even if you're behind in our strategies and history. But why you were sent in as an upperclassman midsemester . . ." He leans back on his elbow. "And then there's the fact that Matteo seems to recognize you, and has some sort of mysterious grudge against you."

"Do you think the Bears killed my aunt?" I say, and my tone shifts.

He frowns momentarily. "I couldn't say. But clearly you think that's a possibility or you wouldn't have done those acrobatics in the dining hall to tackle the most prominent Bear here. But there are a lot of unknowns in this scenario, such as what reason Bears would have for killing one another and holding grudges."

I shake my head and avoid his eyes, not ready to admit how dark my fears are. That my dad and Aunt Jo must have known they were being hunted and so Dad sent me here. And now Aunt Jo is dead, which means the only person left to find is Dad. I get up and start pacing. They could be closing in on him right now. The gravity of the situation hits me hard.

"Yes?" Ash says.

"I'm acting like a selfish wallowing baby. We need to figure out who I am and stop whoever keeps killing people in this school. And fast."

"You're just coming to this conclusion?" he says.

"No. I mean, yes. I mean . . . whether Bears or Lions are responsible for killing my aunt, it's all connected to what's happening here. I'm sure of it. And there is no way I'm waiting around for someone to take out my family one by one."

He gives me a knowing smile. "Took you long enough."

"I'm serious, Ash. Tell me what we need to do and I'll do it," I say.

"Well, first, we need you to go to the dining hall and eat some dinner without attacking anyone. We've got a long night ahead of us."

Thirty-Two

AS I BRAID my hair in front of my vanity mirror, I'm shocked at how spent I look—dried out, as Emily's mom calls it when you've cried so much that you don't have anything left in you. At home, if I felt destroyed over a guy or a bad test, I'd go to Em's house and she'd let me do my crying, and then we'd eat junk food and watch movies until we passed out on the couch. Here, with my crying done, I'm preparing to hunt down information about killers who might be trying to blot out my entire family. I'm not even sure how to process that.

Layla knocks lightly on my bedroom door and I open it.

"I'm ready," I say, and she hands me my cloak.

I put it on and follow her into the common room, where Ash is on the floor peering through the crack under our door.

"Is he waiting for the guard to pass?" I whisper.

"We'll barely have a second to spare. So keep up and stay silent," she whispers back.

I nod at Layla, letting her know that I get the gravity of the situation and won't screw it up.

Ash stands, counts seven seconds off on his fingers, and

silently opens the door. We all jet out and he closes it behind us without so much as a creak. And we're off—down the hall and into the stairwell. Ash doesn't bother to listen at each floor like I did when I was alone. He must know where the guards will be.

We reach the bottom of the stairs and stop. The guard in the foyer is walking into the vine courtyard, and the instant the door closes behind him we run across the stone floor into the hallway near the teachers' lounge. We follow it all the way down to where it dead-ends at a door. The shadow cover is good here, and the only sound is our breathing. However, if someone were to turn the corner there would be no place to hide.

Layla pulls out some kind of multitool that looks like a more complex version of the molded paper clips Ines used in our last challenge. She gets on her knees to access the lock better and slips the tool into the keyhole as I stare down the hallway. Metal clinks and my heart thuds before my brain verifies that the sound is coming from us and not from a guard.

Not four seconds later, Layla pulls the door open. We slip through into total darkness. I put my hand up and my fingers graze the heavy curtain that covers the doorways here. *This door leads outside?* I hear the lock click back into place and I hold my breath.

Ash pulls the curtain back by an inch, and in the dim moonlight I catch a sliver of the outer wall that surrounds our school. Layla taps my wrist and we're moving again, through the curtain and along the tree-lined building. We pass two doors and stop at the third. Layla pulls out her lock-picking tool. I definitely don't remember any of these doors from the inside floor plan. I'm not surprised that there are parts of this castle you can only access from the outside, but I do wonder how bad the punishment will be if we get caught sneaking into them.

Through the trees, I get a better look at the outer wall. It towers over our four-story castle, with round turrets that rise up at each corner. Trees line the outer perimeter and create a tall canopy, just like in our inner courtyards. I wonder how many people have tried to climb their way out of here over the years. I'm sure there is some sort of trap at the top of that wall, and from that height, there's no way you wouldn't get seriously injured if you fell from it.

Layla stands up and opens the door an inch. She nods and we follow her through. And to my surprise, I find myself in a huge kitchen with an arched ceiling crossed with wooden beams. Shelves along the walls are filled with hundreds of jars of spices and stacked plates. Pots of every size hang from iron hooks, while rolling pins and serving platters are left out on a long table to be used for tomorrow's cooking. The kitchen has always been my favorite room in every house, and this one looks like it was plucked from a fairy tale.

The sound of a key sliding into a lock across the room snaps me out of my awestruck moment. I run after Ash and Layla to a door against the right wall. Layla lifts the latch and we practically dive into the dark room.

Layla eases our door closed just as we hear the outside one swing open. Ash pushes us all flat against the wall. My shoulders are pressed between his and Layla's. It's significantly colder in here than outdoors, and I'm sure that if there were any light my breath would be visible. I inhale deeply to slow my heart and anchor my feet in a position where my weight won't shift.

The latch on the door lifts and I hold my breath, not daring to move a millimeter. Dim light spills into the room, and so does an ominously long shadow of a very muscular guard. If he pushes the door open too far, he'll hit Layla, and if he comes in past the door, he'll see Ash for sure.

He moves forward, his candle illuminating the room, and I find it nearly impossible to believe that he doesn't hear my heart. Light flickers off the shelves of cloth-covered ceramic pots. But just as quickly as it appeared, the light diminishes, and the door closes, casting us back into darkness.

Layla was *not* kidding when she said we'd barely have a second to spare. If she hadn't opened a single lock fast enough or if there had been even a moment's delay somewhere, we would have been screwed.

Ash's shoulder pulls away from mine as the outside door closes and locks. I exhale like I'm a deflating balloon. To my left, Layla strikes a match and lights a candle.

Ash heads for what looks like an oversized wooden armoire, with four square doors and one tall, narrow one. My heart thuds. *The cold temperature . . . Oh, please no.* I shake my head, like maybe I can convince Ash by telepathy not to open the tall compartment. Next to the armoire is a long table, and I feel my eyes bulging as I take in two sets of what look like bloody clothes and shoes and a stack of antique hospital tools.

Ash undoes the hooked latch on the tall compartment. My brain screams at me to close my eyes, but I can't manage to look away. And just as I feared, the X guard is standing upright inside, frozen white with his eyes half open. I take two bumbling steps backward and cover my mouth with my hand.

Layla brings the candle close to his face, accentuating his frozen features.

"No bruises or cuts," Ash says in a hushed voice, and inspects the guard's hands. "His knuckles don't have any marks, so there wasn't much of a struggle. Maybe he was outnumbered?"

"Nothing to suggest he took a hit to the face, either," Layla whispers, and leans in to get a closer look at the gash across his neck.

"That's odd," she says. "The cut isn't a clean line. I couldn't tell in the hallway when he was covered in blood."

"What does that mean?" I ask. "Did someone use a serrated blade?"

"No," she says, and frowns. "The wound isn't uniform enough for that, either."

Ash leans closer and his eyes widen. For the first time ever, he looks rattled. "Glass, Lay. I would bet anything that it was glass—sharp enough to cut deeply and easily, jagged enough to make a much sloppier cut."

My chest tightens, and his reaction suddenly makes perfect sense. "The broken glass from my room. Do you think . . . ," I say, and my voice trails off.

"Yes. Someone must have gotten a piece of it before Pippa could dispose of it," Layla says, nodding.

"Wait . . . I don't know if this is a big deal," I say, "but Felix had a cut on his palm in poisons class. I remember thinking that it wasn't there in fencing the day before, which was the day I was actually looking for cuts because of the blood message on my floor."

"Ash, look into Felix's schedule and see if you can find a

reason for that cut, would you?" Layla says. "See if he had any classes between fencing and poisons that involved fighting. Or if there was another occasion where he might have gotten a cut. "

Ash nods, but he's still studying the guard with a look of concern.

"We should check his back," Layla says. "If you two can tip him forward, I'll take a look."

They both turn to me, and it takes every last iota of my self-control not to tell them that it's never going to happen. But there's no time for me to be squeamish, so I force myself forward. Ash already has one hand on the guard's right shoulder and one hand on his chest to support his weight.

I reach my hand into the metal-lined icebox and tentatively touch the guard's left arm, which is hard and covered in frost crystals the way old ice cream containers are.

"You ready?" Ash says.

I gulp. "Yeah."

I press my other hand to the guard's chest and Ash tips him forward. I stumble under his weight and regain my balance, helping Ash bring him to a horizontal position. We crouch on the floor, supporting his stiff body.

Layla takes a good look at the back of the guard's head and runs her hand over it, presumably feeling for bumps that might have knocked him unconscious. "Nothing," she says, and runs the candle over his back. She stops near his left shoulder blade.

"Huh," she says, and we both look at her. "He's got a tattoo, but there's some bad scarring on top of it. . . ."

I lean forward, getting a better look at the scar, and shudder. It appears to be from a burn.

"Can you tell what it was?" Ash asks.

Layla brings the candle near his skin and bends closer. For a few seconds she goes silent and concentrates, moving the candle around to get different angles.

Then she stands up and chews on her lower lip. "Go ahead and put him back," she says, and I start lifting him before she finishes her sentence. We stand him upright and tuck him back into the metal box. Ash grabs the icebox door and latches it.

I wipe my now-wet fingers on my pants and wish I could run full-speed toward a shower. Not that there are any here. I'll have to wait until tomorrow morning and ask Pippa to bring up hot water for a bath. I shake out my hands in front of me like somehow that makes a difference.

Layla's eyes seem far away, locked in concentration.

"Lay?" Ash says. "You know I hate it when you leave me in suspense like this."

But she doesn't respond. She just starts to pace around the small room like she's having a conversation with herself.

I can tell by Ash's face that patience is not his strong suit. It actually makes me feel a little better, though, about all those times Layla has gone silent on me.

After what feels like forever, Layla stops and faces us. "What if we got it wrong?" she asks.

"Got what wrong?" Ash replies, exasperated.

"The guard," she says, and waves her hand at the compartment where his body is. "What if when he told November 'You're next,' it wasn't a threat?"

I look at her sideways. "What are you saying?"

"What I'm saying is that he took a huge risk by speaking to

you," she says. "I told you at the time that guards *never* break that rule. So why would he threaten you verbally when there are so many nonverbal alternatives?"

"Layla, *what kind of tattoo did he have*?" Ash says.

But Layla only lifts her hand and silences her brother.

"Don't forget that he reported me to Blackwood and Conner the night I found Stefano's body," I say.

"Right. And Conner told *you* that the guard went about his schedule differently that night, which we all agree is strange," she says.

I stare at her, trying to follow her logic.

"*Layla*," Ash says more insistently.

She doesn't look at him but stays focused on me. "We already suspect that whoever killed Stefano was actually trying to kill Matteo and frame you, another Bear, for the crime—a *perfect* crime, since it would have eliminated two Bears at once." She nods toward the freezer. "This guard had a Bear Family tattoo on him. He took a different route that night, sure, but somehow wound up at your room the same time you did. Then he gives you a message and winds up dead the same night, *in front of your room*."

I take a step backward and my heart starts to pound. "Pippa thought highly of him," I say in a hushed voice.

"Only another piece of evidence to prove my point," Layla says. "Think about it—this guard had no choice but to report you the night of the murder because you saw him. But what if you were *supposed* to see him?" Layla says. "What if he was trying to get a message to you that night, only you closed the door too quickly?"

I fidget with my hands. "Oh god . . . you're saying that he wasn't threatening me at all, he was *warning* me? Keeping track of me?"

"Protecting you," she says. "And if that's the case, which I very much think it is, then there is every likelihood that's how he died." It's as if her words have punched me in the gut.

"You're saying someone may have been coming to slit *my* throat?" I can't wrap my mind around the idea that it's extremely possible that guard died for me. I feel sick and sad all at once.

"Yes," Layla says, and by her heavy tone I can tell she feels the gravity of it, too.

Ash rubs his forehead.

"But why?" I ask. "Why would the guard decide to protect me?"

"I think she's suggesting that he was likely connected to one of the faculty members, otherwise he would never have taken the risk to speak to you. That someone *told* him to look out for you," Ash says, and I can hear the worry in his voice. "Which means whatever pieces we're missing in this whole mess, whatever is going on here, probably goes beyond the students."

For a moment we just look at one another, the heaviness of that conclusion sinking in.

"I was hanging out with Stefano the night before he was murdered," Layla says, and her voice is soft. "He thought the Lions' network in the school was expanding, that soon there would be no safe place for the Bears or any Family that opposed the Lions. Well . . . maybe this is a good thing. Maybe it means that someone, some faculty member, has decided to fight back against the Lions through the school." I can hear the approval in her voice.

"You were hanging out with Stefano the night before his murder?" Ash says in such a strange way that I look at him. "And he was giving you intel about the *Lions*?"

"Yes, and yes," she answers, and even though it's dim, I can tell she's blushing. She avoids looking at her brother directly.

As I stare at her, the dots suddenly connect. Holy shit. If Layla was hanging out with Stefano at night, it must have been after I went to sleep, because she was in her room at curfew. That means she snuck out. And they would have to have been close if he was telling her secrets, much closer than Ash realized. Was Layla *dating* Stefano? By the look on Ash's face, he's thinking the same thing.

I suddenly feel terrible. I was freaking out because I got his blood on me while searching under that bed, and I was talking about him as a dead body. And all the while, Layla had lost someone she cared about. Maybe a lot.

Ash and Layla stare at each other.

I speak to cut the awkward tension between them. "But why, Layla?" I ask. "Why are the Lions after me, of all people, first trying to pin Stefano's death on me, then Nyx, then sending someone to slit my throat? And likewise, why is someone protecting me?"

"Right," she says. "That's the question. And if we don't find out the answer fast, I think we're going to regret it."

Ash stays silent, still staring at his sister.

Thirty-Three

WHEN I WALK into history class with Layla, I'm surprised to find I'm now doing all the things I thought were so weird my first day—walking silently, keeping track of the other students through subtle glances, and speaking in a low voice. And since we woke up this morning, Layla has gone silent on me again. Not her normal thinking quiet, either. She seems agitated and upset but refuses to talk about it. I can't help but wonder if it has something to do with revealing her relationship with Stefano. Even in the short time I've spent with her, I know that must not have been easy for her. And I'm almost positive that if I bring it up, I will only make things worse.

Brendan is already in the classroom and looks like he got as little sleep as I did. Layla is practically scowling, and everyone seems on edge—the kind of vibe that has you wanting to look over your shoulder or jump when something grazes your arm.

"Shall we begin?" Kartal says, even though it's not really a question. She's standing near her globe and drums her fingers on it while the students take their seats.

Felix and Aarya are the last in the door, and their body language makes me think they might have been fighting.

"Sit," Kartal says to Aarya, and I can tell she doesn't want to. Her fists clench but she drops into her chair.

"Now then . . . The Knights Hospitallers were trained to fight to the death and to the very last man, no matter the odds against them," Kartal says, and glances at Aarya. "And they were geared up to do just that in 1271, when Sultan Baybars attacked the Hospitaller castle Krak des Chevaliers in Syria. Over the course of a month, the sultan gradually drove the knights within the castle walls. But the sultan knew that the cornered knights would never surrender. So he cleverly crafted a forged letter that was supposedly from the Grand Master of the Knights Hospitallers and sent it to them."

She looks around the room and for a brief second her eyes land on me. "The letter told the knights that they had permission to surrender and even contained instructions on how to do so. And wouldn't you know it, the brave knights fell for the forgery. In exchange for their surrender, the sultan spared their lives." Kartal smiles. "It's history's stories of near misses that I love so much—the ones where you think a certain outcome is inevitable, only to be proven wrong. From the outside, the sultan faced what looked like an inflexible situation. But the sultan was creative; he thought past the conflict. What was the key here? What did the sultan do that is worth remembering?"

The class is strangely silent. Where everyone would usually be competing to answer and one-up each other, they now look lost in thought or exhausted. In the wake of everything that's happened, I wonder more than ever if there is a subtle message in Kartal's story.

"November?" Kartal says.

My attention snaps back to class. "He didn't take the knights for granted."

"Explain."

"Well, like you said, the knights were known to fight to the last man," I say, trying to think my way through the strategy psychologically—the way Layla does when she talks about history. "So a typical approach would be to consider that an immovable truth and prepare to meet them in battle. The sultan was special because he gave the knights an opportunity to act differently, to change what everyone else assumed could never be changed."

Kartal spins her globe. "Yes. Very much so. It's not always the situation that's immovable, as you said, but the way people think about the situation. A fresh perspective is often needed."

The door opens then and everyone's head turns as if on cue. Blackwood walks in, and there are two guards behind her. The anxiety in the room noticeably rises.

"Layla and November," Blackwood says. "Come with me."

Sweat immediately breaks out on my forehead, and Aarya gives us a look. We slide our chairs back and follow Blackwood into the hallway. As I pass the guards, I expect to get a needle in my arm and be dragged to the dungeon, but it doesn't come. Instead they walk silently behind us.

I steal a questioning glance at Layla, but she's staring forward, looking as frustrated as she has all morning. The extensive list of rules we've broken and the dead guard in front of our room scroll through my head as likely reasons for being escorted out of class. Blackwood clearly wanted everyone to see, like she's making an example of us.

I take several long breaths the way the deception books recommend, to slow my heart and loosen my muscles. The last thing I need is for Layla to attempt to get us out of something and for me to give it away by fidgeting and looking panicked.

One of the guards opens the door to Blackwood's office and we take our positions, Blackwood behind her desk and Layla and I in the armchairs in front.

"Well," Blackwood says after a long beat of looking from me to Layla. "I'm surprised, Layla. And I'm not surprised often."

I glance at Layla, but her face is neutral.

"I spoke with Dr. Conner a couple of days ago. Do you know what he told me?" she says.

Oh, this is not going to go well. I can already feel it.

"He told you that he saw us coming from the boys' dormitory hallway," Layla says without pause, like Blackwood asked her how her breakfast was. "He insinuated that he found our answer suspicious when he asked us about it."

"Yes. He did," Blackwood says. "As he should."

Layla doesn't respond, and I don't blame her. If she says it's the hallway her brother's room is in, Blackwood will say that she also knew Ash wasn't there. And if she says we were just walking, it will look like she's trying to justify herself, suggesting guilt.

"Are you aware that Matteo had class when you did not?" Blackwood asks.

"I am," Layla says, still with the same poker face.

"After you were spotted coming out of that hallway, Dr. Conner inspected Stefano's room," Blackwood says. "He noticed something askew on Stefano's nightstand. Do you know what I'm going to say now?"

Layla shakes her head. And I can't help but think of Gupta, who would point out that she had answered every other question with a verbal response and no head movement, and that suddenly that had changed.

"He said there was a missing match that Matteo and his butler confirmed had not been used by them." Blackwood keeps her gaze on Layla. It's strange the way she's only looking at and addressing Layla and not me.

"The case of the missing match, *dun dun dun,*" I say. Blackwood's intensity toward Layla is almost overwhelming, and if it's making me uncomfortable, it must be getting to her. I figure I can at least buy Layla a second to gather her thoughts.

And it works. Blackwood turns to me. "You think this is funny?"

"No. Not at all. I just thought someone needed to lighten the—"

Blackwood holds up her hand; she's clearly annoyed. "I'll get to you. Until then, remain silent." There's ice in her tone.

"Copy that," I say, and I swear if her eyes were weapons I would be dead.

Blackwood focuses back on Layla and her expression is unreadable. "When the first homicide occurred last week, I thought that we were looking for one individual. But I now know that assumption was incorrect—that a network of persons is responsible for the recent events, and that if I miss one, the chaos and deaths are bound to continue. Sometimes strange things happen on purpose; coincidences aren't coincidences."

My chest tightens. Kartal said almost those exact words in my first class with her—strange things happen on purpose. And she was talking about coincidences that weren't coincidences. I feel oddly relieved that I was right in suspecting that there was some sort of message or code implicit in those stories and that it wasn't just my paranoia running the show. But now I'm wondering what I might have missed or overlooked by not taking the doublespeak seriously enough. In Dad's games he used to say *Look for the subtle things that are different, a pattern. They'll point you in the right direction.*

"It hasn't escaped my notice that you have been angling to get closer to Matteo and Stefano these past few months, Layla," Blackwood says, and snaps me out of my thoughts.

Layla tenses.

"Interesting that you would embrace a roommate whom Matteo so vehemently dislikes," Blackwood says. "And then you're conveniently in the dining hall when they get into a fight in the hallway." She rolls a pencil on her desk, and besides the crackling wood in the fireplace, it's the only sound in the room. "Then you sided with the roommate whom you barely knew. Seems cold for someone who's supposed to be Matteo's friend."

Blackwood looks up at us, and I can tell by her expression that she's closing in, like a hawk about to swoop. "While your brother and November were in the vine courtyard, where were you?"

"Sleeping," Layla says. Her calm tone remains, but I can hear the slightest difference in it, like she's physically tenser and, even with her great control, it's coming through in her voice.

"Right. Of course. You said that the last time."

I want to jump in and defend Layla, but a distracting comment at this point would likely do more harm than good.

Blackwood shifts her gaze to me. "November, did you break

your bedside water glass the day before the guard was murdered?"

Oh no. "Yes."

She sits back, like she knows she's won. "Did Layla help you clean it up?"

Pippa saw Layla help me. There's no way around this. "Yes."

"Did you see Layla take any of the glass?" Blackwood asks, and folds her hands.

"Take any of it? No, definitely not," I say.

Blackwood straightens the ruffles on her shirtsleeve. "The guard who was killed in front of your door had his throat slit with a piece of glass," she says, and I'm fairly certain that if I were the fainting type, this would be my moment. "And *your* glass is the only one in the entire school that has broken all year."

I can tell Layla's scared.

"Now, did *you* take any glass, November?" Blackwood asks.

"No," I say too fast.

"Then the only conclusion I am left to make is that it was Layla."

"It wasn't," I say to Blackwood. "Layla didn't take the glass. I didn't, either. But I'm sure it wasn't Layla." I know I'm not helping, that I have no proof to back me up, but I can't just sit here and let Blackwood corner her.

"As much as I'd love to listen to your endless sputtering, November, I'm afraid I must get on with it. You're going to the dungeon, Layla, for the murder of an Academy guard," Blackwood says, and I almost fall out of my chair.

"*What?*" I say, practically spitting the word. "You don't have proof that Layla did anything!"

Blackwood's look is dangerous. "You are sorely mistaken if you believe I need to justify my decisions to you. And if you continue arguing with me, I can promise you that will only make things worse for Layla." She looks past us, like she's done with our conversation, and raises her voice. "Guards!"

They open the door, and Layla looks at me with genuine fear. I jump in front of her, blocking their path. The guards look at Blackwood. She nods at them and a split second later they have us both pinned and are sticking needles in our arms.

My vision blurs and the world goes black.

Thirty-Four

I TOUCH MY head, which pounds like I got dropped on it. I'm on the couch in my dorm room; the curtains are drawn, and the fire is big and bright the way it usually is after Pippa lights it in the early evening. *But how did I get* . . . All at once, the events from the afternoon flood my memory.

I jump up and scrub my hands over my face to wake myself up. *Layla*. I need to help Layla. This is my fault. *I* snuck out that night. *I* got Layla involved. I stare at the fire, all the awfulness of these couple of weeks coming into focus. Layla's in the dungeon. Aunt Jo is dead. Someone's trying to murder me. And Dad is god knows where, potentially being hunted and running for his life.

"November?" Ash says softly, and appears in Layla's bedroom door.

I don't jump this time. I want to apologize for what happened to Layla, tell him I tried to stop the guards, but an apology doesn't fix anything. "Blackwood threw Layla in the dungeon" is all I manage to say.

"I know." His gaze is intense again, and I don't blame him.

"When I heard at lunch that Blackwood had removed you two from class and that you never returned, I came here looking for you both. But I only found you, sedated on the couch. Which told me Layla was most likely in the dungeon and that you'd likely been sedated because you were trying to prevent the guards from taking her."

I nod and exhale, relieved that at least he knows I attempted to stand up for her.

"Tell me everything about your conversation with Blackwood," he says. "Don't leave anything out."

I recount the meeting for him almost word for word, start to finish. He lets me speak, not commenting until I'm done with the story.

"Something's weird about it," I say. "There's no reason for Blackwood to punish Layla in front of me. It would have been easier just to leave me in class."

As Ash considers what I'm saying, I can almost see the wheels turning in his head. "Maybe Blackwood wanted you to hear it, to know about Dr. Conner discovering the missing match and about the piece of glass," he says.

"But why?" I ask. "Unless she wants me to know because she's also the one who told that guard to look after me? Could she be the faculty member Layla was speculating about who's fighting back against the Lions? But how does that make any sense if in the same conversation she dragged Layla to the dungeon?"

He shakes his head and I fidget. We're both quiet as we analyze the situation.

I look up at him. "Did you find out anything about that cut on Felix's hand?"

"Yes and no. He didn't have any classes where he might easily have come by the cut, which makes it suspect. But I couldn't really get many details on him, either. He may not be a powerful Lion, but he's still a Lion, and no one feels safe speaking against them right now."

"I get that," I say. "The question is, what happened to the glass after it left this room? And is there any way to get Layla out of that dungeon?"

He shakes his head. "We'd have to find it first. The dungeon is either under the castle or possibly under one of the outer perimeter walls. That's why they use the sedative anytime someone gets locked up. They don't want us to know where it is."

"Okay, then let's tackle this one piece of missing information at a time," I say. "And fast, before someone else gets killed. Pippa should be coming soon to turn down the beds and refill the water. You stay here and get her to tell you everything about that glass. If we both leave, we'll miss our chance to talk to her."

He looks at me questioningly. "*Both* leave? And where are you going?"

I swallow. "To find Matteo," I say, fighting to keep my voice calm.

He looks at me for a long moment like he's trying to decide something, or maybe he's registering my fear and that I'm doing it despite that.

"Be careful," he says so genuinely that my stomach flutters.

There's a beat of silence and I nod.

I turn around, grab my cloak from the armoire, and exit into the hallway. The cold air and the idea of confronting Matteo send a shiver down my back.

* * *

Minutes later, I'm standing in front of Matteo's room, my hand hovering to knock on the door and my heart racing. The only problem is, if I knock and he slams the door in my face, I'm screwed.

From down the corridor comes the sound of boots on stairs and I don't hesitate—I lift the latch and walk right into his room.

Matteo's on his couch, staring at his fireplace. "Get out," he says without even turning toward me. The sight of him makes my nervousness soar. I take two more steps but don't dare move far from the door.

"I'll get out if you tell me what you know about me." My voice sounds louder and my tone more forceful than I thought it would.

He turns to me and for a brief second he looks surprised. "I'm sick of playing games with you, November. Save us both the energy of getting angry and turn around and leave," he says, and the disgust I usually detect when he's speaking to me isn't there. He almost seems worn out.

I've only got one shot at this. "You don't trust me. But consider this: Layla does. And you know better than I do how much Layla cared about Stefano. Do you really think she would trust someone who killed her boyfriend? Of course she wouldn't."

I watch as Matteo clenches his hands and then releases them again. It seems like he's trying to keep himself from getting worked up.

"Ever since Stefano's murder we've been trying to figure out why Charles attacked your friend. Layla, Ash, me—we've been sneaking around this creepy castle, putting ourselves at risk trying to *help*." My voice becomes more insistent. "The least you could do is stop making things harder!"

Matteo gets up off the couch so fast that I take a step backward. He crosses the room in a few long strides.

"How dare you come into my room and tell me what I'm doing or not doing? If this whole situation is anyone's fault, it's *yours*," he says, and his broad chest rises and falls quickly. "What made you think you could just walk into this school, an exact replica of your mother? You can't be stupid enough to think no one would notice. Anyone who knew her recognized you immediately. This is your mess!"

I look at him closely, trying to make sense of his words. "This is *exactly* what I mean. You're assuming I know something I don't. How do people here know my mother?"

A warning flashes in his eyes, telling me to back off. "I'm doing my best not to kill you right now. But you're not making it easy. You should have stayed in whatever hideout you came from."

"Are you kidding?" I say, matching his tone. "Gladly! Fire up the goddamn plane. I don't want to be at this insane school any more than you want me here. Blackwood refused to send me home. So you can mistrust me until the end of time, but it won't change the fact that both of us are stuck here together. Only one of us knows anything about my family's history. And it's not me."

He takes a step backward, getting a good look at me. "Bullshit."

"No, not bullshit. I wish it were like you all thought. I would *love* to be playing a game right now, masterfully manipulating people and scheming about my next move. But instead I've been kept in the dark my entire life and am trying desperately to learn my way around this place and to avoid getting murdered at every turn, all because of something to do with my parents that I know nothing about. In fact, as far as I can tell"— I point at him—"*you* are the one person who reliably knows who I am. But the moment you saw me, you punched me in the face. So I've been left on my own here. Some Family you are."

Something in his expression shifts, only I can't quite read his emotions.

I hold eye contact with him so that he knows I'm completely serious. "Stefano is dead," I say in a calmer voice. "And without Layla and Ash, I would have been dead by now, too. So, yes, I'm in your room yelling at you to explain what I'm missing here. Because as far as I can tell, this whole mess circles around me and my parents and very possibly *you.* I'm over not having answers. The only way I'm leaving this room without an explanation is if I'm dead."

He scowls and stays silent for so long that I wonder if he's coming around or deciding to in fact kill me.

"When you attacked me in the dining hall . . . ," he says, and his voice is less angry than it was before. "Somebody died that day. Who died?"

"My aunt," I say, and my voice deflates as I picture Jo's face. "My mom's sister."

His eyes widen and he runs a hand through his hair. "Magdalene?"

The sound of my aunt's name coming out of his mouth all but freezes me. "She, well, she went by Jo, actually. Sh-she—"

336

I'm stuttering, unable to make sense of his personal knowledge of one of my most important people.

"—gave the name to herself after she read an American novel called *Little Women*," he says, finishing my sentence.

My eyes tear up and I will them to stop. The last thing I want is to cry in front of him. "Yeah," I say quietly. "How could you possibly know that?"

"My mom used to tell that story," he says.

I look at him sideways. "Your mom knew my aunt Jo?" I say, trying to grasp what that could mean.

"Knew her? My mom is Jo's *sister*—the youngest of the three," he says, and it feels like someone sucked all the air out of the room.

"You're lying," I say, pressing my hand into my chest in a desperate attempt to get control of my heart and the crack I feel forming there.

He shakes his head.

My mom and Aunt Jo had another sister. They had a younger sister, and Matteo . . . "You're my *cousin*?" I say, and my confusion and anger surge anew. I shake my head to blink away the tears, but they're only getting heavier. "When did you know? How could you not tell me this!" I'm stamping toward him, fuming. "My god, you punched me!"

I swing at him and he leans out of the way.

"You made me a target!" I yell, and swing at him again.

He catches my wrist. "*You* made *us* a target!" he yells right back at me, and releases my hand. "Stefano is dead because you came here. So don't tell me what I did to you."

The more I look at him, the more I realize how much his features remind me of my mom and Aunt Jo. How could I not have seen that before? "Why were my parents in America?"

He looks at me with caution.

"I'm serious. Tell me why my parents were hiding in the country. Tell me why I didn't know I was Strategia."

He frowns. "You didn't know you were—"

"No. And spare me the endless 'That doesn't make sense' responses," I say. "I know better than anyone that it doesn't make sense. But I have a right to know who I am and why I grew up the way I did. And don't tell me you don't know, because I can see on your face right now that you do."

"I'm not telling you Family secrets," he says.

"These are *my* secrets! I have more of a right to them than you do and you know that," I say.

Matteo looks at me like he's not sure.

I exhale. "Look, my mom died when I was six, and although I was always told it was an accident, Aunt Jo was vehemently convinced it wasn't. Now my aunt gets murdered—*our aunt*. And I'm guessing that whoever is trying to destroy my family will go after my father next. If they haven't already. And if what's going on in this school is related to their deaths, and I'm nearly positive it is, then I damn well need to know. All I have to go on right now is that the Lions hate us because we're trying to stop them from taking over all of Strategia."

Matteo scoffs. "You are a Lion," he says, and I open my mouth and close it again. His comment, while confirming my suspicion about my dad, throws me. How can I have all these identities that mean so much to everyone here that I've never known anything about?

"I'm also a Bear," I say, and raise my chin. "Just like my mom and aunt. And even if my dad was born a Lion, in his heart, he wasn't one of them."

Matteo steps away from me and for a split second I'm terrified that he'll go into his bedroom and lock me out. But instead he heads for the fireplace, staring at the logs for so long that I take a few steps toward him.

He nods to himself like he's made a decision. "Twenty-five years ago there was a group of students here who were the best this school ever had."

"I've heard the teachers talk about them," I say.

"Right," he says. "Your mom, my mom, Aunt Jo, Blackwood, your father, and a couple of others were part of that group. But there were two who were better than all the rest—your parents."

"*What?*" It takes me a second to wrap my mind around what he's saying. "Not the . . . the scroll in the library?" I ask, remembering my visit there with Ash. "That was *them?*"

He nods, and the look he gives me tells me to shut up and let him finish. "Your parents—the firstborn of the Lion Family and the firstborn of the Bear Family—started at Academy Absconditi the same year. My mother says everyone anticipated fighting, considering it's what our Families do. And they did at first, but over time they also fell in love."

My stomach twists uncomfortably. Not only were my parents the best, but they were also both firstborns? The magnitude of information my dad kept from me is staggering.

"My mother said your parents thought they could change Strategia politics for the better," Matteo says. "But they soon found that the decades of fighting between the Lions and the Bears, and the centuries of the power imbalance, were going to make things nearly impossible. Initially your grandparents refused to come to an agreement about what the terms would be if they were to get married. Jag demanded that your father and mother stay with them and that she give up her standing as a Bear, and your mom's parents wanted the opposite. They fought viciously among themselves for months, but to everyone's surprise, they did eventually agree to sit down and try to compromise."

Jag is my grandfather. Oh, holy hell. "And what happened?" I ask quickly, with some amazement that my parents were actually doing something to fix things. "Did they get their Families to agree?"

Matteo sighs, like he understands the larger question I'm asking. "At the time, some people thought that your parents would restore order and put an end to the Lions picking off members of other Families."

"By your tone I'm guessing that I'm about to find out how they went from uniting their Families to hiding," I say.

"Your mother killed Jag's brother—"

"Wait, *what*?"

Matteo puts up his hand. "Patience really isn't your strong suit, is it?" He pauses, daring me to interrupt him again. I swallow and shake my head. "What I was saying was that your mother killed Jag's brother and any shadow of an agreement that our Families had fell apart."

My mother. A *killer*?

As if he can sense my shock, he continues, speaking quickly, almost reassuringly. "My mother always said the reasons were complicated. And if she knows more, she's never told me exactly what happened. But needless to say, the Lions put out a hit on your mother."

Even as Matteo is talking, I'm wrestling with the impossibility that this is my mother, my *family*.

"As for your father, he fought back against Jag and the Lions, and it earned him a contract on his head as well. So they ran." Matteo shrugs, as if running from trained assassins is what everyone does when things get bad. "As for our Family, well, the Bears felt betrayed that your mom left instead of coming home to them. And they . . . they refused to protect them."

My eyes widen. That's why Aunt Jo blamed her family for Mom's death.

"The way I heard it, the Lion assassins came back one by one without finding either of your parents. Or they didn't come back at all. So to save face, the Lions convinced the rest of the Families that your parents were tragically murdered. But meanwhile the hunt went on," Matteo finishes.

"But they did kill my mother eventually," I say quietly.

"Yes," he says, and there's some regret in his voice. "But none of the other Families know that except us and the Lions. And since then, the animosity between the Lions and Bears has only gotten worse. When I hit you that day outside the dining hall, I . . ." He falls silent then and returns his gaze to the fire.

"It's okay," I say, and my voice is heavy. "Thanks for telling me the truth."

"You are . . . welcome," he says, but doesn't look at me. Under all his anger and bravado, there's such a deep sadness.

"You should know," I begin slowly, trying to find some way to match his honesty with another truth, "that Charles wasn't trying to kill Stefano. He was trying to kill you and make me take the fall for it. After your explanation just now, it makes a hell of a lot of sense that the Lions would want to divide us. I also think you should know that the guard who was killed outside my door had his neck slashed with a piece of glass. As far as we can tell, the weapon is still out there somewhere. So I guess what I'm saying is . . . be careful."

Matteo looks up and his sadness intensifies. "They were trying to kill *me*?"

I nod slowly. I feel awful for telling him. I know how I would feel if something happened to Emily, especially if it had something to do with me. But after what he's just confided in me, I can't *not* tell him. There is every chance someone will try again.

"How do you know this about Stefano?" Matteo asks, and I can almost hear his heart breaking.

I explain the blood under Stefano's bed, the guard's tattoo, and all the strange details we've uncovered. He listens to everything I have to say, and by the time I'm done speaking, his jaw is tight and his forehead is creased in concentration.

"I was going to come back here that day after class," he says. "But Blackwood had given me a third mark for punching you and sent me to the outer perimeter."

"That's what Layla figured," I say.

Matteo rubs his neck and looks at me like he's trying to decide something. Finally he sighs and drops his arm. "And I wouldn't assume I'm the only one who knows who your parents are. Blackwood has to know. Probably Conner. Brendan and Nyx were Charles's best friends, so they definitely know. Felix. And I'm sure there are others."

"Felix?" I repeat, suddenly remembering the creepy "I *know*" that he hissed in my ear at my first lunch.

"Yes," Matteo affirms, and rubs his neck again. "The thing is . . ." He pauses for a moment, like he's debating whether he should keep going, and I sit very still, hoping he will. "Felix's father was one of the assassins sent to kill your parents. One of the ones that didn't come back. There are likely other Lions here, too, who have lost a relative trying to take out your parents. No one knew you even existed, though, until you showed up," he says.

My mouth is suddenly dry and it's hard to swallow. My parents *killed* Felix's father? No wonder he hates me. Not that *his* father wasn't trying to kill *them*, but still. I should feel excited about getting another piece of the puzzle, but the entire conversation fills me with dread. Coming to this school was like starting a wildfire that immediately raged out of control. Not to mention that I remind people of the past in the worst possible ways.

"November?" Matteo says.

"Yeah?" I look up, snapping out of my thoughts.

"You should know that I didn't punch you because I was angry," he says. "What happened with your mom . . . You're still a Bear. I punched you because I was told to."

"Who told you to punch me?" I say, my brain starting to whirl once again. "Was it Felix?"

"I can't tell you that," Matteo says, and I can see by his face that he's not going to. "But I just thought you should know."

I open my mouth to argue, but he looks so lost in his thoughts that I suspect he's thinking about Stefano again.

"Now it's time for you to go," he says, and I do.

As I close the door behind me, I can't help but wish things were different. I finally have another family member who's more like me than I want to admit, and he also wants nothing to do with me. I can't really blame him, though. He's right. If I'd never come to this school, Stefano would still be alive.

Thirty-Five

"ASH?" I SAY, when I'm back in my room. I wait a beat, but there's no response.

I check the window and under the beds and return to the empty common room. On the floor in front of the fireplace, written in ash, are the words *Be back soon.* I smile at the cleverness and rub out the message with the bottom of my boot.

My conversation with Matteo cycles through my thoughts. My parents were next in line to lead their Families. They were the best in this school. I can't even imagine what their lives were like before they had me and before they became the Romeo and Juliet of the Strategia world. I need to talk to my dad. I have so many questions, so many missing details from Matteo's story to fill in.

Sending me to the Academy makes no sense at all. My family was in *hiding*—why put me in the one place where I'd be exposed to the very people who are a threat? Matteo was right that I resemble my mom: if he could pick me out, surely others can, too. I keep thinking about what Blackwood said, that strange things happen on purpose. Matteo said Blackwood knows who I am, which she must if she attended the Academy at the same time as my parents. But why let me in? She must have known that the shit would hit the fan as soon as the Lions and the Bears recognized me.

I head for the breakfast table and pull out a chair.

But Blackwood also gave me information about the glass and the match, and she quoted my history teacher. Plus, Ash told me that she's a Bear herself. I tap my fingers on the table. There has to be a specific reason, a message she was trying to communicate. Strategia aren't random; I've learned that much. So I'm just missing the pattern, some subtle difference, as my dad would say.

I think back to my first history class, when Kartal said strange things happen on purpose. She was talking about coincidences in historical contexts and how people love to believe them and exaggerate them. And she said that if you could pull off a crime and make it look like a coincidence, it was a brilliant achievement. Was she trying to tell me something? What if she was hinting about the murder happening just after I arrived, and people wanting to link it to me and exaggerate the details—which, as it turns out, wound up being true?

Then there was the story of the decoy body being dropped to the Spanish during World War II with fake plans to invade Greece. The entire plan relied on the fact that the people who found the body wouldn't do the inspection they needed to do. Just like I didn't examine Stefano thoroughly when I discovered his body, not like Layla would have. And it wasn't until Layla asked the right questions that we figured out Stefano had been killed hours earlier and planted in that hallway, eventually leading us to his room, and to the fact that Charles was actually after *Matteo*.

My pulse begins to race. Then there was my poisons class. Hisakawa said that poisoning is truly great when there's no evidence left behind. And that if you can manage them, the best poisons of all are emotional and psychological. Was she talking about me and Matteo? Someone had clearly been trying to pit us against each other from the beginning. And if I hadn't forced myself to talk to Matteo, I still wouldn't know who my parents are, which is obviously key to understanding how this whole mess started.

I hit my fist on the table. Why hadn't I been paying closer attention? Ash had made it clear to me that the Academy wasn't about academics, it was about learning to read the signs. But I was so caught up in my own fears and frustrations I couldn't see what was right in front of my face.

I put my head in my hands. Moment after moment comes flooding back to me. Kartal talking about the sultan who sent the letter to those knights, and how he gave them the opportunity to act differently, to change what everyone assumed couldn't be changed.

I chew on my thumbnail angrily. What or who is the inflexible thing in this situation that needs to be approached differently? There's the hatred between the Lions and the Bears, but that's not something I can fix in this school. It has to be something more specific.

My door opens and I look up at Ash.

"Oh, good. You're here," Ash says, and I can see the concern leave his eyes.

"I spoke to Pippa," he says, and takes the seat across from me. "At first she said she didn't see anyone and took the glass immediately down to the kitchen to be disposed of. But when I pressed, she acknowledged that she actually stopped a couple of times to check on other rooms. I made her walk me through her route, and I've got to say that there was ample opportunity for someone to steal a piece, even though she claims she kept a close watch on it."

"My money is on Felix," I grumble.

Ash pulls back and looks at me. "What do you know that I don't?"

"This has all been about killing me, right?" I say. "Charles killed Stefano to pin it on me, and if it had worked, I would have been the one executed. Then Nyx tried to skewer me with a sword. Then someone came to slit my throat with a piece of glass but wound up having to confront the guard instead. Like Layla said, Brendan rarely does things himself. And of all the possible suspects, Felix definitely has a reason to want revenge. My parents killed his father."

Ash's eyes widen. "How do you know that?"

"Matteo told me."

"Matteo *told* you," Ash says like he doesn't quite believe it. "Matteo went from punching you to suddenly telling you secrets?"

"Not that this makes it any better, but he was told to punch me," I say.

"He was what? Why would . . . Maybe Dr. Conner? It could be some kind of new assessment tactic," Ash says, and a hint of concern reappears in his tone.

"Maybe," I say. "But that punch earned Matteo a third mark and landed him in the outer perimeter—a punishment

347

orchestrated by *Blackwood* that just might have saved his life. My guess is that she was trying to keep him out of harm's way. Maybe trying to keep him safe and test me at the same time."

Ash looks at me questioningly for a second. "He told you more, didn't he?"

I nod slowly. I've barely begun to process it all myself.

Ash waits for me to say something, and when I don't he says, "Did he tell you who you are?"

"Yes. My dad is a Lion, like we suspected," I say, stretching out my sentence and trying to figure out how to approach the rest of my answer. "And considering what my parents did, it makes sense that the Lions want to kill me badly," I add. I want to tell Ash that I'm Matteo's cousin and explain why I'm a target, but I need to think it through first. If I've learned anything from Ash, it's that personal information is dangerous and should be shared precisely and with caution.

He half laughs. "Look who's guarding Family secrets now. You're becoming more of a Strategia by the minute."

"It's not that I'm not going to tell you," I say. "I plan to tell you. I just haven't made sense of it all myself yet." I pause. "Besides, aren't you more worried about getting Layla out of the dungeon?"

"As far as I'm concerned, they're related," he says. "And just because I don't flaunt my emotions doesn't mean I'm not worried. You know that." He leans back and shifts his weight. His voice has a tightness to it, like I've offended him.

"Sorry, I shouldn't have said that," I say. "I'm just on edge and I can feel that we're running out of time. I mean, how long do you think it's going to be before someone tries to kill me again? Tonight? Felix is still out there. Brendan. God knows who else is part of this."

Ash takes a breath. "Understood."

I crack my knuckles. "What about Aarya?"

"What about her?" Ash says.

"Felix is likely involved. But something tells me that Aarya isn't, at least not the same way. In fact, from everything I've seen of her interactions with Brendan, I'd guess she hates the Lions." I pause, considering the situation. "And then there's Ines," I say.

Ash looks at me like he's not sure where I'm going with this, or maybe he is but he doesn't like it.

"The Lions are killing off the top students, right? And Ines is one of the best. She's also Aarya's closest friend. Won't Aarya want to protect her best friend? Maaaybe we can convince her to take a stand with us, help us get a grip on what she knows about this whole situation," I say.

Ash is already shaking his head. "Aarya wouldn't do that in a million years," he says. "Believe me, if I thought there was any way she would cooperate, I would have asked her by now."

"But you can't know that for sure until you try," I insist. "I didn't think there was any way Matteo would talk to me, and I managed it."

"Matteo and Aarya are fundamentally different people. Matteo has a temper and is too emotional, but he's a good person. I wouldn't have let you go to his room alone if I thought otherwise. But in my two and a half years at the Academy, I've never once seen Aarya do anything for anyone but herself. She would take whatever opportunity you give her and flip it on you," Ash says, and all at once I'm reminded of the knights and the sultan.

"The inflexible one . . . ," I say under my breath.

"The inflexible what?" Ash asks, but I'm already on my feet.

Of all the people who could appear immovable, stubborn, and ready to fight to the death, Aarya is the most fitting. I don't know why I didn't think of her as a possibility earlier.

"I know this sounds crazy, but my gut is telling me that getting Aarya on our side is important," I say, and take a deep breath. My voice has gone from frustrated to excited. "I can't put my finger on what she might contribute; I just know I need to convince her to tell me what she knows."

Ash groans. "I don't know how else to make this clear: *Aarya will not help you.* She'll only find a way to hurt you," he says with a serious tone. But of course he would be serious. If Ash weren't completely convinced that she was inflexible, Aarya wouldn't be a contender for being able to act differently. It's like Kartal said: a fresh perspective is needed.

I stop pacing and look at Ash. "Would you say that Aarya cares about Ines more than she does about Felix?"

"November . . . ," Ash says, and stands. I can see it written all over him that he's going to try to talk me down.

"You told me once that Felix was in love with Aarya but that it was never going to happen. So answer the question. Does she care about Ines more?"

"If I had to guess, I would say she does," Ash says.

"Okay. Good," I say, and run into my bedroom. I pull a piece of paper out of my bedside table drawer. On it I write:

Ines is in danger. Meet me in the trees right after curfew and I'll explain.

Ember

I figure if I sign that ridiculous name she'll know it's really me who wrote the note. I hand it to Ash. "Can you slip this to her? I know you're good at this sort of thing because of that game you and Layla played when I first got here."

He looks at the paper and glances up at me. "You're not seriously going to do this, are you? If someone's going to talk to Aarya, I should be the one to do it."

I shake my head. "You can't, Ash. It has to be me. You don't see her the way I do."

"No, I don't," he says, and he's getting more frustrated by the minute. "I see her for exactly who she is. I can read her. I've known her for years. I've seen people go up against her over and over, and she always wins because she's ruthless and because she's *talented*. You're too forgiving. You're too trusting. Layla warned you that you weren't good enough to go up against Aarya, and I'm telling you that meeting her in the trees after dark is a fast way to get yourself killed."

I take a deep breath, willing myself to be calm. "I know you think all that, which is exactly why I have to be the one to talk to her. I'm not saying there's not a risk, but if there's even a slim possibility that she has information we need, this can't wait," I say. "I get that you're trying to protect me, and I appreciate it. But I have to do this."

"Seeing Aarya in a more forgiving light isn't a *reason*," he says.

"Blackwood had me in her office when she punished Layla for no reason that I can tell other than to give me information about the glass and the match," I say. "And—"

"You're saying you think Blackwood is trying to help you?

Why would she lock up my sister to help you? She's toying with you," Ash says.

"Helping or toying—it really doesn't make a difference. The point is that she gave me information. And Blackwood's not the only one. That guard who protected me. Kartal and Hisakawa. They all said things that directly related to the murder and the situation with me and Matteo. And in Kartal's last class, she said something about taking people for granted. Not in the typical sense, but in the way that if you see people as ruthless and vicious, you can't *unsee* them behaving that way. She said sometimes having a fresh perspective on a person is the only way to influence change. If you ask me, that sounds like Aarya," I finish.

Ash is quiet for a long time, and emotions dance in his eyes like lights on a pond. "So let me get this straight. You're going to risk your life because you think your teachers are giving you hidden messages in their classes?"

"Yes. Exactly. And if I were anyone else, you wouldn't doubt what I was saying. You're only questioning me because I wasn't raised the way you were. But that doesn't mean I'm wrong. So if you won't deliver my note, I will," I say, and hold out my hand so he can give the note back to me.

His eyes flash anger. "You know she's not going to come alone," he says. "So even if by some miracle Aarya doesn't try to kill you, someone else might."

"I know," I say. "That's why I chose the trees—they're my best terrain. It's the only advantage I can give myself. Well, that and I could really use you there with me."

His eyes widen slightly like he can't believe what I'm saying. "You thought I wouldn't be?"

"I hoped you would be," I say.

He rubs his forehead. "How is it that sometimes you understand so much and other times you understand nothing?"

"Look," I say, "if it doesn't work and Aarya throws me out of the tree, then I'll admit I was wrong and you can call the shots for the rest of the night. But you're wasting time right now and we need to deliver that note."

He folds the note up and looks at me like he wants to say something, but changes his mind and walks out of the room.

Thirty-Six

I'VE REVIEWED MY strategy over and over in my head, although it's hard to plan for someone like Aarya. I glance at the door for the hundredth time. Ash should have been back by now.

On top of my anxiety over meeting Aarya and over the network of people clearly trying to kill me, my thoughts keep going back to my parents and everything I don't know about them. What they were like when they were my age, whether they liked being Strategia, how many assassins they ultimately had to kill to protect themselves and me, where I factored into the decisions they made. It's almost more than I can take.

My door opens and I jump up from my seat near the fireplace.

Ash wears the same worried expression he had when he left. "It's done," he says quietly as he latches the door behind him.

"And? Did she say anything or give any indication that she would show up?" I ask, searching his face for clues.

"No. But we're talking about Aarya, and this is an opportunity to get you in a vulnerable position. I doubt she'll miss it," he says.

Ash removes his cloak and rolls up his sleeves. I give him a questioning look. He's not getting ready to spar with me, is he?

I flip my braid over my shoulder, and just as I do, Ash aims a punch at my stomach. I block and immediately adjust my stance so that I'm not open to him. Well, I guess that answers that question.

"Mediocre defense," he says, and takes a swing, this time at my face.

I dodge his fist.

"If I were Aarya, that punch would have hit you. You can't be that slow," he says. "And if she comes after you in the trees, it's mostly going to be hand work. She might manage a kick if she's able to brace herself, but otherwise you can expect that any attack will be aimed at your upper body."

I jab at him, but he easily steps out of reach before I'm halfway there and grabs my wrist, yanking me off balance. I stumble forward. He hooks his arm around my neck in a loose choke hold, pulling me into his chest.

"Don't counter unless you absolutely have to. I've told you that," he says roughly, and releases me. "You'll instantly put yourself at a disadvantage. You're fast and you learn quickly, but you need to be ready. You need to pay attention to visual cues."

"But I saw your shoulder move and—"

"That's not what I'm talking about," he says, and it's obvious that he's still frustrated about the Aarya meeting. "I gave you three cues that I wanted to fight and you fixed your hair instead of getting yourself into a defensive position."

Wow. He's in a mood.

"Okay, well, what were your cues?" I spit back at him. "Rolling up your sleeves?"

He cocks an eyebrow at me. "You're frustrated. That's good," he says. "Maybe now you'll pay better attention."

Man, I wish I could fast-forward to being a better fighter so that I could knock him out.

"I taught you what to look for when you're already fighting—which foot is back, where your opponent's eyes go before they take a swing, and which muscles tense. But what you don't know are the signs that tell you someone *wants* to fight," he says.

"Are you getting any of those vibes from me right now? Because you should be," I say.

He lifts an eyebrow again. "Look for your opponent's chin to jut out or their jaw to clench—like this," he says, gritting his teeth and lifting his jaw in my direction. "When people are angry, they frequently grit their teeth. And jutting your jaw is a territorial gesture—a sign that you're threatening someone's personal space. Now, it'll never be as pronounced and obvious with Strategia as with some idiot in a bar, so you're going to have to be alert for a more subtle version of it."

I nod. "That makes sense. Charles did that before he threw the knife at me."

"Exactly," he says. "Another thing to look for is the nostril flare. It's a survival mechanism to get more oxygen into our lungs and get the blood flowing before a fight. The same is true of pupil dilation—they'll expand to take in as much information about an opponent and the surroundings as possible."

"Got it," I say, nodding.

"Another thing you might detect is someone puffing themselves up, trying to look as imposing as possible. The more space someone's body takes up, the more testosterone they produce—giving both men and women strength and speed. If you're paying close enough attention and wind up spotting a couple of these cues, then you need to move immediately. Don't let Aarya get a hit in. You'll greatly regret it."

"And what if I only see one cue?" I ask.

He frowns. "One isn't enough of an indicator. It might just mean that she's angry rather than planning to hurt you. So whatever you do, don't mirror any of her behaviors. It will only escalate the situation. Keep your posture relaxed and open."

"I can do that," I say.

"And again, don't counter unless you have to," he says. "Just get away from her and let me deal with it."

I nod. "I appreciate it. Even with the bad attitude that's putting me on edge."

"*Attitude?*" His eyes widen. "You're really not taking this seriously enough."

"Not true," I say, matching his frustration. "I'm nothing *but* serious about this. I know this is risky. I know people are trying to kill me. I just don't need to suffer over it until something's actually happening or I'll tense up and screw myself."

His mouth opens and closes, like he doesn't know what to say to me.

"And it definitely doesn't help anything to have you mad at me," I say.

"Mad at you? November, I'm not mad at you," he says, and pauses. "I'm *worried* about you. I . . ." He looks away.

"What?" I say.

He makes eye contact with me. The butterflies I felt earlier return tenfold, and before I can reconsider what I'm doing, I take a step toward him.

The emotions on his face shift from frustration to desire and back again, like he's having an argument with himself over me. "I care about you," he says, and his voice is quiet. "I care what happens to you. The last thing I want is for you to get hurt." His words are slow and weighty. I get the sense that he hasn't really cared about anyone in so long that he's almost scared to admit it out loud, that caring for someone means so much responsibility that it's overwhelming. He smiles a small heart-wrenching smile. "I don't know what I would do if I lost you."

For a split second he looks at my lips and I can see the question on his face.

My heart pounds and I stare at him, completely lost in his eyes. I want to tell him that I feel the same way, that I don't know what it all means, and that this has never happened to me before. Instead I move closer.

He lifts a hand and gently brushes my cheek with the back of his fingers, sending a pleasant shiver down my neck. In turn, I reach out and place my palm against his chest. I can feel his heart under his linen shirt and it's racing almost as fast as my own. He runs his finger over my bottom lip and slips his other hand behind my neck.

When his lips press into mine, it's with such surprising emotion that a thrill pulses through me, weakening my knees. He pulls me toward him and my arms lift to wrap around his neck.

His hands move through my hair and onto my back and I press closer into him. All those times Emily talked about being knocked over by a kiss, I never understood, until now. Our connection is overwhelming, like a floodgate opening that I didn't even know was there.

All at once he releases me before I can steady myself, and I'm left with a tingling body and no words. I blink at him in confusion.

There's a beat of silence.

"I didn't mean . . . ," he says, and he looks vulnerable. "I'm sorry."

"Why are you sorry?" I say.

He smiles and shakes his head. "You're right, I don't know why I said that."

I grin. "I'm pretty sure you just scared the crap out of yourself by having a real emotion."

He laughs but also looks a little sad. "You might actually be right."

"Well, you're not the only one who's scared by their feelings right now," I say, and realize my cheeks are getting hot again.

He doesn't respond right away. He just looks at me, his eyes burning with thoughts I wish I knew. "November, there's something . . ."

I wait a beat.

"Ash?" I say, hoping he'll continue.

Ash opens his mouth to respond, but before he can get a word out there's a muffled sound from the hallway—a guard patrolling.

"It's time," he says, and all the fear I was putting off earlier immediately comes rushing back.

Thirty-Seven

ASH GRABS MY cloak from the armoire and drapes it around my shoulders. "Last chance to change your mind or let me go in your place," he says, pulling my braid out from under the collar. I shake my head wordlessly. Even that simple touch sends a shiver through me.

"Stubborn," he whispers, and for just a moment we stare at each other.

He puts on his own cloak and the mood shifts. "I'm not going to take the same route or Aarya will spot me. I'm going to go around and enter through the garden lounge."

"Okay," I say, and I hate that just the mention of Aarya made my voice catch. I secure my cloak at my neck and lift my hood, not enough to obscure my vision, but enough to hide me in the shadows.

Ash opens the door. "Count to twenty-five and then go." He takes one long last look at me. "And be careful," he says before silently slipping into the hallway.

I force myself to breathe to get more oxygen into my muscles, like Ash said, and to focus my racing mind.

Here goes nothing.

I step through my door and move silently into the hall and then down two flights. I stay in the shadows as the guard in the foyer exits the courtyard door, and I wait a beat before slipping out the door myself.

I stand in the pitch black of the vestibule, the stone of the archway cold beneath my warm fingers, and count off a few seconds like Ash did. When I'm sure the guard is far enough away, I slide behind the curtain, careful not to rustle the fabric, and into the dark courtyard.

The grass is spongy beneath my boots and silences my steps as I run toward the trees. I stop at the vine near the middle of the back wall that Ash and I used last time and scan the dark branches above me. But there's no sign of Aarya.

I climb up the vine and make my way through the branches at a measured pace, being extra cautious with my footholds and listening for noise of any kind. The sky bench is empty when I reach it, so I position my back against the tree trunk, eliminating one direction I need to watch. I sit in a relaxed way, even though my nerves are buzzing like a hive of bees. I make note of all the branches I can move to and the nearby vines I can grab, in case I need to run for it.

"Well, well, the note was real," Aarya says, and drops down from a higher branch onto the bench.

My heart skips a beat. Ash's warning about Aarya's talents and her ruthlessness rings in my head.

"You wouldn't have come all the way out here if you thought the note wasn't real, would you?" I say, trying to show her that I'm calm and comfortable.

She balances on one foot, like she's walking on a thin ledge.

"It's not really *all the way out here*. If you'd wanted to make it challenging, you should have asked me to meet you in the dungeon."

I look at her sideways.

She grins and drops into a sitting position about three feet away from me. "I can see by the look on your face"—she points at me, moving her finger in a circle—"that someone told you they didn't know where the dungeon is . . . Ash, maybe?" She takes a dramatic breath, like "Isn't it such a shame that you're so gullible?"

My stomach twists. Ash knows where the dungeon is and didn't tell me? *Wait, this is Aarya,* I remind myself. *Don't let her distract you right off the bat.*

"Ines—" I say, determined to bring the conversation back under my control.

"Yes, Ines. Let's talk about Ines." Something dangerous flashes in her eyes.

Talking to Aarya is like walking a tightrope.

"It's no secret that Lions are killing off the best students from the Families that won't follow them," I start, trying to keep my voice neutral.

Aarya picks at the bark with her fingernails like she doesn't have a care in the world. "Did you really call me up here to tell me things I already know? I've concocted a few colorful reasons for this meeting in my head, and if the truth proves *less* interesting than those, I'll just need to find *another* way to amuse myself." She turns to look at me like a cat that just saw a mouse, and I force myself to lean back against the trunk in the most relaxed pose I can manage.

"Ines is one of the best students at the Academy," I say. "I

362

know you know that. Which puts her directly at risk. Layla believes someone here is trying to prevent the Lions from killing students. I want to know who it is."

Aarya tilts her head, and I know I've finally got her attention.

"But Layla's in the dungeon right now because Blackwood thinks she killed that guard—"

Aarya scoffs. "Yeah, right, that's *clearly* the reason she's locked up."

I stare at her, confused. "Do you know something about Layla being in the dungeon that I don't?"

Aarya looks at me like I'm an idiot. "Everyone knows Layla didn't kill that guard."

I frown. "Then why would Blackwood put her in the dungeon?"

Aarya rolls her eyes at me.

"So you don't know," I say, and shrug. "You're just trying to pretend you have information that I don't."

Annoyance flashes in her eyes and I can tell that she hates that I just doubted her. Then all of a sudden her expression calms. "You should really ask your boyfriend why she's in there. Or do you guys not talk about the deals he makes with the headmaster?"

My stomach twists, and something must show in my expression because she looks far too amused.

"It seems someone's about to have a fight. I should have brought popcorn." She laughs. "Do you need a minute? Are you going to cry about it?"

My fists clench. I can't let her get under my skin like this. "You want to talk about screwed-up friendships?" I ask. "What about Felix?"

Her eyes widen ever so slightly. "What *about* Felix?" she says, and gets to her feet in one sudden movement.

I focus on maintaining my composure. "Just that it must be difficult being friends with him when he's clearly aligned with the Lions, who probably have Ines on their target list?"

I know I've hit a nerve when I see her nostrils flare, and I instinctively look for Ash.

"You think Ash can get to you before I can punch you in the windpipe?" she hisses, and I hate that she's able to read me so well. "Because I seriously doubt it."

My heart pounds for all it's worth. "No, I don't," I say evenly, because it's true and because threatening her won't get me anywhere. "Believe what you want, Aarya. But first know this: That guard's throat was slit with a piece of broken glass. Then Felix had a cut on his hand the morning after the guard was killed. Now, maybe there's an explanation for that cut, but maybe there isn't."

She moves ever so slightly toward me and I wince. I can't tell by her expression whether she believes me. And even if she *does* believe me, maybe she doesn't care and will stand by Felix no matter what he did. But he's a Lion. Can she really think he wouldn't help his Family if they demanded something of him?

"As far as I can tell," I go on, "that throat slitting was actually meant for me. Maybe you don't care about me, fine. But if Brendan and the other Lions are pressuring Felix, how long do you think it will be before he's pushed to do something to harm Ines?"

"He would never," she growls, and her chin juts in my direction, telling me that even though she may not think Felix would

364

do anything to Ines, she also isn't arguing with me about his role as a Lion.

"Maybe not," I say quickly, and stand, spreading my hands out to show her I'm not challenging her. "But as long as the Lions have a strong network within the Academy, people like Ines are in danger. I'll do everything I can to stop them, but I need you to keep Felix off my back."

She starts to laugh, and I'm so surprised by her reaction, I almost fall off the branch. Except there's nothing humorous in her laughter; instead, it has an undercurrent of viciousness. "I'm shocked. Didn't Ash tell you I would never make that deal? Not in a million years. And whatever fantasy world you're living in that made you think I would give you information is amusing, but completely warped—which, coming from me, is saying something."

I maintain eye contact and don't back down, even though I'm a ball of nerves. "Ash told me exactly that. And I told him he was wrong about you. Ines saved your life that night in the teachers' lounge. She cares about you. And you care about her, too. I don't know why everyone in this crazy school acts like that's a bad thing. You *should* care about her. That's what friends do. And yes, you're definitely off your nut, but as far as I can tell you're also one of the few people who haven't bowed to the Lions. You're brave and you *do give a shit,* as much as you pretend you don't. Even Conner—"

"If you think you can stop Conner when even Blackwood can't stop him, then you're completely unhinged," Aarya interjects. "This Pollyanna cluelessness is getting old. Find a new act."

My eyes widen. *Conner?* For a moment I'm speechless, considering I was about to say that Conner had warned me about trusting anyone. But that's not what Aarya's saying at all—she's suggesting that Conner's in league with the Lions. I mean, if some of the faculty members were trying to send me warning signals, others—like Conner—might have had altogether different, maybe even malicious intentions. I look at Aarya, wondering if she could possibly be telling me the truth. Conner was helping to inspect swords the day Nyx tried to skewer me. And the day that Charles stood accused at the assembly, I swear Conner looked at me like I was to blame. In fact, when I stop to think about it, he's somehow been involved with everything that has gone wrong since I got here. The weight of the realization shakes me.

"Oh, great, now I have to suffer through waiting until you piece together what a shit Conner is?" Aarya sounds like she might push me off the sky bench. "Let's get on with this. You say Felix tried to kill you. Then what's the reason? There must be a reason."

I don't hesitate. "Revenge. Felix's father was sent to assassinate my parents and my parents killed him."

Aarya snorts. "That's not a reason—everyone knows the risk they're taking when they're sent to assassinate someone. I find it hard to believe that Felix would help the Lions because his father failed at his duty." She sounds angry. She watches me and licks her lips. "No, I think there's more."

I do everything I can to appear calm.

"There's something you don't want me to know," she says, and tilts her head, like she's trying to see me from different angles. "Felix knows who you really are, doesn't he? And it must be something terrible, otherwise you wouldn't be here trying to make ridiculous deals with me."

For an awful second, I blank on what to say. I haven't even had time to process this myself.

"Nailed it!" she says. "I have to admit I'm a little miffed he kept his discovery from me. But I'm sure that can be corrected." She stands and turns.

Shit. Shit. Shit.

"Wait," I say, and I grab her arm, even though I know it's a bad idea. She whips around and shoves me back into the tree trunk, grabbing my wrist and twisting it, sending shooting pain up my arm. I know that if I try to get free of her grip or fight her, Ash will be here in a second and my opportunity to talk to Aarya will disappear.

"If you walk away after what I told you about Felix," I say through clenched teeth, "it's the same thing as helping the Lions, and it'll be on you if they decide to go after Ines next."

She applies more pressure, and I have to force myself not to yell out in pain.

"I would *never* help the Lions. Do you hear me?" she seethes, and releases my wrist just at the point I'm convinced it will snap.

I pull my wrist into my body. "You're angry about the Lions, yet you won't tell me what you know and help me stop them? And don't bother saying you don't know anything that will make a difference, because you're way too good for that."

"I'm not taking your ignorance on as a pet project. Don't confuse me with Layla," she says.

My heart pounds. I can't believe I'm about to do this. "You want to know who I am? That matters to you so much? Well, I'll tell you. Maybe it will compel you to stop being so selfish!"

She looks at me like I'm a species she's never heard of

367

before. "You're going to tell me who you are even though you don't have an agreement from me that I'll help you?" She sounds genuinely confused, but I can tell by her tone that she's at least listening.

I know the gamble I'm taking and I also know that it's my last card to play. "Yes. Exactly. Because even if you won't do the right thing, I will. Everyone at this school who is talented and won't fall in step with the Lions is in danger. Ines is. Layla is. *You* are. You know this better than I do. And if I can't save my own ass, maybe at least I can save theirs. And yours."

Aarya frowns.

Even though the night air is cold, I wipe sweat from my forehead and take a deep breath in an attempt to calm my heart. "My parents are the ones on that scroll in the library who took all those titles—the firstborn Bear and Lion who fell in love and then disappeared."

She opens her mouth to say something, but I stop her.

"Wait. I know you're going to say it's bullshit. I get it. But just ask Felix. Or Matteo and Brendan, Blackwood or Conner. You asked me once how I got in midsemester at seventeen. Now you know—my parents were the best Strategia the Academy has turned out in generations. And yet no one knew I existed before I showed up here. *I* didn't even know who my parents were." I swallow, and Aarya blinks, just once, so I know she's listening. "So why are all these people trying to kill me— some girl no one's ever heard of?" I continue. "It's not because my parents fell in love. It's because my mom killed Jag's brother and the Lions told everyone some bullshit story that my parents were dead to cover up the fact that they'd failed to track my family down. Except they eventually succeeded. They killed my mom when I was six years old, and since then my dad has been hiding me . . . right up to the point that he sent me here."

I take a deep breath and fix her in my gaze. "I can't change the past. But if there's one thing I'm going to do before I leave this school, it's stop the Lions and anyone who's colluding with them from blotting out the good parts of Strategia. Because a world without my mom, with no Laylas or Ineses and all Brendans, is a terrifying place to live. So I, for one, am going to fight back." I can't believe the words that are coming out of my mouth, but the moment I say them, I know I mean them.

Aarya stares at me for so long that I think she might be frozen. "Aarya?"

"Shut up, November. Just shut up."

I swallow, wondering if she's planning to punch me in the throat after all. But after a few more seconds of deadpanning, she sighs and her shoulders drop.

"I broke into Conner's office not that long ago, okay? I've never trusted that bastard. Blackwood caught me, but as far as I know, she never told Conner I broke in. I've always wondered why." She pauses. "He keeps a knife hidden under his desk and he has poison in one of his drawers. Not the amateur assessment poison that will give you a stomachache, the real deal." She looks at me and I get the sense that she's expecting a big reaction. When it doesn't come, she rolls her eyes like I'm an idiot. "Obviously, students aren't allowed to keep weapons, but it's not unusual for us to try. But faculty *really* shouldn't have weapons. It makes them a threat and undermines the entire point of keeping this Academy hidden. And he's *the head of assessment*. No. My creepy tolerance is high, and this soared right past it."

I shift my gaze from Aarya to the tangled tree branches, trying to process what she's saying. This has all been so foreign to me that the difference between students and faculty having weapons didn't occur to me as a particularly huge deal. However, anything that freaks Aarya out is enough to send your average person into a faint.

Aarya snaps her fingers in front of my face and I look up at her. "Conner's bedroom is attached to his office through a door behind his desk, so if he thinks you're after him, chances are he'll wait for you in his office, where his weapons are stashed, and then you're as good as dead."

I stare at her, stunned. I don't doubt that she'll find a way to hurt me with the information I just revealed about my family, but she actually told me something she didn't have to. Somewhere under all her meanness, she actually has a conscience.

"And if I ever hear that you've repeated what I told you, Ember, I'll make you suffer," Aarya says, and turns around.

I gulp and she climbs to a higher branch and disappears into the blackness of the trees.

Thirty-Eight

ASH DROPS DOWN onto the sky bench. There's so much I need to tell him about Conner and my growing suspicions about what's been going on in this school, but instead I just frown.

"I need to ask you something," I say.

"We should get out of here first," Ash says.

I ignore him. "Do you know where the dungeon is?"

"What?" he says like he's not sure what I'm asking, but his eyes search me the way they do when he's looking for something specific.

"I'm serious. You told me no one knows where it is. But do you know? Did you lie to me?" But he doesn't need to answer, because I can see the recognition on his face.

He exhales quietly. "I didn't want you to think that the way to solve this was to get Layla out of the dungeon. It would have put you at risk."

"Because you were the one who made the deal to put her in there in the first place?" I say, and give him a demanding look.

"It's not that simple. Let—"

"You let me worry about her like that when you knew all along what was going on?" My tone is getting more indignant by the second.

He rubs his forehead. "If you'll let me explain—"

"How am I supposed to trust you now, Ash? How do I know you didn't lie about everything else?" I expect that he's going to argue with me, try to convince me there was a good reason for him to lie and that everything else he said was true. But he just stands there.

"November, there's something I need to tell you," he says slowly when he finally does speak. "I just . . . I need you to know first that I have a plan. That I'm going to fix this."

"What do you need to tell me? And what are you going to fix?" My words come out too fast.

"I'll tell you everything, but please hear me out before—"

I know Ash wants me to listen, but his expression is so serious that my mind is frantically trying to sort out what's going on and I just start talking again. "Tell me this: Did you know Conner has been helping the Lions kill students?" Until the sentence was out of my mouth, I wasn't even sure I believed it could be true. But someone on the staff has been helping the Lions. And after what Aarya told me about Conner's secret weapon stash, and from my various encounters with him, it's the only thing that makes sense.

"Let's go back inside," Ash says, attempting to keep his voice measured, but I can see the distress in his eyes. "I can't explain this quickly."

I pull back from him. "Oh my god. You *did* know about Conner. And you said *nothing*?" My pulse quickens. "Next you're going to tell me you've been helping him." I give a nervous huff because obviously that's out of the question, but Ash just fixes me with a solemn expression.

"This is not . . ." Ash rubs a hand over his face.

"You're not denying it. Ash, why aren't you denying it?" There's panic in my voice.

"If you'll slow down and come with me, I'll tell you everything you want to know." His tone is apologetic.

"There isn't a chance in hell I'm going anywhere with you until you answer me. *Were you helping Conner?*"

He exhales and there's pain in his eyes. "Again, it's not that simple."

My heart pounds so hard that it hurts, and all of a sudden it feels like there's no air to breathe. I grab a branch to steady myself. Everything I thought about Ash, everything I felt—it's all based on a lie.

"The day you arrived here," Ash says quietly, "Conner came to me, told me that since our Family didn't form an alliance with the Lions he had received word that my sister was on their kill list." I can hear the fear in his voice, but I fight back the urge to let it affect me. "Layla's brilliant, the smartest person in this school. She was always a possible target, and at first I thought he was just manipulating me with the *idea* of a threat. But I read him, November. He meant every word he said. He told me he was in a position to see that she was removed from the kill list, but that there would be a price, that I would have to do something in kind. And that something turned out to be . . . maneuvering you."

"So you what? You cozied up to me, got me to trust you, all

so you could hand me over to them?" My throat tightens and I attempt to swallow the hurt that's trying to strangle me. "The night that Stefano died, the hallway—"

"Yes, I told you to take that hallway, but I didn't know what you were going to find there. I swear," he says, and his eyes are pleading for me to understand. "Dr. Conner never told me."

I feel sick. "You were part of the plan to kill Stefano? The guy your *sister* had feelings for?"

"No! Of course I didn't know that Stefano would be murdered. And I didn't know that the intended target was Matteo. I never would have agreed to help Dr. Conner if I'd known any of that," he says.

I stare at Ash in horror, replaying everything that's happened these last two weeks in my head. "If that guard had been on his normal route instead of trying to protect me, would he have been in that hallway? Would I have been caught with Stefano's body?"

"Yes," Ash says, and it comes out in a whisper.

I put my hands over my face. I don't even know how to process what he's telling me.

"November—" he says, and reaches toward me.

"Don't you dare come near me," I say, so angry that I'm practically shaking. "When you sent me down that hallway, you had no idea what was waiting for me. There could have been someone with a knife waiting to kill me! You know that, right?"

"Yes," he says. He doesn't even try to deny it.

I walk back and forth. I open my mouth once but close it again. All this time, the missing information, the things that didn't add up—those things were Ash. And deep down, I knew it. I felt that I shouldn't trust him from the start, and yet I let myself. "So you came to me and offered to partner up to find the murderer when you already knew who it was. Why? Because you were trying to get information out of me to report back to Conner and the Lions? You . . . betrayed me."

"I *didn't* know it was Charles. Dr. Conner didn't tell me anything of the plan other than that I was to lure you out after curfew and send you down that hallway," Ash says, and his voice is getting more pained.

"All those questions Conner asked me about you . . . He *knew* you were playing me." My voice shakes and I press my lips together, trying to get myself under control.

I glance at Ash. He looks like he wants to reach out to me, which only makes me feel worse.

"And in that assembly, when Charles threw the knife at me? Did you take the hit to get me to trust you so that you could ask me about my father?" My voice cracks and I try desperately to shake away my emotion.

"No, no way," he says, and his voice is so genuine that I want to believe him. But how can I? "I blocked that knife because I wanted to. And that information was for me. I was trying to figure out why Dr. Conner was going through so much trouble to kill you. Trying to set you up for Stefano was one thing. But between Charles and the stunt that Nyx pulled with the sword . . . Dr. Conner is clearly fixated on you, or the Lions are, or both."

"So now what?" I ask, exasperated. "Am I supposed to believe that you aren't working with Conner anymore?" There's disgust in my voice. "What about this deal to put Layla in the dungeon to keep her out of harm's way? Was that a deal you made with Conner, too?"

"No, it's a deal I made with Blackwood," Ash says flatly. "If I had to guess, you're right that Blackwood's trying to stop Dr. Conner. But think about it: She can't just eliminate him from the school, not with the hold the Lions have over it. And if she killed him, it would set off a much bigger war. So I made a deal that I would protect you if she would protect my sister."

"And she agreed?"

"Not at first. Initially, she laughed. She said you didn't need protection, that you were deadlier than I was. So instead I promised her that I would do what I could to stop the Lions. While Dr. Conner's alive, they'll never give up trying to hurt you."

My head is whirling. "Blackwood said I was deadlier than you? That's not even possible. And don't you dare try to say that this is to *help* me." I almost choke on the word.

"This is why I didn't tell you," he says, and looks like he needs for me to understand. "You see things as good and bad, right and wrong. And being a Strategia means living in a world made entirely of shades of gray, where everything is a trade-off."

I shake my head, my anger high in my throat.

"And of *course* this is to help you," he says, and his voice is insistent. "I wish I didn't care. I wish I could hand you over to the Lions and be done with it all. But I can't. I won't. When I told you how I felt about you, I was minimizing it. I'm not good at caring about other people. I wasn't encouraged to have best friends like you were—none of us were. Mine was burned alive in her bed. So, yes, I'm bad at this. Yes, I made a mess of things. But I've also been doing everything in my power to keep you and Layla safe. And I don't know how to make sense of it, or how to explain it all to you, or how to tell you that after I've only known you for a short time I'm completely—" He stops himself.

He takes a breath. "If I could take back what I did, I would. I've made a mess of things. But I swear I will make it up to you, November. Just give me a chance."

I stare at him for a long time, trying to hold back the flood of tangled emotion that threatens to let loose.

"Okay," I say, my voice as restrained as I can manage. "You've said your piece. I'm leaving."

His eyes are so sad that I can barely look at him. He bends down and pulls a dagger out of his boot. He offers it to me hilt-first.

I stubbornly shake my head, but he grabs my palm and places the dagger in it. I yank my hand away from him and shove the dagger into my boot, not because I want to take it but because I can't stay here with him a second longer and argue about it.

"Please just—" he says, but I raise my hand and stop him.

"Don't," I say, and grab a vine. I begin to lower myself with shaky hands. It takes everything in my power not to cry.

I move through the trees slowly, and the farther I get from him, the more it feels like someone is strangling my heart. I also can't help but wonder how much of this Layla knew.

I'm nearing the ground when a twig snaps above me. I look up and can't see Ash, but I know with certainty that he wouldn't snap a twig. He's as silent as I am in trees.

A branch creaks to my right, jolting me with fear. With the dim light and the thick canopy of branches, everything is lost in shadows. I could scream in frustration. All I want to do is walk away so I can process this horror of a night. But if someone else is up there, Ash is alone to confront them. And as angry as I am, I can't let him fight while I run off.

I pound my fist onto a branch and squeeze my eyes shut. *Damn it all. I really hate you, Ash.* When I open my eyes again, I scour the trees in the direction the creak came from, searching for any sign of movement.

There isn't enough of a moon to see well, but there also isn't wind to mask sounds. I take a breath and focus, listening. For a couple of seconds, there's nothing but the occasional buzzing of insects in the forest. Then suddenly there's a thump nearby and the sound of boots hitting bark.

I whip around to my right, and sure enough, I catch a glimpse of a dark figure moving through the trees above me.

I'm creeping silently along the branch when I hear another dull thud, not like boots this time, but the unmistakable sound of a fist connecting with flesh. It's followed by another thud and a grunt.

I stop abruptly. On a smaller branch above me, I can just make out Ash struggling with the cloaked figure. My stomach bottoms out as I realize *he doesn't have his dagger.* I see Ash throw a punch and his opponent jumps out of the way and down two branches. Ash pursues, and once again my view is blocked.

I hustle from branch to branch until I'm near the center of the courtyard, then grab a vine and climb up it so fast that I burn my hands. I catch sight of Ash again just as he lands a kick. I want to yell to him, to tell him that I'm coming, but breaking his concentration in the trees would be the worst thing I could do.

Ash's opponent recovers his balance and tackles Ash. They collide and slam into the branch below them.

I scurry across the branch about ten feet above where the finally close enough to make out gloom—*Felix*. He gets to his feet, him. *Get up, Ash!* My heart pounds on

Felix steps back and kicks Ash so h impact of his boot on Ash's ribs. The blow off the branch. He quickly grabs at a vine, like a loose hold, only to smack into another through the darkness below.

"No!" I shout, and Felix whips around at the voice, his eyes locking with mine. But I don't care th me. I've been hunted and chased the whole time I've this school and *I'm done.*

I jump down two branches and land in front of Felix.

He wipes blood from his mouth with the back of his han and studies me smugly. "Well, you just saved me the trouble of dragging you from your room."

His right shoulder twitches, but by the time he swings, I'm already blocking. He follows with a left hook to my face but I manage to dodge it, too.

"Let's hope you're better against me than your father was against my parents," I say as I yank Ash's dagger from my boot, slicing it diagonally toward him as I stand.

He jumps out of the way, cursing. "And let's hope you're better than your dead mother," he says, and swings at me again. I deflect with my left and slash him across his shoulder with the knife.

But he doesn't look angry or in pain. In fact, he grins at me. For a split second he goes blurry. *What the hell?* He's staring at

d I follow his eyes only to discover a needle sticking
y thigh. *Oh, shit.*

branches dance in front of my eyes and I drop the knife
he sends a hard kick to my stomach. But instead of try-
move out of the way, I take the impact with a grunt and
age to wrap my arms around his leg and hold on. Only, my
rdination is failing me and I stumble, knocking him off bal-
ce and both of us off the branch.

"I'm taking you with me," I mumble incoherently as I cling
o his leg.

He grabs on to a vine to slow us, but we're falling fast, hitting
branches on the way down. I try desperately to keep my eyes
open, to maintain a hold on his leg, but my eyelids are impos-
sibly heavy. They flutter one last time and the world goes dark.

Thirty-Nine

WHEN I COME to, colors swim in front of my eyes and pain radiates from my shoulder, ribs, and head. Noise fades in and out. I crack my eyelids open a little farther and can just make out a patch of maroon fabric . . . a couch maybe?

I try to sit up, but I'm already sitting. I force myself to blink, and it takes me a moment to make sense of the shapes in my vision. I catch sight of my arms, which are bruised and cut up. My wrists are zip-tied to the arms of a wooden chair, and since I can't move my feet, I assume my ankles are tied to the chair legs as well. If I struggle or move around, the ties slice into my skin.

Suddenly I'm inhaling something awful that's reminiscent of ammonia, and the fog in my brain starts to clear. A man stands in front of me, waving a small glass vial under my nose. My chair is against a wall, and now I can make out a heavy desk to my right and a fireplace to my left.

I cough and turn my head away from the smell, fully awake.

The man corks the vial and slips it into his blazer pocket. I focus my eyes on him and it suddenly occurs to me where I am, who he is. *Oh no.*

Conner watches me curiously as the events of the night begin to come back to me: Aarya, Ash, Felix . . .

"Well, there you are," Conner says, perfectly at ease.

"What did you do? Where's Ash?" The fear in my voice is apparent and I'm sure he doesn't miss it.

Conner smiles. "It's amazing to me that you would worry about someone who was helping to *kill* you." He makes a tsking sound, as though it's all such a shame. "Just like her father," he says under his breath, but I can tell it was meant for me to hear.

I freeze at the mention of my dad.

Conner gives me a knowing look. "And that's another thing. You're far too easy to read. It's actually disappointing. One would think the Strategia in your blood would have manifested itself more, but alas." He clasps his hands behind his back. "Yes, I know your father, November. And when I saw you, the exact image of your mother, I was expecting someone polished and poised. A true opponent. But you?" He laughs. "I'm not saying you're not like them. After all, you've certainly managed to inherit their *worst* qualities."

I hate the way he's talking about my parents. He's clearly trying to get a rise out of me.

"It makes you angry when I talk about your father?" Conner says in answer to my thoughts, and puffs out his chest. "Well, then I imagine you're not going to enjoy our time together very much."

My fists clench, making the zip ties dig uncomfortably into my skin.

"Now, November," he says slowly. "Where *is* your father?"

I struggle against the restraints, pain be damned. "I don't know," I say, because it's the truth.

I look at his desk on my right, but it's too far away to get the knife Aarya said was hidden under it.

Conner sighs. "You may not know where he is at present, but you can tell me where you live."

Suddenly it's hard to breathe. If I give him my address in Pembrook, the people I love are in danger—Dad, Emily.

Conner smiles. "I see you understand the question now. Based on the assessment I gave you and your skill sets, I'd say your father has hidden you away in some sleepy town in the country that you don't leave. Probably has a mundane job that never raised any flags. Near a forest—lots of light and trees."

I cringe, remembering the yellow and green I chose on the color test my first day here—what else did I give away during my interview with him?

"Your aunt wasn't easy to find, either, even in a small city," he says casually, like he's merely commenting on the weather. "But your father . . . he has managed to elude us for a very long time. Then again, our Family always was excellent at deception and disguises."

My chest tightens at the mention of Aunt Jo and tears sting my eyes. "I'll kill you!" I blurt out.

"Right. Right. That would be an excellent idea," Conner says, and he has the same amused expression he wore when he thought he was catching me in a lie. "Now that you've said your piece, let's get back to the question at hand."

I've never wanted to hurt someone so much in my life. My skin is practically crawling with the need to strike out at him.

But Conner isn't the only one who can read people. The more pain he thinks he's causing me, the happier he gets. So losing myself to anger is going to get me exactly nowhere. If there is one thing I've learned here, it's that you can't think your way out of a situation when you're overrun by emotion. I take a calming breath. *He doesn't know where Dad is,* I reassure myself. *He doesn't know about Pembrook.*

"Silence? Is that your choice?" he asks.

I'm too far from the fireplace to burn these zip ties off. And even if I could somehow get over there, I would seriously burn myself before I could melt the ties.

Conner strokes his beard and paces in front of me, seemingly relaxed. "I knew when I offered you those two chairs during our first assessment that you didn't like having your back to the door—you don't like being vulnerable to the unknown. You prefer details, information. You gauge your surroundings and exits, like you're doing here right now," he says. "But you also didn't want the chair that I was standing behind—you don't like being pushed by other people or dominated in any way. So you made your own seat."

I swallow. It reminds me of what Dad told me about thinking differently. He knew I would go up against other Strategia eventually—and the only real advantage he could give me was to *not* think like them, *not* fight like them.

I want you to think of unusual and creative solutions. And I want you to see the world in your own unique way. If you learn to hit a certain way in boxing or to jump a certain way in wushu, your brain will immediately default to them as an answer. I don't want you to rely on the same answers every other person does. I want you to make up your own. If you learn how to approach a fight from an unexpected angle, you will become the weapon your opponent can't predict.

"Again I will give you two choices," Conner says, and watches me. "Only this time you will not have the simple luxury of choosing your own seat."

"You know, it's weird," I say, stalling for time. "You tell me I'm a weak opponent, and yet you've failed three times to kill me. And yes, I figured out you were behind all of those attacks before you got me in this chair. So if I'm bad, you must *really* suck."

Conner's lip curls and he slaps me across the face. My head whips to the side and my ears ring, but I manage not to make a sound or show him that he's hurting me. My mouth fills with blood and I spit it toward him.

"We have lots of time, November," Conner says with a flash of annoyance. "How painful you make this is entirely up to you."

Conner steps behind his desk and presses on a panel. Just like Aarya said, a door behind him swings open. He watches me as Felix limps into the room, dragging Ash.

My hands grip the chair arms so hard my fingernails gouge the wood.

Ash's hands are tied behind his back and his ankles are bound. He's bloodied and covered with scrapes and bruises, but he's breathing. Felix dumps him on the stone floor about ten feet away from me.

Conner chuckles and the hair on my neck stands up. "It seems Ashai betrayed us both. But judging by the concern on your face, I'm a lot less forgiving of his betrayals than you are."

Ash told me we needed to leave the trees. He told me he had a plan to fix things. But I wouldn't listen. I insisted on arguing with him there. My stubbornness gave Felix the opportunity he needed to ambush him, and now . . .

I strain against the zip ties on my ankles, but there's no give.

"Now, this is an easy choice," Conner says, and one side of his mouth twitches upward—the microexpression of contempt that Brendan showed in deception class. He goes to his desk and pulls open a drawer. I watch as he removes a false bottom and pulls out a small green glass bottle. *Aarya's warning.* My stomach tightens nervously.

Conner returns to Ash's limp body and takes the vial of smelling salts out of his blazer pocket. He removes the cork and waves the salts below Ash's nose. Ash's eyelids barely flutter.

"You're going to have to choose a seat this time, November, with no option to make up your own," Conner says. "The question is, are you going to watch Ashai writhe in pain, dying in slow agony? Or are you going to tell me where my brother is?" He says this last part slowly, making sure he has my full attention.

I can't breathe and I can't make sense of what he's telling me. *"Brother?"* I choke on the word. "But. That can't be true. I'm not . . . You're not . . . No."

Conner's eyes brighten happily, like this is the moment he's been waiting for.

"My dad doesn't have a brother," I say, willing it to not be true. I refuse to be related to this maniac.

For a split second Conner mirrors my confusion. "Oh, now this is just depressing." He waves the smelling salts under Ash's nose again and Ash's eyes flutter slightly more than they did the first time.

Anger flashes across Conner's face as he looks back to me. "Off he ran with that witch of a Bear after she murdered our uncle . . . in *front* of me, no less. And who do you think got blamed for not stopping her? Then he chooses *her* over his own brother, leaving me in the wake of destruction and ruining my reputation in our Family. And he has the nerve *to pretend I don't exist*?" Conner's voice is getting louder by the second. There's something dangerous about the way he looks at me, like he's seeing not me, but someone else.

Conner rises and kicks Ash in the stomach. I wince and want to yell at him to stop, but I know it will only make things worse. Ash coughs and Conner kicks him again, harder. Ash groans and opens his eyes.

I start talking fast, trying to bring the focus back to me. "No. Nothing. He didn't mention you once. I mean, I don't really blame him. I wouldn't mention you, either."

Conner hurls the vial of salts and it smashes against the wall next to me, spraying me with the pungent liquid and burning my cuts so badly that my eyes tear up. I look at the glass from the broken vial on the floor and Conner follows my line of sight. He nods at Felix.

Felix walks up to me but still won't look me in the eyes. Nevertheless, his right arm twitches, and I brace myself as he punches me in the stomach. The impact is so hard that I gasp for breath.

"November?" Ash mumbles, and his eyes widen.

"Now," Conner says in a calmer tone, and smooths his hair, like he didn't just have a freak-out. "As I was saying before. Location or Ash?"

Ash looks from me to the glass bottle in Conner's hand, and the realization of what's happening shows on his face. "Don't do it, November," Ash says, and I can tell by his voice that he's in pain. "Whatever you do, whatever he does to me, don't tell him what he wants to know."

Conner nods like this is all playing out beautifully. "Are you really going to let someone who cares about you so much die?"

I take in a ragged breath. "Ash . . ."

"No," Ash says resolutely. "This was my fault. I screwed up, and he's playing us both. Just look at him. It's all over his—"

Conner kicks Ash again, and he coils in on himself in pain.

"It's a simple choice," Conner says as he uncorks the poison.

I open my mouth but no sound comes out. I'll never be able to forgive myself if I let Ash die. But if I tell Conner about Pembrook, who's to say they won't find Dad or kill the people I love as revenge?

"I can't hear you—" Conner starts, but stops abruptly because there's a scratching sound that seems to be coming from the door.

Felix slaps his hand over my mouth and nose, making it impossible for me to scream.

"You breathe a word, and he dies," Conner hisses. "Do you understand?"

I nod and Felix lets go of my mouth.

There's another scratch, almost like a cat asking to be let in.

"Go handle it," Conner says, and Felix makes his way to the door.

He opens it just a crack and peers out. "There's no one out here," he says in a confused voice, and closes the door again. But the second it clicks into place, there's another scratch.

Felix opens the door a little wider and a hand reaches into

the room, grabbing Felix by the collar and slamming his head into the side of the doorway. Conner's eyes widen as Felix collapses on the floor.

Conner recorks the poison and moves quickly to his desk.

"Well now, y'all are havin' a party and ya didn't even invite me?" Aarya says in a terrible cowboy accent as she drops down from above the doorway. She leans against the open door as if she doesn't have a care in the world.

Conner runs his hand under his desk.

"Looking for this?" Aarya asks, and twirls a knife in her hand.

Conner's jaw tightens. "You don't want to pick this fight, Aarya," he says. "There are people in this school you don't want to lose."

Aarya nods. "You're right. I don't want to pick this fight." She pulls back her arm, but instead of throwing the knife at Conner, she turns and throws it at me. I gasp as it lodges in the arm of the chair, close enough for me to slide the zip tie on my left wrist along its blade and snap it.

"But *she* does," Aarya says.

Conner darts toward Ash. I grab the knife and quickly slice through the remaining restraints. I stand unsteadily, knife in hand, as Conner grabs Ash's jaw, forcing his mouth open and letting the bottle hover over his lips.

"Think carefully, November," Conner says. "You won't get to make this choice again."

I focus on Conner.

"Is it really worth it if you also kill Ashai in the process?" Conner says, like suddenly he's a reasonable person.

"November, throw it," Aarya says.

Don't fight like them, November, fight like you.

I exhale and slowly drop the knife. It falls to the stone floor with the grip resting on the toe of my boot.

Aarya moves forward.

"Stop, Aarya," I say with force, and she does.

Conner looks at me like I'm a complete idiot. "Maybe you were right. I have no idea how we could possibly be related." He tips the poison into Ash's mouth and squeezes a hand over his mouth and nose, forcing him to swallow.

"No!" I scream.

Ash coughs and gasps on the floor. Conner stands just as I slam my foot down on the broad side of the knife blade, flipping it into the air, where I snatch it by the handle and throw it so fast Conner doesn't even have a chance to take a step toward me. It's a clean shot and lodges deeply just below his shoulder.

His eyes widen and he takes one stumbling step. I run at him and dive for his knees, tackling him to the floor. His back hits the stone hard and he groans. Aarya is by my side in a second. She pins Conner down.

I grab the poison bottle from the floor near Ash, who looks like he's in untold pain.

"Now you get to choose," I say to Conner. "Live or die?" And I pour what's left of the poison into his mouth.

I yank the knife out of his chest and he fights back a scream.

"Let go of him, Aarya," I say, and she looks unsure but does it anyway.

Conner's back arches and his eyes bulge. His shaking hands immediately go to his inside blazer pocket and he pulls out a vial.

He struggles to uncork it and brings it to his lips, taking an unsteady swig. I immediately snatch the vial from his grasp and watch him closely to make sure it's the antidote and not more poison.

Slowly relief spreads across his face. Aarya's eyes light up like this is the best game she's played in ages.

I run for Ash and kneel down next to him, carefully lifting his head. "Hold on. Just hold on, Ash. Don't you dare die." I pour the rest of the antidote into his mouth and he chokes.

The moment I'm sure he's swallowed it, I move to his hands and feet, slicing the restraints. Aarya watches Conner as he desperately tries to stop the blood he's losing from the knife wound.

"Holding a late-night assessment session, Dr. Conner?" says a familiar voice, and Aarya and I look up. Blackwood stands in the open doorway with two guards behind her, taking note of the entire scene. She steps over Felix's passed-out body, but the guards don't follow her in.

I'm not sure if I'm relieved to see her or if I hate her for showing up when it's all over. Ash did say she would assume no responsibility for it one way or the other.

"I'll take it from here, girls," Blackwood says.

Ash pushes himself up into a sitting position, some of the pain gone from his eyes, but he looks totally spent. I try to help him stand, but he shakes his head and does it himself.

"Stubborn," I say under my breath.

I stay next to him to make sure he doesn't fall. He seems to be regaining his strength by the second, but he's still wobbly.

"I'm going to take *this* with me," Aarya says, and grabs Felix's ankles.

"That depends," Blackwood says. "Was he helping you or was he helping Conner?"

"Neither, really," Aarya says, and for the first time ever, she looks vulnerable. "He stumbled into a situation he couldn't handle and got knocked out like a dumb—" Aarya stops herself and coughs.

Blackwood turns to me.

I look at Ash. He was once on the wrong side of this, too. And it didn't stop me from doing everything I could to save his life. He could easily have been in the position Felix is in right now.

I make eye contact with Aarya and nod. "It's like Aarya says. He just got caught in the middle. Conner has a bad habit of blackmailing people."

Blackwood nods at Aarya, who doesn't lose a second. She pulls Felix into the hallway and past the guards, whistling as she goes.

Blackwood makes her way to Conner, who's dragging himself across the floor, leaving a trail of blood.

"One way or another we're going to find your father," Conner says through clenched teeth. "And when we do, you'll wish I'd killed you in this room."

"Very moving last words," Blackwood says. "But I think the material point is that if someone finds him, it won't be you." Blackwood glares at Conner like he's a loathsome parasite and she's trying to decide what to do with him.

I don't spare him another glance. Aunt Jo was right about Dad's family—*good riddance.*

"After you take Ashai to the infirmary, November," Blackwood says over her shoulder, not taking her eyes off Conner, "please meet me in my office. . . . And close the door on your way out."

Forty

ASH IS DOZING in the infirmary. He tried to stay awake to talk to me, but whatever the nurse gave him knocked him out cold. He only mumbled an incoherent sentence or two before his eyes fluttered shut.

I watch his chest rise and fall and I exhale audibly. If Aarya hadn't showed up when she did, I honestly don't know how much I would have lost tonight. Probably both our lives, and maybe my dad's as well.

"We should get your cuts cleaned up," the nurse says, and I turn around. She wears her long black hair in a braid that reaches her waist. A single gray streak near her temple makes her look like a sorceress. And she's petite, but her voice is raspy and commanding.

"I know. And I promise I'll be back. But Headmaster Blackwood told me to come see her first," I say, and she gives me a stern look.

"Get on with it, then," she says, and I do.

I make my way through the silent hallways, passing three guards as I go. They all watch me, but no one looks at me like

I shouldn't be there, which makes me think they already know what happened with Conner.

I take the three flights slowly, my body more bruised and achy than it was even half an hour ago. And when I reach Blackwood's office, two guards stand outside her arched door. One of them opens it for me, but neither guard follows me in. Blackwood must want total privacy, and I don't blame her, considering her role in all of this.

The familiar smell of woodsmoke fills the air. I take a seat in the armchair just like I did my very first day, and I find myself blurting out the first thing that comes to mind. "Did you try to send me messages through some of my instructors?"

Blackwood raises an eyebrow and considers me. "I may have suggested a few lessons to help you acclimate."

I would laugh at that tempered answer, but I'm too pooped and sore to muster a laugh. "And when Matteo punched—"

Blackwood cuts me off. "Now, I know you have questions, and truthfully, you are entitled to ask them. However, please do me the favor of listening first." She leans back in her chair.

I thought that tonight would have softened her toward me, but she's just as formal as ever. I quietly nod my agreement.

Blackwood folds her hands over her lap. "Your father contacted me when your aunt was murdered, looking to secure an immediate safe house for you."

My heart sinks. When Conner relayed the news that Aunt Jo was dead, a part of me wondered if it had happened just then or if it had occurred earlier. And if she was killed before I was admitted, that explains why Dad gave me no warning, no chance to say goodbye to Emily or my other friends. He must have been on high alert the entire time, wondering just how fast he could get us out of there before someone descended on our house. I shudder at the thought of Strategia in Pembrook, and even though I've considered it before as an awful possibility, the idea has just graduated to an insistent fear.

"As I told you when you first arrived, we do not typically admit students your age. But with you, nothing is typical. We've made exceptions in the past for the children of leading families, and even though you have no formal standing as yet among the Strategia, you fit that qualification in two Families, not one."

I swallow. I was so convinced I didn't belong here that I hadn't really considered who I might be in the Strategia hierarchy.

"Did my dad know his brother was—"

Blackwood gives me a look and I close my mouth. "Your father and I made a deal. I told him his brother was working here and my suspicions about his involvement in several student deaths. In exchange for your protection, he agreed that you would assist in flushing Dr. Conner out—under my guidance, of course."

I shake my head, scarcely able to process what she just said. "Whoa, hold on. That is one hundred percent not the reason I thought I got in here. My dad made a deal that I would flush out *Conner*? What was the point of sending me here for protection if I was just going to be exposed to a different kind of danger?"

"I can't speak for your father," Blackwood says. "But what I will say is that you were more than up to the task. You not only confirmed my suspicions about Dr. Conner, you exposed his guilt beyond any reasonable doubt. And of course, you know our policy for grievances committed against another person."

I would respond to that, but I have no words. *An eye for an eye. Which means as punishment Conner is now . . . and I was the one who . . .* I can't wrap my mind around it. Conner was a threat, I know that. But I threw the knife and the rest . . . Well, I suppose only Blackwood and the guards know the details.

And I don't even know where to begin with the way Blackwood and my dad apparently see me—as one of them, as Strategia.

"Your father was always exceptionally good at reading people, and while you may lack skill in that area, I not only see what he sees in you, I think you have hidden talents that haven't even surfaced yet."

I tuck my hair behind my ears, flustered. "Then why didn't he take me with him? He could have *explained* things, helped me learn things."

Blackwood sighs. "Even though you're well trained for having been raised outside of our society, and you think in your own unique tactical way, you lack a deeper knowledge about the Strategia way of life. This was the best place for you to acclimate. It was how your father—and your mother—learned their way as well."

I want to argue, but I know she's right. Dad had no time to make a decision and he did the one thing he thought would make me safe and prepare me.

I examine Blackwood. "You knew my dad, didn't you?"

For a moment she hesitates, then sighs. "Before this, I hadn't spoken with him in more than a decade, but yes, I knew both of your parents quite well at one point."

I can tell by her tone that she not only knew them, but that they were close. "Why did Conner hate my parents so much?"

She nods, like she was expecting this question. "Your mother and father were special. They thought they could bring balance and equality back to Strategia, and they had every intention of devoting their lives to it as leaders of their Families. And even in the short time after they left this school, they made some headway. They got the impossible to happen—their Families came to an agreement. But as you might expect, there were members on both sides who were unhappy with their union and felt that balance would never happen or would ultimately mean relinquishing power. Dr. Conner and Jag's brother were two of those people."

"This was the uncle my mother killed?" I ask.

"Was *accused* of killing," Blackwood corrects me. "No one actually knows what happened. The only thing we do know is that Dr. Conner was present. There was a great deal of suspicion at the time about how the events unfolded, especially since Dr. Conner walked away without so much as a scratch and without confronting your mother. Jag blamed Dr. Conner for not stopping her—he called him the great shame of the Family. As a result, after your father disappeared, Dr. Conner wasn't named as the next leader, even though he was next in line. He became reclusive and removed from Strategia society. He changed so much that I barely recognized him when he was assigned to be the assessment officer here."

I sit there for a moment, trying to make sense of my tangled Family history, where people are constantly killing one another. "Thanks for explaining," I say, and shift to what I most want to know. "Do you know where my dad is right now?"

She shakes her head and her eyebrows furrow ever so slightly. "I haven't heard from your father since your admission."

I frown. "Okay, then can we get in touch with him and find out?" My fear of Strategia in Pembrook comes back full-force.

Blackwood shakes her head.

My heart begins to pound. "Well, did he leave any information for me? A message? Anything that would tell me how I can find him?" My voice is rushed.

"No, I'm sorry."

I stand up, overwhelmed and unsure how to proceed. "But the Lions could be hunting him down right now," I say emphatically.

"You've completed our agreement," Blackwood says slowly.

I look at her questioningly. "What's that supposed to mean?"

"It means that you may stay here and continue your education as your father wished, or you may leave if that's what you feel is necessary."

"I can go? You're letting me go?" I say more to myself than to Blackwood.

Blackwood hesitates. "Technically, you can go. However, I must advise you that there is still a great deal for you to learn and your skills are severely lacking in several areas. But more importantly, you know very little about the Strategia world at large."

"Maybe so, but there's no way I can stay here while my dad's out there all alone. Especially knowing what I now know," I say. "What happened here with Dr. Conner seems to be just a microcosm of what's happening out there."

"The school doesn't involve itself in outside politics," she says, even though we both know that the situation between her and Conner was completely political. "I'll just say again that it would be prudent if you made additional alliances here and learned as much as you can before you leave."

I take a good look at Blackwood. Her hair is pulled as taut as ever, her look as inscrutable as it was on day one, and I now know that her frilly white shirt, spilling out from under her crisp black blazer, is the perfect metaphor for who she is. She's clearly trying to help me, to tell me what I need to do, but she won't say it outright.

"Okay," I reply, even though I'm not sure yet what she means.

Forty-One

WHEN I FINALLY crack my eyes open, my bedroom curtains are drawn and a candle is lit next to my bed. I'm not all that surprised that I slept through the day. I pull back my covers and inspect the bandages on my arms and legs. There are cuts and bruises all over me. As I step out of bed, I wince.

I walk slowly into the common room, everything aching, but the pain is more manageable than I would have thought. Maybe I've just fallen out of so many trees at this point that my body has gotten used to it.

The fire is big and bright and the room feels cozy. But I stop dead in my tracks when I spot Ash and Layla playing cards at the table next to the window.

Layla! She puts down her cards and comes right up to me.

We stand there awkwardly for a second and she looks like she wants to give me a hug but doesn't know how to approach a gesture like that.

"How long have I been out?" I ask, and my voice has a morning roughness to it.

"It's just after eight at night," she says, and starts to lift her arms, but then seems to decide against it and puts them down again.

I would laugh at how awkward she's being right now, but it would hurt my ribs. "Layla, if you don't woman up and hug me already, this friendship is off," I finally say, and lift an eyebrow.

Her smile widens and she carefully wraps her arms around me, like it's the first hug she's ever given. She's about the same size as Emily, and just the thought of Emily and Pembrook makes my heart ache.

"Thank you for saving my stupid brother," she says into my shoulder.

I nod against her head and we stay like that for a couple of seconds.

She releases me and her eyes are teary, but she tries not to let me see. "Let's get you to the couch," she says, and walks next to me in case I need support.

I lower myself slowly onto the cushions. Ash joins us, and he looks as banged up as I feel. As he sits, we make eye contact. He looks so genuinely happy to see me that my stomach does a quick flip.

"How in the world are you up and about right now?" I ask him, looking at his bandages.

He grins. "You seriously thought some poison and these little cuts would set me back?"

Layla rolls her eyes. "What he means is that he came here so I could play nurse to him and he could wait for you to wake up."

But Ash doesn't respond with a joke the way he normally would. He just looks at me like he can't believe I'm real.

Layla glances from Ash to me and back again. She clears her throat. "Pippa stopped by to bring you dinner. She asked me to let her know when you woke up," she says, and stands. "So I'm just going to, uh, go do that." It's obvious that she's leaving the room to let us talk, but neither of us tells her not to go.

Layla closes the door behind her and Ash and I are left on the couch. He stares at me, those intense eyes burning into my own.

I sigh. "Blackwood gave me a choice," I say, not sure how to approach this topic. "She said I could stay here or I could leave. That I'd fulfilled an agreement she made with my dad, so my next step was up to me."

Ash nods at me like he figured as much. "That makes sense."

"That makes sense to you?" I ask, wrinkling my brow. "It doesn't really make sense to me."

"Well," Ash says. "Aarya more or less told the entire school who your parents are. And the heroic story of how she saved you—emphasis on *heroic*. Now she's growling at Brendan every time they pass each other in the hallway."

"Oh," I say, not sure how to process that. "And Felix?"

"Well, that one's a little fuzzy. Aarya's been vague about how he was involved, although I think people already have their suspicions. But everyone knows that Dr. Conner was vicious. Felix may have had a grudge against you over what happened with his father, but my guess is that Dr. Conner had something he was holding over him, just like he used Layla's safety to manipulate me."

"I figured as much," I say. "That's why I didn't out him to Blackwood, even though I'm sure she knows. Speaking of Blackwood, she also told me that I'm not trained as well as I should be and that I should make alliances. Do you know what she meant by that?"

Ash smirks. "She meant that while you're good—great, even—you're not ready to navigate the outside Strategia world by yourself. You'll need the help of the Bears and possibly some of the other Families as well," he says, casually acknowledging that he knows I've decided to leave, even though I haven't told him yet.

I exhale. "I have to go find my dad," I say. "I'd never forgive myself if I didn't and something happened to him." And even though I feel good about my decision, I'm sad, too. I know there's every chance that I'll never see Ash or Layla again.

We're both silent for a beat.

"I know," he says.

A lump forms in my throat and I attempt to swallow it down. "Ash—"

"So when do we leave?" he says briskly, and for a brief second, I think I misheard him.

I stare at him in shock.

"What?" A mischievous grin creeps over his face. "You didn't think I was going to miss out on you single-handedly taking on the Lions, did you? Besides, it's like the headmaster said: you need alliances."

I don't know whether to kiss him or to cry. "I can't ask you to leave this place you fought so hard to get into and, more importantly, to leave Layla."

"Well then, it's a good thing you're not asking and I'm volunteering," he says with a smile.

"I'm serious."

"So am I," he says. "Layla and I were always going to lead our Family together, as a team. She's memorized practically every lesson we've ever had here. She'll just fill me in on anything I miss. And with Dr. Conner gone, she's safer now than she's ever been in this school."

"Okay. But you know there's a high possibility we won't live through it," I say.

"And there's one hundred percent certainty that *you* won't unless I come with you," he retorts. "You don't know any of the Strategia safe houses in Europe, and you won't find them on your own because they're hidden. Plus, you don't know the first thing about where to get information and who to trust."

So that's what Blackwood actually meant when she told me I wasn't prepared. "Why, Ash? Why do this?"

"Do you really need to ask?" His eyes drift down to my lips and my stomach flutters. *"Amantes sunt amentes."*

Before I can work out the meaning, he smiles. "Lovers are lunatics." He gently pushes his fingers through my hair and pulls me close. For a split second his mouth lingers an inch away from mine and his breath is warm on my lips. My stomach drops like I'm free-falling.

"You ruined our first kiss," I whisper. "Don't screw this one up."

He grins. "I promise to practice constantly until I get better," he says, and presses his lips onto mine.

Acknowledgments

I woke up one morning after having a dream about this story, and it was My Pirate who listened to me brainstorm and encouraged me to grow my idea into this book. In fact, he always listens, he always encourages, and he is always my very first reader. We have been together for nearly twelve years now, and I'm still continuously amazed by how wonderful he is. Here's to twelve bazillion more (because I plan on stalking him through the afterlife).

Of course, there's also my mama, who is an integral part of every book I write. She takes care of me when I'm on deadline, supports all my wacky ideas, and makes the most yummy writing snacks ever! She is a delightful part of my life, and I'm thankful for her every single day.

Then there's my Ro, who is the best agent on the planet. But more importantly, she is a dear friend and an exceptional human being. It's truly a blessing to know her.

And my lovely editor, Mel, who sprinkles magical story dust on every book she touches and makes them so much better.

I suppose it would be possible to write stories without her, but I wouldn't want to.

My dear CPs Kerry Kletter and Jeff Zentner are not only brilliant, but they're generous. More than once I've asked them to read something for me in a pinch, and they always show up. I could not be more grateful to have these two by my side.

Kali Wallace and Audrey Coulthurst are my go-tos for hashing out ideas, sympathizing with writing woes, and, when all else fails, crafting truly delicious cocktails. Ravenclaw forever.

And Anya Remizova, who is always there for me and listens to me talk endlessly about writing, even the inane parts. She's a true friend, and I'm honored to know her.

The entire team at Random House is a big piece of wonderful. They bring so much joy to my world and make it possible for me to do what I love most—tell stories.

Clementine Gaisman, who has me smiling every time she pops into my inbox.

And Jason Dravis, who takes my books and casts them on new adventures.

On top of all these awesome people, I also have the most beautiful and supportive family, filled with truly eccentric loves who provide me with inspiration and, in the case of my uncle Rob, even some super-helpful sneaky strategies.

And I have the biggest-hearted readers in my FAMB group, who brighten my days with their enthusiasm for books and all their kindness.

A huge thank-you to everyone here who has contributed so much. My books wouldn't be what they are without you, and neither would I.